BLEST THOSE WHO SORROW

a novel by Pat McGauley

AUTHOR'S NOTE
This is a work of fiction. Names, characters, places, and incidents either are the product of the author's imagination or are used fictitiously, and any resemblance to actual persons, living or dead, events, or locales is entirely coincidental.

Copyright 2004 by Patrick McGauley (Number pending)

Manufactured in the United States of America through Bang Printing (Brainerd, MN). Published by Pat McGauley Publication (Hibbing, MN, 55746).

Without limiting the rights under copyright, no part of this publication may be reproduced in whole or in part in any form without the prior written permission of both the copyright owner and the publisher of this book.

ISBN: 0-9724209-2-4

Library of Congress Control Number: 2004095931

First Edition, Summer of 2004

DEDICATION

Friendships are golden. This book is dedicated to Ed Beckers.

How blest are the poor in spirit;
The reign of God is theirs.

Blest too are the sorrowing;
They shall be consoled...

From the Beatitudes
Gospel of Matthew (6: 3,4)

Prologue

THE OLD MAN HAD FALLEN ASLEEP in his well-worn chair. Having paused only occasionally to relight his Meerschaum pipe, Claude Atkinson had been relating his absorbing narrative for nearly three hours. In that space of time I had glimpsed the age in his once piercing blue eyes, heard the frequent rasps in his labored breaths, and sensed the newsman's urgency to share this unique blend of history and commentary with me. Perhaps, somewhere in the depths of his thoughts, a keen reality inspired his flow of memories. I wondered if Claude was sensing that this might be the last of his many stories.

Or perhaps his depletion could be attributed to the unseasonable heat of this late August afternoon. In the cluttered living room where we had been visiting, humidity hung in the air like the fog that sometimes obscured the names and dates he labored to remember. There was no breeze to flutter the chenille curtains hanging in limp defeat over an open-screened window. At times, the small, dimly lit space had become almost too uncomfortable for the two of us to keep our focus on the story. I prayed his drift away from our conversation was due to the draining heat more than to his failing health.

While the old man rested, I reviewed the copious notes resting on my lap. In scanning over the pattern of dates, I realized that Claude's incredible story was nowhere near finished. He had been pouring his thoughts and memories as if composing a dear friend's obituary for tomorrow's newspaper. Staring back at me from the first page of scribbled anecdotes, I was reminded of a pearl of wisdom that the sage had shared before beginning his rambling discourse hours ago. All that I had written down from this fleeting remembrance were the two words story and fish. As best my memory would allow, I penciled the clever analogy on the back of my tablet:

Writing a story is like catching a fish. After casting and trolling for a time, you finally get the anticipated tug. Once it's on your line, the real struggle begins. The goal, of course, is to get the elusive creature in your boat. But it fights you with a mind of its own—going one way, then another—shooting near the surface, and then plunging into dark depths. You fight it. At times you feel a slack and think you've lost it, but then it pulls in resurgent anger—battling you more than ever. So, you keep reeling, and hoping, and praying that you'll be able to keep it on your line and somehow tame its defiant spirit. If you have enough skill and energy and perseverance—perhaps that fish can become your trophy.

Was the old man trying to tell me something I needed to know? Did his analogy apply to all things in life that we desire? From experience I had learned how elusive a story can be. Perhaps the same is true of love, and of spirituality, and peace of mind.

Claude Atkinson was somewhere in his eighties now. Before nodding his large gray head and resting an angular, deeply furrowed face upon his narrow shoulder, he had been recalling events which followed the political campaign of 1932. The esteemed former newsman and historian loved politics with a passion. With a tone of remorse in his voice, Claude remembered an occasion of twenty-four years ago as if it were yesterday. "But Kevin didn't take our advice... No, that's when I first recognized the young man had his father's stubbornness—and a dose of his old man's pride as well," Claude had observed. Kevin was the son of one of Hibbing's most powerful and tragic pioneers, Peter Moran. "For several years afterwards, Kevin struggled with aroused demons in his Moran blood. He kept everything pretty much to himself, though. Like his father, he chose to live in a private hell of his own making."

Having written a story about Kevin's father in the early days of Hibbing, I could surmise what those demons might have been. Peter Moran had wealth and ambition in near equal measure. He had everything—and, in the end, had nothing! Perhaps, Claude would tell me later that the son had fallen to similar depths. I hoped that would not be the case. Kevin, I was certain, had better stuff than his father.

In a story sequel to Peter's rise and fall, I endeavored to chronicle the life of his son. Kevin Moran was an intriguing personality, and I was enamored with his forthright integrity. After all the credible things I had written about young Kevin, was Claude going to put an unwanted damper on all of my perceptions? Had I missed something in the essence of Kevin's character? The young attorney had everything, too: a beautiful wife and son, a majestic hotel, and wealth which allowed him comfort in those Depression times. How could he possibly let all of that slip away? I prayed that my surmise of where Claude's story seemed to be going was wrong. And, I prayed that there would be time to finish our conversation.

Claude Atkinson's devoted son, Marc, entered the stifling room while I ruminated over the unfolding story of Kevin Moran. Unloosing his father's tie and removing the plaid blanked draped across the old mans spindly legs, Marc whispered, "There's so much more he'll want to tell you about. Dad's memory is still just as sharp as a tack. I've been eavesdropping, you know." Marc smiled, "Can you come back in the morning? I can see that Dad's exhausted himself for now."

That evening, in my room at Kevin Moran's grandiose Androy Hotel, I tried to put my thoughts and notes in order. While attempting to 'get his fish in the boat', Claude's story had gone in a myriad of directions—into the past, and oftentimes near the fringes of the present. I had so many questions but was reluctant to interrupt the flow of where he had been taking me. Perhaps, everything would make better sense if it were sorted out at a later time. But I had the distinct impression that Claude had learned much about what Kevin was going through back then from Tony Zoretek, Kevin's beloved father-in-law. Tony and Kevin had always been as close as any two men can ever hope to be. Although I had never met Tony in person, I had developed the highest respect for him. After my visit with Claude, I would try to spend some time with the prosperous local contractor. Earlier, Marc had informed me that Kevin and his wife, Angela, were presently vacationing with their two children in California.

I circled something confusing near the last pages of my notebook. It was an unexpected reference to Angela Moran that seemed strangely out of place in the story. While focusing on Kevin's political exploits, Claude had made frequent allusions to Angie's 'issues'. What riveted my attention was this obscure quotation, "It wasn't until Angie's 'missing time' that Kevin got a grip on what was really important in his life..." Missing time? I had the feeling that when he resumed the story, Claude might have much more to say about Angela Moran. I could not escape the impression that this may become more Angie's story than Kevin's.

Other things puzzled me as well. Were Claude's comments really the pearls of wisdom I imagined them to be—or were they subtle warnings? Understandably, he had talked a great deal about his hometown of Hibbing, Minnesota. He knew more about the aging iron-mining hub than any two living people, and had written more about that city than I might ever hope to accomplish. I found what he had to say about Hibbing's 'old days' truly fascinating. Ultimately, the people and the events occurring in this place had become the essence of my first two novels. I knew that Claude had read them both, but had carefully reserved any critical judgments. "I don't know if folks outside the Range (Minnesota's fabled Mesabi Iron Range) will really care very much about these stories. You need to have been here to appreciate the melting pot of immigrants from Austria, Italy, Finland…and thirty other foreign lands. You had to have walked into the perilous depths of these gaping pits to have any legitimate feelings for the labor and the strife of those beleaguered mine workers. You had to experience the presence of our colorful personalities, like Peter Moran and that 'Little Giant' Victor Power, to get your emotions stirring." He had paused reflectively for a long moment when he recalled those things. "Be careful, my friend… Don't fall into the trap of trying to write historical novels. Unless you have felt the passions of these people and their times first hand, you're going to fall on your face."

I pondered those words for nearly an hour. Was I being lured into a realm that I might never comprehend? Claude, of course, had been here through it all. So had Tony Zoretek, a Slovenian immigrant and miner who had risen above the grueling open pits and found success on the coattails of ambitious Peter Moran years before. Their children, Kevin and Angela, however, were relative newcomers. And Old Hibbing was only a ghost of its former self. The original city had been forced to move two miles south of its former location where splendor and squalor existed side by side. Like myself, this new generation of 'Rangers' had little memory of what had transpired in the first half century of Hibbing's unique history. Was I, however, unconsciously attempting the impossible in telling stories about things I might never fully understand?

In writing *To Bless or to Blame*, I sought to capture the ribald spirit at loose in the early century of this booming mining center. In my pages were sagas of power, lust, tumultuous labor strife, human failures, unrequited love affairs, and the compelling personalities behind them all. In my sequel, *A Blessing or a Curse*, my historical endeavors were much simpler, and probably more superficial. Hibbing and Duluth remained backdrops while I unfolded the 'coming of age' for a new generation of Hibbing residents. By the second quarter century of the story, Peter Moran had left the stage, yielding the major dramatic roles to Kevin and Angela. There is a poignant irony here: Peter's son became the husband of the daughter of Mary Samora—the woman Peter loved but could never win.

If the story Claude would unfold the following morning had the same measure of history and personal drama as those I had already borrowed from his narratives—there would certainly be another book. Maybe more than just one. Claude's story of that afternoon had been lodged in August of '32—the calendar on the desk in my hotel room read August of 1956. A gap of nearly a quarter century remained to be filled.

Peering out of my window over brightly lighted Howard Street three stories below, my thoughts were in turmoil. So much had changed over the years. In the old city of Hibbing, with some ninety saloons and taverns with brothels upstairs in nearly half of them, red ore-dusty Pine Street was the commercial artery. It was a masculine place where many different languages were spoken along the busy streets. An untamed dynamic hung in the air like the dust from the tumultuous mining operations nearby.

But this city, bustling with nighttime automobile traffic and neon lights, had evolved into a totally different creation. Gone was the strident fervor of a past which I could only imagine. In its place were the qualities and characteristics of life one would find in any American city of its size. Yet, a city is much more than mortar and brick and tree-lined streets and rows of diverse houses. A city claims the substance and personality of its residents. Despite all the changes, Hibbing, Minnesota, was still a blue-collar mining town with a uniquely rich and charming ethnic heritage.

Where would this next story take me? Somehow, I had a gut feeling from what Claude had already told me, that the lives of Kevin and Angela Moran might stretch far beyond this majestic Howard Street hotel. They were both, in every respect, talented and aspiring young people. It seemed only reasonable to assume that their future held yet untold mysteries. Still lingering in the back of my thoughts were the three words I had circled with bold stroke in my notebook...*Angela's missing time*!

BOOK ONE

Angela and Kevin Moran

A Lapse in Memory

Two distinct and utterly frightening sounds pierced her ears!

Having just finished nursing her year-old son, the woman was in the grips of an overwhelming melancholy while sitting at her kitchen table. The early September morning was gray and chilly. Her husband's recent depression and withdrawal were weighing heavily in her thoughts of the moment. Being unsettled and possessed with anxiety—the shock of those two sounds—at that precise moment—must have caused her blackout…But she couldn't remember!

Everything in her world was suddenly blurred in a cloud that folded across her mind from every direction.

The paralyzing blast, followed by the shattering of glass, became locked somewhere within a tightly sealed and unconscious realm of her mind. All that her interrupted memory would allow was the sight of his ashen face. He was standing helplessly in the doorway of the library, just a few feet down the hallway from where she lay on the tiled kitchen floor next to her screaming son.

In the weeks that followed, she chose to repress the blackout incident and go on with her life as if nothing more than a faint had happened. But, she knew that whatever had happened was far more serious. In concealing her fears about that nightmarish episode, she would be untruthful to her husband for the first time in their years together. Yet she rationalized the unnerving incident by believing that whatever she did not know for certain might not hurt her—ever again.

November 9, 1932

As she regarded herself in the vanity mirror, Angela Moran winced at the lingering pain in her temples. The sudden headache had drained her lovely face of color, leaving her body almost numb. What had just happened? Glancing down, Angie noticed the spilled bottle of red nail polish on the oak vanity top, and then the fingernails she had started to glaze. Confused and troubled, she wondered again about her unexplainable lapses in memory.

Looking up once more, she recognized that her complexion was unnaturally pale. The mirror reflected a face that had been recently made up with a blush of rouge on her high cheekbones, a light touch of lipstick on her full mouth, and a mascara highlight upon long eyelashes above wide-set, dark, ovaline eyes. Such dark, vacant eyes!

Why had she dressed in her finest outfit—a black serge dress with an open-buttoned bodice? Why was she wearing her exquisite natural pearl necklace with its matching earrings? Where was she planning to go at this hour of the day? What hour was it? Looking through the large bedroom window to her left, Angie realized that it was already night time. The small timepiece on the nearby dresser read seven-thirty. Angie puzzled. That dreaded *something* had struck her…again!

Where had her thoughts been only moments before this lapse? Obviously she had bathed, dressed in her finest, and begun her final touching up…but—

She forced her mind back in time. Had it been two months already?
The vague memory of lying on the floor, her husband's consoling voice while stroking her face, and him pacifying their frightened son. Despite her every effort to unlock the mystery, Angie could not recall any further details of that September morning's episode.

Daily she prayed her rosary to the Virgin Mary. Prayers for her health and prayers for the courage to tell Kevin that something was seriously wrong with her. Yet, for unknown reasons, Angie continued to keep her tormenting secret from the man she loved more than life itself.

"Are you ready, Angie?" Kevin's question echoed up from the wide hallway below the staircase. Ready for what?—she wondered to herself.

"I'll be just a few more minutes, sweetheart," she called to her husband over her shoulder. "Are we running late?"

"I told your dad we'd pick them up about eight." He replied with a trace of impatience in his voice. Kevin considered that Angela had been 'getting ready' for more than an hour. Unusual for her.

Them would be her father, Tony Zoretek, and his wife, Becca. Angie's mind processed one connection…but not the other. Why Tony and Becca? Out to dinner? A movie? Appraising her elegant dress once again, she wondered—where?

Angie's right hand nails were already dry, as were three fingernails on her left hand. As she finished painting the remaining two nails, she regarded the diamond ring and smiled to herself. The ring held memories of her deceased mother, Mary Samora Zoretek, and was a gift from her father. Shimmering on her finger next to that precious memento was the wedding band from Kevin. How lucky she was. How richly Kevin, and their year-old son, Patrick, had blessed her life. Pleasant thoughts, however, did not mitigate the sharp pain splitting across her head like the part in her long dark tresses. "Jesus, Mary, and Joseph—" she mumbled a quick prayer under her breath, "…help me find the key."

Angie could feel Kevin's presence in the room without seeing him in her mirror. This uncanny magnetism between them defied any reasonable explanation. The two of them had such a marvelous chemistry—almost a communion without any need of words to express itself, or any sight to make it visible. If only she could read his mind at this moment. Angie needed to find out what had been planned for their evening with her father and Becca, but how could she grasp what it was?

Kevin regarded his beautiful young wife from the bedroom doorway.
Angie was his most precious treasure. Recent months had made him realize more than ever before how important she was to his happiness, his completion as a man. Beyond her radiant loveliness, Kevin was enchanted with her blithe personality, her quick intelligence, clever sense of humor, and winsome charm. She was always spontaneous, positive, and confident —especially at those times when he allowed himself to become timorous or doubtful. Angie was everything Kevin could ever want in a woman.

"You're staring at me, Kevin." Angie commented without looking up from her delicate hands. "I thought you were in a hurry to get me out the door and off to dad and mom's house."

"You are so beautiful! How can I help myself from staring!" he said while gazing at his wife's reflection in the mirror. "We can always be fashionably late."

Angie smiled to herself at Kevin's thoughtful compliment, dabbing at the pool of red on the vanity with a tissue. "I've made a little mess here, I'm afraid," she troubled over the spilled bottle. Still, she could not remember how the accident had happened. "I'm sorry I've kept you waiting, but…" Angie would try to find out what was happening. "I've been in and out of the closet, I'm not really sure if my black dress is appropriate or not."

Kevin was wearing his navy pinstriped suit, a crisp white shirt, and a stylishly coordinated burgundy silk tie. Her husband was strikingly attractive. Tall, chisel-featured, auburn-haired, Kevin Moran cut an imposing posture.

"Is everybody going to be formally dressed tonight?" Angie tried an open-ended question as she fished for some thread to grasp onto.

"I would think so. Probably everybody but our guest of honor that is." Kevin laughed more to himself than to Angie at his observation. "If Melvin were closer to my size, I'd gladly give him some of my suits. Lord knows he's going to need a whole new wardrobe when he gets to St. Paul."

Angie's puzzled expression became a wide smile in the mirror's reflection. Quick to grasp Kevin's reference to their friend Melvin, and then to St. Paul, she figured out where they were going tonight! Everything became immediately clear in her mind, and with her realization, the headache perceptibly eased its grip. "I'm so looking forward to congratulating Melvin on his campaign," Angie said in a tone of sincerity, a sparkle now in her eyes. Finally out of her closet of amnesia, she breathed a sigh of relief, "But he couldn't have done it without your help, my dear."

Kevin glanced at his pocket watch: 7:45. He and Angie would be more than a few minutes late but he didn't care. Walking over to the vanity, he placed his hands gently on her delicate shoulders, and kissed her soft hair, "Melvin would have done the same for me, sweetheart. We both know that. He's a good man, Angie. I'm looking forward to the celebration."

As Angie adjusted her string of pearls she kissed Kevin's hand. "Just give me two more minutes, Kevin…maybe you could bring the car around to the back door."

Kevin nodded without reply. As he did so, he noticed what he thought was the line of a dried tear on his wife's unusually pale cheek. Had she been crying?

"Are you feeling well, honey?" Kevin paused, his sudden frown betraying his concern. "Were you just crying?"

"Only a lash I tried to remove from the corner of my eye," she lied. "In trying to get it out, I must have brushed the nail polish bottle with my elbow and spilled it—how simply careless of me."

Kevin's intuition caused him to doubt. For the past two months there had been an unspoken and subtle tension between them. Ever since that morning in the library—ever since that damnable lie he had told her! Maybe tonight he could be more honest with her about the torment that haunted his thoughts so much lately. Maybe he could get their relationship back to where it had been before the political campaign. Those months had driven a discernible wedge between them. His life's priorities had been warped by a personal ambition that Angie had been forced to suffer.

The most shameful moment in Kevin Moran's twenty-four years was, at the same time, perhaps, his most triumphant. Despondent over the pain his election campaign had caused those he loved—Angie more than anybody—and the public smearing of his character, Kevin had sought the refuge of his library and closed the door on everything disturbing him. On that September morning he had decided to withdraw from the race, a race he so deserved to win. A decision, like so many others, that was both selfish and made despite Angie's advice to the contrary. A decision he'd reached without due regard to the counsel of his closest friend and mentor, Claude Atkinson. The retired editor of the local newspaper had expressed his willingness to go an extra mile for Kevin. In the depths of his self-pity, Kevin had taken a loaded pistol from the bottom drawer of his desk and for a brief moment, contemplated the easy escape from his torment. It had only been a few fleeting seconds, but each one seemed swollen with his father's memory—a remembrance which had weighed heavily on his psyche since childhood. With that grim reflection came the realization that the blood of his deceased father pulsed in his veins…Kevin recognized, perhaps for the very first time in his life, that there was a serious defect in his nature: A lack of courage to cope with adversity!

In an emotional outburst over this touch of reality, he fired a shot at the framed and yellowed photograph of his father which hung on the wall opposite from the desk where he was sitting. The pistol blast split the silent space as shards of glass sprinkled over the hardwood floor. Outraged at himself, Kevin stood and hurled the firearm through the window, and wept uncontrollably in self disgust.

When the gravity of what he had nearly done began to sink in, Kevin raced from the library to explain the frightening incident to his wife. He found Angie and his infant son lying on the kitchen floor. While reviving Angie and quieting son Patrick, Kevin fabricated a story about what had just happened in the library. "I was rehanging that old photograph of my father and dropped the hammer on the floor…I lost my temper and threw the hammer and broke the damn window!" He knew his explanation was flawed, but in that moment of stress it was the best deception he could concoct.

Kneeling at her side and stroking her face, he apologized. "It must have scared you half to death. I'm so very sorry, Angie."

Groggy and confused, Angie only nodded.

Later, after putting Angie to bed and Patrick in the playpen, Kevin frantically cleaned up the mess of broken glass and pulled the heavy drape over the library window. Then, racing out the back door to retrieve the pistol, he headed along the pine ridge and down the long hillside to the small pond on the western edge of their sprawling property. Once there he tossed the .38 caliber Smith & Wesson as far as he could. Watching the splash, Kevin mumbled to himself, "Never again…" His reference had double meaning—one of the pistol that would rust away and never be found, the other was a cutting self-reproach for his vulnerability.

As he wandered back up the hillside, Kevin resolved further—*never again* would he lie to Angie. Yet, from somewhere in the back of his thoughts, he knew that a lie was like a single leg on a table—it would take more than one to make it stand.

"Kevin?" Angie turned to face her husband. "Are you going to bring the car around to the back door? I'm finally ready to go."

Interrupted from his reverie, Kevin offered an almost enigmatic smile, "Sorry, sweetheart. I was just thinking…" Knowing that where his thoughts had been could not yet be shared, Kevin finished what he'd started to say moments before "…thinking about how richly God has blessed my life, in so many mysterious and marvelous ways."

"You were thinking of your lovely, vivacious wife then, weren't you?" Angie chided.

"Sometimes I believe you can read my mind, sweetheart."

The drive from the Moran's Maple Hill estate to Hibbing was nearly three miles. As Kevin drove east on gravel-surfaced Townline Road, Angie watched the swirls of snowflakes dancing in the glowing headlamps. Winter would soon be closing the door on what had been a moderate autumn in Northern Minnesota. A slight smile creased her face at the thought—Angie always loved the isolation and temperament of the long winter months. Although frigid and blustery, the long white period which lay ahead promised tranquility of mind and spirit along with an inspiration to become more deeply in touch with her creativity. Angie Moran was becoming recognized as an accomplished artist.

Looking off to her right, Angie noted a hovering stand of Norway pines along the roadside. It was at this exact location nearly six years before where she had had her terrible accident. A chill worked its way up her neck. The memory of the incident which happened during her rebellious teenage years still lingered. Angie had stolen her father's car with the idea of running away from home that night, but ended up in the Rood Hospital with a splitting headache, a broken collar bone, and various bumps and bruises. She remembered the flashing white tail of the deer, the sudden impact, and banging her head against the steering wheel as she lost control of he car and crashed into the pines. The broken clavicle mended easily, but ever since that night, she had occasional, sometimes excruciating, pangs which stabbed across her temples.

Angie frowned over the transient memory. Perhaps that accident, more than anything else in her sophomore year, put her in a tailspin of dropping grades and estrangement from friends that continued until only months before her graduation from high school. However, while 'grounded' for the remainder of the school year, Angie developed a meaningful friendship with the doctor who would, only thirteen months later, become her stepmother.

Turning north on First Avenue Road, Kevin contemplated the ensuing evening while Angie gazed absently out the window at passing scenery silhouetted with stands of tamarack and leaf-stripped poplar. With the snowfall tapering off, the clearing clouds allowed a full harvest moon to enhance the early November evening. His thoughts drifted from the tranquil moment to the speech he would be expected to give at Melvin Alto's victory celebration. As he was often wont to do, Kevin pondered how different things might have been if...if his name and reputation had not been slandered by unscrupulous political opponents; if he hadn't quit the campaign. So many *ifs*—and, among them all, the *if* of his troubling deceit. If he had been honest with Angie about what had happened that morning, maybe his guilt would go away. As it was, the lie had become a subtle veil between him and the unconditional love he owed to his wife.

Kevin's surname had been Schmitz while growing up in a blue-collar West Duluth neighborhood. Shortly after his birth, he was adopted and his 'parents' kept his birthright identity carefully locked away from any possible awareness. The scars of that rueful deception still had not healed. It was not until his graduation from Denfeld High School that the truth about who he *really* was had been awkwardly revealed. Since that moment of truth, and the new life he carved for himself, Kevin wondered if assuming his father's surname had been a blessing in his life— or, a curse. Only time would reveal the truth.

Kevin's father had left him a multimillion dollar inheritance—but along with that incredible wealth, Peter Moran's enemies were visited upon the son. After graduating from the University of Minnesota with his degree in law, Kevin settled on the very same soil as his father. Hibbing, Minnesota (a mining town that his obsessed father had largely built through his varied enterprises) became both his home and his challenge in life. Bright, energetic, and perceptive, Kevin Moran built a reputation of credibility for himself and his new family, by quietly using his fortunes to help his adopted community cope with the severe economic hardships of the emerging depression. Kevin's philanthropy and commitment were largely accomplished from the background of his daily social life—the young millionaire chose to keep all his charitable deeds as private as possible.

But, when he decided to make an ultimate contribution to the people he cherished and served, his placid life began to dramatically unravel. In seeking public office, Kevin Moran would become a threat to the political clique that 'called the shots' on Minnesota's Mesabi Iron Range. As a threat to the status quo, a conspiracy of conservative power brokers targeted young Moran for ruination.

Angela broke the silence. "Now that all of this is over—the election stuff, I mean—what are you going to do, Kevin?" Her husband had been wrapped up in political activities of one kind or another for several months. In the back of her mind, Angie hoped that he would consider returning to the regular hours which his law practice afforded. She desperately missed his presence at their dinner table, his companionship around the house, and the intimacy they enjoyed when their life had been centered and balanced.

Kevin smiled, reached across to find Angie's linen gloved hand. "It's been hard on you...on *us*..." he emphasized *us*, and finished the acknowledgment with a question he already had an answer for, "Hasn't it been, Angela?"

Angie sensed that when Kevin used her full first name, his mood was more serious than superficial. "I'd be less than honest," Angie squeezed his hand and frowned. "Yes, Kevin, you know it's been difficult. And, on *us* far more than just myself. I'm glad you put it that way." Angie swallowed hard at the next words she would say. "I've never told you this before, but...maybe, I need to tell you something that makes me feel—well, feel really selfish. There was a time, Kevin, before you withdrew from the campaign when I actually..."

Kevin could have finished Angie's confession, but chose to allow her to purge the thought for herself.

"...When I wanted you to lose!" Angie looked at her husband, expecting some sign of surprise, disappointment.

But there was no change in his somber expression. "Just between the two of us, so did I. Only for a moment or two, mind you—but, I was beginning to think that if I were elected it might be too great a price to pay." Slowing the car so he might stretch this time with Angie, Kevin continued. "Please don't think I wasn't painfully aware of all the time I would have had to spend away from you and Patrick if I'd won."

Kevin's admission allowed Angie to summon an additional measure of candor. "You might have been thinking about that, Kevin, but you surely weren't living the daily isolation like I was. And you weren't communicating any concerns about our family to me. There were times when I really believed you were insensitive, and too full of yourself to realize what was really most important in life."

"That's putting it mildly, dear. Selfish might be the better word."

Angie nodded her agreement but conceded. "We both were selfish, I mean. And, insensitive to each other at the same time. Let's be careful, both of us, not to let that happen again. It's the worst possible thing."

Kevin pulled over to the side of the road, shifting into neutral, and turned in his seat so that he could meet Angela's eyes directly. "Let me make that promise to you right here and now." He could feel the swell of emotion in his throat. "You mean more to me than anything in the world, Angie. Sometimes I wonder why I do the selfish things I do. It's like I have this strange obsession inside me. I've told you enough about my father, or what I've managed to learn about him from others over the years. He was impulsive, self-centered, and ambitious! And look where it got him!"

Angie knew enough about Peter Moran to understand the dangerous behaviors to which her husband had alluded. She mitigated the sharp edge on Kevin's insinuations, "Let's not be too harsh on him, Kevin. I've been told that your father was one very charming gentleman, too. And very generous to those he loved, besides." Angie smiled, leaning forward to kiss Kevin softly on the lips. "I think Peter might have swept me off my feet if I'd ever known him. What do you think about that?"

Kevin could only laugh at the crazy notion. "Thanks for saying that, sweetheart. You've got a way of putting a positive slant on everything. I do just the opposite most of the time, I'm afraid."

"Aren't I just the most lovable woman in the world, Kevin?"

Kevin pulled her close and kissed her with an ardor that caused Angie to gently push herself away. "Let's save that passion, young man…for a few hours, anyhow."

~

Tony Zoretek consoled his wife with an amused smile, "They're only fifteen minutes late, Becca. Little Patrick probably delayed them; I'll bet anything that's what it is. You know how hard it is for Angie to leave that son of hers, even for a couple of hours.

Becca, sitting on the arm of the living room sofa, regarded her tall husband pace from the front window to the foyer and back again. She couldn't help a soft laugh at the sight, "Who's walking around like a new father in our hospital's maternity ward, Tony? Come over and sit down with your favorite doctor and let her give you a small dose of patience. They'll be getting here soon enough."

Tony paused as he passed Becca, leaned over and brushed a light kiss on her dark hair. "Did I tell you that you look gorgeous tonight?"

"Maybe two or three times, but it's like music to my ears every time you say it."

"Speaking of music, what's Marco doing upstairs?"

Marco was Tony's twenty year old son, already an accomplished musician with his own little swing combo band. In his second year at the local junior college, Marco's world was far different from that of his father. Gregarious Tony Zoretek, a highly successful building contractor and real estate developer, loved the outdoors and sports, while Marco could spend hours alone in his room with his phonograph and wide assortment of musical instruments. And, Marco had never so much as attempted deer or duck hunting nor had he gone on fishing trips with the men in all his years. Even attending ball games with his father or Uncle Rudy was a reluctant chore for young Marco.

"I think it's his new clarinet. Your son, need I remind you, is determined to be a one-man orchestra some day."

Tony nodded his awareness of Marco's talent, "He's really good, isn't he Becca? I mean, that melody he's playing right now is…"

"Soulful? Yes, he's marvelous." Becca finished her husband's thought as she often did. In their years together, the two of them had developed concordant marital patterns where they almost thought as one.

The lilt of the Louie Armstrong rendition of *Stardust* caught her breath.

Becca Kaner Zoretek had married Tony, a widower, six years before. These had been the six most delightful of her nearly forty-four years. A physician at the Hibbing Rood Hospital, Becca had established the largest practice in the bustling mining community of twenty thousand people. To many, she was simply known as 'the good doctor'. Her commitment to the women, and their mine-working husbands, was almost legendary. And, nearly half of the children in town had entered the world through her two caring hands. Hands that tended to their every illness and broken bone thereafter.

It was Becca who had been working at the hospital on the night when Tony's wife, Mary, died of the pandemic flu outbreak in October of 1918. Through the difficult years following, it was Becca more than anybody else, who kept Tony from losing his tenuous hold on life. Although the two of them would never have children together, both Angela and Marco were as close to her heart as her own children might have been. Winning their affection, however, wasn't an easy task, but surely an accomplishment of love conquering mistrust and apprehension.

Angela was an especially difficult conversion, but over the years had become Becca's closest friend.

Taking Tony's hand and meeting his deep-set green eyes, Becca hummed the *Stardust* melody. "So you think I look pretty good tonight. I have to be as stunning as I can, you know. I'm going to be on the arm of the most handsome man in Hibbing at Melvin's party."

Tony smiled at the compliment, "Gorgeous doesn't do you justice, my dear. Maybe stunning is a much better choice. That dress you're wearing is simply fantastic."

Becca laughed, "Angie's wearing one that's almost identical tonight. We planned it that way when we were shopping together." Becca stood to brush wrinkles from the front of her black dress, "Hers is serge rather than velvet, with an open neck and puffy sleeves; and she's wearing her pearl accessories." Becca's dress buttoned to her long neck and had fitted sleeves. Her accessories were an emerald necklace and matching ring. "So I'm glad you like the way I look because your two women are going to look a lot like twins."

"I think Kevin and I are the two luckiest men in the world."

"I'll second that, Mr. Zoretek…if you don't mind." Becca saw the glow of headlamps approaching, "Now, if you can act on that precious sentiment of good fortune, my wrap is in the foyer closet. Kevin and Angie are here."

SHADES OF WHITE

The Androy Hotel was the landmark, and the towering anchor of bustling Howard Street—Hibbing's main artery of commerce. Kevin Moran's concealed ownership of the modern, majestic, hundred-room hotel had been an issue in the contentious political campaign which had been decided the previous Tuesday. A campaign in which every aspect of his personal life had been exposed like a public surgery.

Kevin's vast inheritance enabled the young attorney to enjoy a comfortable lifestyle during these difficult Depression times. There were, however, only two conspicuous purchases he'd make in the six years since his eighteenth birthday. And both were linked with the legacy of his deceased father. Kevin had moved the Peter Moran mansion from North Hibbing to its present location on Maple Hill, south of the city, and had purchased the imposing Androy Hotel from out-of-town interests. Kevin once suggested to his friend, Claude Atkinson, "It's my dad's money after all, and it's only fitting that I use the bequest to keep his house from being demolished, and to keep a luxurious hotel in the family name. (Peter Moran's elegant European-style hotel had been reduced to ashes in a horrendous arson fire shortly before his untimely death in 1908).

To some, the Androy Hotel might have been considered a far too elaborate setting for this evening's campaign victory celebration of Iron Range blue-collar Democrats. But Kevin Moran insisted upon sending the conspicuous message that change was in the offing—borrowing the concept from the tradition of Andrew Jackson's memorial inauguration at the White House. This evening was, to his way of thinking, a triumph of the working class over the wealthy elite of the iron mining hub city.

In the grand ballroom, nearly two hundred well-wishers were paying tribute to the newly-elected young representative from nearby Chisholm. Melvin Alto was a champion of the working man and the struggling local merchant community. Mesabi's blue-collar mine workers, public employees, and small business owners had formed the Democratic coalition which had elected Alto to office. Hibbing's wealthy nabobs—the mine owners and managers, along with major materials suppliers—were the Republican power structure that Melvin Alto overwhelmed at the ballot boxes. In light of that reality, Kevin had imparted to Melvin on the previous day that, "Were it not for Prohibition, we'd see far more beer mugs than martinis at our victory party."

"What a wonderful turnout for Melvin!" Kevin commented as he escorted Angie into the crystal-chandeliered opulence of the Androy's main ballroom. Not a building north of Duluth compared with the refinement afforded by Moran's esteemed hotel.

Smiling, Angie nodded without reply, linking her arm with that of Becca walking beside her. The two women added a striking elegance to the crowded scene of mingling partisans.

The red, white, and blue campaign banners of Franklin Roosevelt and Floyd Olson hung from the ceiling alongside those of Melvin Alto, adorning the frescoed walls with splashes of garish political color. Tonight all of those present would celebrate a triumph for mainstream America!

"There's Melvin...over by Steven and Senia." Tony gestured to his left as he placed a large hand on Kevin's shoulder. "Let's head over that way and offer our congratulations before Mel gets swallowed up in the crowd."

The foursome moved through the throng shaking hands and offering pleasantries to their friends as they made their way toward the guest of honor. Tony Zoretek knew everyone in the room in one manner or another, while Kevin was still learning names and the kinship connections that went with them. The tall contractor had affectionate hugs for Norm Dinter, Lud Jaksa, Con O'Gara and their wives. And Becca, walking at Tony's side, was like a magnet to so many of the guests that the procession toward Alto's group only inched its way along.

Steven Skorich, a respected labor organizer and small businessman, spotted Tony making his way in his direction. "Anton, c'mon over here—Becca, Kevin, Angie...we've been waiting for the four of you to show up." Steven used the name 'Anton' affectionately—Tony was his nephew.

"Uncle Steven," Tony waved, while encouraging his small entourage along. "Fashionably late is all; at least that what Angie's told me," he called in Steven's direction over the noise.

Claude and Dora Atkinson had joined Melvin and Mia Alto in Steven's small cluster. Claude's son, Marc, and mayor-elect Frank Molinaro were conversing in happy tones nearby.

Melvin stepped forward, meeting the eyes of Kevin with a wide, infectious smile, "All this is like a wedding reception, Kevin…and, I've finally found my best man."

Kevin understood the 'best man' compliment immediately. When he had withdrawn from the campaign and thrown his support behind Melvin, the tight race turned dramatically in Alto's favor. In doing what he had, Kevin became the king maker! He embraced the smaller man and whispered, "I couldn't be happier, Mel. We're going to have the best damn representative in Minnesota to fight our causes—I mean that with all my heart."

Placing his hands on Kevin's shoulders, Melvin's smile radiated sincerity, "Were it not for you, my friend…"

Overhearing Mel's comment, Angie interrupted the two men, hoping to temper the emotion of the moment. Taking Mia's hand in hers, she complimented, "What a handsome couple the two of you are. Your dress is exquisite, Mia; a perfect match for your blue eyes. And, Melvin—what a nice looking suit and tie."

"Thanks to Tony and Becca. They took us shopping yesterday and—" Mia's smile was one of modest embarrassment, "We owe so much to all of you. Can we ever thank you enough?"

Becca interrupted in an indignant tone, "Nobody owes anybody anything, Mia. We're friends, and friendship has no boundaries. We all know that, for heaven's sake! And, when Melvin's down in St. Paul, we're going to pitch in and help you run the creamery business."

"Remember, I want to drive Mel's 'Alto Dairy Company' truck at the first chance, Becca," Angie laughed. "And Kevin's going to milk some cows—what do you think about that, Mr. Moran?" She nudged Kevin in the ribs playfully.

As nine o'clock approached, the gathering began to settle around the linen-covered banquet tables adorned with patriotic centerpiece arrangements. Kevin had insisted upon serving a meal of venison stew, partridge breasts and breaded walleye filets along with wild rice and Slovenian *sarmas*. His favorite sweet, *potica*, rested on crystal platters in thick slices with rich slabs of Alto's Creamery butter nearby.

Father Potocnik of the Immaculate Conception Church, along with Pastor Lundstrom of First Lutheran, jointly offered a blessing over the food, and those who shared this marvelous bounty, invoking Jesus' name with ministerial reverence. "And we ask that God's guiding hand be upon Melvin Alto and all elected officials as they legislate on our behalf." "Amen," added Rabbi Rothstein at their side as co-celebrant.

After everybody had eaten their fill and the dinner plates had been removed from the tables, the clink of spoons on glasses resonated through the room. "Speech! Speech!" In unison, countless voices appealed toward the head table where the honored guests were seated. Whistles and hoots followed in a boisterous demand… "Speech!"

Melvin Alto stood, gesturing for the crowd to allow some decorum. "I'll only say a few words if my friend, Kevin Moran, will speak first."

Prepared for the invitation, Kevin shook Melvin's hand and rose to the podium which was centered behind the broad table. Shouts of enthusiasm greeted Kevin's appearance, continuing for a long minute, as he returned their recognition with an exuberant waving gesture.

"Melvin…Mia…Angela…members of the clergy," Kevin nodded to his right, "And our dear friends—thank you for what you've done to make this evening…this celebration of victory…possible! Democrats have been swept to power at every level of government, and we're here to acknowledge this triumph for the American people, all Minnesotan's, and especially our beleaguered brothers and sisters across this great Mesabi Iron Range!"

Loud applause echoed throughout the room.

Kevin paused before resuming his oration. With a confident demeanor, he offered a brief summation of election returns, concluding with Melvin Alto's thousand vote plurality in the sixtieth legislative district. In a softer tone, Kevin lowered his head perceptibly, "When I think of victory, my friends, I am always reminded of Victor." With his reference to Hibbing's nationally recognized former mayor, Vic Power, a hushed silence hung over the assembly. Power had died unexpectedly in April of 1926, but his memory continued to be held in highest esteem among Range mine workers. "Yes, I can feel the spirit of that great man in our midst this evening. 'Power to the people' he promised us, and power to the people he delivered!"

Melvin was clapping enthusiastically when Steven Skorich stood at the head table, encouraging a standing ovation to the invocation of Vic Power's famous campaign pledge. Everybody stood, whistling and cheering at the top of their voices.

Kevin waited for the clamor to dissipate before continuing. "Friends, it is my sincere pleasure to introduce a man who, like his father, and his father's friend, Vic Power," Kevin pointed toward elderly Martin Alto, "is a fighter for human rights and dignity."

More cheers erupted. "And, I can assure each of you, we now have a man who will work shoulder to shoulder with Governor Floyd Olson to make Minnesota work. This man, as we all know, is our own—Melvin Alto!"

After five minutes of jubilant acclamation, Melvin began his own speech. The thin, blond-haired Finlander was the son of an activist mineworker, and owner of a successful creamery business in Balkan Township north of Chisholm. Young Alto was a political newcomer, but a man of unquestioned character and credibility in every respect. During the campaign he made no empty promises about putting people back to work, or getting the sluggish economy back on its feet. Rather, the erstwhile dairyman promised only to listen and learn—and to always give his best effort. For the first time in recent history, the Hibbing region would be represented by a person who did not have the 'puppet strings' of powerful mining company managers attached to him. At Kevin's suggestion, Alto had linked his own campaign with the broader theme of Roosevelt's 'New Deal' and Floyd Olson's populist platform.

In his laid-back style, Melvin repeated his campaign promise: "I'll give you my ears and my voice…you give me your prayers and support. We've got to work together—always…asking the Good Lord to stand behind us all every step of the way."

Watching the festivities from a doorway at the back of the huge ballroom was the Androy Hotel's manager, Armando Depelo. 'Mando', as the handsome and well-dressed Italian was widely known, had been employed by Kevin Moran for nearly three years. That reality had become increasingly distasteful to Depelo. While most of the well-wishers were drinking soft beverages and coffee, Mando served liquor to his friends from a private room nearby. His insidious activity was both illegal and contrary to Moran's clear instructions that hotel security personnel confiscate any spirits on the premises.

Prohibition had been profitable for Mando Depelo and his ill-reputed colleagues in the Hibbing underworld. Most of the local 'bootleggers' were small timers with their own small distilling operations. The Italians made wines while the Austrians were often moonshine cookers. But Fort Francis (on the Canadian border) was only a hundred miles to the north. Because of its proximity, Hibbing had gained a reputation as a major outlet for barrels of fine Canadian whiskeys which made their way to Duluth, the Twin Cities, and Chicago. As a member of the police commission, Depelo was in a perfect position to manipulate trafficking and subvert enforcement of the Volstead Act. The Feds would shut down an occasional 'two-bit' still while turning a blind eye on Depelo's larger operations. Mando had no respect for Prohibition or any other law.

The hotel manager already had had more than enough to drink this evening, and purposely remained in the background so as to avoid any reprimands from the celebrated political dignitaries whose interactions he studied from a distance.

"Hey, Zench...get your ass over here!" Depelo's face wore a scowl. "Vinny over there says you refused to fill his flask when he asked you. I'll fire your black ass if you don't do what my guests ask...do you understand me, 'boy'?"

Gary Zench, an honor student in his second year of junior college, worked afternoon shifts as a 'jack-of-all-trades' at the Androy to help pay a share of the monthly rent on his small room on the hotel's fourth floor. The young man was as determined to learn every aspect of the hotel's operations as he was determined to please his employer. Gary had been a childhood friend of Kevin Moran in West Duluth and was now the only black face in the ethnic melting pot of Hibbing. "Can't do that, Mr. Depelo, sir. Mr. Moran was very clear about drinking. 'Absolutely no liquor' he told the staff, sir." Gary bit off the 'sirs' he felt required to use as an ending punctuation to every sentence.

Depelo gave the young man a cold stare. He despised the Negro, but knew better than to make a scene. It was well understood at the hotel that Gary Zench and Kevin Moran's friendship was deeply rooted. Depelo had made the mistake of calling Gary 'nigger' in Kevin's presence once—only once! (Kevin had taken him by the shirt on that occasion and told him that he'd better not use that despicable expression again). So, Depelo had used 'boy' instead.

Gary Zench was Mando's height, with an angular frame, and the complexion of a mulatto. At twenty-five, he had made more than his share of mistakes while growing up in an abusive home, but was determined to make a respectable life for himself with the opportunity an education would provide. (Gary had served five years at the St. Cloud Reformatory for his involvement in a Duluth robbery, had been paroled, and then moved to Hibbing). His new life had been made possible by Kevin's benevolent intervention in Gary's troubled affairs.

Gary met Depelo's hard eyes with a challenge of his own, "I'd like an apology, sir. If I heard correctly, you said something about my 'black ass'. That's disrespecting me, sir. We're not supposed to use that kind of language in Mr. Moran's hotel, sir."

Depelo never engaged in an argument he couldn't win, and as much as he disliked the Negro, he chose to back away from this confrontation. "If I did, and I'm not gonna admit that to nobody, then…I shouldn't have done it. That's all I got to say, Zench." He looked away from the dark eyes that had locked with his for a moment, "Maybe you ought to help out in the kitchen or bus some of the tables, 'boy'—you ain't no help just standing around."

Gary gave the manager a wry smile. He considered telling Depelo to brush up on his English or to come up with something more creatively degrading than 'boy', but squelched the notion. "That's exactly what I was doing, sir—that's before you told me to get my dark buttocks over here. If this little scolding's all you wanted, well, you've got that off your mind for the moment. And I've gotten the closest thing to an apology that I'll ever hope to get."

Gary sensed that Depelo had been stung by his remark and he couldn't repress his satisfied amusement, "Now, if you'll excuse me, I'm being paid to work this banquet, sir…and that's what I intend to finish doing." Before leaving, however, Gary added, "You might want to be more careful about dispensing booze, sir. Mr. Moran would be very displeased."

Depelo watched the young man walk away. His eyes moved from Zench to the head table where Kevin Moran was finishing his speech. "You really think you're something, Moran," he mumbled under his breath.

Vinny Gabetti wandered over to Depelo's side, "That nigger kid givin' ya a bad time, Mando? I'd like to meet him in the alley outside some night. Like I just tol ya, Mando, the sonofabitch wouldn't get me no booze—now I gotta go get some myself, for chrissakes!"

Mando nodded at his balding, fleshy-jowled countryman without reply. He wasn't in the mood for any more conversation about the incident. Something else had seized his attention. His eyes were riveted on the beautiful dark-haired woman sitting at the head table near the podium where Moran was speaking.

Armando Depelo had grown up as a close family friend of Angela's parents, Tony and Mary Zoretek, and had known her since she was a little girl. Tony's younger brother, Rudy, had been Mando's best friend for years. But, Angela was always much too young. She was a grade-schooler, when he graduated from high school, and by the time Angela was a senior, Mando was already unhappily married and disconnected from her family. "My God how I'd like to get my hands on her gorgeous ass," he fantasized his secret lust.

Part of Depelo's hatred of Kevin Moran was rooted in the fact that his employer had inherited wealth almost beyond comprehension from his late father. Another part of the complex pattern of jealousy stemmed from Kevin's tight relationship with the Zoretek's. To Mando it seemed that younger Kevin was like a member of their family—something of a golden son to Tony. It wasn't only the Zoretek's that Kevin captivated, however, almost everybody else in this town had readily taken a shine to the young Moran. Since coming to Hibbing, the 'do-gooder' and benefactor for so many community charitable activities had become somewhat the 'prodigal son' returned to have celebrity status lavished upon him. Mostly, however, the germ of Mando's covert envy was his obsession with Kevin's wife, Angela. Watching her smile and applaud her husband's speech, Mando cursed under his breath again, "Enjoy your moment, Moran. One of these days you're gonna fall on your face, and I'll be there to piss all over ya."

~

Winter's talons clasped a sharp grip upon Northern Minnesota in mid-November. Arctic winds swept the landscape with a fury that defied any human activity out-of-doors. Minus twenty dipped to minus thirty degrees when December took its place on the calendar. Horrific wind chills surrendered their grip to weeks of snow! For many dark gray and endless days, the skies emptied countless inches of icy flakes, creating a blanket of white nearly two feet deep. When the snowstorms were driven by fierce westerlies, enormous drifts brought days of virtual paralysis.

Angie Moran was enthralled by the majesty which was manifest through the long winter months. The many different shades and tones of white inspired her artistic inclinations. Angie loved to sketch and paint the abstract concepts which the varied winter landscapes offered in marvelous abundance.

From her living room window overlooking the vast Maple Hill acreage, a sweeping vantage down a pine ridged western slope, Angie could behold the many contrasts of January's white brush strokes. There were the white emptiness of the open fields, the white pillows of snow on spruce branches, the white bark of the birch tree stands highlighted by naked hardwood clusters, the white line of picket fencing which angled off to the east of the property, and, as a backdrop to these varied complexions were the wispy white clouds stretching toward the distant horizon. Angie found beauty and intrigue in the manifold shades of white that converged in wildly imaginative design upon the coarse canvas surfaces resting on her easel. In her every aspect winter was a queen in robes of white.

While Patrick napped in his nursery across the hallway from her upstairs studio, Angie mused to herself over her abstruse oil painting depiction of icicles dangling from the limb of a naked birch. The snarly tree stood only a few feet from the south facing window to her left, and had captured some snow melt from the eaves of the house.

What was it about white? What did her fascination with the color without color say about her personality? There had to be something hidden deep in her psyche to explain this arcane seduction. But…what could it possibly be? Perplexed by the enigma, she resolved to pose this question to her mentor, Jacque Grojean, when next she visited his 'artiste shoppe', as the little Frenchman called his studio nestled between taller buildings on a Hibbing side street. White was virginal, pristine, placid…even indefinite. Yet none of those traits seemed a plausible personality definition—if anything, Angie was a virtual contradiction of all these characteristics.

Suddenly, her contemplation was broken by a cry from Patrick's room. Putting her brush and smock aside, she rinsed her hands in a white porcelain bowl and dried them with a white towel. White everything, Angie smiled at the irony…but, her awakened son was hungry. Her studio was an escape—her boy was the center of reality in her life.

In the months since the tragic Lindbergh kidnapping, Angie had suffered nightmares in which she envisioned a ladder leaning against the Moran's house below Patrick's nursery window. The isolation of Maple Hill was both alluringly tranquil most of the time, but eerily unnerving at others, "Mommy's coming, my pumkin…"

If Angie Moran didn't quite have a grip on some elusive aspects of her personality, her life was undeniable complete, spiritually connected, and centered on her chosen priorities. Without trace of any doubt, her son and her rejuvenated relationship with Kevin, offered her the fulfillment she needed. Only one room in the illusory house that was her self, continued to cause Angela anxiety. Why were there lost moments in her life…? Where were the missing pieces in her puzzle?

'LIFE'S LONGING FOR ITSELF'

August 18, 1934

The early morning sun rays crept slowly over the eastern bank of lofty Norway pines into the airy sitting room where Angela Moran nursed five month old, Mary Rebecca. She was humming a lullaby to the wide-eyed infant cradled in her arms, and gently pushing her stockinged feet into the rhythm…"on the treetop", while the nursery rocker creaked in soft cadence. Angie ran her fingers over the baby's silky locks arrayed upon the perfectly formed little head as she intoned "when the wind blows"…The Kilim-pillowed rocker had been a gift from Kevin when Maribec, as the girl had already been nicknamed by her proud father, was born on March 18.

How the past two years had flown by! As the infant's eyes closed, Angie contemplated this early Saturday as well as the many past Saturdays of her contented life on Maple Hill. The lovely home that centered her life, however, would never define Angela Moran. Even during her pregnancy, she remained active with charitable activities in the community, attended mass regularly, and found ample time to work with Jacque Grojean in the artist's downtown studio.

Although life was comfortable for her and Kevin, the grip of America's Depression caused untold misery for so many inhabitants of iron mining-dependent Hibbing. Unemployment had idled more than seventy percent of the area's population, and the social malaise of poverty was everywhere in evidence. The Morans and Zoreteks, blessed with considerable financial resources, endeavored all they could to alleviate the widespread economic hardships of their friends and neighbors.

On most occasions, Angie was the catalyst and her husband the funds provider for helping those in dire need.

On an early Thursday morning shortly after Christmas the previous year, a passerby reported seeing flames from the northwest corner of the sprawling Memorial Building. In minus thirty-three degree temperatures, Hibbing's three fire departments, with assistance from nearby Keewatin firemen, fought the blaze which had started in the kitchen. Their valiant efforts, however, were to no avail. Within two hours the entire building became consumed in a roaring conflagration. Barney Vesel, a butcher by trade, was one of the first of nearly 250 citizen volunteers to join nearly one hundred professional fire fighters. Barney lost fingers on both hands from frostbite. Although the young father of three could no longer cut meat at Khort's Market, he could be trained to take care of horses and maintain a barn. The Moran's employed him as a handyman at their Maple Hill residence.

Jalmer Norgren was only thirty-four when he became disabled in a mine blasting accident before the heavy layoffs in 1930. He and his wife Thelma had seven children between six and sixteen. Since his accident, Jalmer had been employed as the Androy Hotel's boiler room attendant. Despite the handicap of having only one arm, Jalmer proved to be a competent and dependable employee of Kevin Moran.

Eleven year-old Sarah Laudner had leukemia. The Mayo Clinic treatment costs accumulated to thousands of dollars. Angie had driven Sarah's parents the eleven hour distance to Rochester on two occasions. Kevin quietly paid all the transportation, lodging, and medical bills. And, ten months after Sarah's last trip to Mayo, Kevin paid for the child's funeral.

The previous autumn, tragedy struck the family of Arvid and Eila Maki. Arvid was accidentally shot in the groin by a companion while deer hunting near Kitzville Location. Arvid bled to death. Along with Becca Zoretek, Angie organized a benefit dance at the Finnish Tapio Hall. Kevin and Tony pledged a match to every dollar raised so that the surviving Maki family could avoid foreclosure on their house in Park Addition. Bake sales and craft bazaars raised additional funds. Only weeks ago, Kevin gave Eila a job in the Androy laundry so that she could keep up with her bills and put food on the Maki's table.

Every Christmas, Kevin Moran was Santa Claus to the Vesels, Norgrens, and Makis…as well as the Sorci, Pontinen, Morelli, Prebich, and Whitcombe families. On Easter Sunday, Kevin became the mysterious 'Easter Bunny' and delivered baskets of candies to nearly fifty Hibbing children.

Doctor Becca Zoretek had been reprimanded for her billing procedures by the Rood Hospital's chief-of-staff. It was discovered that many of her needy patients had not been charged for services in several months. Tony, Becca, and Kevin covered the expenses.

Tony Zoretek's construction company, strapped by the lack of contracting work, continued to maintain its payroll by putting his carpenters, masons, and laborers to work on community development projects. During the years of the Depression, Zoretek Construction Company had actually increased its workforce from sixty to eighty employees—and had managed to keep every worker busy five days a week.

In October of the previous year, Angie had organized her female friends from various churches into what she called the 'Women of Winter' to knit warm woolen sweaters, mittens, and scarves for the needy children in Hibbing's schools. In addition, the women assisted elderly residents with shopping, housekeeping, and laundry chores and volunteered time at the local orphanage.

Angela heard the footsteps only moments before feeling the soft kiss on her neck. "Good morning, sweetheart."

Kevin pulled up an easy chair, handed his wife a cup of freshly brewed coffee (saturated with cream and sugar), and plucked his daughter from Angie's lap. "I can tell I'm interrupting some serious thinking, Angie. What's on the mind of my lovely bride this morning?"

"Nothing, really. Just adoring my little pumpkin, that's all. And thinking about Patrick's birthday party tomorrow. Can you believe our little boy's going to be three years old, Kevin? Where has the time gone?" Kevin smiled at the thought. The past two years were like a blur to him as well. Having put politics behind him, he had returned to the Peterson and Raukar law firm under a part-time arrangement and was doing mostly *pro bono* work for those who could not afford the legal fees for probates, real estate matters, contracts and simple litigations. Also, Kevin had involved himself more in the daily operations of the Androy which was limping through the difficult economic times. Most of his time, however, was spent in various church and community development activities where he could see improvements made in daily lives of people. "Yes, it does, Angie...seems like only yesterday." He cradled his sleeping daughter while smiling upon her perfect features. "She's the picture of her mother, that's for sure."

"People said that when I was born—that I was the picture of my mom. I guess I was, too. But Maribec's got your nose, Kevin, and your chin as well. Look at that little dimple."

Kevin looked at Maribec for a long moment, then at Angie. "Mary was the most beautiful woman I'd ever seen; I can still remember her loveliness from my childhood. And her goodness."

At the mention of goodness, a troubling thought slipped into Angie's mind. She had been only seven when Mary died suddenly sixteen years ago. For months afterwards, she believed that her mother spoke to her within the privacy of her bedroom. Angie remembered her mother's consoling voice and how she recorded those secret conversations in a notebook kept hidden in her dresser drawer. After telling her father about the wondrous 'voice' one morning, Mary's consoling words were never to return. It was then that Angie truly experienced the loss of her mother's presence in her life, and began a period of estrangement from her father and friends that lasted for months.

"I hope and pray that our little girl grows up to be as wonderful as her mother," Kevin commented pleasantly. Then, noticing the traces of a frown on his wife's face, inquired, "What's wrong, dear?"

Obviously disconcerted, Angie looked beyond Kevin trying to measure what might be his reaction to what she was about to say. "...And I hope that she doesn't."

Kevin wondered at her faraway look without reply.

"I've told you often enough about my childhood. For nearly ten years I was a very unlikable person. I was berating Becca all the time, telling my father he was being disloyal to mom. Running away and crashing the family car, dropping out of school activities and allowing my grades really suffer from neglect. I've tried to erase those memories of high school and my belligerence at home, but I can't. I think my Dad and Becca are saints for bearing through it all. And you…" Angie explained, as she had many times before, how much her love and infatuation with Kevin had been her saving escape throughout those difficult times.

Kevin also had remorse. While growing up in West Duluth, he had put his adoptive parents through a private hell of their own on so many occasions. Art and Sarah Schmitz were good people doing their very best to cope with an awkward situation. Where Angie had largely withdrawn from the world, Kevin however, had chosen to challenge it—to be conspicuously successful in everything he did. In both academics and sports, he excelled, and with achievement came a maturity beyond his years.

Kevin stood, placing Maribec in the nearby bassinet, and knelt on the floor while placing his hands along Angie's hips. "We've both had our share of things to regret, sweetheart. But, somehow, we've managed to make something good of our lives. I believe that with all my heart. We've become decent people, Angie. And we're going to be the best parents our children could ever have."

Angie stroked Kevin's auburn hair pressing his head softly into her lap. Her husband always seemed to know the right thing to say at the right moment. "Our children have our blood, Kevin. That's a miracle for sure…and there's nothing we can ever change about that. But, does that reality spell things like 'always' or 'never'?

Looking up and meeting her dark, ovaline eyes, Kevin understood the concern underlying his wife's question. Would the two of them shape the lives of their children or did Patrick and Maribec have some arcane predestination? While in college he had read something by Kahlil Gibran and the message still lingered somewhere at the edges of his memory. In his work, *The Prophet*, Gibran's wisdom on life had touched Kevin deeply at the time…

Your children are not your children.
They are the sons and daughters of Life's longing for itself.
They come through you but not from you,
And though they are with you yet they belong not to you…

In a tone soft and barely audible, Kevin said, "We can probably only give them the right direction, Angie. And pray that God's hand does the rest."

Among Kevin's favorite childhood memories were his birthdays. On his special February day, 'relatives' from Hibbing always made the trip to Duluth. The Iron Range contingency included Angie and her brother Marco along with their parents Tony and Mary, Tony's brother Rudy, Steven Skorich (Tony's uncle), and Senia Arola (his late father's friend—although Kevin didn't know that until many years later. Nor could he have known that his 'relatives' were not really related him in any biological way.) Kevin's birthday always outshone his Christmas. Consequently, birthdays were a tradition that Kevin made every effort to continue celebrating with his extended family. On this occasion of Patrick's birthday, the traveling family members, however, were coming from Duluth, not traveling to Duluth.

Art and Sarah Schmitz traveled to Hibbing with Father Pat Foley (Kevin's devoted mentor during those often turbulent St. James parochial school days and throughout his teenage years) and Kevin's favorite Denfeld High School teacher and neighbor, Mr. Barker. The foursome would be arriving shortly before noon.

Standing beside Tony Zoretek and gazing into a cloudless, azure, Sunday morning sky, Kevin was in a celebratory mood. The two men absorbed the rich aroma emanating from the barbecue pit. Kevin had placed the seasoned pig on a spit the night before, and had been carefully attending to the roasting since early morning. Angie and Becca were in the kitchen putting the finishing touches on a large bowl of potato salad.

Kevin lifted his glass mug of beer to offer a toast, "Here's to a wonderful day with my favorite people in the world."

Putting his hand on Kevin's shoulder, Tony clinked his glass of lemonade with the host, "And especially to my grandson, Patrick."

Kevin smiled, drawing a deep swallow, "It's been a lot of years since we could legally have any liquor at a birthday party, and you…Tony…I wonder, have you ever had a drink in your life?"

"Once or twice, I guess. I've always had more fun watching other people drink—often to foolish excess. Besides, I much prefer a cold glass of milk…or lemonade. I swear Angie managed to get her mother's recipe—this is delicious!"

Much to the delight of most Americans, Prohibition had finally ended the year before. Despite his abstinence, Tony was pleased when the Volstead Act was repealed. He had close friends who had been financially distressed by Prohibition and deplored the criminal activity that the era had inspired. "Kevin, were it not for alcohol, you and Angie might not be living in this beautiful house. Have you ever thought of that?'

Kevin nodded at the reality, "My dad made a good share of his fortune—and now, mine I guess—in the liquor business before he died, didn't he?" Kevin was well aware of Peter Moran's diverse enterprises. Lifting his mug again, he looked heavenward and smiled, "To my dad, he's to bless…and probably to blame, for everything my life's about."

Tony knew without explanation that Kevin's unusual toast referred to how the Moran name had been slandered in the political campaign two years before. "I'll drink to every blessing in your life, Kev. But I'd go lightly on any blame. Were it not for your dad…well, I might never had learned carpentry…and never—" Tony's eyes sparkled, "never been able to make the birthday gift I've brought for little Pat." Tony had spent hours in is workshop crafting a wooden fire truck replica, complete with attached ladders, and a roll of cord for hosing.

"Speaking of carpentry, Tony, yesterday afternoon I sneaked away from the office and drove out to Sturgeon Lake. Even with the rain it was great to be out there for a couple of hours." Kevin owned forty acres of pristine, wooded lake shore property next to a smaller tract that belonged to the Zoreteks. Kevin smiled at his memory of the experience. "I've got a huge favor to ask of you."

"Thinking about building a cabin?" Tony could read Kevin's thought. "Yes, I am. I'd like to surprise Angie with a lake home. There's this spectacular ridge…it would be just perfect." The west facing hilltop, nearly sixty vertical feet from the sandy shoreline afforded a marvelous view of the lake. For Kevin, a lake home on their remote property would be a pleasant retreat from his hotel and community activities. And for Angie, an ideal place for her to create some dramatic landscape scenes.

"And you'd like some help building a place…am I right?"

"You're the best carpenter I know." Kevin explained his imagined cabin and offered to help out with the construction. "I'd like a tower on the west end for an art studio—but, I'd like the whole project to be kept as a secret from Angie."

"They're here!" Angie called to the men from the rear deck of the house. "Father Pat's car is coming up the driveway."

"So, we'll just keep this cabin business between the two of us, right, Kev?" Tony took Kevin's arm and the two of them wandered up to the house to greet their guests.

Shortly after everyone's arrival, Kevin made a point of spending some private time with Art and Sarah by inviting them to take a hike down the slope of his property to the horse barn on the lower pasture a quarter mile from the house.

Placing his arms around their shoulders as the walked between him, Kevin gave the elderly couple a gentle squeeze. "Thanks for coming, Mom and Dad." Kevin seldom used the familial expression, but it rolled easily from his tongue this cheerful early afternoon. "We've shared a lot of birthdays together, haven't we?"

"Twenty five of yours and now three of Patrick's," Art recalled.

"And we'll celebrate lots more, Kevin," Sarah chided with a wide smile. "We don't get to see you, Angie, and the grandchildren often enough. If it weren't for birthdays…"

"Sometimes we feel so out of touch with you, son—I think that's what your mother's trying to say." Art was a small man with sparse and wispy blond hair. Since his retirement two years before, his health had been failing. "Not complaining, mind you, it's just that…you're all that we've got in the world."

Kevin choked on his emotion of the moment. He could feel the frailty of Art's bones in his fingertips. "I know that, Dad. Angie and I were talking about that just the other day, and we both wish the two of you would take us up on our offer to move you both up to Hibbing. We've got lots of room here, or we could easily find you a nice little house in town. You know we'd love to do that."

"No, I don't think so Kevin, we're pretty well settled in where we're at now. These days, houses in West Duluth are hard to sell, and besides, when you get to be our age, any change from the old routines becomes kinda frightening," Sarah explained. "We're much too comfortable at home; your dad has become more involved in St. James parish things these past two years, he still bowls on Wednesdays, and plays poker with his old friends from the shipyards."

Art nodded, "Mom's right about that, Kevin. We've lived in the old neighborhood pretty much all our lives and we're pretty much beyond wanting anything more than what we already have."

Kevin knew that they lived minimally on their meager savings, and had always refused any financial assistance from him. But, the previous week, he had purchased something that Art and Sarah did not have. "I know you drove up here with Father Pat, but I hate to admit—I've never had much confidence in the old priest's driving." Kevin casually observed, setting up his surprise.

Art puzzled at Kevin's remark; Father Pat was heavy on the gas pedal at times but still very alert at sixty-two. "If Father didn't drive us, Kevin, we'd never have been able to get up to Hibbing. You know I can't hardly trust my car to drive downtown these days."

Turning the corner of the barn, Kevin stopped abruptly, reaching into his pants pocket. "I thought so. That's the problem—the reason why the two of you don't come and visit as much as we'd like. You ought to sell that rusty old Chevy of yours, Dad." He handed Art the keys, "Now you won't have that 'car's not running very well' excuse any more."

Parked in the shadows behind the barn was a shiny, new black '34 Ford sedan.

Art and Sarah were speechless.

After the Moran's scrumptious pig barbecue in mid-afternoon, Kevin took Father Pat aside. The tall, gray-haired priest had been the first, and on many past occasions, the only person with whom he could confide his innermost concerns. Pat had been his most trusted confidante since Kevin was a youngster.

The clergyman spoke first, "That was quite a nice gesture on your part, Kevin. Art and Sarah have never been more surprised. But Art told me after your little walk that even more than the new car, his heart was warmed by your calling him and Sarah, Mom and Dad. Those simple words mean more than you can imagine to both of them."

Kevin nodded his understanding of that reality.

"So, what's on your mind, young man? I've had the feeling all day that you've got something to tell your old friend. Am I right about that?"

"As a matter of fact, Father Pat, there is something. Another favor I'd like to ask of you." Since his conversation with Angie the day before, Kevin had been tormented with an issue in his life that he had never been able to resolve with any measure of satisfaction. In recent years he had managed to unfold a reasonable impression of his often maligned and ambitious father, Peter Moran. But his mother had always remained an enigma. All that Kevin had learned could be summarized in a few brief sentences. He knew her name was Barbara Chevalier, that she lived on Wadena Street in West Duluth, and that she and his father were unmarried when she died in childbirth. Father Foley had been at the scene when his mother died, and had told him the few facts that allowed this meager biographical sketch.

"You know that you can ask me for any favor, Kevin—helping out is what I do best. Tell me, what is it you want?"

Kevin felt a lump form in his throat, "I've got to know more about my mother. Lately she's been on my mind a lot. Anything beyond what you've already told me would help, Father."

"I've been waiting for you to approach me about that matter for more than a few years. Let's the two of us go for a little walk."

Foley explained the vague details he could recall from many years ago. On earlier occasions he had told Kevin that back in February of 1907, his mother had been at heaven's doorstep when she telephoned the rectory. "It was a Doctor

Dorsher who arrived at about the same time as I did that day—lucky for you he got there when he did, I might add.

"Before placing you with the Schmitzes, I had to do some legwork of course. County adoption procedures have a complexity all their own." Patrick Foley went on to tell Kevin all that he had learned while doing his necessary background investigations nearly thirty years before. Barbara had been an abused child who ran away from home to live with an aunt in Cloquet when she was seventeen. While there, all she found was more cruel rejection. The aunt sent her to a grandfather, living in Morgan Park at the time, who didn't have any sympathy to give the poor young woman. Foley's description from that point was rather intangible. Family and relatives had apparently shut young Barbara out of their lives.

"I don't know when or where she met your father, Kevin, but I do know that Peter took very good care of her—at least financially. He must have been all she had to cling to in a life that had treated her badly. Apparently your dad bought Barbara the house on Wadena Street and found her a job with an insurance agency in West Duluth. The two of them were very much in love—I'm certain of that. But, for some reason which I've never been able to quite understand your father never married her. It seemed to me that Peter distanced himself from Barbara when she needed him most. He was very busy with his Hibbing affairs—the new hotel and other business matters—"

"He probably learned that she was pregnant and couldn't deal with it, Father. That's my theory, anyhow. He was a very self-centered man."

Foley knew that to be true. "Your father could deal with almost everything, Kevin—unless it was personal, I guess. We tangled on more than one occasion about placing you for adoption." Foley chose not to mention that Kevin's father adamantly denied paternity, and had threatened the priest with a lawsuit if the matter was made public.

"She was a beautiful woman, wasn't she?" Kevin wanted to avoid discussing his father's shortcomings any further. "You told me that my mother was quite attractive once."

"Barbara was that—strikingly so! And from what her employer told me, very bright, dependable, and pleasant. I'm sure that there are many of her qualities in you. I wish I could tell you more about her, but I'm afraid…" The priest paused in their stroll without completing the thought.

Kevin took his hand, "What you've just told me is probably all that I'll ever know."

"That may well be the truth. Her relatives, at least all those I've ever known about, have all passed away, Kevin. And to my knowledge, Barbara never had any close friends."

Kevin met his eyes levelly, "But she's in heaven, isn't she, Father?"

"Of that I have no doubt." Foley placed his hand on Kevin's shoulder, "We can only pray that she's found your father somewhere up there, and that the two of them can look down together upon what you've done with your life…and share in that immense pride."

"And share in their grandson's birthday," Kevin added with a smile.

After everybody had left, Angela and Clara Motter, the Moran's housemaid and nanny, worked in the kitchen putting leftovers in the icebox, scrubbing pots and pans from the afternoon's party, and polishing glassware; Kevin played with Patrick on the living room carpet while Maribec watched from her playpen. The youngster was enthralled with the red wooden fire engine his Grampa Tony had carved for the boy's birthday present. "Of all the toys, Patrick seems to enjoy this one the most," Kevin called toward the women in the kitchen.

"Whee…" Kevin pushed the truck across the floor toward his son. And, "Wheeee," the pajama clad toddler emulated his father when sending the toy speeding back. "Wheee!" the three year old repeated excitedly as the truck's wheels caught his father's foot and turned over on its side…

"Boom! Dada…truck go booom."

"Well, my little man, it's about time to give mommy a kiss g'night. We can play with your toys some more tomorrow." He set the fire truck aside and picked up the boy, raising him high above his head as he did so.

"Horsey ride, Dada…"

Kevin set his son upon his shoulders and walked toward the kitchen, "Back for you in a minute, pumkin," he smiled at Maribec who was beginning her familiar hungry whine. After two steps, however, the phone on the foyer table sent its shrill jingle into the room. "I've got it, honey," Kevin said, lifting Patrick from his shoulders to the floor. "Run to your mommy…"

Giving the boy a pat on the behind, Kevin picked up the receiver: "Morans, Kevin speaking, Mildred," he told the operator. He paused, listening—"It's for you, Angie."

Draping a dish towel over her shoulder, Angie took the phone. "Evelyn? Is that you…Evelyn?" Angie's face distorted in pain as she listened to the voice on the other end of the line. "Yes…Yes…You poor woman. Yes…Oh, my God."

Kevin wondered at the name, Evelyn. Evelyn Hayes? He listened intently to Angela's end of the conversation as Patrick tugged at his trousers and Maribec screeched. "Fytuck, Dada," the boy whined. "Play fytuck."

Angie clutched the black phone with white knuckles, her distress growing as she listened. "Last Friday…?"

"Are you sure it was—? I mean, absolutely positive, Evelyn…?"

"He actually made that threat…?"

"Have you told the police…?"

Kevin tried to imagine what had happened—threat, police? Angie was obviously very distraught. "Is that Evelyn Hayes?" he whispered over Patrick's fussing.

Angie nodded, "Yes, Evelyn…I'll talk to Kevin right away…"

There was a long pause as Angie listened. "Yes, he'll know what to do…" she assured. "This is so terrible, I can't believe…"

Putting down the phone, Angie's eyes welled with tears. She stood speechless dabbing at her eyes before turning to Kevin. "Let's put the children to bed. I've got some tragic news—and I promised Evelyn that you would help her out."

Two Tragedies

Evelyn Hayes was folding linens in the ironing room near the steamy laundry in a downstairs area of the Androy Hotel. The single mother had been twenty minutes late for work that Friday morning and felt obligated to make up the time after her coworkers had left for the weekend. Glancing at the wall clock, Evelyn brushed a lock of her dark hair to the side of her face—it was nearly four-thirty. Two more sheets and she could leave. For Evelyn, it had been a long week with her two children sick at home suffering the discomforts of a flu virus. Fortunately, Evelyn's mother was once again willing to baby-sit so she could get to work. Jobs were a precious commodity in these difficult times and Evelyn had been late for work on other occasions.

Spreading the last linen on the broad tabletop, she startled at a sudden draft in the still room. Before she could turn toward the door...a thick hand covered her mouth! She felt the press of a man's body behind her—locking her into a viselike grasp. Then, a wet tongue licked her neck.

Evelyn's heart caught in her throat. Dropping the linen, she used every measure of strength she had to free herself, trying desperately to gouge her teeth into the flesh of the unseen assailant's hand. One of the man's arms released its lock on her neck; the freed hand found her breast and squeezed painfully.

Terror stricken, Evelyn felt the man's hardness rubbing brutishly against her bottom. She tried to scream, but no sound escaped her choked throat. Her molester was overpowering every fiber of her resistance. Evelyn's mind raced...who could be assaulting her? Then, as sudden as the attack, came an instant memory—the smell of a familiar cologne... At that moment, Evelyn Hayes knew!

Feeling herself being pushed roughly to the cement floor, she frantically kicked out at ankles, legs, anything to prevent the inevitable. Her every squirming, wrestling effort, however, seemed to no avail. The strength of his grip was incredible and she could no longer keep her feet planted in resistance. Forcefully twisting her body around, the man's right hand released her breast—moving swiftly over her belly and grasping between her legs. The other suffocating hand retained its pressure over her mouth. The fighting was draining the last of her strength. Evelyn made a deliberate effort to relax and conserve whatever measure of final resistance she could. Dropping her arms limply to her side allowed the overwhelming man to force her down to the floor, roll her violently onto her back and press her under his weight. For the first time, she was able to see into his crazed, dark, and familiar eyes. Finally, summoning every last fiber of her strength, she locked her knees tightly together, and—with a free hand—tried to gouge his face. Her swat was deflected.

His right hand came off her mouth, slapped her face—liquored breath stung in her nostrils…"Please don't do this to me—let me go…" she breathed her hopeless appeal in gasps. "…Please!" She sobbed in deep, anguished tones. By now, however, Evelyn was feeling the immobilizing numbness, and nausea of defeat. The large man was on top of her, pressing his knee down between hers and separating her thighs. Closing her eyes on the horror of the moment, she could offer no more resistance…powerful fingers were tearing away her undergarments.

The last words Evelyn Hayes would remember from that late August Friday afternoon were more frightening than what had just happened to her. "You say a word about this, bitch…and you'll never see those bastard kids of yours again!" snarled Armando Depelo.

∼

Kevin shook his head in disbelief as Angela revealed the sordid, but understandably scant, details of her conversation with Evelyn Hayes. The described incident troubled him at several levels of thought, and far more deeply than he would admit.

"Why didn't she tell me about it, Angie? I'm her employer, and I would hope to believe after all these years, her friend as well." Kevin had kept Evelyn working despite several poor performance reports and a history of being late and missing scheduled shifts. Perhaps more than anything else, he always had a soft spot for people who had been dealt a difficult hand in life. The woman, he knew, had had more than her share of tough luck and had complicated her misfortunes by earning the reputation of a 'loose woman' in their woefully unforgiving community. Hibbingites could tolerate many sins—but a woman's promiscuity was not one of them.

"And why did Evelyn wait until Sunday night to tell someone?"

"She was ashamed, Kevin. Ashamed that she was raped—as sad and unbelievable as that may seem. You know as well as I that most people think she's a tramp. And, consider who raped her—one of our seemingly respectable businessmen. That despicable, loathsome—!" Angie almost swore in her unbridled anger. "I've never trusted that filthy man. Sometimes I've actually had the feeling that he's undressing me with his eyes." (Angie would not reveal that the hotel manager had once touched her in a provocative manner). She lowered her eyes and dabbed against welling tears, "How can a man…?"

Kevin took her hand in his own. "It's not something a *man* would ever do, sweetheart. Only an animal would victimize a woman—a perverted animal at that."

Looking Kevin straight in the eyes, Angie asked, "What are you going to do about this?"

"Everything I can, Angie. Beginning right now."

Kevin got up from the sofa, walked over to the phone, and got the operator on the line. He asked for the Hayes residence. "Evelyn, this is Kevin Moran." After a long moment of silence (Angie sensed that her high school classmate had broken down when she heard Kevin's voice) Kevin spoke into the receiver again. "Now…now…I know how terrible you feel." Then he corrected himself, "No, I don't *know* how you feel at all, Evelyn. I can never know that! All I do know is that something horrible has happened and we've got to pick up the pieces somehow."

Angie sat on the edge of the sofa so as to hear every word Kevin was saying. A feeling of confidence welled inside her breast. If anybody could help out this broken woman, it was her husband.

"I want you to stay home this week, Evelyn. Don't even think about the hotel right now. I'll tell Gary to make certain that you get a full paycheck."

Moments later, Kevin was off the phone, but continued to stand by the foyer table. "She's devastated, wants to leave Hibbing at the first opportunity—insists that nothing is to be reported to the police. I hope I was able to settle her down a bit." Shaking his head, he added an incomplete thought, "How can anybody…?"

Angie walked over to her husband, placed her hands on his arms, "That was good of you to do, honey: To share your concern and give her time off. How will she ever be able to go back after this?" Absorbed in thought over the next phone call he would have to make, Kevin didn't reply to Angie's question. It was after eight o'clock, a Sunday night, and he was exhausted from the events of the day. Deep furrows creased Kevin's brow as he picked up the phone.

Angie could hear her husband's hoarse voice, could read the depths of his emotion as he waited for the party to answer. She listened to Kevin's end of the conversation:

"Depelo, we've got to talk..."

"Forty-five minutes..."

"No, it won't keep until tomorrow..."

"My office at the hotel..."

Before saying a word to Angie, Kevin was back on the phone asking the operator to connect him with the familiar number—884. "Gary, I need your help tonight."

Gary Zench was Kevin's most trusted friend. The two of them had grown up together in a West Duluth neighborhood and their lives had been entwined since childhood. In June, Gary had finished his college degree in accounting and married his sweetheart of many years, Nora Pratt. After graduating from the business university in Duluth, Gary returned to Hibbing and assumed the position of chief bookkeeper at the Androy.

"Sure thing, boss," Gary said good-naturedly. "Overtime pay is always welcome in this household. Nora's already claiming we've got us the start of a family going on...In fact, she's got an appointment with Becca tomorrow."

When he learned the gravity of the situation, however, Gary's light tone became immediately serious. "I can run things at the hotel better than anybody, even Depelo—you know that, Kevin." He swallowed hard, "I'm sorry about all this, it's got to be hard on you—and Evelyn, I can't imagine. I'll be there before nine."

Angie gave Kevin a warm hug at the door, kissing him softly on the mouth before he left for his impromptu meeting. "I'll say a prayer."

Smiling, Kevin cupped her chin in his hand, "You always do."

Watching his car lamps wind down the gravel road, Angie said her prayer for Kevin...and for Evelyn Hayes.

Although never close, Angie and Evelyn were Hibbing High School classmates as juniors. Evelyn, however, missed her senior year. The story around school was that Evelyn had transferred to a Minneapolis school to help care for her ailing grandmother. Naturally, nobody believed that story. Most everybody knew that Evelyn Hayes was a loose girl, and suspected that she had gotten herself pregnant. Those suspicions were confirmed two years later when Evelyn and her daughter returned to Hibbing. And, two years later, Evelyn had a second child out of wedlock.

Rumors follow a bad reputation like a long shadow. Evelyn's son was dark complected and shared few common features with his blond-haired older sister. Becca Zoretek, never one to spread gossip of any kind, once confided to Angie that Johnny Hayes was the son of Armando Depelo. If Becca made that contention, Angie had no doubt about its veracity. "Forgive us our trespasses as we forgive those who trespass against us…" Angie moved her fingers over the rosary beads in her lap.

Their meeting was brief and heated. Depelo immediately denied the allegation as "absolute bullshit", and told Kevin "I'll see you in court, you sonofabitch!" Before slamming the door behind him, Depelo took a moment to stare first at Gary, then Kevin, "Gonna let a *nigger* run this hotel, huh? Zench'll run it all right—into the fuckin' ground, Moran!"

Kevin angrily started up from his chair to grab Depelo, but Gary restrained him from making any physical assault. The incensed confrontation left both men emotionally drained. This was going to be an ugly ordeal before it was over. Collecting his thoughts for a moment, allowing the episode to settle, Kevin felt the heat inside his tight chest ebb. What had just taken place pained him beyond words. Kevin had just terminated his manager—an old friend of the Zoretek family, and a man in whom he had vested great trust over the years. Gary Zench would take over the hotel operations beginning on the following Monday morning.

"There's a lot of cold hatred in that man, Kevin," Gary met Kevin's eyes. "Every time I'm around him I can feel it—like an ice cube down the back of my shirt."

~

Probably the last person Kevin expected to see early on Monday morning was his first Androy office visitor. Recently appointed police chief, Keirnan McGinnis stood with erect posture by Kevin's office door, his navy-blue cap held stiffly at his breast as if the officer were in an academy dress inspection line. McGinnis was popular Mayor Frank Molinaro's choice to bring respectability to the formerly Prohibition-corrupted Hibbing department. Being an 'outsider' on a force of cronies, the St. Paul native was a highly unpopular selection. Kevin, however, had publicly supported Molinaro's appointment and genuinely liked the affable Irishman.

"All due respects, sir..." He said almost apologetically, "But, I'd like a few minutes of your time, Mr. Moran." McGinnis seemed almost ready to salute the tall businessman whom he held in highest regard. The chief was Kevin's height, with wiry red hair, and a narrow nose which added an almost comic fullness to his slickened handlebar mustache.

Kevin wondered about the purpose of the officer's early and unexpected visit. Had Evelyn Hayes decided to call the police?

"C'mon in, Keirnan. My time is always yours."

Behind the closed door, McGinnis fidgeted with his cap for a long moment. "Sorry to bother you, sir...but I'm afraid I've got some tragic news to burden you with this morning." Keirnan McGinnis could hardly maintain his composure as he explained what had happened the night before.

Kevin slumped in his chair. Reaching for his handkerchief in order to dab at his eyes, he put his head in his hands..."Eternal rest—" he mumbled his quick prayer. After a few moments Kevin raised his head, "Thanks, Keirnan, I'm sure this is the most difficult part of your job. I really appreciate your coming directly."

Father Pat Foley had been killed in an automobile accident on Stebner Road, on the northern perimeter of Duluth. Apparently the car in which he and Mister Barker were traveling, left the roadway, rolled over, and crashed into a telephone pole. Kevin's former teacher, Robert Barker, was not seriously injured.

After McGinnis left his office, Kevin immediately called Angie asking her to let Tony and Becca know about the tragedy, then phoned Art and Sarah Schmitz. His Duluth parents had taken their new automobile on a different route into the city the night before and had only learned about the accident moments before Kevin's call. "The whole neighborhood's in grief this morning. We'll keep you informed about funeral arrangements, Kevin," Art promised through his sobs.

After offering his condolences, Art paused for a significant moment. "Sarah and I were just talking...if you hadn't given us the new car..."

Kevin knew the end of Art's thought, "Don't even think that way, Dad. God wanted Father Pat last night. It's as simple as that."

Art demurred, "You're right, I'm sorry." His apology was rooted in the very same soil of countless other apologies. For years Art had been guilt ridden over his failures as a person and as a father to Kevin. 'I'm sorry' had become a pervasive pattern in their formerly estranged relationship. But Art could not change his colors and needed to continue his thought—another apology of sorts—that he and Sarah had discussed only minutes before his call. "This may sound foolish, Kevin, but I have always been aware that Pat Foley was not only the clerical *father* in your life, but..." Art's emotion strained his voice, "but the nurturing father that I always wanted to be. At times I was probably jealous, but mostly I thanked God for Pat's role in your life every day."

Kevin knew the admission to be true (he and Angela had named their son after the beloved priest) but he wanted to mollify Art in his own grief. "Dad, he was like a father to both of us—all of us, for that matter. But you and mom were there every day for me. Pat always had hundreds of souls to shepherd."

After blocking out Wednesday and Thursday on his calendar for the anticipated wake and funeral, presumably at Foley's St. James church, Kevin contemplated his loss. Memories of childhood flooded his thoughts. Were it not for Patrick Foley's guiding hands, Kevin's life might have been far different than what it had become. Pat always had a way of helping him sort things out, always had a way of helping Kevin make good decisions.

Kevin's desk phone rang. His secretary wanted to remind him of the staff meeting he had arranged with his key hotel employees: "Your conference is scheduled for ten, Mr. Moran…but I can't seem to locate Mr. Depelo."

"He won't be attending, Doreen," was her employer's only reply.

Kevin scribbled some comments he might choose to make on a tablet resting near his elbow. Distracted by the tragic news of minutes before, he found it too difficult to concentrate on his meeting's agenda. His staff would probably be shocked by the change in management and the prospect of working for a much younger man, a former handyman—a black man! The reason for his abrupt decisions could not be revealed at this meeting, but by day's end, rumors would be rampant. The Androy, like the small town of Hibbing, had more than its share of tongue waggers and gossipmongers. Kevin's hotel was a focal point of community life and employed more than sixty of its residents; anything that happened there would be big news.

Already knowing what he was going to say and how he would frame it for is staff, Kevin pushed his notepad aside. This was going to be a very difficult day he realized. He would need to spend some time with Gary on management details later this morning, and before lunch, he needed to go the Blessed Sacrament Church, say some prayers, and light a votive candle for his departed friend.

On his desk calendar, Kevin had penciled in the Chamber of Commerce meeting for noon. (The Chamber office was on the first floor of his enormous hotel, and the luncheon would be in the nearby dining room). He and Tony always sat at the same table with Armando Depelo and either Frank Molinaro, or Claude Atkinson. What would Tony think? The other businessmen? Depelo's absence would be highly conspicuous.

Later, Kevin would try to convince Miss Hayes to file charges against Depelo with the police. In the afternoon, while the Hayes children were taken to Bennett Park by their grandmother, Angela had arranged for the two of them to visit with Evelyn.

The knock on his door interrupted the swim of thoughts washing across Kevin's mind. It was nine-thirty. The door opened on Marc Atkinson of the *Hibbing Daily Tribune*. "Got a few minutes, Kevin? Just wanted to stop by for a chat," the tall, thin newsman asked in a voice tinged with some anxiety. His and Marc's relationship had a checkered past, but their differences had evolved in an awkward fashion toward friendship and mutual respect in recent years. Marc's father, Claude, had been (like Father Pat while Kevin grew up in Duluth) an important mentor during Kevin's years in Hibbing. Kevin loved the old gentleman dearly.

Kevin's first thought was that the news of Depelo's termination had already reached the newspaper reporter's office. "What's up, Marc?"

"Nothing serious, Kevin. Just father and son issues…and you know our history better than anybody."

Kevin nodded knowingly, stood to shake Marc's outstretched hand, "By all means, Marc, sit down." He didn't have much time for chitchat, but out of courtesy—"So, what's the old patriarch up to these days?"

Mark lit his pipe bowl before explaining the reason for his untimely visit. A pipe fill suggested more time than Kevin had to spare. Regarding the reporter, Kevin was reminded of the many similar features shared by father and son.

Inhaling the rich aroma of tobacco, Kevin ventured a guess, "Having another episode with your old man?" Marc and Claude had opposite perspectives on almost everything.

"Worse than just another episode, I'm afraid. I've learned to cope with the daily arguments pretty well by now." Marc leaned forward in his chair, spoke in a softer voice—almost a whisper. "Dad's in a bad way. Has been all summer, but it seems to be getting worse. Mom asked me to talk to you about his health. He won't see a doctor, even though I think he's been in love with Becca since she first came to town," he laughed easily at the notion: Most men in Hibbing were infatuated with the lovely 'good doctor'!

Marc's mom was Dora Atkinson, a well known woman's activist and close friend of Senia Arola, Kevin's trust fund advisor, and a dear 'aunt' throughout his complicated growing up years. "Drinking, depression, or heart trouble?" Kevin posed the three most obvious questions. Claude had been in a funk ever since Marc sold the family newspaper to the competing, and larger circulated, *Hibbing Tribune*. But, despite Claude's objections, that decision had been Marc's to make.

Kevin remembered having talked with Claude for hours about the inevitability of his cherished newspaper's demise. The *Mesaba Ore* had been unable to effectively compete with its primarily local news format, and the vital advertising dollars were going to the more diversified Hitchcock-owned newspaper. "Your dad's got a stubborn streak thicker than a layer of iron ore, Marc—we all know that. What makes Dora think he'll listen to anything I've got to say?"

Marc nodded his acknowledgment of his father's stubbornness. The son, however, was of a totally different ilk—generally reserved, self-conscious, and agreeable. Claude had forged a statewide reputation for journalistic integrity that Marc would never be able to duplicate. The father was a legend, the son a reporter of modest talent and insight. And, Claude Atkinson's shadow had been like a wet blanket upon Marc's newspaper career.

"Mom thinks my dad's got heart trouble. Lack of energy, poor coloring—you know, the things one gets concerned about. I can't even get him to argue politics or baseball these days."

Kevin laughed. Marc was a Roosevelt critic and Giants fan; Claude, on the other hand, admired both Franklin and the Yankees. "Does he still smoke his Meerschaum pipe, have his whiskey highball every night, and keep watch with the owls?"

"Those things will never change, Kevin. I'll never know where he got those bottles of whiskey from during Prohibition...and he's usually up beyond midnight, and still wakes up the roosters in the morning. Like always, I guess."

Kevin was more concerned with Claude's apparent depression than with his smoking or drinking. "I'll try to stop by tonight or tomorrow and say hello—give your dad a lecture if you think he needs one. Tell Dora to keep a pot of coffee on the stove."

"I'll tell Dad you're coming over," Marc replied appreciatively. "That's sure to brighten up his day."

Kevin considered the opportunity of the moment as Marc stood to leave, "Being you're here, Marc, I've got something to share with you, myself." Kevin could trust Marc to keep a confidence. "I'll wager that before you leave the *Tribune* office this afternoon there's going to be some front page news about the operation of my hotel." Kevin measured the reporter with intelligent eyes, "Just between the two of us for now, but if there is a story coming, I want *you* to report it. Okay? I'll make that clear with your boss, Hitchcock."

Marc nodded appreciatively.

"I had to let Armando Depelo go. I can't get into the details, but for the record, let's just say I've lost confidence in his management. He's got a lot of friends in Hibbing and one of them is the owner of your newspaper."

"God, Kevin! Mando? I'll say he connected. Mayor Molinaro is one of Depelo's best friends, and Ian Roberts, Trembart, even Hitchcock and Gerard. You mean to say you just up and fired Mando Depelo? You can bet that's going to be big news."

"Probably bad news for me. I felt compelled to do it, Marc. I know Depelo's not going to sit back and do nothing."

"Thanks for the heads up. Let me tell you..." Marc offered his hand across the desk, "If you felt compelled to do it, then it was the right thing to do. I'll never doubt your integrity, Kevin."

Kevin smiled, "There was a time—wasn't there, Marc? A time when we didn't trust each other at all. We've come a long way, my friend."

As the two men released their handshake, Mark nodded, "A very long way, Kevin. Thanks again. I'll keep the Depelo business under my hat until you say otherwise."

~

Having two children to attend to, Angela's Monday morning got off to a typically early start. After feeding Maribec and Patrick, and getting Kevin out the door, she poured herself a cup of coffee. Angela considered calling Evelyn Hayes and reminding the distraught woman that she and Kevin would visit her that afternoon.

Then, Kevin's unexpected call! The tragic news hit her hard. If she hurried, Angie could get into town in time for morning mass. "Clara," she beckoned the maid into the foyer when she hung up the phone, "Father Pat was killed last night...his automobile..."

Clara rushed to Angie's side, "I'm so sorry, my dear..." Seeing the pain in Angie's eyes, the five words were the only consolation Clara could offer. Yet the housemaid knew that Angie needed a shoulder to cry on more than anything else. "What can I do?"

Drying her swollen eyes, Angie drew a sigh, "Will you take care of the children—I'm going to drop everything and get into town. I'll probably be away most of the day, Clara."

From mass at the Catholic church, Angie drove to the little art studio on Fifth Avenue. Angie had been living on the edge of her consuming fear that something...some unknown something, might trigger that dreaded headache again. Any blackout stimulus would most likely come from an unexpected and tragic event—a death, an accident, or...? On this August Monday morning it had been nearly two years since her last episode, but—?

Jacque Grojean's shop was Angie's customary escape from stress. The diminutive, one-eyed artist was one of her favorite people and had always been able to lift her sagging spirits. But the usually good-natured old Frenchman was not himself this morning. When Angie entered the studio area in the back of the shop, Jacque hardly looked up from the newspaper spread out on the paint crusted table.

Reaching around behind him, Angie gave the man a quick hug while planting a kiss on his long, always wildly unkempt hair. *"Bon jour, mon ami!"* Angie offered her usual greeting...but Jacque only grumbled an acknowledging, *"Oui."*

"Your pupil can always sense when her maestro is in a foul mood, what's troubling *mon ami* this morning?" Angie forced a lightness into her voice even though a pain throbbed in her temples.

"The news from Europe, *mon cherie*, always so…what can I say, *decouragement*? I am reading about that German scoundrel again this morning, and my stomach—it turns inside me." He pushed the paper away and offered a weak smile. "Perhaps I am more sensitive to all of that man's power lust than most, my dearest. But France, you know…we have had our troubles with Germany before, and my native country is not strong like this America of ours." Jacque had been a United States citizen for most of his adult life but still had relatives in Paris. "It's this Hitler, *Fuhrer* he wants to be called! The tyrant has made himself the President now, more power—more ambition, more everything…He scares me, terribly so, I'm afraid!"

Angela was not an astute student of history but knew that America had come to the aid of France once before. "We will not allow that Hitler to give *your* country any trouble, Jacque. He'd better darn well know that!"

Jacque gave Angie an amused smile, "America is *my* country, *mon cherie*, but…I pray that you are right." The Frenchman's expression changed, "Still, I must be honest with you; there are days when I long with all my heart to be with my family in Paris. As much as I love this great land of ours, I must be buried in the soil of my parents. Once a Frenchman…"

"Don't talk like that, Jacque. The thought of losing you…well, I've had enough sadness for one day already." Angie told her friend about the Foley tragedy of the night before.

Jacque listened with a pained expression, "Angie, I always have a happiness inside me when a saintly person passes away. I believe that another angel is born and those who are left behind have an easier time making their own way to heaven. You see, those departed will pray for us every hour of every day, and they are so very close to the ears of God."

Angie had tears in her eyes, "Thank you, Jacque. What a beautiful thought. I must share it with Kevin; the good priest was like a father to him."

Jacque took her hand, 'Be assured that what I say is true…and, when I am gone, you will have my prayers always guiding and protecting you—wherever you may be." He choked on his next few words, "For you are like a daughter to me—you know that, don't you, *mon cherie?*"

Angie only nodded; there were no words she could say.

Monday Luncheons

Armando Depelo waited at his table in a dimly lit corner of the posh Algonquin clubroom upstairs of a major downtown bank building. The space was elaborately appointed and the decor impressively masculine—oak wainscoting, red wallpaper, and trophy wildlife adorning the walls. The club's membership fees were steep, allowing only the wealthiest of Hibbing's elite to join. Depelo's luncheon guests on this Monday would be a group of Hibbing's most conspicuous power brokers: Attorney Elwood Trembart, Oliver Mining Company official—and Elwood's son-in-law—Ian Roberts, and real estate broker, Alphonse Gerard. The realtor, a retired mining nabob, owned much of the area's lucrative mining properties, and was reputed to be Hibbing's richest citizen.

Although Armando Depelo was neither bright nor well spoken, he was clever and well-connected. He would take advantage of this luncheon meeting to tap the minds of his colleagues. An angry bile stirred in his stomach. Depelo was determined to pay back Kevin Moran—one way or another, and earlier that morning, he had set one wheel of that revenge scheme into motion.

It was only eleven-thirty and Depelo was fifteen minutes early, giving him opportunity to browse Sunday's *Hibbing Tribune* issue which he had brought along with him to the table. After unfolding the newspaper to the sports page to check the major league baseball scores and standings, he returned to the front page stories. The article on the lower right caught his attention and brought a smile of amusement to his handsome features. Al Capone was being transferred "with great secrecy" from an Atlanta penitentiary to the new Alcatraz Prison in San Francisco Bay—a prison that authorities called impregnable.

Depelo had met America's 'Public Enemy Number One' years before in a remote lodge on Lake Vermilion, near Tower in the northern Minnesota wilderness. The Chicago gangster had impressed Depelo more than any man had before—or since. "Impregnable? You show'em impregnable, Big Al. You're a better man than all of those asshole Feds put together," he mumbled under his breath. Prohibition times had been exciting for Armando Depelo. Back then, he had some muscle—being a bootlegging kingpin always carried the respect of intimidation. Also, there was the liquor money constantly bulging in his wallet. Regretting those years of squandering his small fortune, he was now faced with having to earn his living respectably.

Governor Floyd Olson's speech at the weekend meeting of the Minnesota Federation of Labor was also front page *Tribune* news. The Governor's popularity was ebbing, and tied to the fate of Minnesota's populist governor, was that of young Melvin Alto. Olson had been roundly criticized for his comments suggesting that the Federal government take over idle plants and employ the unemployed workers, and further that the government distribute commodities. "Fuckin' socialist bastard!" Depelo despised Olson. But a comforting thought crossed his mind as he continued reading the article. Perhaps in the fall elections, Depelo's clique would be able to dump Alto and replace him with one of their own people. Maybe even his friend, Ian Roberts.

"Mando…the Tigers are three games up on the Yanks, and you're going to owe me five bucks when the season's over," Ian Roberts announced approaching the table. He and Armando were both baseball fans and often wagered on games. Wearing a natty beige suit, Roberts always dressed with impeccable taste. "Did you read the Olson speech story?" Ian Roberts asked cheerfully, noticing the paper spread over the table. "The Guv's going down, my friend. Just wait and see."

Depelo shook Robert's hand and turned to Ian's father-in-law, and old political sage, standing at Ian's elbow. "What do you think, Elwood?"

Elwood Trembart was in a typically foul mood. "Never underestimate Olson!" the attorney commented with a scowl.

Depelo quickly folded the paper and pulled out a chair for Trembart. "Thanks for joining me, fellas. Gerard will be a few minutes late, I'm afraid." Depelo ignored Ian for the moment and met Trembart's eyes. He would skip the politics and baseball small talk and get right into his personal issue. "I'm…well, kinda in a bind today—need some good legal advice, Elwood."

"You're in a bind and I'm starved, Depelo. Let's order a sandwich. Alphonse may not get here for another hour," Trembart grumbled.

"I've got Rueben sandwiches coming from the kitchen in a few minutes, Elwood. I know that's your favorite—along with some fried potatoes and soup."

"That's good. The most important matter's taken care of then," he said with noticeable sarcasm. "Now, what's your problem? I've got a one o'clock meeting at my office."

When the three of them were seated, Depelo stammered, "Moran fired me last night, Elwood. Right outta the fuckin' blue!"

Trembart gave Depelo a twisted smile, "Moran doesn't do anything 'out of the blue'—you ought to know that by now. What did you do to *deserve* it, Depelo? Get your sticky fingers in the Androy till?" Elwood always found a sense of satisfaction in clever barbs, and power in using other people's surnames.

"I didn't do nothin'. Honest to God!" Depelo's lie in God's name came without a flinch. "He's slanderin' me, Elwood. Claims I..." he swallowed hard as his mouth dried. After sipping from his glass of water, Depelo continued, "Claims I raped an employee at the hotel. Can you believe that? Said his wife had a phone call from some bitch that worked in the Androy's laundry room."

Depelo explained the meeting of the previous night in Kevin Moran's office. "And he had the balls to bring his *nigger* buddy with him."

The sandwich platters were served—beginning with Mr. Trembart—by a uniformed waiter who must have been trained in the Algonquin Club's pecking order. Elwood took a bite and dabbed a small piece of cabbage from his chin with a linen napkin. He wouldn't respond to Depelo's story which was thinner than the butter knife blade he used to slice a large piece of fried potato.

"Sounds like slander or something to me," Ian Roberts broke the pause in their conversation. "Doesn't it, Dad?" Ian looked to Elwood for approval of his simple legal observation. "We can sue Moran's ass, can't we?"

Elwood shook his head, glowering at his son-in-law, without offering a reply. The two younger men were wet behind the ears and grasping at straws. As he often did, the old attorney worried over the naivety of Ian and Depelo's generation. He was 'old school' tough—they were too accustomed to having things handed to them.

"Thing is, Elwood, I don't want no trial or nothin' like that. You know, that's awfully messy stuff for everybody concerned. Can't we just lean on him—force

Moran to give me my job back? I mean, he can't just fire me because some woman—a woman that always hated my guts, by the way…"

Trembart eyes burned scorn at Depelo, "Why are you afraid of going to court? Why does this woman 'hate your guts', Depelo? I'm missing some critical details here."

Depelo shrugged his shoulders, "Most things get settled out of court, don't they? That woman ain't even got the guts to tell her crazy story to the police. With her reputation, hell…nobody'd ever believe her."

"Apparently Moran's wife believed her. And, I'm getting tired of your references to 'her'—who's the woman you're talking about?" Trembart bit off the question with irritation.

Depelo looked first to Ian, then back to Trembart, "Evelyn Hayes."

Trembart smiled to himself. Evelyn Hayes was a damn good-looking woman. More than once he'd fantasized taking her into a backroom somewhere. And, Mando's reputation as a womanizer made his slur of the woman's character a moot point. "So, what's the Hayes woman got against you, Depelo? Why would she fabricate such a story?"

Depelo felt himself being painted into a corner by Trembart's inevitable questions. If the rape allegation were investigated by the police, the terrible truth would likely be uncovered. "I wrote her up for being late a few times. Told her that if it happened again, I'd can her fat ass. She got pissed—said she'd go to Moran. Maybe Moran's screwin' her on the side—who knows? Anyhow, maybe she made up this story just to get me in trouble with Moran. See what I mean, Elwood?"

"Let's cut the bullshit, Depelo. Either you give me the straight story or I'm out the door." Elwood pushed away from the table in an obvious display of disgust. "What's the Hayes woman got on you?"

Depelo gave Trembart a defeated look. Time was running out and the attorney had evidenced neither support nor sympathy on his behalf. Trying to hide a look of defeat at Elwood's question, Depelo admitted, "I kinda fucked up a few years ago."

"Haven't we all? What is it—something related to the bootlegging and prostitution bullshit you've been involved in, Depelo? Hell, that's history now—nobody gives a shit about that anymore."

"No. It's something personal, Elwood. I'd really like to leave it that way—personal, you know?"

Trembart's heavy brows dropped as he leveled his derision toward the humbled man across the table with a favorite dismissal: "Do I look like a mushroom to you? Do you think I somehow flourish in the dark?"

"No, sir. Not at all. I'm sorry if I've offended you. But, God…if Carol ever found out about what I did back then, she'd divorce me in a heartbeat. That's what I mean about personal, sir." Depelo tried to be more carefully respectful of the attorney across the table. "I made a mistake in my personal life, sir. A serious mistake!"

Trembart enjoyed watching Depelo squirm in his chair. "Well? Am I supposed to make three guesses?" He leaned back in his chair, crossing his arms.

Depelo gave Ian Roberts a suffered glance. "Ian knows, sir," Depelo said.

Ian recognized his friend's dilemma, interpreting "Ian knows" as an invitation to intervene and convey details of the 'mistake' in Depelo's life.
"Don't get upset over what I tell you, Dad. Mando…well, Mando might have been the father of Hayes's boy. That would have been what, eight years ago already?" He looked to Mando for confirmation. "Might have been, Dad—nobody's certain. He had a little fling, you know how that goes."

"A little fling?" Trembart glowered at his son-in-law. "Is that what you young fellas call it these days? A little fling? Tell me, Ian…if you were cheating on my daughter and something like this came up in conversation—is that what you would tell me? Just a little fling, Dad? And that maybe…just maybe, a little boy might have happened because of your innocent philandering? This is making me sick!"

"I'd never do that to Molly, Dad. You know that." Ian gave Elwood an indignant frown. "Never!"

Trembart stood, "I've go a one o'clock appointment. I'll excuse myself and let the two of you figure out what you're going to do about this mess. If you decide to bring charges against Moran, Depelo…well, I'd take him to court in a heartbeat. You both know enough about my hatred of the Morans without my reminding you. If and when it comes to knocking Kevin Moran off his high horse—"

More than anybody else, Elwood had sabotaged Kevin Moran's political campaign two years earlier. His grudge against Kevin ran deep in his marrow—back a quarter of a century—to a time when the senior Moran had foiled Trembart on a million dollar land deal.

"Yes, sir." Depelo stood at the table. Not knowing what else to say, he offered a befuddled smile…"I'll pick up the tab—I hope you enjoyed the sandwich, Mr. Trembart."

Elwood only shook his head at the remark. The sandwich on his plate had been uneaten except for his first bite. And, he enjoyed Ruebens with a passion! "Maybe Alphonse will finish this sandwich for me. I see old moneybags coming in the door right now."

As Trembart and Gerard visited in the doorway, Depelo turned to Ian's ear, "I don't think that went very well, Ian. Maybe your idea of talking with Elwood about this wasn't a very good one." He glanced furtively at Trembart and Gerard, "I think I'm getting this Hayes business cleared up by my self without any legal stuff."

Ian gave his friend a puzzled look.

"I don't think Evelyn'll be talking to anybody else…for a long time," Mando informed. "She's got kids to take care of, you know." Depelo had already taken steps to cover himself. After lunch he would make three more calls, one to Evelyn's mother, another to his attorney friend, Bob Peterson, and the last to Chief Keirnan McGinnis. He smiled inwardly at the thought of what was coming up in Kevin Moran's afternoon.

As Gerard approached, Ian whispered a quick question. "Why'd you ask Alphonse to join us? He's not a lawyer and he doesn't need to know any of this Hayes business."

Depelo laughed sarcastically, "I need a job, stupid. I have debts, and I don't have a rich old man like you do."

Kevin was late for Monday's weekly Chamber of Commerce luncheon at the Androy. Spotting Tony Zoretek sitting alone at their reserved table, he shook hands and offered his apology, "I stopped by the church to say a few prayers and ran into Father Potocnik. He'd already heard about Father Pat and was devastated. The two of them had known each other for years."

"So am I, Kev. What a loss for all of us. Father Foley was a beloved man—a saint! I'm sorry…I know how close the two of you were."

Kevin gave Tony's hand a squeeze, "A saint for sure. I'm going to miss that old Irishman more than words can say." Kevin had left his emotions, and his tears, in the church. "Father Potocnik says it's going to be one of the largest funerals in the history of the Duluth diocese. I'm sure he's right about that." (Kevin would learn later that afternoon that he had been selected as one of the priest's pallbearers). "We'll have to go to the wake together on Wednesday—the four of us."

"And stay overnight for the funeral on Thursday," Tony added somberly. "How are Art and Sarah taking the news?"

"Okay, I guess. I'll have to talk to them again later tonight."

Tony nodded, looking up and over the gathering. "I'd hoped to see Claude here this afternoon. Our meeting agenda is right down his alley. And, I haven't seen Mando anywhere—he's usually here before me." The four men often sat together for Chamber functions.

Swallowing hard, Kevin met his father-in-law's eyes, "That's a long story, Tony. I'll fill you in later…but I'm afraid we won't be seeing Mr. Depelo here very often in the future."

Tony puzzled at the reference to Mando, "Mr. Depelo? Where did that come from? I've never heard you call Mando…"

"We've got an issue—a huge issue to say the least. I pray that I did the right thing, but truth be known—I had to fire him, Tony."

Tony's discretion regarding whatever had happened was evident in his nod. "Later then. Whatever the issue, I'm sure you've done the right thing."

Marc Atkinson approached the two men, "Dad's not going to make it, so I'm pinch-hitting; mind if I join you? Dad wants me to take notes and give him a full report later," Marc said.

The special Chamber guest and speaker was Ashton Hoyt, a top executive of Pickands-Mather Company—one of the major mine owner-managers in the Hibbing district.

"I'd be surprised if Hoyt gives us anything but a rosy picture of iron mining recovery, Kevin," Marc intoned. "These Cleveland bigwigs all sing the same song."

Prematurely gray-haired, tall and thin, Ashton Hoyt had a distinguished air about him: A confidence tinged with the arrogance of wealth and power. While the mining executive brushed a crumb from his expensive double-breasted gray suit, adjusted his reading spectacles, and cleared his throat, the luncheon crowd offered a rousing applause.

"It's always wonderful to visit your fair city and see so many of my old friends…" Hoyt smiled graciously at his audience. "I cannot help but marvel at how prosperous Hibbing always seems to be. Despite our nation's economic woes these days, well, I wish more of the 'gloom and doomers' could walk down Howard Street and see your vitality for themselves—and feel your community spirit. Yes, my friends, iron ore mining is continuing to keep this local economy afloat."

Applause was sporadic.

"Some look at a glass of water..." Hoyt lifted his glass as a timely prop for his ensuing observation, "Yes, some would want to tell you that the glass is half empty. Well, let me assure you that it's not 'half empty'—no, the glass I'm holding before you is half full! It's all a matter of perspective, isn't it?"

Kevin rolled his eyes at the timeworn analogy. He knew that the speaker's next observations would have to do with optimism versus pessimism.

"Let me assure you at the onset, I'm an optimist!" Hoyt's voice rose like that of an erstwhile politician at a partisan rally. Glancing down at the notes on the podium in front of him, Hoyt was ready to provide the inevitable statistics which would support his contention that things were not as bad as some would have you believe.

Adjusting his glasses on his narrow nose, Hoyt continued, "In our nearly fifty operating mines we have approximately five thousand men employed at a daily wage of five dollars." Hoyt added his estimate that the tons of ore shipped during the '34 season would approach fifteen million. "Down some from a few years ago—the 'high demand' years—as I like to call them...but, nevertheless, very impressive numbers, all things considered."

"Are those rose-colored glasses Hoyt's wearing?" Marc Atkinson whispered to Kevin behind his cupped hand.

Elaborating from his opening observations, Hoyt explained the supply-demand scenario, emphasizing the problem of "cheap iron ore competition from our Canadian neighbor to the north." Pausing for dramatic effect at his remark, the speaker only received scattered claps as evidence of their concern over an obvious issue. "And let's not forget that the eastern steel mills are becoming obsolete. Our basic industry is going to be financially stressed to modernize operations from top to bottom over the next few years."

Kevin had the ear of many local mining officials and knew that Hoyt's numbers were purposely inflated. The 'high demand' years which the speaker alluded to were the pre-Depression years. He and Claude had examined some production and employment numbers just days before Hoyt's visit. Claude was an historian and an astute observer of all things related to iron mining. Only seven years ago, the Mesabi Range had more than seventy operating mines employing nearly ten thousand workers, and shipped close to thirty million tons of ore. Also, the prevailing wages back in '27 were close to fifty cents a day more than they were now. Kevin's figures were in sharp contrast to those of Ashton Hoyt.

When Hoyt had finished his thirty minute speech and opened his presentation to questions from the audience, Kevin was the first businessman on his feet. Hoyt acknowledged the hotel owner by his first name, "Kevin, let me tell you that your hotel is the finest in northern Minnesota. I always enjoy your superb accommodations here." Hoyt added another pleasant compliment, "And, your high school down the street, built by the mining industry as a tribute to the value of education in the life of a community, is unsurpassed anywhere in America."

For the first time that afternoon, Hoyt had struck a positive chord. Applause mixed with whistles spread widely. Hibbingites regarded their high school with an ardor bordering on reverence.

Kevin smiled, "Thanks, Ashton. Yes, we're awfully proud of all our community schools, and their teaching staffs as well. And, you're right about the vitality and spirit evidenced in our city." His comments received a louder response than any Hoyt had shared.

"My question, Mr. Hoyt, is simply—where is the industry's priority when demand for steel picks up? Will you folks out East, who make all the critical decisions for those of us here in Hibbing, be focusing on renovating the steel mills, or boosting the output from our mines?"

Hoyt seemed noticeably uncomfortable with the question. Rather than tell any unmitigated truths, he hedged his answer. "Of course both are high priorities, Kevin. It's much too early to say which will need the greatest initial attention…but if the mills are improved, they will have a greater capacity for your iron ore," Hoyt smiled self-assuredly.

Claude and Kevin had discussed the steel mills only recently, "I'm aware of that fact, Ashton. But, correct me if I'm wrong, aren't there seven steel mills shut down as we speak? Two of which, in Gary and Bethlehem, were built with new technologies only five years ago?"

Hoyt stammered, "Why, yes, of course…we'll have to look at returning to full production capacity, too."

Kevin sat down to a round of applause. Hibbing Chamber activists were not narrow-minded myopics. To a person, the local businessmen knew the entire industry picture and were quick to recognize a snow job.

When he returned to his office, Kevin's thoughts wandered from the Chamber meeting to his grief over Foley's death. Perhaps the twenty minutes in church had not purged the void he felt. At the door, Kevin's secretary, Doreen Boyum, handed him his batch of mail and phone messages. "You had a call from Evelyn Hayes' mother, Mr. Moran. She sounded out of sorts; said that her daughter and the two children left her house after a phone call earlier this morning. She wants you to call her back as soon as you can. Your wife called an hour ago to tell you she's having lunch with Miss Arola, and these others…" Doreen paused as Kevin rifled through the slips. Her employer's grief was clearly apparent, "My condolences, Mr. Moran. Father Foley will be in my prayers."

After a brief hug, Kevin closed the door saying, "I've got a ton of things to sort out, Doreen. Give me some time without interruption, please." Kevin's thoughts were swimming with all the events of this, still only half spent, Monday: Foley's death, Depelo's termination, the staff meeting and follow-up with Gary Zench, the Chamber session—he had lost the Evelyn Hayes tragedy somewhere in a far corner of his thoughts. Looking at the note, he picked up his phone and gave the operator the Hayes number.

"Evy didn't say where she was going, Mr. Moran. But she took the kids and packed a lot of clothing," Esther Hayes said in a worried voice. "She told me to tell you not to come by the house this afternoon. 'Tell the Morans to leave me alone' is what she said. I just don't know what…?"

"Did Evelyn say who called her? Or, where she was going, Esther?"

"No, sir. I asked her…but she wouldn't tell me anything." Esther Hayes paused, "But she was awfully upset—I can assure you of that."

Angie Moran had promised her friend, Senia Arola, to join her for lunch at Con-Ed's Cafe, and now almost wished she hadn't made the earlier commitment. Her thoughts were consumed with grief over Pat Foley and Evelyn Hayes, and at this moment she would much rather be with Kevin than anyone. Crossing busy Howard Street, she spotted Senia leaving her small office around the corner at Fourth Avenue East. The tall, gray-blond Finnish woman still walked with the long confident strides of her younger years. Senia's typically conservative gray suit, like most of her wardrobe, was expensively well-tailored. At fifty-three, the professional woman had retained the posture, bearing and self-assurance of a lady who was always in control of her world.

Senia Arola had learned of Patrick Foley's death from Becca Zoretek only an hour before. Although never a religious woman, Senia had paused from her work of the moment and said a prayer. Her career, and her passion had always been accounting; she had come to prefer numbers to people. In recent years she had been self-employed. Her lifelong friend and companion, Steven Skorich, worked as her partner two or three days a week, depending upon his faltering health. Although their business activity was generally slow these days, Senia had few financial concerns of her own. She came from a wealthy family in Finland, continued to manage the considerable Moran estate, supervised Steven's mineworkers investment account, and handled most of the Zoretek Construction business.

Intelligent, self-assured and perceptive, Senia Arola had experienced more than her share of grief over the years. Life had been filled with unrealized dreams and profoundly unsettling experiences. She had loved three men in her lifetime, and was left with nothing more than bittersweet memories of each. Her tears of rejection had been spent, and the pattern of her independent lifestyle now centered almost entirely on her work.

Senia left her position as vice-president of the large Merchants and Miners Bank upon learning that her employer had betrayed her unequivocal trust. (Harvey Goldberg had been among those who conspired to defeat Kevin Moran in the '32 election). When learning of Goldberg's unethical activities, Senia resigned from the bank and went into business for herself. Miss Arola was an uncompromising and unforgiving woman. Over all her years, however, the deceased Duluth priest had been one of the very few men whose trust and integrity had never failed her.

"Senia, I'm over here," Angie hailed from the sidewalk in front of the new J.C. Penney store.

Senia waved, crossed the intersection and offered her elbow to the younger woman. "How's Kevin taking the news, Angie?" Senia's relationship with Angie's husband was one of the brightest spots in her otherwise unfulfilled life. Kevin was the son she never had, and his welfare remained both a promise to the young man's father, and a personal obsession like none other.

"He's going to be all right, Senia. Pat's in heaven where he can keep an eye on everything now." Angie shared Jacque's perspective with a smile. Kevin's going to miss him a lot, that's for sure, but…as we both know, my husband always tries to put a positive twist to everything."

Senia believed that she knew Kevin's nature better than most, and secretly wished the young man's father had possessed a measure of his son's optimism. "If only...?" she often thought to herself. One of the three men Senia had loved was Peter Moran. Refocusing her attention on Angie walking beside her, Senia commented, "I haven't talked to Kevin yet today, but I thought I'd stop by the Androy after lunch and offer my condolences. Such a tragedy!"

Remembering that she and Kevin were going to visit with Evelyn Hayes after lunch, Angie suggested, "Then I'll walk over to the hotel with you, Senia. Kevin and I have an appointment together this afternoon."

It was nearly two o'clock when Kevin's office door opened and Angie and Senia entered the lavishly-appointed room. Like his father, Kevin appreciated fine art work and antiques—the walls and shelves reflected his taste for Matisse prints and ancient Chinese ceramics. Rising from his paperwork, he gave each woman an affectionate hug, offering overstuffed leather chairs to the two ladies. "I called your office, Senia...no answer, of course. Angie must have told you about..."

"Becca called this morning, Kevin. I'm so very sorry..." Sensitive to the woman's grief, Kevin took her hands in his, "You and Father Pat shared a lot over the years—I don't know what I might have become without the both of you." He swallowed at the lump in his throat, "We all know he's in a much better place now. And that's what life's all about—getting up there." He looked toward the ceiling as he spoke, "That's the reward for a job well done."

After Senia left for her office, Kevin explained his earlier conversation with Evelyn Hayes' mother. "She just took off, Angie. Esther told me her daughter got a disturbing telephone call early this morning, packed some things, took the children, and was out the door."

Angie pondered the unexpected news. "Armando Depelo! I'm sure of it, Kevin. He must have threatened Evelyn...threatened to harm her children. Do you remember me telling you that last night?"

Kevin nodded, "My thoughts exactly. She's probably scared to death about what he might do."

"Should we go to the police?"

"Without divulging any specifics, I asked Esther if her daughter said anything about an incident at the hotel last Friday night. She said no, but added that Evelyn hadn't been herself all weekend. Said that her daughter was really depressed."

"What would the police do if we reported the incident?" Angie's concern brought deep furrows to her brow. "Would they arrest Depelo?"

"Not likely, sweetheart. They would contact Depelo, probably write up a report with his denial, and begin looking for Evelyn."

"Of course he would deny everything."

"Sure he would, and try to make the two of us look like fools in the process. No, I think we ought to keep things to ourselves for right now. I've told Gary not to breathe a word. When we find Evelyn the whole matter will be in the hands of the police." Rape, Kevin knew, was a crime that rarely made a statistic—a secretive crime, so riddled with shameful consequences that it seldom went reported. In suggesting that he and Angie keep the matter to themselves, Kevin was subconsciously attempting to shield his wife from getting too involved in Evelyn's personal crisis.

Kevin's phone rang.

"Keirnan. Twice in the same day, what's up my friend?"

Angie watched the color drain from her husband's face as he listened to the police chief. Had something terrible happened to Evelyn?

"I can't believe what I'm hearing, Keirnan. That's absolutely preposterous! Yes…I'll be over there in just a few minutes."

Kevin put down the phone, drew a sigh—"You won't believe what's just happened, Angie."

Under Suspicion

Chief McGinnis squirmed uncomfortably in his wooden swivel chair. "It's only routine in matters like this, Mr. Moran. The questions, I mean. You're a lawyer…you probably know the process much better than I do."

Kevin's face wore an expression of disbelief, "I understand, Keirnan. Let's try to get to the bottom of this absurd allegation."

As the police chief nervously dipped his pen in an ink bottle, tiny droplets of black spotted the blank page of paper on his desk. "Maybe we can clear up this unpleasant matter right away: Where were you on Friday afternoon, sir—around four or five, and afterwards?" He would try to frame his inquiry as professionally as possible and mask his nervousness.

Kevin's mind processed the inevitable question and how his answer would most likely be construed. "Out at my lake property by myself, just looking around."

Keirnan looked up without asking why? 'By himself and just looking around' was awfully vague. He would get more clarification as the interview progressed.

"I've owned a property out there for years and have been thinking of building a summer place. I was doing a little visual surveying on Friday."

Trying to force a smile, the chief failed miserably. "Lovely area, Mr. Moran…So, just getting some ideas, then?"

"That's all."

Hoping for more than a two word response, Keirnan scribbled something down. His next question choked in his dry throat, "That's quite a time period to be out there 'by yourself'. You did say there was nobody with you, didn't you, Mr. Moran?" Keirnan looked up, "Did anybody see you while you were 'looking around'?"

"Not that I can remember. I wanted to do this by myself." Feeling a dull pang of worry, Kevin pressed his memory for details of the previous Friday afternoon. He had purposely kept his Sturgeon Lake excursion to himself—and to his knowledge, nobody had seen him. "I don't believe anybody really knew what I was up to…and I can't remember seeing anybody at the lake. It was raining, if you remember. Rather unpleasant to be out."

Keirnan puzzled, imagining the scenario while scribbling and avoiding eye contact with his friend. "Rained for about an hour—wouldn't you say?"

Impatiently, Kevin folded his arms and leaned back in his chair. This interrogation was not settling well. Keirnan was only doing his job, but—"Why isn't Depelo here? You'd think he'd have the guts to be here and face me with these insane allegations."

"I agree. Asked him to come over…but, well—" Keirnan stammered, "He says you'd be awfully angry with him for quitting his job. He thought it best to avoid another scene."

"Quitting his job? Is that what he told you? Hell! That really angers me, Keirnan. The truth is, I *fired* Depelo last night! That's the fact of the matter. Fired him for…" Kevin caught himself. He'd told Angie that they would keep Evelyn's story to themselves. "…for personal reasons."

"Personal reasons?" Keirnan looked up from his notes.

Loosening his tie and running his fingers through his thick auburn hair, Kevin leaned forward, "He's lying through his teeth, Chief. Gary Zench was at the meeting when I terminated Depelo."

Looking away from the eyes of the man he deeply respected, he was going to be candid with Mr. Moran about everything Depelo told him. "Depelo claimed that you would probably say that, sir. Told me he and Mr. Zench had bad blood between them and would corroborate anything you told the police. But that's none of my business at the moment." Keirnan hoped these personal issues could be ironed out later.

Kevin considered the chief's 'business of the moment'. "Am I to understand, Mr. McGinnis…that Depelo simply called you on the phone at one o'clock this afternoon with his slanderous fabrication and then…then, you—believing his preposterous story—told him that you'd call me in for questioning? Is that about it?" Kevin's voice had a hard edge.

McGinnis felt like a man pressed in a vice. Since his arrival in Hibbing he had been of the belief that Depelo and Moran were not only business associates, but the best of friends. "Not at all, sir. My first priority, of course, was to try and locate Miss Hayes. I talked with her mother before calling you, sir. But, it seems…"

"I know, Evelyn Hayes and her children have left town."

"And, how might you know that, Mr. Moran?" Keirnan puzzled.

"I've talked with Esther Hayes myself."

"Yes. She told me that. Early this morning—am I correct?"

"No, I returned her call to me after lunch—about one o'clock. Angela and I had planned to meet with Evelyn this afternoon. So Esther wanted me to know that her daughter had left town."

Keirnan scratched his head in obvious frustration. "I'm confused Mr. Moran. But, did you say your call to Mrs. Hayes was 'after lunch'—not earlier—say, around seven this morning?"

"Yes. My secretary at the hotel can verify that."

"I see." McGinnis' face contorted as he wrote something down. "Mrs. Hayes told me that you called and talked to Evelyn both late last night and early this morning. She claims that your call must have upset her daughter terribly, because—it was after your morning call that Evelyn started packing. Perhaps you can appreciate my confusion over these conflicting accounts, sir. She didn't say anything about calling you at the hotel or your return call this afternoon. I'll have to get back to her about that. I wonder why…?" The chief turned another page in his notebook and jotted the reminder.

Kevin could feel the heat on the back of his neck. The lawyer in him believed that he had already said enough and that anything else he might add to this inquisition might be self-incriminating. "Allow me to summarize this misunderstanding, if I may, Keirnan? Esther Hayes told you that I called her daughter early this morning—not this afternoon—and she failed to tell you about her call to me."

"That's correct, sir."

Kevin pushed his chair away from in front of McGinnis' desk. "I think that we've covered about enough. Something very convoluted is going on here and I'm not going to answer any more questions without another lawyer present. These charges are too serious for any more 'she said' and 'I said' dialogue."

Kevin would explain this bizarre frame-up to his veteran law partner, Bob Peterson.

"I'd encourage you to see an attorney, Mr. Moran. I believe that Mr. Depelo has retained his lawyer as well."

Kevin stood to leave, "I'd suppose Depelo contacted Elwood Trembart even before he called you."

McGinnis swallowed the knot in his throat, "No, sir. If I understood Mr. Depelo correctly, he said that I would be hearing from Bob Peterson."

Located on the second floor of the eastern wing of Hibbing's impressive city hall building, the police headquarters (and jail facility) were swamped with post-weekend activity. Angie waited anxiously on a wooden bench outside the police chief's door for her husband to finish his business with Keirnan McGinnis. She had never been in the department before and found the routine interactions intriguing. From where she sat she could see the hallway to the lockup wing, hear the ringing of telephones, and observe the men in blue woolen uniforms scurry from one exigency to another. Angie contemplated crime in her community for the first time. A man the desk sergeant called 'Spurge' was being discharged for a Saturday evening assault at the Red Rock Tavern. Another named Lavigne was being booked for trespassing and property destruction. The oldest son of Lars Udahl, 'Lefty', was still intoxicated and behaving disrespectfully—"His dad's on the way over" a young officer informed the desk sergeant while trying to restrain the obnoxious youth. Angie felt a pang of remorse for the man's father who had struggled raising three children on his own after his wife's death years before. She made a mental note to tell Kevin about this episode and ask him to give Lars some support.

Looking down the hallway, she wondered who was in jail. At times she heard the vulgar language of angry voices echoing into the waiting area. As she sat looking at the large wall clock behind the main desk, Angie began to feel a biting discomfort wearing on her nerves. The boisterous scene became almost intimidating, frightening. And, the cops' casual stares almost saying "What's she in here for?" gave Angie a feeling of cheapness and violation.

On their way from Kevin's office to the city hall—across the street from the hotel—Kevin said nothing more than "Depelo's up to something very nasty," and promised to clarify what was going on after he'd talked with McGinnis. The wall clock moved slowly, Kevin had already been in the chief's office for twenty minutes.

When he emerged from behind the closed door, Kevin's face was drawn and flushed; his tie hung loosely from his unbuttoned collar. "What was that all about, Kevin? You were in there for quite a while...does it have to do with Evelyn Hayes?"

"Let's get out of here, Angie. I could use some fresh air...I'll tell you what's going on when we get outside."

In front of the city hall building were banks of lush flower gardens, tall shady trees, and oak park benches. Kevin and Tony had contributed to the public works beautification project the previous summer. The afternoon sun hung in a cloudless powder-blue sky and a gentle southwestern wind wafted the scent of roses across the lovely landscape. The setting was ideal for casual idling, but the tension in Kevin's stomach obscured the loveliness.

Leading Angie by the hand to a bench resting below a stately pine on the east side of the lawn, Kevin sat down beside his wife, breathing deeply to mitigate his stress. "Depelo's going after me, Angie." Taking out his handkerchief and dabbing perspiration from his forehead, Kevin explained what his meeting with Keirnan had been about.

"I'm under suspicion for raping Evelyn Hayes last Friday! Can you believe that?" Kevin bit off the question. "Depelo called McGinnis earlier this afternoon with what he called 'some messy business involving one of Hibbing's most prominent citizens' and asked Keirnan to initiate an immediate investigation."

"He what?" Angie's mouth dropped. "You can't be serious?"

"I'm serious all right. Depelo told the chief he got the story from Evelyn herself on Sunday afternoon. Said that he called me, asked for a meeting at the hotel that night...and when I denied everything—he quit his job and told me he was going to the police. How's that for a convoluted story?"

"He's twisted everything around. I can't believe..."

"Fear and revenge bring out the very worst in a person, and if you stir in hatred along with it..."

"Well, we'll just have to talk with Esther Hayes. She'll clear things up in a hurry," Angie's voice was determined. "Let's go right now!"

"Not so fast, sweetheart. I'm afraid Depelo's a few steps ahead of us. He's already gotten to Evelyn's mother—she's even corroborating his story of what happened. He must have threatened her somehow. I can't believe what's going on. This has been a day from hell!"

"How can Keirnan believe all of these unfounded lies! He knows you well enough to realize…"

Kevin tried to laugh through his growing distress, "Depelo's not only a very clever man, but a former police commissioner with a ton of contacts in the department—and a smooth talker as well. He probably even wept when he told McGinnis that he quit his job at the hotel because 'he couldn't in good conscience work with someone who had violated a woman—an employee, at that'. I'm paraphrasing what's in the rape report Depelo gave the chief."

"This is all such—it's so horrible!" Angie was furious; her voice trembled. "What did McGinnis say when you told him about Evelyn's call to our house last night? How she described to me about being raped by Depelo in the laundry room—and his threats to her children!"

Looking ashamedly away and averting Angie's eyes, Kevin shrugged his shoulders, "I didn't tell him anything, Angie. For some reason…" His explanation caught somewhere in his throat—"I guess I felt that this wasn't the right time or place to divulge any confidences. Isn't that what we agreed back at the office?"

Angie shook her head in disbelief, "You didn't tell him?"

"Maybe Keirnan's questions were unsettling me. Maybe I felt like I was walking blindly into some kind of trap. Maybe lots of things! And, I didn't want you getting dragged into the middle of everything right now. Sounds crazy, I know… What else can I say?"

Angie couldn't believe what she was hearing. Kevin seemed at a loss for words to explain himself.

Looking for Angie to respond and reading her expression of incredulity, he continued, "Do you think I was wrong to keep your conversation with Evelyn to myself? I mean, how would I look if I countered Depelo's accusation against me by saying 'Wrong Chief, it was really Depelo who raped the woman—just ask my wife, she's sitting outside right now.' Can't you understand how foolish that would look?"

Angie gave her husband a disturbing stare. Kevin was asking her if he'd done the right thing and his question bothered her. Where was that unflappable confidence that so defined everything that he was about. His demeanor almost suggested that he was a boy talking to his mother. Truly, Kevin was not himself at this moment. And, why had he waited until after this meeting with McGinnis to say anything? On the walk over to the police station, Kevin had not said a word about the allegation. Shaking her head at Kevin's last words, Angie asked, "Who cares how 'it would look'—?"

Kevin only mumbled, "It'll come up later, I guess."

"Please look at me when you're talking, Kevin," she implored. "You seem…really out of sorts. Did Keirnan make you that nervous? Why didn't you just laugh in his face and tell him that Depelo was trying to cover his behind and that he was angry about your firing him? Why didn't you lay it all out on the table and tell him to investigate Depelo—not you?"

Kevin sat for a long moment without reply, nodding absently at the clear logic of Angie's words. He probably had made a culpable impression on the chief. Keirnan's first question had rattled him more than he would admit. That inevitable and damnable question!—his response flashed again in his thoughts, *"I'm afraid that nobody knew…nobody saw me."* Kevin wondered if he should tell Angie about his Friday afternoon excursion, then chose against the idea. "I guess I really messed things up…didn't I, sweetheart?"

"That's putting it mildly. For a trained attorney, you really…" Angie swallowed the cutting remark she'd started…"What are you going to do now? Go back into Keirnan's office? Tell him what really happened?"

"No…but maybe I should get an attorney of my own to resolve this mess before it gets out of hand. And, it's imperative that I find Evelyn Hayes. I'll talk to Gary when I get back to the hotel."

Angie could only shake her head at the wound of his words. 'Talk to Gary,' not her? He seemed vexed, anxious, and on the defensive. Even worse, Kevin had used the word 'I'—not 'we' in considering what to do.

"Let's the two of us go over to Bob Peterson's office right now, then.
He's your friend and a darn good lawyer to boot. Then he can get back in touch with Chief McGinnis and begin to straighten out this 'mess' as you choose to call it."

Kevin took Angie's hands in his, "Not Bob Peterson, sweetheart."

Angie gave Kevin a startled look, "Why not your partner?"

Armando Depelo had finished hatching his scheme after having lunch with Ian Roberts. In his call to Evelyn Hayes at seven that morning he'd promised to "hurt her really bad" if she said another word to anybody.

"I wouldn't lay a hand on the boy—you know that—but you and that bastard daughter of yours…that's another story." Mando's tone intimidated the frightened woman.

Evelyn knew that Mando Depelo was capable of delivering on his threat. "I'll do whatever you say. Just don't hurt Nancy or me."

Depelo insisted that Evelyn take the children and get out of town for a while. "I've got a friend in Duluth who'll put ya up until it's the right time to come back to Hibbing. And, if you talk to Angela Moran again, I'm going to make her live miserable, too." He concluded his threat with a chafing order, "So, get packing, bitch!"

Depelo's friend in Duluth was an old partner in crime, Sam Lavalle. Lavalle had done time in Stillwater Prison before hooking up with Depelo's bootlegging operations ten years ago. On more than one occasion, Depelo needed a competitor (or a stoolie) rubbed out of the picture. Whenever he needed a hit man, or any dirty work accomplished, Sam Lavalle was willing to get the job done for him. Always simple and clean, no questions asked, cash in advance.

Ian Roberts had told Mando after lunch that "Maybe Elwood's not the lawyer you want if you're going after Moran. El might be so blinded by his personal hatreds that he'll lose any kind of perspective."

Depelo agreed. Bob Peterson was a partner of Kevin Moran—but the respected lawyer owed Depelo money. "I don't think our esteemed Mr. Peterson would like it to get around town that he's got a serious gambling problem—or that he got something under the table during my Prohibition wheeling and dealing."

All it took was a twist of the arm and Bob Peterson assured Depelo that he'd be willing to do the legal work Depelo needed. Bob's personal, but unspoken, displeasure with Kevin Moran stemmed in part from his partner's *pro bono* legal assistance to people who ought to have been paying something to the firm for their services. Pete, as he was known to most, would never admit to something else—a colleague's success and wealth bred a subtle contempt in his stomach. However unjustifiable, Pete's quirk of jealousy ran deep in the lawyer's psyche. For years, Bob Peterson had also quietly resented the fact that most clients wanted Moran's services and not his own. The junior partner had proven a far better litigator than he was.

When Depelo called Esther Hayes, the mother was beside herself with grief over Evelyn's sudden departure and whereabouts.

"Look, Esther, I know what happened to your daughter and I'm the only one who can take care of her—she needs protection right now."

After her initial disbelief of Depelo's story, "But that just can't be the truth, Mr. Depelo—I know Mr. Moran...he's always been fair to Evelyn." Armando, however, became very persuasive. "If anything happens to Evelyn it will be on your conscience. You've got to help me before your daughter, and God forbid, even the kids..." Within a few minutes, his clever talking had Esther believing his story and willing to do exactly what he wanted her to do."

"When this ugly business is over, we're going to have a chunk of that Moran money in our pockets, Esther," he assured her.

Having set his scheme in motion, Armando Depelo's last phone call was to Chief McGinnis. Puffing on an expensive Havana, Depelo finished his conversation—"Keirnan, my friend, I want you to know that we all think you're doing one helluva job. Once you get Kevin Moran we'll have rid our fine community of a serious problem. I realize you're still new to things here, but Mayor Molinaro and I could really tell you some stories about how the Morans got all their money." Getting carried away with what he perceived as a marvelous deception, Depelo couldn't help stretching his story. "We've always suspected Moran's links to bootlegging and prostitution using his hotel as a front. He's smooth—hides behind that respectable wife and family of his, but..."

The chief scratched his head in disbelief at all he was hearing. True, he had much to learn about Hibbing, but if his fledging respect for Kevin Moran were undermined, his mission to bring respectability to the force might never be accomplished. This town, he believed, had even more per capita corruption than St. Paul! "I'll talk to Mr. Moran this afternoon."

~

Father Patrick Foley's untimely death was a front page story in Monday's edition of the *Hibbing Daily Tribune*. Marc Atkinson wrote the extraordinary obituary with a sensitivity and emotion that would be pleasing to his father.

> *The loss of a beloved man brings the deepest human remorse. Late Sunday evening, the Good Lord took one of his own into the realm of heaven. Father Patrick J. Foley, pastor at the Duluth Cathedral of the Sacred Heart, died tragically in an automobile accident near Duluth. The widely respected priest was sixty-three.*

Father Pat, as he was affectionately known by thousands, came to the Diocese of Duluth from County Clare, Ireland, in 1896. During the years of 1900-1903, Father Foley was the pastor of our Blessed Sacrament parish. He was transferred to St. James in West Duluth after his Hibbing assignment. In 1922, Foley accepted his Bishop's call to the Cathedral where he had served the Catholic community of Northern Minnesota in an administrative capacity.

In light of Father Pat's passing, this scant biography seems almost trite. Over his many years of service to God, the priest has been a friend and mentor to hundreds of Protestants and Jews as well as those of his own denomination. Father Pat was a frequent visitor to our fine community where he had numerous close friendships. In fact, Foley was returning to Duluth from Hibbing yesterday. His passing will be especially difficult for Kevin Moran and his family who were hosting their son's birthday party attended by the priest.

Funeral arrangements are pending as this issue goes to press.

Father Potocnik of Blessed Sacrament Church has told this reporter that the burial will likely occur on Thursday. Potocnik will relay any and all information as it becomes available from the Bishop.

It is with heavy hearts that we all say good-bye to this holy soldier and shepherd of souls.

Traveling with the priest in yesterday's fatal accident was retired educator, Robert Barker. Fortunately, the passenger's injuries were not serious, and Mr. Barker is recovering satisfactorily at St. Mary's Hospital.

ALONE ON A HILLSIDE

Kevin Moran's Tuesday afternoon call caught the Duluth attorney by complete surprise. Making an immediate connection with the well-known Hibbing surname, memories of her father's stories flooded into Colleen McIntosh's thoughts. The caller's father, Peter Moran, and her own father, Jim, had been best of friends many years before. "I'm sorry, Mr. Moran. I'm just so very surprised to hear from you..." Colleen apologized. "If I'm not mistaken our fathers were old friends."

Kevin laughed easily at her recollection, "From what I've been told, that's an understatement, Miss McIntosh."

Needing to discuss his situation with an attorney, Kevin had confided his dilemma in vague terms to Senia Arola that morning. His personal accountant and lifelong confidant always afforded him good advice. It was Senia's belief than an out-of-town lawyer would be in Kevin's best interest considering the potential 'politics' of any legal issue in Hibbing. Having followed the career of her old Duluth friend's daughter, Colleen, Senia was of the opinion that the McIntosh woman was among the sharpest legalists in Northern Minnesota. "I know just the person to contact, Kevin..." Senia advised.

"As soon as I heard your name, my dad's old stories came immediately to mind...thus, the little delay on my end of the line, Mr. Moran. I must apologize—I'm not usually..." Colleen laughed easily over the awkward beginning to their conversation.

"Kevin, please, Miss McIntosh." Kevin, distracted by the lilt of the attorney's laugh, attempted to frame his thoughts. When on the telephone with a stranger, he always tried to form a picture in his mind of the person he was talking to. Small talk about their respective fathers seemed inappropriate at the moment, however…"I want to congratulate you on your winning verdict in the Luddington case," he said.

Colleen's practice focused largely, but not exclusively, on women's rights issues. Two weeks before, she had concluded her successful prosecution of a major Minneapolis grain-milling corporation for job discrimination.

"It was a lot of work…Mister Moran." Using the man's surname seemed awkward in light of his suggested informality. Realizing that Kevin was a respected attorney in his own right, she wondered about the reason for his call. "But, justice was served in the end," she responded assuredly to the compliment. Two of her thirty-seven years had been devoted almost exclusively to the complex case.

"I would certainly agree with that. Margaret Staples deserved the jury award," Kevin said. (Miss Staples, a University of Minnesota business graduate, had been passed over in a controversial Luddington promotion. The junior executive position had been given to a far less qualified man. Colleen McIntosh had made a convincing case for gender bias and her victory was a watershed decision in the Federal District Court in St. Paul).

Kevin chose his next words carefully. "Miss McIntosh, I have a legal issue myself and would appreciate any consideration your schedule might allow. I'm of the belief than an attorney who seeks to represent himself has a fool for a client." Although Kevin's observation was almost a cliché in law school, it was, nevertheless, the truth—and the purpose for his call.

Colleen McIntosh, pinning the phone between her chin and right shoulder, automatically slid her large yellow legal pad toward her left hand so she could write down any relevant details. "I'd be more than happy to help if I can, Mr. Moran." With her understanding that the call was professional and not personal, the surname rolled more easily from her tongue.

For several minutes Kevin followed his outline of notes while explaining the Evelyn Hayes matter: The Sunday phone call to his wife, Kevin's termination of Armando Depelo, Evelyn's strange disappearance, the rape accusation, and, finally, his frustrating visit with the Hibbing police chief the day before.

Colleen bit nervously at her lip as she scribbled across the tablet. Moran's depiction was precise, methodical, and uncommonly articulate. Most importantly to her, the man's words rang with sincerity. She pictured the man as she listened to his voice—a masculine and self-assured voice! When he had finished, she regarded her tightly-scripted notes and placed bold check marks next to every *why* on the page. She had some questions for Mr. Moran.

Why did he think it advisable, or necessary, to have an attorney at this point in time? No criminal charges had been filed.

And, if he wanted representation, *why* not his legal partner of several years, Bob Peterson? Peterson, she knew, was a senior member of the bar and well-respected in northeastern Minnesota.

Below the second why she had penned, '*Why* me?'

On her second page, four additional question marks caught her eye: Angela Moran? Gary Zench? Friday afternoon? Full disclosure?

Deciding to postpone any inquiry regarding her questions about legal representation, Colleen focused on the second page. "Can you clarify a few things for me, Mr. Moran?"

Kevin cleared his throat; Miss McIntosh was using his proper name, choosing not to reciprocate his earlier invitation to be less formal. That reality impressed him. "Yes, most certainly, Miss McIntosh."

"Did you speak at all with Miss Hayes on Sunday night?"

"No—my wife, Angela, took the call." Then, Kevin corrected himself, "Let me take that back...I did call Miss Hayes right back. Expressed my concerns about what had happened to her, told her to stay home for the week. I didn't get into any details about the incident with her, however."

"Your wife had been given the details—is that correct?"

"Yes."

Colleen chose to avoid descriptions of the sordid act for the moment, moving to her next question: "Did Mr. Zench stand to benefit from Mr. Depelo's termination?"

"I suppose you could infer that...I asked Gary, Mr. Zench, to assume the role as hotel manager."

Recognizing that the credibility of anything Zench might say about the hastily summoned meeting would be impugned by the fact that he was being promoted. Kevin commented, "A very good question, counselor."

Shaking the compliment, Colleen pressed on to the two most difficult questions. "Are you in the habit of leaving your office without mentioning where you are going to anybody—such as your assistant or personal secretary?"

"No. Usually I'll tell Doreen Boyum or Gary where I'm going."

"Usually?"

"Most of the time."

"Had you told your wife, or anybody else, that you were going out to the lake on Friday afternoon?"

"No..." Kevin expected the question and knew that his answer would invite conjecture. "I enjoy doing that sometimes, I mean...just taking off and wandering around by myself. I've been that way since I was a kid—always needed some space or privacy to collect my thoughts. Do you understand? My life gets awfully cluttered with people and activity—a long walk away from it all is rejuvenating."

Colleen sensed the honesty in his words, "Yes, Mr. Moran, I can relate to that very well." Although she could understand...most people would probably consider such behavior as out of the norm.

"Why did you drive out to the lake so late in the day? It must have been getting dark while you were surveying your property. And, with the rain and all, it would seem an unlikely day for such an excursion."

"It didn't really get dark until after I'd done my surveying and it only rained for an hour or so—but I carry a lantern in the trunk of my car...and I know the lay of the land like the back of my hand. In fact there's a narrow deer trail from where I parked my car to the ridge overlooking the lake."

"That's fine...but nobody saw you from the time you left Hibbing—at about four o'clock—until you returned home somewhere around ten?"

"Not that I'm aware of. That reality bothers me, too, Miss McIntosh. I passed a few cars going in the other direction, but—"

Colleen had a female client waiting outside her office and wanted to conclude this conversation without sounding unforgivably rude. Offering any advice at this juncture would be premature, and Kevin had not requested any specific legal assistance. Besides, having another member of the bar as a client was always a discomforting situation. "One more question, Mr. Moran, and then I'll have to get off the line. I'm sorry...but, briefly—why didn't you tell Chief McGinnis about the rape allegation Miss Hayes told your wife about? I'm unclear about your reasoning." She chose the word "reasoning" over "judgment".

Kevin admitted to the attorney, as he had to Angie the day before, "I just wasn't thinking clearly enough at the time, I guess. I was a little overwhelmed by the accusation...even nervous." As he recalled the interrogation he realized that his omission didn't make much sense. "You know how, when something comes flying right out of the blue, something really upsetting..."

Colleen empathized with the beleaguered man, "We all have those feelings at one time or another, Mr. Moran: Moments when we're caught completely off guard."

Later that afternoon, Colleen sipped coffee at her desk while reviewing the notes from her earlier conversation with Kevin Moran. She remembered concluding on a rather ambiguous note: "I think the ball is in the court of the Hibbing police department right now—not ours." She had informed Kevin that locating Miss Hayes and getting her statement was the first priority. "After that we can discuss this matter again." When she asked if there was anything specific he wanted her to do, Kevin had told her that he simply wanted to give her the relevant information.

Looking up from her papers, Colleen recalled her final words, "Get in touch with me anytime…"

Colleen McIntosh was thirty-seven, never married, and committed to her profession. Her older sister, Anne, often kidded her as being "The only virgin your age in Duluth." Ever since her freshman year at college, Colleen had regarded life as a perpetual competition to succeed. And the competition she faced was mostly from men. Competition for grades was later compounded by the competition for a job in a first-rate law firm—and from that time on—further competition with men in the courtroom. Over the course of her twelve years in the legal profession, she had established her own law firm—McIntosh and Associates—and gained a remarkable reputation as a hard-nosed litigant.

By age thirty, Colleen had realized that she intimidated most men—men who were looking for someone to have their children, make their meals, and maintain their households. (In the culturally defined scheme of things, 'the man brought home the bacon')! Colleen McIntosh did not meet these requisites of 'womanhood' by any measure. Conspicuously tall for a woman at five feet ten inches, narrow-hipped and small-bosomed, the cinnamon-haired attorney was viewed by many of her peers as standoffish, even tenacious. And when she talked with men—it was in an eyeball-to-eyeball, no-nonsense dialogue of equals. To other woman, Colleen's striking facial beauty made them wonder "Why isn't she married?" Being attractive, educated, *and single*—seemed both unnatural and upsetting in contemporary society.

Despite all her successes, Colleen McIntosh often felt unfulfilled. It wasn't so much that she wanted a husband or marriage...a strong and sensitive companion might pleasantly fill the void of lonely nights and lost weekends at the office.

She pushed her notepad aside and gazed out the window at the gray afternoon. As was her end-of-the-workday custom, Colleen telephoned her father before heading from her posh third floor Superior Street office to her comfortable London Road home. Jim McIntosh was her favorite person in the world. (Her mother had passed from breast cancer while Colleen was in college.) "Dad, you wouldn't believe who I talked with this afternoon..." She went on to explain her conversation with the son of her father's old friend without sharing the details of Kevin's dilemma.

Jim McIntosh smiled inwardly at all the memories the name Moran evoked from years before. How much like his father was the son, he wondered? If Kevin had Peter's kismet, misfortune might be his traveling companion throughout life. A life that could very well be short and tragic. "If he's a chip of the old block, Colleen, he's probably handsome, bright, and equally charming."

Colleen laughed at her dad's insight, "And, I suppose you're going to tell me, ill-fated as well."

"You said it, sweetheart, not me."

∼

"Have you ever lied to me, Kevin?" Angie's question caught him off guard as he was knotting his tie in the wide mirror of the bedroom dresser. The two of them were getting ready for their trip to Duluth with Tony and Becca. Father Foley's wake ceremony would be held at the Cathedral on the central Duluth hillside that evening, with the funeral the following morning at St. James in the western part of the city.

"Where did that question come from, sweetheart?"

"I just wonder about you sometimes. Like last Friday night...then again yesterday. Both times I called the hotel and no one seemed to know where you were."

Tightening the knot under his crisp white collar, Kevin sat down on the bed and regarded his wife brushing her long hair at the vanity. Angie was wearing the new lavender linen suit he had purchased at the Itasca Bazaar the week before. "I drove out to our lake property on Friday...just to get away for a while. And, yesterday—let me see; I took a walk up to Bennett Park, visited for a few minutes with Senia, and dropped by Claude's house for coffee."

Angie turned to face Kevin, "Out to Sturgeon Lake by yourself—late at night? Getting home well after ten, Kevin. What on earth for?"

"Why not? I'm not scared of the dark," he made light of his clandestine excursion.

His answer, however, brought a deeper frown to Angie's face, "And I suppose the walk yesterday was just your need to get away for a while, too. What I'm not understanding…is…what do you need to get away from? What's bothering you? You haven't been yourself since—since seeing McGinnis on Monday." That reality, however, did not explain Friday's wandering off by himself, coming home late with wet and muddy shoes. Angela chose to let the matter drop for the moment, "So how are Senia and Claude?"

"I talked to Senia about getting an attorney if I should need one."

"What does she think?"

"She gave me the names of a couple of lawyers in Duluth…that's all. She thinks it's best to find someone out of town. I agreed with her."

"Are you going to follow up on her advice?"

Kevin felt ashamed of his half-truths. If he started keeping secrets from Angie now—where would it end? He had been in a funk even before the McGinnis interrogation. This dark mood probably went as far back as that September morning nearly two years ago. Kevin couldn't really understand or explain what this change in temperament was all about. At times he wondered if his father's ill fortune had become some compelling shadow over his life. His walk to Bennett Park the day before was actually a trip to the cemetery only a block away from the wooded sanctuary. Lately he had been spending lost hours at the grave site of the father he never knew…but seem obsessed with. More than once, he tried to pray for some spiritual insight, but nothing gave him peace. And now, Father Foley, one of the few people who might help him understand this perplexing magnetism, was gone.

"Kevin? What's the matter? You look like…"

Kevin had been staring out the window. "I'm sorry, sweetheart. What was it you just asked?"

"Nothing. I'm ready—let's get the luggage packed into the car. I'll go over my list of things for the children with Clara downstairs. Patrick's napping right now, so let's give him a kiss good-bye before heading over to my dad's."

Kevin stood, stepped toward Angie, put his arms around her narrow shoulders, "Just a minute Angie; I did call a lawyer in Duluth." He swallowed hard, "I'm worried about what's been going on…not only the Evelyn Hayes business, but strange things inside me. I don't mean to shut you out…Sometimes I pull away from the one I love and trust the most, even when I know that I should be pulling you closer to me." Kevin kissed her on the mouth, "Don't let me do that to you, honey. Whenever you sense I'm slipping off somewhere…anywhere…pull me back. Please!"

Angie felt warm tears on her cheek, "Kevin, as much as you want to figure things out for yourself—as much as you want to explore those depths inside of you—remember…you'll find what you're looking for by reaching out to me, or anyone who loves and cares for you, much better than by plunging into yourself alone. Let me help your search. Let me be your spiritual mate, Kevin. Don't ask me to pull you back—pull me into your thoughts instead."

Kevin could feel tears welling in his own eyes, "I do need you, my love. More than you will ever know."

~

The Patrick Foley funeral ceremony swelled St. James Catholic Church far beyond capacity with mourners clustered in the entryway, down the wide concrete steps outside, and onto the sidewalk lining Fifty-Seventh Street. Following the mass and burial rites in Oneota Cemetery, hundreds gathered for the reception in the school gymnasium adjacent to the church.

Kevin mingled with many old friends he had grown up with during his childhood years in the West Duluth neighborhood. Hud Tusken and his wife, Kathleen, had traveled up from Minneapolis where he was a teacher and coach at Benilde. Huddy and Kevin had been best of friends and teammates at Denfeld— Kathleen (Murphy) Tusken had been Kevin's first crush and scholastic rival while in school at St. James. Teasing Kathleen, Kevin asked the lovely brunette, "Have you mastered the spelling of *vacuum* yet?"

Kathleen laughed easily at the memory of losing a tense spelling contest to Kevin on that word many years before.

"Yes, I have—'smarty-pants'—and I can spell *guillotine* as well!" She feigned a slashing cut toward Kevin's neck. Strikingly attractive, Kathleen also had a sense of humor. "Hud and I still relive those wonderful times here at St. James, Kevin, and we remember you every time we do."

"Ah, yes...the memories! They're everywhere—this school, the neighborhood—we were blessed, weren't we? And to have had Father Foley in our lives, well...what more can I say?"

Nodding in her agreement (and after more good natured banter about old times shared), Kathleen suggested, "Kevin, you must introduce me to our wife sometime this afternoon."

"Angie would love to meet you both. I'll try to fine her..." As he glanced over the sea of mostly familiar faces, Kevin was struck by another woman toward the back of the room. Tall and thin, the red-headed woman in an elegant black dress looked like Helen of Troy as he had imagined that legendary woman's beauty. For a brief moment, their eyes met, but the woman turned suddenly away and became lost in the swell of people.

Angela was commiserating with Art and Sarah Schmitz while her husband was renewing old acquaintances in the crowded room. She enjoyed watching Kevin as he mixed and mingled. Her heart was always warmed by his easy manner of meeting people, conversing, and finding humor in past memories—even those that did not include her. Whenever Kevin laughed, Angie was at her happiest.

She smiled when she saw Kevin give a hug to an elderly nun who had shuffled up to his side. "Is that Sister Anne de Poris, Sarah?"

"Yes...however did you know that? She was Kevin's favorite teacher here at St. James."

"Sixth grade, if I remember correctly," Art added, looking in the direction of the small-framed woman in black habit. "She's retired now."

Kevin embraced the frail Benedictine Sister warmly, "Sister Anne, how wonderful to see you!"

The diminutive nun's eyes sparked, "Kevin Schmitz, what a handsome young man you've become. And successful from what I've been told. I always knew you would be."

"Mostly, I have my father to thank for whatever success I've had, Sister. He gave me a pretty good start in life." Kevin easily dismissed his own achievements by acknowledging his inheritance. "And I've got Father Foley to thank as well; were it not for his wisdom along the way...well, we both know that he was something of a guardian angel in my life."

"In all of our lives, Kevin. God has a special place for that man."

Sister Anne regarded the tall man with intelligent eyes, "How are you, Kevin? Have you found happiness as 'Kevin Moran?'? (As her student years before, Kevin had been Schmitz). I pray for you every day—for your happiness, I mean. We old nuns are prayer warriors, you know—with memories like an elephant as well. There's hardly a former student from my years of teaching that I don't remember and pray for." She beamed her truth. But, that Kevin Schmitz was among those most frequently prayed for remained an unspoken thought. She had been among the first to recognize and encourage Kevin's unique potentials.

"I couldn't be happier, Sister. You'll have to meet my wife, Angela—she's a big part of my happiness. And we have two children already—Patrick was named after Father Foley, and Mary after Angela's mother."

Sister Anne knew Kevin's story better than the young man realized. Her closest friend, Sister Bridgette, had retired to the Blessed Sacrament convent in Hibbing several years before (a move that Anne was considering herself). Bridgette, an avid reader of the *Hibbing Tribune*, had kept Anne well informed on Kevin's busy life—his family, political activities, hotel ownership, and various community involvements were as familiar to the old Benedictine as they might have been if Kevin had lived in Duluth all these years. Somewhere, locked behind his deep-set, expressive green eyes, however, she saw traces of pain. "I would love to meet your wife, and your children, too." She explained that she was thinking about moving to his Iron Range community "one of these days".

"That would be wonderful, Sister Anne," Kevin's surprise was evidenced in his wide smile. "Come, you must meet Angela. I've told her so much about you."

Angela and Sister Anne both found an immediate and unexpected bond. Angela was charming—and Anne was charmed. "I pray with the very same rosary that Kevin won in your sixth grade class room for winning a spelling contest, or something..." Angie stretched her memory for recall of the story.

"For being my most outstanding student," Sister Anne said. "I haven't forgotten. Your husband was one of my all-time favorite pupils."

Kevin, standing up from the table across from his wife, blushed. "It took me a few years to get my bearings, I'm afraid. Kevin Schmitz wasn't always the model pupil I assure you. I spent more than a few hours in the principal's office during my early grades."

Art and Sarah laughed easily at their memory of Kevin's deportment issues as a youngster. "Father Pat had to straighten him out once or twice," Art said.

"If you all don't mind, I'm going to excuse myself so the two of you can get better acquainted." Kevin smiled toward his wife and the Sister. "I'm willing to bet you've got quite a bit in common. I think I'm going to take a little walk and get some fresh air."

Kevin's insight was prophetic. In his absence, the two women's conversation was animated and quickly ranged from Kevin's student days to other topics of interest. Like Angela, Anne had a passion for painting. "I've heard of your wonderful artwork and I'm anxious to see some of it for myself," the nun complimented.

After they had talked about the importance of prayer in their daily lives, Anne turned to Art and Sarah who were talking with another couple at the table and suggested, "If you'll excuse us, I'd like to show Angela my former classroom. I think Kevin's initials are still engraved near the inkwell of his old desk."

Kevin departed the school and headed north toward his old neighborhood haunts of years before. It felt refreshing to breathe in the crisp afternoon air after nearly two hours inside the stuffy gymnasium. Being enclosed for more than a few hours seemed to motivate the restless spirit which had become his aggravation in recent weeks. The need to cut himself off from other people and find a solitary respite where he might mull over his thoughts tugged at him like an invisible hand. As he walked up the street, Kevin's mind wandered from Pat Foley, Sister Anne, Hud and Kathleen—to the striking redhead who had caught his attention earlier. There was something magnetic about that woman. It troubled him that he could not put a finger on what it was. Although he had never laid eyes on her before this afternoon, there was, nevertheless, a mysterious familiarity beyond his comprehension. Dismissing the thought, Kevin smiled inwardly at the apparent connection between Angie and Sister Anne. Women had a manner of bonding, he believed, that men rarely experienced. In his own life, women had been able to help him understand complexities with a greater depth than the men he was closest to—Angie more than anybody, but Senia and Becca, too. He wondered about his mother. How much of an influence would she have been in his life? How different might he have become if…? In the very last conversation Kevin had had with Pat Foley, he had asked the priest about Barbara Chevalier. Perhaps Kevin was destined to take that mystery with him to his own grave.

Far too often these days, Kevin found himself wondering why his life had become such a roller coaster of ups and downs. Why he was allowing his torments to consume hours of his thoughts? Why was this incomprehensible self-searching so important? His roots, his purpose in life, and his annoying comparisons with the father he never knew? Even more than his present dilemma regarding Evelyn Hayes, personal tribulations and misgivings were his rue. As he walked aimlessly, dismay and doubt flooded his thoughts.

From the rock outcroppings near the rugged hilltop, he could look down over the blue band of the St. Louis River, the mammoth ore loading docks, intricate railroad track network, and busy Grand Avenue. He and Gary Zench had spent hours lazing in this very spot on long summer afternoons talking about their families and the adolescent issues in their lives. Not far from where he sat was the old Zench homestead—a ramshackle structure that defined the poverty of his friend's mixed race family. As close as he had become to Foley, Tony, and Claude Atkinson over the years, perhaps it was Gary more than any other man in his life who really knew where he came from and what he was about.

Unseen, from a window down the street, the eyes of Thelma Barker watched the solitary figure sitting on the distant ledge. Her memory strained, "Could that be Kevin Schmitz up there?" The elderly woman was certain that it was. Smiling to herself, she remembered seeing the tall man as a boy—sitting for hours by himself on that very same boulder.

"Where have you been, Kevin?" Angela's expression wore a frown. "We've been looking all over for you." Angie had noticed that Kevin's trouser cuffs were soiled, his shoes muddied. "It's been nearly two hours. You just vanished …even Art and Sarah had no idea—"

Most of the people had already left the school and the tables were being cleared. "I'm sorry, sweetheart. I just took a little walk up the hill. Lost track of time along my memory lane trip, I guess."

∼

On the Friday following the Foley funeral, Tony Zoretek and his brother, Rudy, drove out to Sturgeon Lake, north and west of Hibbing, to survey the site Kevin had told Tony about at Patrick's birthday party the previous Sunday. "He wants to build a lake home on that pine ridge, Rudy—the one with the spectacular view of the lake." Tony gestured toward the promontory draped with stately white pine and birch.

Rudy had been out to the Moran property before and knew the site from memory. "He wants to surprise Angie, huh?" Rudy repeated his brother's comment from moments before. "She'd love it out here, wouldn't she? Everything you see is like a picture waiting to be painted."

Tony smiled at the thought. His daughter was an artist and his son a musician. Sometimes he realized that his younger brother was more like himself than either of this own two children. Tony and Rudy not only loved sports, but hunting and fishing and all activities outdoors. "You're right about that, Rudy. There'll be more than a few landscape portraits coming from Sturgeon Lake when Angie gets her paint brush and easel set up out here."

"After we do our surveying, I hope we've got an hour or so to wet our lines from the shore," Rudy said. "I have a feeling there might be some walleyes off that point between Kevin's property here and your place up the shore."

"I wouldn't have it any other way."

While standing on the hillside, Tony heard the rustle of bushes behind, "Someone's coming our way, Rudy—wonder who…?"

"'Lo fellas…what'cha up ta this afternoon?" A thickly bearded man asked in a gravely voice as he approached.

Tony recognized the unexpected intruder. 'I might ask you the same question, Oscar."

Oscar Berquist was a recluse who had lived in the Side Lake forest for as many years as anybody could remember. The eccentric trapper and woodsman was almost legendary. It was known that Berquist, perhaps in his eighties, had been a foreman in the old Daly Moran lumbering operations in the years before the city of Hibbing had been platted.

"Just looking over this property, Oscar. Might be building a little lake home up here later this fall," Tony informed the stocky, disheveled old man.

"Don't like that idea none," Berquist said gruffly, "This here's good trappin' country ya know. Don't take kindly ta folks messin' up where the wildlife's been livin' all these years. Yer kinda folks belong in da city."

Tony laughed easily, "There's lots of room out here, Oscar."

"Never enough. 'For ya know it, things'll change—never be the same agin. First it's that resort o'er at Pine Beach, then cabins goin' up here and dare…dis place gonna be a playgroun' fer you rich folks. That's what I baleeve—ya can like what I'm sayin' or not."

Rudy, taken aback by the ragged old-timer's reference to 'rich folk', attempted to placate the hermit who most believed lived somewhere in the nearby Beatrice Lake area. "A little house on these eighty acres won't disturb your wilderness hardly at all. I've heard a person could walk a hundred miles toward Canada from here without seeing another human being."

Oscar Berquist knew that to be true. "Seen that Moran kid up here da other day—wanderin' about in the rain 'til after dark. This here's his property ain't it?"

"Yes it is, Oscar." Tony answered. "You worked for Kevin's grandfather years ago I'm told."

"A better man never walked dis here earth than Daly Moran—dat's the truth. Never had no damn use fer his son, Peter, though." Oscar spat the juice from a plug of tobacco, "Never met dis…what'z his name…Kevin? Heard he's got lots'a his ole man's money though."

"Maybe you'll have a chance to meet him one of these days. I'm sure Kevin would enjoy hearing some of your stories about his grampa. He was born long after Daly died out west."

"Mebbe so." Oscar shrugged his broad shoulders in agitation. He'd spoken his piece and felt no need to waste time with city folk. "Enuff jawing. Gonna be movin' on, fellas. Ain't got nothin' else to say, 'cept I don like what I'm hearin' about what yer up ta. God din make dis place for rich folks ta ruin with no buildins'."

Tony appreciated the old timer's perspective but couldn't help a rejoinder. "Now Oscar, we both know how the old loggers clear-cut this very countryside we're standing on—back in your day—don't we?"

The question did not evoke any reply. Oscar knew that these lands had been ravaged by his own hands as well as those of the huge lumber operations less than fifty years ago.

Oscar Berquist picked up his deerskin sack filled with traps, slung it over his shoulder, and walked away as silently as he had come.

∼

On Sunday morning two boys rafting across a misty bay off the St. Louis River near the western Duluth neighborhood of Riverside, found the body of a woman floating in the reeds. After racing home in white-faced horror to tell their parents, a call was made to the police.

Detective Carver Blake's preliminary identification of the drowned woman that afternoon was linked with a Friday report from the Piedmont Orphanage where two children had been dropped off at the building's doorstep by an unidentified woman. The children were Nancy and John Hayes from Hibbing. For two days the Duluth police had been searching for the missing mother, and had been in close contact with Hibbing police chief, Keirnan McGinnis.

McGinnis placed a call to Kevin Moran at two o'clock on that rainy Sunday afternoon. "Some tragic news again, Mr. Moran." The chief explained what he had just learned from the Duluth homicide investigator. "Just between us…they told me that the woman had been murdered before being dumped in the river. She'd probably been dead for a couple of days from the report I've been given."

Waiting for a reply, McGinnis heard an audible gasp but no words. Filling the momentary lull, he added—"So, I guess this *other business* we talked about last week is going to be in limbo? Evelyn Hayes is never going to tell a living soul about anything again."

Kevin was too dumbfounded with grief to say anything for a few seconds. 'Other business! Evelyn murdered! "What about the children, Keirnan? What's going to become of them?" He finally blurted.

"Evelyn's mother is on her way to Duluth as we speak, sir. She's going to bring the children home…and, I would guess, try to tell them what happened to their mother. I pity that task."

After expressing his heartfelt sympathy for Mrs. Hayes and the two kids, Kevin hung up the phone. He would talk to Esther tomorrow and offer to make certain that her daughter's children would be provided for in every possible way. The tragedy turned his stomach—did Depelo have anything to do with what had happened? Murder? Was his antagonist capable of such a wretched thing? Kevin had heard rumors of his former friend's flaunting of the law during Prohibition, but regrettably, had never confronted him with the allegations. Yet, it was well understood by most; the illegal trafficking of liquor involved some dangerous characters and countless mysterious deaths and disappearances.

"Angie!" Kevin called from the living room toward the kitchen, "I've just been given some more terrible news."

MOTIVE AND OPPORTUNITY

Visibly shaken, Angie's jaw dropped as Kevin told her Keirnan's tragic report. Tears streamed from her dark eyes and down her cheeks, "Oh, no! That poor woman—the children. Kevin, I can't believe…"

"Now nobody will ever know the truth, will they?" Kevin's voice held a somber tone, but one of relief as well.

Distraught over the tragedy and Kevin's casual observation, Angie virtually exploded, "Never know the truth? I can't believe what you've just said, Kevin Moran. I know the truth—so do you! Evelyn Hayes told me the truth. I have no doubt in my mind about that. How can you be so—so offhanded about it?"

"I only mean that—well, McGinnis thinks I might have… "

"Finish your thoughts for heaven's sake! You might have what—raped Evelyn Hayes at your hotel? Angie's voice trembled at the audacity of such a notion.

Kevin felt the sting of ire in Angie's voice, "Keirnan hasn't said as much, but he certainly did put me through the wringer last week. Now, I wouldn't be surprised if he considers me a suspect in Evelyn's murder."

"We both know who the prime suspect is. Armando Depelo would do something evil like that—without any conscience or remorse—we both should know by now that he hates you! He would stop at nothing to destroy your reputation if he had half the chance—just like those other political sharks did two years ago." She sank back in the sofa, dabbing at her eyes, "Something about that man has always frightened me."

Angie considered telling Kevin what that something was, but repressed the revelation. It had been on New Year's Eve, three years before, at the Androy Hotel's annual party. After the stroke of midnight, in the mayhem of revelry, Depelo had kissed her. His kiss was wet and repulsive and his hand had brushed lightly across her bottom as his arm encircled her. She pushed herself away and nearly slapped his face. But, as violated as she had felt at the time, Angie never spoke a word about the episode to anyone.

Keeping secrets from Kevin deeply disturbed her. Angie had lied more than once—never blatantly, but by omission. Was that just as bad? What were Kevin's secrets from her? Angie believed that a relationship without complete trust was a relationship at risk. Why had she kept things locked inside like a surreptitious diary from him? Even important things like her headaches and blackouts remained darkly concealed in her private torment.

Kevin sat close beside her but felt miles away, stroking his chin in contemplation of something he, too, seemed unable to share with his wife. Angie, however, was perceptive. Lately, though she didn't probe, he knew she wondered about strange ideas lurking about the edges of his mind. His demeanor had been noticeably remote and self-absorbed. Angie remembered his disappearance after the funeral…had asked him more than once where he'd really gone—and why? Her questions seemed unusually laden with suspicion.

"I'm going to the police station, Kevin!" Angie finally blurted. "That's all there is to it. McGinnis needs to know the truth—right now, before he develops any more misconceptions from the Duluth police or hears any more lies from Depelo."

"No. That wouldn't be prudent, Angie." Kevin said with a slight tremor in his voice as he turned away from his thoughts to face his wife.

"What?" Angie had never been told not to do something she thought was right before. Never!

Taken aback, Angie repeated, "What?"

"You heard me, sweetheart. This Hayes business is already a can of worms—don't you understand that?"

"Then let's get it cleared up before it becomes a can of snakes and tell McGinnis about Evelyn's call last Sunday night. If you won't do it, I'll dump the can on his desk, and get him pointed in the right direction."

Kevin took her hand, "…Please—not right now. Let things cool down a bit. Then, we can both go to the police."

Angie shook her head, "We've waited too long already. If you think things are going to 'cool down' you're mistaken. There's going to be an investigation of Evelyn's death…and your name is more than likely to come up. You know that, Kevin."

Kevin nodded without comment. Angie was right.

"Well?"

"I'll see Keirnan tomorrow."

"If you think its right to wait that long," Angie reluctantly demurred to her husband. Biting her lower lip and shaking her head she said, "I'll wait with you. But I have a strong gut feeling that delaying isn't going to cool anybody's suspicions."

∼

Upon learning that his hired *job* had been taken care of, Armando Depelo traveled to Duluth on the Wednesday night of Patrick Foley's wake.

Depelo, however, had no intentions of going to any church ceremonies. Armando had a much more covert meeting to attend to. Sam Lavalle was waiting over a double Seagrams for his Hibbing visitor at a back table in Sam's former tavern on Central Avenue.

After bowling in his Wednesday night league, Art Schmitz and Jerry Oelrich often stopped at the Central Bar for a few glasses of Grain Belt beer. From his bar stool, Art discerned the familiar face of Sam Lavalle in the shadowed corner. Lavalle was a convicted felon and still held a grudge against Schmitz for testifying against him in a bungled kidnapping case many years before. "Let's drink up, Jerry," Art whispered toward his friend's ear, "I see Lavalle over there and I don't want to get my butt kicked by that thug tonight."

Oelrich glanced over his shoulder, "Who's the guy with him, Art? I ain't seen him in here before."

Art did not recognize the well-dressed Hibbing businessman, "I have no idea, but I'd bet he's not the kind of guy either one of us wants to meet."

"Just a minute, Art," Oelrich strained his neck to better view the pair of men in the corner. The men's lavatory door had swung open casting a beam of light toward the corner table. Before Lavalle could turn away, Oelrich got a quick glimpse of a transaction. "Lavalle must have won a bet or somethin', that other guy's payin' him off. And that's one helluva wad of money Lavalle's tuckin' in his pocket."

"Let's go, Jerry. It's none of our concern what kind of business those two fellas are up to."

~

Kevin was feeding Patrick from a bowl of oatmeal when the telephone rang. "Who'd be calling this early?" he wondered aloud. It was only seven on this dreary Monday morning and Kevin was helping Angie with the children's breakfast.

"I'll get it, Kevin." Angie pushed away from the table with Maribec cradled in her arm.

When she returned to the kitchen, Angie's face wore an anguished expression. "That can of worms you talked about the other day is sitting on the police chief's desk. He wants to talk with you this morning, Kevin. It seems that something's already developed in the Hayes case…he was deliberately vague about what that might be. I asked him what he wanted to talk to you about, but…" She put her daughter in the highchair, untied her apron, and riveted her eyes on Kevin.

"But what?"

"Only that you might be able to 'shed some light' is what he said."

Turning away from Angie's stare, Kevin resumed feeding his son without any further comment. He knew what Keirnan wanted to find out.

"I'm going with you, Kevin. I've got a few things to tell our new Chief of Police. This Evelyn Hayes matter has gone too far to suit me."

"Always good to see you, Mrs. Moran," the chief's surprise at seeing Angela was undisguised. Keirnan McGinnis stood respectfully from his desk. "And you as well, Mr. Moran." The lanky cop pulled a second chair up toward the front of his cluttered oak desk for Angela. "Why don't you both make yourselves comfortable? Can I get either of you a cup of coffee?"

Both Morans nodded negative to the gesture.

"That's fine," Keirnan said sitting down. "This matter should only take a few minutes."

Kevin pushed the extra chair so that Angie could be seated, but chose to stand himself. Leaning on the corner of the chief's desk, Kevin said "Let's get right to whatever 'this matter' is all about, Keirnan," the sharp edge of directness cutting upon his remark.

McGinnis didn't like confrontation and regarded Kevin's posture as a subtle form of intimidation. "Please sit down and let me explain exactly what's going on."

When Kevin was seated, Keirnan swallowed hard. "As you might expect, the Duluth police asked if there might be any suspects in the Hayes case (he had hoped to find a better word than *suspects* but couldn't come up with one) here in Hibbing. A logical question, of course, under the circumstances. They're trying to identify any people who might have any kind of motive…"

Kevin's face colored at the word *motive*. With Depelo's rape report on record, he would obviously be considered as a prime suspect. Shaking his head, he said, "I know where you're going with this. You gave the Duluth police my name—didn't you?"

McGinnis could not deny it, "I'm sure you can understand, Mr. Moran… considering our conversation of…" he looked down at the notepad in front of him, "…of last Monday."

Kevin nodded without reply.

Trying to avoid Kevin's intense stare, McGinnis looked toward the window, fidgeted with a pencil, and swallowed. "Being that you were a pallbearer in the Foley funeral on Thursday, well, that would have placed you in Duluth last week…wouldn't it?"

"Yes, we all—Angie, the Zoretek's, and myself—went down on Wednesday for the wake. Spent the night at the Hotel Duluth, and were at St. James Church the following morning."

"Yes, that's what I have here in my notes," McGinnis pointed his finger at his tablet. "And, after the cemetery burial rites, all of you attended a reception at the St. James School?" His statement of fact was framed as a question looking for acknowledgment.

"That is correct."

Angie had waited long enough to enter the dialogue. "Are you suggesting that Kevin is a suspect in the Hayes murder?"

McGinnis squinted, tugging at the tip of his waxed mustache, "I must admit that the Duluth police are of that impression. You see…" The chief attempted to explain investigative procedure as carefully as a civics teacher stressing the two essential criteria of *motive* and *opportunity* in his discourse.

"Do you mean to imply that Kevin's being in Duluth on Wednesday and Thursday constitutes some kind of opportunity?" Angie blurted her question in disbelief.

Uncomfortable with what he had to say, "You see, we're—the police, I mean—dealing with two gaps in your husband's whereabouts, Mrs. Moran. One of those is the Friday night before Miss Hayes's disappearance (he would take every pain to avoid mention of the rape allegation on that night) and the other is last Thursday afternoon."

"Last Thursday? What do you mean?" Angie was confused.

As Kevin listened to the chief's explanation he knew exactly what was coming next. He turned in his chair to face his wife. "You remember I took that walk, Angie."

"Yes, but—"

McGinnis interrupted the couple, "The Duluth police interviewed some of the folks who were at the funeral reception, Mrs. Moran. It would appear that your husband was gone for quite some time—about two hours, according to Detective Blake of the Duluth department. I've got the names of the people that Blake talked to written down right here." He pushed the notebook toward the edge of the desk for both to see.

Kevin had a sinking feeling. As with his dubious trip to the lake property on that Friday evening, he could not remember anybody seeing him walk up the West Duluth hillside on the previous Thursday afternoon. He recalled wondering where everybody was while looking down upon empty streets and yards. "About two hours, Keirnan—that's about right. I grew up in that neighborhood and just wanted to look around. It was nothing more than a nostalgia trip."

Angie gave Kevin a worrisome look. She remembered his muddied shoes and dirty pant cuffs upon returning to the St. James School. Earlier, Kevin had called this whole matter a can of worms, and she was now beginning to fully comprehend the gravity of what he meant.

"For the present, I just wanted to confirm the information I've been given by Inspector Blake—do you understand my position? Rest at ease Mr. Moran—Mrs. Moran—there are no formal charges pending—but I must be candid with you both…a thorough investigation is underway as we speak."

Angie could not contain her frustration any longer, "While all of you are investigating my husband, Mr. McGinnis, let me suggest that you put the name of Armando Depelo on your list of suspects. He's the one that had better be able to explain his whereabouts on that Friday night when Evelyn Hayes was raped. Yes, I'm telling you right now…Mr. Depelo raped Evelyn!"

McGinnis nearly spilled the bottle of ink resting near his elbow.

"Yes, you heard me right! Evelyn Hayes told me exactly when and how it all happened. You have my word of honor on that!"

McGinnis turned over a fresh page of his notepad, dipped his pen; "Please tell me everything you remember, Mrs. Moran."

Angie explained her conversation with Miss Hayes on that Sunday night and of her appeal that Kevin help the woman deal with her trauma.

Bewildered, Keirnan McGinnis frantically scribbled without interrupting the graphic details of her story.

When Angie had finished by telling the chief of the appointment that she and Kevin had made for the following Monday afternoon, McGinnis looked at Kevin with a puzzled expression. "Please help me with my growing confusion, Mr. Moran. Why didn't you tell me any of this when we first talked in my office last week?"

Kevin shrugged his shoulders, "I guess I just didn't think it was necessary at the time. And, having fired Depelo the night before…In retrospect, I realize now that the omission was clearly an error on my part." Kevin leaned forward, "Keirnan, maybe the truth had to come from Angie first—not me. If I had counter-charged Depelo right away…it would look like a pissing contest—pardon my language, but I fully expected that Evelyn Hayes would clarify what happened."

"Then she disappeared—and you…" Keirnan hoped that Kevin would explain why he hadn't come forward earlier.

"I got…wrapped up in my own feelings—a dear friend had just been killed in an automobile accident."

Keirnan found Kevin's admissions to be almost unbelievable. Moran was too bright for such illogical errors in judgment, and was a credible attorney besides. "My condolences," he said weakly, not wanting to invite a diversion to this investigation.

Kevin nodded. The police officer was doing his best in a most awkward situation.

"And it was because of your wife's conversation with Evelyn Hayes that you found it necessary to terminate Mr. Depelo's employment, sir?"

"Yes. As I told you before, Depelo's contention that he quit as my hotel manager is an outright lie. Just as his allegation that I violated Miss Hayes is a blatant fabrication. Apparently he's bent on smearing my reputation as well as covering his own a—" Kevin caught himself, "In covering his assault of Evelyn. He's as clever as he is deceitful, Chief McGinnis. I'm quite certain that he told the woman to leave Hibbing and then proceeded to intimidate Esther Hayes enough to make her change her story when she spoke with you. Keirnan, you're dealing with a complex pattern of lying and conspiring here."

McGinnis scratched his head. Feeling as if he was caught in an unsettling limbo—somewhere between two of Hibbing's most influential citizens—the chief was at a loss over what he might do about it. Being newly-appointed and without very much in the way of a viable support system was one problem— lacking any performance credibility in his short tenure was another. His greatest dread was getting himself into a no-win scenario, and that seemed exactly what he was now getting himself into. The gray areas of coincidence and circumstantial innuendo were an investigator's perpetual nightmare.

"I've got a lot more questions right now than answers, Mr. Moran," he nodded at Angie and respectfully added, "Mrs. Moran." Standing from behind his desk he concluded, "I'll have some follow-up investigating to do and I'll get back to both of you as soon as I have a better grip on things." He offered his hand to Angie, then Kevin—"I should probably advise you not to disappear again without letting anybody know of your whereabouts, sir."

Kevin understood the rationale, "I'll keep in touch, Keirnan."

Keirnan caught Kevin's elbow as Angela was leaving the office, "One other thing..." the chief swallowed hard on his heartfelt consolation, "Mr. Moran, I want you to know that I'm not your adversary. Okay?"

Louie Bosch was the *Hibbing Tribune* reporter who generally covered the local police beat. One of Louie's inside connections on the department was Officer Fran Kauchik. Bosch was hanging out at the front desk when he saw the Morans enter the office of Chief McGinnis.

"Probably had to do with the Hayes case," Louie commented to Kauchik, "She was Moran's employee at the hotel, wasn't she?"

Fran Kauchik nodded absently while rifling through files in his desk drawer.

"See what you can dig up for me, Fran. Our mutual friend Mando told me that he'd pay us a little something for finding out whatever we can about the Hayes murder."

"It's the second time in a week that I've seen Moran in here. Brought that good-lookin' wife of his along both times." Fran scratched his head at the memory of watching Angela Moran while she sat on the bench outside the chief's office a week ago. "Last time she just waited around like she was lost or somethin'. A real stunner, that woman—I wouldn't mind...you know, Louie."

"I think I do, Fran. She's one helluva looker, I agree." Louie Bosch rolled his eyes, "Like I said, find out what's going on. I can smell a story going on here."

When he noticed the Morans leaving McGinnis' office, Louie abruptly excused himself and rushed toward the downstairs front door of the building. Assuming the couple would be leaving through the City Hall's east door, he might be able to do some tailing. A good reporter had gut instincts and Louie sensed he was onto something.

Standing in tree-shadow outside the city hall building, Angie inquired, "What are we supposed to do now? Just wait until we hear from McGinnis again? There must be something…? Did you tell me that you talked to a Duluth lawyer last week—I can't remember?"

"Senia gave me a name—McIntosh," Kevin mumbled and silently cursed himself for holding back disclosing his conversation with the attorney the past week.

"McIntosh?" The name rang familiar in her memory. Angie followed women's rights issues in the newspaper…"Colleen McIntosh? The woman who won the Luddington case a few weeks ago?"

"Senia thinks a female attorney would be great with a jury in this kind of case. And I've heard she's a strong litigator," Kevin said impatiently, hoping to divert Angie's attention from the matter for right now, "I'd better get over to the office—Mondays are hectic, sweetheart. We usually have our staff meetings and by now everybody's probably wondering where the boss is."

Angie felt snubbed, "That's it then? Kevin, an employee of yours has been murdered, McGinnis tells us that you're a suspect, and you give me a brush off—! Like, Angie you can find something to do with yourself while I get back to work!" she fumed. "I'm confused…offended, Kevin! I ask you about getting an attorney and you dismiss my concern with 'I'd better get off to the office' to be with Gary?"

Contrite, Kevin took Angie's hands in his own, 'I'm sorry if it sounded like I wanted to get rid of you or gave the impression that I'm not too overly concerned about Evelyn…I apologize, that was insensitive on my part. Do you think I should contact McIntosh?"

For the second time in as many weeks, Kevin was asking her what he should do and his question was unsettling. "What do *you* think, Kevin? That's what matters most right now."

"What would I tell her? There are no charges against me. So far it's only…coincidence and conjecture. What Keirnan's looking at now is all circumstantial. Calling an attorney might seem like a panic reaction."

"Or, good judgment. The 'circumstantial' you're referring to seems like some pretty serious stuff to me. You're being investigated—can't you get that through your thick skull? We're talking about rape and murder for God's sake!" Angie surprised herself at the angry tone of her words. "I'm having great difficulty in understanding what's going on in that head of yours. Do you just want me to go home and take care of our children, do some housekeeping, paint a picture…or get started on dinner? Pretend that nothing out of the ordinary is going on in *our* lives?"

Kevin met her fiery eyes, "I'll call Colleen McIntosh."

Letting go of Kevin's hands, Angie indignantly turned away. "I'll take the car home. If you need a ride after work—give me a call."

Sitting behind an open newspaper within earshot on a nearby bench, Louie Bosch had no difficulty in hearing the heated Moran conversation.

The Monday issue of the *Duluth News Tribune* cited a reference to the body of a woman found in a bay off the St. Louis River near the Riverside neighborhood. The article outlining preliminary details was located on the front page. Colleen McIntosh bit at her lip. Any story involving potential violence to a woman stirred her emotions. Before leaving home for her office, she made her first call of the morning. The receptionist transferred her to Inspector Carver Blake at the Duluth police department.

"No details, ma'am—we've just informed the deceased woman's mother and our investigation is very sketchy at this point," the detective said. "Sorry, but I'm not at liberty to say anything more."

Colleen was an expert interrogator and not so easily put off. "Look, Inspector, I'm an attorney and anything you tell me is 'off the record'—you can be assured of confidentiality."

Blake had seen Colleen McIntosh in the courthouse on many occasions and didn't need any reminder that she was a lawyer. She was the kind of woman one did not easily forget. Blake realized that his job was always made easier when people owed him some favors. So, McIntosh might prove helpful to him at some unforeseen point, "Ask me any question that I can answer with a simple 'yes' or 'no'—okay?"

Having opened a door to some dialogue, Colleen pressed, "Was there any apparent violence involved?"

"Yes."

"Is there any evidence that she was raped?"

"No."

"Was the woman from the West Duluth neighborhood where her body was discovered?"

"No."

"From Duluth?"

"No."

"Cloquet?" Colleen knew that the currents could carry a body from the wood processing community several miles up the river. And, there had been reports of a missing woman from the Fond du Lac Indian Reservation.

"No. It's not the Indian woman, if that's where you're going."

"But, the victim is from out of town, though?"

"Yes. We think the body was dumped in the river near Riverside."

Blake had departed from his strictly defined yes or no format with his last two answers and Colleen sensed she had forged a small opening in their perfunctory dialogue. She pressed, "Dumped? Do you think she was murdered?"

"Yes."

"Does the mother...you did say that the victim's mother has been notified...does the mother live in Duluth?"

"No, again. Look, Miss McIntosh, I'm willing to put you in the pipeline and keep you informed as we find out more. How's that?"

"What's the harm in giving me a name, Detective? If the woman is from out of town...?"

Carver Blake considered the question. It didn't seem likely that the Duluth attorney would have any significant interest in what could well have been a Hibbing homicide. "Okay, and that will have to do for right now. The woman's name is Hayes—Evelyn Hayes."

Colleen's next question surprised the detective, "That would be the missing woman from Hibbing...wouldn't it?"

"How and the hell..."

"Thanks, Inspector. You've been most helpful. Please keep me up to date as promised—and I owe you one." Colleen knew the wheels of the complex legal system in St. Louis County best functioned on the traditional lubrication of favors and pay backs.

Her second call in less than a week from Kevin Moran did not surprise the Duluth attorney. Her curiosity, piqued from their earlier conversation, had inspired Colleen to do something she still felt guilty and confused about. After reading about the Foley funeral the previous Monday, and learning that Kevin Moran was one of the pallbearers, Colleen had taken an hour from her busy work schedule to travel to the St. James Church. "Curiosity killed the cat!" she told herself—but…Colleen made the drive from downtown to West Duluth in time to briefly visit at the reception in the school's gymnasium. Mingling in the crowd, the tall attorney had no difficulty in locating Kevin Moran. For one brief moment, she caught his eye. He was even more handsome than she imagined. Embarrassed over what she was doing, she slipped away from the gathering and returned to her office. Colleen had hoped to see what Mrs. Moran looked like, but…

"Hello, Mr. Moran." Her voice was controlled, professional. "I expected you might call."

"Something terrible's happened, Miss McIntosh. Evelyn Hayes is dead!" Kevin wanted to keep a nervous edge from his voice but failed. "I've just finished an interrogation at the Hibbing police station."

Colleen would not play any guessing games, "I've already talked with Detective Blake, *Kevin*…" the first name slipped out unexpectedly. It was too late to correct the error, but she would be more careful, "I saw an article in the morning paper and called the Duluth police only a few minutes ago. Tell me what you know, *Mr. Moran*."

Kevin explained that foul play had been determined and that he had been questioned as a 'possible suspect'. "I'm afraid I've got another hole in my story, Miss McIntosh. I was in Duluth last Wednesday and Thursday for a close friend's funeral."

"That would be Father Foley?"

"Yes…The priest and I…"

Colleen offered her condolences, "He must have been a beloved man. I saw the obituary in the paper. My father knew him quite well, but couldn't get to the funeral. I'm sorry about his untimely death…"

"Thank you, he was very special in my life. Anyhow, this detective down there, Blake, has already questioned a few people who were attending the Foley funeral. He's learned that I was gone from the reception for a couple of hours, and naturally that raised some interesting speculation."

"Another little walk by yourself—to clear your mind, Mr. Moran?"

"No more than a short walk I assure you. I've mentioned my little idiosyncrasies before."

"Yes, you have. And, I suppose nobody can verify where you were for those two hours?"

"That's about it. The Hibbing police chief claims that Evelyn Hayes could have been killed at some time on either Wednesday or Thursday. To say the least, that leaves me in a difficult situation."

"Where exactly did you go, Mr. Moran? I want you to try to be as specific—step-by-step, minute-by-minute—as you can. That's critical."

Colleen began scribbling as Kevin explained in careful detail.

When he had finished, the attorney said, "I'll go out to West Duluth this afternoon and begin knocking on doors. Perhaps someone…"

"I probably sat on the ridge up on Fifty-seventh for more than an hour, Miss McIntosh. I hope someone saw me—though I can't remember seeing a solitary person the whole time I was gone."

"We'll see. In the meantime, I'd like you to retrace your footsteps out to your lake property on the Friday night. Try to find anybody who might have seen you out there. We've got two huge empty spaces to fill."

"Huge is an understatement!"

"Am I to understand, then…you are retaining me as your attorney?"

"Absolutely!"

Colleen leaned back, remembering his face, wondering how he was dealing with the stress in his life. "I'll take the job," she wanted to use his first name but didn't. "Keep your chin up. And, please don't say anything further to the police without letting me know."

"I'll keep in touch, Colleen."

Louie Bosch wrote the article on the Evelyn Hayes murder for the Monday afternoon *Hibbing Tribune*. As was the reporter's controversial style, he would mix facts with his own speculations—a technique that often got him in trouble with the newspaper's owner—but, at the same time, sold papers.

The body of Hibbing native, Evelyn Hayes—age 27—was discovered in the St. Louis River in West Duluth yesterday. Miss Hayes had been missing for one week and her disappearance was under investigation by the Hibbing Police Department. Although authorities have not issued any details of the Hayes death, an unnamed source at the Hibbing department has suggested to this reporter that murder is a distinct possibility. The officer's information is based upon a verbal report from a Duluth homicide inspector.

Miss Hayes, the mother of two children—Nancy Elizabeth aged eleven and John Albert age nine, had not been seen since early last Monday morning. The deceased woman's mother, Esther Hayes, refused to make any comments at this time. We have further learned that the two Hayes children had recently been placed in a Piedmont (Duluth) orphan's home last Wednesday.

Evelyn's employer, Mr. Kevin Moran, has been interviewed by Hibbing Police Chief, Keirnan McGinnis on at least two occasions this past week relative to the disappearance and death. Chief McGinnis assured this reporter that information in the case is incomplete and highly sensitive. McGinnis would not indicate if there were any suspects at this time. Mr. Moran would not return our calls before this issue went to press.

Funeral arrangements are pending at Dougherty's Funeral Home.

A Blessing and a Curse

August, 1936

Over the past two years, Kevin had made a point of visiting his old friend and mentor, Claude Atkinson, on Monday afternoons after the weekly Chamber meeting at the Androy Hotel. (The old newsman's health had noticeably improved and his sagging spirits enlivened since his earlier bout with depression). Their meetings in Claude's living room were mutually satisfying—Claude enjoyed the opportunity to vent his frustrations and offer his insights on a "world in crisis" as he was wont to call contemporary affairs, while Kevin considered their time together as his "two hours of enlightenment and bonding." More often than not, Marc Atkinson joined his father and Kevin in their animated discussions.

Marc had quit his position with the *Hibbing Tribune* eighteen months earlier and had used the money he'd saved—mostly from the sale of the family newspaper in 1930—to purchase a small book store near Senia Arola's accounting office on Fourth Avenue. His small business venture had rejuvenated the young man's spirits, and since being out of the reporting business (or out of "my father's notorious shadow" as he once told his friend, Kevin) Marc had forged a more affectionate bond with his usually cantankerous father.

In his years with the defunct *Mesabi Ore* newspaper, Claude had become a local institution and a voice of conscience for his many readers.
Stepping aside ten years earlier was the most difficult decision he'd ever made. But, the narrow faced, sixty-eight year old pundit still possessed a keen intellect behind his riveting blue eyes. His wife had ceded their small living room to Claude's literary pursuits some thirty years before and had allowed her husband to make the space into a personal library which their small house could hardly accommodate. (Dora's private space, for quilting and macramé, became an unused bedroom upstairs). So, large bookcases lined two walls from floor to

ceiling of the living room. A collage of yellowed photographs and maps were haphazardly cluttered upon the walls. Claude's well-worn chair in the corner of the room had probably never been occupied by anyone other than himself and his father who had passed away in 1894.

"I disagree with you, Dad!" Marc said emphatically. "Europe's becoming a power keg, just like it was before the World War. You have to agree with me on about that."

"They have to remain neutral—regardless of the temptation to openly oppose fascism in Spain, Marc. Let cooler heads prevail."

"Britain and France are scared to death of Hitler," Marc argued. "If they don't get more involved in what's going on over there pretty soon, we're going to see another world war. Heed my words! Spain has become no more than a staging ground for the armies of Germany and Italy—everybody can see that," Marc's voice raised an octave for emphasis.

The three men, as had been their custom for months, were talking about the explosive political situation in Europe. Hitler's power had been dictatorial for three years and his Nazi Party now controlled all aspects of German economic, social, and religious life. Huge arms production and public works programs were reviving Germany's sagging economy, military conscription was being rapidly escalated, Jews were experiencing unheard of discrimination, and only months before, Hitler's Nazi forces assumed occupation of the Rhineland without opposition.

On another front, Fascist Francisco Franco's rebellion had initiated a bloody civil war in Spain. "I read that Mussolini's sent Italian troops into Spain to help Franco overthrow the government, and that the Germans are providing most of the war munitions," Kevin said. "I think I have to agree with Marc; the democracies can't just sit on their hands like they're doing these days. Hitler's taken part of Czechoslovakia already, and Mussolini's rolled over Ethiopia—what's everybody waiting for?"

Claude's long fingers stroked the beginnings of a gray beard on his cheek, "Waiting for diplomacy, Kevin, not escalated intervention like Marc seems to advocate."

Before moving their discussion on to the human atrocities and political purges occurring in Joseph Stalin's Russia, Kevin suggested another hypothesis. "One day Hitler and Stalin are going to look a map of Europe and decide how they want to carve it up between themselves."

Both Claude and Marc frowned at the young man's alarming vision.

Marc caught his father's eye, "And what's going on with Japan can't go unnoticed either. They have already taken control of Manchuria and seem hell-bent on invading the rest of China. Hirohito is determined to see his 'rising sun' over the entire Pacific some day."

Claude nodded his large gray head without reply.

"Maybe your man Roosevelt ought to spend more time on what's going on with the rest of the world, and less time on his tyrannical efforts at centralizing all the powers of government here in the United States. Maybe we've got a despot of our own running for reelection this fall!" Marc's perspective struck a nerve in his father sitting across from him.

Claude leaned forward in his chair, "Just a minute!"

Kevin would arbitrate the anticipated argument, "Now, now—you two guys save your heated FDR debates until after I'm gone—I always get caught in the middle." Kevin drew a sigh, "But, Marc's made a good point. The President is talking neutrality at every opportunity, just like the British and French are doing."

"FDR needs time to get this country on its feet, Kevin. Once our economy has recovered—and, believe me, he's the only one that can make that happen—then…then, America can flex its muscles a bit," Claude commented with a measure of passion in his voice.

"I'll just hope that a world war isn't what it takes to get our miners back to work again, Claude. And I have my doubts that massive public works is the answer to our problems. Private initiatives and diversification need to happen on the Iron Range." Kevin did not have to mention the obvious: Seventy per cent of the Mesabi work force was unemployed.

∼

"If it weren't for the women in this town…I think we'd have bread lines halfway down Howard Street", Senia remarked, looking up from the stack of corduroy, wool-lined, winter coats of various sizes which were arrayed on the long work bench in front of her. Senia Arola, Becca Zoretek, and Angie Moran were doing their Monday afternoon volunteer work in the construction warehouse that Tony had allowed the women to use for their clothes and food distribution program.

Angie nodded her understanding of the point Senia had made, "In a way, I envy them. Their stubborn resolve, commitment to family, downright skill at making something out of next to nothing. Just look at the three of us…so well-off, comfortable. We're all growing flowers in our back yard gardens—not vegetables like most folks are doing."

The harsh reality of Angie's reference stunned Senia's conscience. Perhaps their charitable work paled in comparison to what other women were doing every day of their lives. Hibbing's mothers grew vegetables and were masters at canning everything that they grew in order to put food on their family tables through the long winter months. Wild blueberries, raspberries, and strawberries were picked and preserved along with tomatoes, beans, carrots, and countless other garden crops. And, they tended chickens in back yard coops, fed pigs, and managed to maintain their homes as well. "If I had to, I'd be doing the same as any other woman, Angie. So would you. As it is… well, none of us really have anything to be ashamed of. We're doing more than our share to help put food on a lot of tables, too. And clothing on the backs of the children."

Becca was unloading twenty-pound sacks of flour from Tony's pickup truck while Angie and Senia conversed. The flour along with corn meal, sugar, and rice had been purchased by Tony and Kevin at a Duluth commodities market the week before. Overhearing Senia's defensive comment, Becca put down the sack she was holding and walked over to the older woman's side. Sensitive to her friend's solitary life—without husband or children—she was quick to perceive the Finnish woman's indignation. "You've certainly got that right, Senia. This food and clothing didn't come from the government, and none of us have any apologies to make for our good fortune. It would be awfully easy for us to sit back in comfort and close our eyes to the hardships of others, but we have chosen not to do that! It's the goodness in our hearts…not the obligation of our circumstances."

Noticing the trace of tears in Senia's eyes, Angie attempted to reconcile any misunderstanding her comment might have provoked. "Yes, each of has chosen to share the bounty our Good Lord has given us. I don't think there's anything wrong with feeling somewhat proud of ourselves, ladies. And, believe me, I don't have an ounce of guilt over growing day lilies rather than cabbage in my garden! Flowers are as much a gift from God as vegetables, and we have chosen to make our little corners of the world as beautiful as we can."

Senia smiled her understanding of Angela's spirited pronouncement, "And I choose to have a bar of chocolate after dinner—without the slightest trace of guilt. And, furthermore, I will refuse to eat a plate of sauerkraut until the day I die: Come hell or starvation!"

(Sauerkraut, sarmas, potatoes, and thin soups along with bread were staple meals in most households during the Depression).

"And, I would starve along with you if I had to eat polenta (a corn meal mush) for breakfast every morning," Becca admitted while pointing her finger at a bag of corn meal and making an abhorrent expression.

Despite having two healthy and happy children, a spacious home, and all the trappings that her husband's wealth provided—Angie Moran had been unhappy for several months. Ostensibly, no one could see the pain, but her life issues brought self-searching and confusion.

Angie's recent paintings were the best she'd ever done, and her reputation as an artist had grown well beyond the Hibbing area. (At the Twin Cities Art Exposition in June, her oil 'Birch Ice' had won the coveted blue ribbon and a cash prize of $200.00).

A part of Angie's melancholy was probably linked to Jacque Grojean's return to Paris the year before. Also, there was the lingering stress of Evelyn Hayes' unresolved murder investigation which had put her and Kevin through another highly publicized rumor mill. Despite the utmost consideration and courtesy provided by Chief McGinnis, Angie always felt the questioning eyes of Hibbing upon her.

More than anything else, however, Angie's *secret* problem continued to mystify and haunt her thoughts. Only a month before, when two-year old Maribec slipped and fell down the staircase—bruising her face on a railing—Angie had another blackout. The scream from her daughter lying on the floor brought an immediate, excruciating ache to her temples, splitting through her head like a dagger. Clara Motter found Angie unconscious on the floor beside Maribec only moments after the incident.

Angie was easily revived with a cool, damp cloth—and had no memory of what had happened. Awakening to the whimpers of her daughter on the landing beside her, Angie wondered why she was lying on her back with her head resting in the lap of her bewildered housekeeper.

Clara wanted to call Becca at the hospital, but Angie wouldn't allow her to do so. Recognizing that she'd had an 'episode' and thinking quickly—"It's nothing, Clara…I must have tripped on the rug trying to break the baby's fall," Angie lied. Sitting up by herself, Angie regarded her daughter, "And Maribec seems fine—we've both got a little bump on our heads, that's all."

The little girl, more frightened than injured, was quickly pacified when given her favorite stuffed animal to play with on the living room floor. "And, Clara, I'd rather you didn't say anything about this accident to Mr. Moran. He'd probably have all the rugs glued to the floor!"

Kevin would consider doing something just like that, Angie knew, "Or he might go so far as to tear out the staircase and install an elevator!"

Her husband's protective nature was that way: Always doing what he thought would please his wife and make her life more comfortable. Angie pondered that thought in depth as if doing so for the first time. *Always giving!* Giving seemed to have become the manner in which he chose to please every one around him—even himself.

After Jacque had unexpectedly decided to return to France to care for his aging mother, Kevin immediately stepped into the picture and purchased the small art studio for Angie. That spontaneous decision, he must have perceived, would be exactly what Angie hoped he might do. Yet, she and Kevin hadn't even discussed the matter between them beforehand. "I know it's been a special place in your life and you can always hire someone to run the shop when you've got other things to do," was Kevin's simple rationale when closing the real estate deal.

And the new cabin at Sturgeon Lake. Kevin had asked her father to build the lake home as a surprise for her, and had added to the elaborate construction what he called an 'art tower' on the far corner of the structure. The tower was intended to be her 'studio on the lake'.

Bouquets of flowers from Kevin arrived at the Maple Hill home two or three times a week—and for no special reason. Sometimes he bought her expensive jewelry or purchased stylish new clothing (always in her size six) just to make her happy. Kevin gave her everything!

Everything, that was, except himself.

Angie troubled over that thought, and pondered even more deeply over the growing void in their relationship. It wasn't that they didn't have sex anymore; Kevin remained sensitive to her every need for intimacy, but outside of the bedroom there was a constant and unspoken strain between them. Kevin had become a shell of his former self. Remote and seemingly self-absorbed, her husband had built silent walls. When they talked, it was always about their children, or mutual friends, or local activities that were happening: "How was your day…?" became a reporting ritual of insignificant details at their dinner table every evening.

Their dialogue had become almost predictable, even superficial. The night before, Angie remembered, they had talked for nearly twenty minutes about the weather!

Angie knew they were not communicating about the most important aspects of their lives—feelings, needs, fears. Was this troubling void between them her own doing? Had she become a boring person to be around? Had her successes distanced her from Kevin? Were her own secrets and private concerns building the subtle barriers they found a sense of security hiding behind? Communication, she knew well, was a two way street—but had she made a wrong turn somewhere? As she probed her feelings and fears, one question kept creeping into her thoughts: Did all relationships have secrets? Were there unspoken and private realms between any two people—places kept guarded and silent through good times and bad? Was absolute honesty something husbands and wives were incapable of sharing with one another?

Maybe she was being too negative, doubtful, unfair—stress often had that effect on her. "Think positive!" Angie scolded under her breath. Think of the Kevin that is so good, so compassionate, so concerned with the welfare of others: The Kevin who was Santa Claus and Easter Bunny to so many Hibbing children! Then, a memory from only a few days before slipped into her thoughts. She and Kevin had been walking down Howard Street after having a pleasant luncheon together. A boy of about eight or nine stepped out from a recessed doorway in front of them with his dirty hand outstretched, "I'm hungry!" was all the youngster said.

Kevin took the boy's hand, "Come along with us, young man," he instructed. Then, with the boy in tow between the two of them, Kevin led the trio around a nearby corner and into the open door of General's Budget Market. Three bags of groceries later, they were knocking on the boy's front door.

Mrs. Gustavson, wondering if her son had gotten himself into trouble again, was taken aback when Kevin said, "Young Joseph told us that you could use these groceries. You must be proud of this son of yours, ma'am."

Kevin, as Angie recalled the touching incident, seemed to have enjoyed that half-hour episode more than anything else since…since when? Maribec's second birthday the previous March?

Angie's torment of the moment, however, did not pass so easily, despite her positive recollections. Kevin was troubled and she had been unable to do anything about it. Angie's thoughts were suddenly interrupted by the ringing telephone.

"How's my precious little girl tonight?" Her father's affectionate greeting always lifted Angie's spirits.

"My glass is about half-full, Dad. Kevin's out at the lake again—I swear that cabin you built for us has…" Angie couldn't find the words to finish her thought. Has what? Been her husband's private sanctuary —or divided the two of them even further than they had been before?

Tony could always read between the lines of his daughter's thoughts. Since she was a little girl, he was the one person capable of prying Angela loose from whatever might be troubling her. He might have finished what she had started to say about the lake place, but chose not to do so. Tony was perceptive enough to realize that Kevin had changed, and had withdrawn into himself of late. He knew that his son-in-law was spending more time at the lake than at home where he belonged. "Talk to your dad, sweetheart. 'Half-full', whatever that's supposed to tell me about what's going on—doesn't seem like a very pleasant place for my daughter to be. How about letting me in on some of what's on your mind, Angie."

"I got another dozen roses from Kevin this afternoon, Dad—and a lovely note saying…let me see, it's right here on the table…

> *Going to replace some planks on the dock this afternoon and paint the shed. I'll be staying overnight and check in tomorrow—maybe we can have dinner at the hotel.*
>
> *All my love…K.*

Tony could hear the pain in Angie's voice as she read the note. To try and persuade his daughter that having a wilderness cabin was simply a man's infatuation would neither be honest nor satisfying. "Angie, I want to tell you something that I probably haven't ever felt the need to tell you before." Tony had a lump in his throat, "Are the children in bed? This is going to take a few minutes."

Tony's mind probed back into the distant past—through nearly thirty dust-covered years—to when he was a young man down on his luck. To understand Kevin, Angie ought to know more about the man who was her husband's father. Ultimately, Peter Moran's wealth had been his undoing.

Tony began his lengthy discourse with an observation that Angie needed to comprehend at a depth beyond that which she already understood—a truth about what Tony often considered to be the *blessing and curse* of being a Moran.

"Wealth is a dangerous thing to deal with. It can become intoxicating…and isolating. Neither Kevin nor Peter ever allowed themselves to be intoxicated by their fortune, but—they might have allowed it to swallow them up. Unknowingly, perhaps."

Tony had dealt to a much lesser degree with the same issue in his own life. "Money is never a source of happiness, honey. Never! We've all learned that. But, sometimes, we aren't aware of how it can distort our perspectives. I think Peter believed that his generosity was the best expression he could give to show the love he felt for others…I even think that his magnificent hotel was more than a personal ambition satisfied—it was his monument to the community he loved. Mind you, that's not to say that Peter's enormous ego wasn't a major part of the whole undertaking. He always seemed to confuse loving with giving."

Angie tried to draw parallels in her mind without comment.

Tony laughed inwardly at some faded memories, "Peter used to buy me things—new clothes and theater tickets to wear my new duds to, and tools when I was learning to become a carpenter, baseball equipment that I couldn't afford. These were affectionate and well-intended gestures for sure, but at the same time, empty ones as well. He confused giving material things with giving himself…Kevin, I think, is prone to doing the same thing. Like his father, he's never really learned that we are loved for who we are, and not by what we give. When Peter needed—I mean, really needed, a payback for all he had given to so many—there was nobody there for him. I was involved in my own things, Senia was doing hers…he must have felt so cheated and…"

"Alone!" Angie offered an ending to what she anticipated her father was about to say. "Did you feel guilty, Dad? That you somehow had failed Peter? Misunderstood him?"

"All of that, Angie…and more. All of us realized our remorse too late."

Angie and Kevin had often talked about Peter's fortune and how the two of them were determined to use the inheritance to better the lives of others. But, had they both regarded their philanthropy as an obligation? Were their benefactions truly from the heart? Or, were their motivations more like those of Peter Moran? Tony's insights on Kevin's father caused Angie to wonder…"Dad, would you break the ice for me and talk with Kevin about these same things that you've just shared with me? I think Kevin and I have some soul-searching to do."

"I'll get out to the lake in the morning right after early mass. It's been much too long since the two of us have had any meaningful conversation." Tony considered his promise. He would be careful while 'breaking the ice' not to lecture Kevin, or in any way try to tell the young man what he should do. Such advice would certainly do more harm than good.

"I don't have to remind you that Kevin is more like a son to me..." The incomplete admission pained him. Truly, Kevin was more like Tony than was his own son, Marco, in so many ways. Kevin and Tony were made of the same solid stuff. "Maybe your brother will ride along with me. He could do some hiking along the lake shore—maybe even take a dip while Kevin and I visit. I'd enjoy Marco's company. Besides, he could help me split some wood and do cabin chores while we're out there." Tony muffled a laugh, "And, would you believe, I've got a shed in need of painting and some planks to repair on my dock —just like Kevin?"

Angie missed her father's humor. Biting at her lip, she took a deep breath, "Dad, I've got to share something else with you, too—before you hang up…it's…it's been tearing me apart inside. I haven't had the courage to tell anybody about it. Not even Kevin! Maybe I've been a big part of our problems by harboring a fear that Kevin has something to do with what's been going on with me." She caught her breath, "I don't really know and that scares me—everything about it scares me, Dad!" Angie explained the blackouts she'd been having to her father. "Please don't tell Becca about any of this yet. I still believe that if things get better with me and Kevin everything will go away." As candid as she had been, Angie did not express her fear that one day she may have a debilitating blackout—one that seriously cut her off from reality.

Experiencing a sense of relief over having at least opened a door on her secret agony, Angie was, nevertheless, exhausted and disconcerted. She considered spending an hour in her upstairs art studio unwinding from her stress of feeling unmasked and vulnerable. Although Tony would not disclose her condition to Kevin, sharing her concealment with her father was an admission that Angie had placed more trust in him than in her own husband. That realism was deeply disturbing!

Angie had started an oil painting while visiting the lake only three weeks before. The work had been etched in charcoal upon the canvas and some preliminary strokes applied to what, in her imagination, would become 'Whitecaps'—an abstract depiction of a churling wave. As was her unique style, the primary accents would be the frothy whites of a majestic breaker rolling toward a singular shoreline rock.

In early October, only six weeks from now, Angie would be the featured artist at an art exposition in Duluth sponsored by the London Road Women's Society. 'Whitecaps' might be her hallmark painting for the showing. Angie locked the downstairs doors, made certain that the windows were secure, and turned off the living room lights. Once upstairs, she contemplated the two doors—one at the end of the hallway opened on her studio, the other led to the master bedroom. Considering her two options, Angie realized she was too tired and mentally exhausted to summon any creativity. Her decision was an easy one.

Angie dreamed that Saturday night—a fragmented dream that she would never remember. A dream that would cause her to wildly toss and turn and awaken at three in the morning in a cold sweat.

~

The sound was clearly a gunshot. Shards of glass glistened in the air of the sun-drenched room, creating an almost surreal ice storm. A man was running away from the storm. It was Kevin. She found herself entering an endlessly dark tunnel. She was with somebody. As she traveled through vague places she looked for a ray of light. Any light that would lead her out.

Her riches and circumstance were almost sinfully exhilarating. She was always dressed in elegant fashions from Paris and Milan, her simple rings replaced with diamonds set in Florentine gold, her home was a castle overlooking the vast ocean. Her husband had more wealth than could be imagined and his sole obsession was to lavish his wife with gifts and treasures beyond estimation. She traveled by train and ship to exotic, winterless places with splendorous surroundings.

Kevin was standing in a shadow on some distant ridge—looking for, but unable to see her. She was gone from the beach. For some reason he was crying—pain radiated from his deep-set, but vacant, green eyes. Jacque was seeking her, too. Smiling as if he knew something that Kevin did not. And a small woman. A nun in a black habit. Sister Anne was on her knees in prayer.

Then, they were all gone—Kevin, Jacque, Sister Anne, the wealthy man who showered her with everything she could imagine. Her husband?

Sitting upright in her disheveled bed, Angie wiped at her brow with the corner of a wrinkled cotton sheet. The bedroom clock on her vanity read three.

∼

Kevin had considered driving into Hibbing and attending Sunday morning Mass but had chosen against it. The bright August sunshine and pine-scented air were far too captivating at the moment. He might find more fulfillment in giving a solitary homage to his God in these pristine surroundings than anywhere else. It was easy to rationalize that his Creator would be satisfied, even pleased, to be revered in this natural sanctuary of His own omniscient creation. Any church ceremony, to Kevin's way of thinking this morning, would be much too stuffy and ritualistic to give him the peace of mind he so desperately needed.

But Kevin was at a loss for any meaningful prayers, and allowed his thoughts of reverence to fade into the warm breezes flowing up the hillside from the lake below. He was too consumed by his own interpretations of life to consider anything sacred or spiritual.

Lately, Kevin had absorbed himself in punishing thoughts—troubling contemplations of personal insufficiency and doubts about his place in the scheme of things. All of his accomplishments were under critical scrutiny. Life, he reasoned, had been a wondrous platter served to him without any effort of his own. His father had built a town and a fortune with his own two hands. While Kevin…? What had he created? The son had come along many years later and inherited the millions of Peter Moran's insightful providence—without sweat or sacrifice. Aside from his insignificant life triumphs in academics and athletics years before—a university scholarship and a law degree—what substantial accomplishments had he attained? Where was his own mark on the world? How did he stack up in comparison to the firebrand that was Peter Moran? How might he be judged?

Kevin stroked his unshaven face, wiped his eyes with the sleeve of his rumpled light woolen, plaid shirt, then sipped at his cup of coffee. From his porch he could hear the distant splash of waves over a segment of rocky shoreline at the edge of the sand beach. Blending with the gurgle of waves was the resonant call of a loon, a whistle of wind rustling the leaves of trees hovering high above the cabin, and the creak of his old rocker on the wooden deck boards. The world around him was a peaceful enchantment—in a serene harmony that conflicted with his disquieting reflections.

Often when he sat on the porch, Kevin would ruminate, losing his thoughts within the clouds. The morning sky was blessed with huge banks of billowy white shapes floating high across the blanket of blue. His vivid imagination was stirred by perceptions in the changing configuration—an elephant's trunked head transforming itself into a dog—a terrier with a blunt nose. Shifting his gaze to another fluffy cluster, he saw the semblance of a face—a countenance with vaguely familiar features. Was it God's face looking down upon His realm...or Foley's...or that of Peter Moran?

Kevin's meditation of the moment, however, was suddenly shattered! The sound of an automobile approaching up the driveway on the far side of his solitary perch overlooking the vast blanket of blue water disturbed his contemplation. "Damn!" Kevin cursed under his breath, "Who in the world—?"

When he wandered around the cabin to see who was there, however, Kevin's scowl turned to a wide beaming smile—"Tony, what a nice surprise," he called toward the approaching man. "What brings you out to paradise this morning? Have you got a list of cabin projects to take care of today, too?" The Zoretek's simple lake home was about a quarter of a mile down the shoreline from the Moran's more pretentious hilltop residence.

"Not really, Kev. Just came out to visit with you for a while. I dropped Marco off at our cabin so he can commune with nature for a couple of hours."

Kevin regarded his friend with an enigmatic smile, "Just out to talk, Tony? Is something the matter?"

Tony considered his response carefully, choosing to throw an initiative in Kevin's direction: "I guess that's up to you to tell me. You sure spend a lot of time out here by yourself. Gosh, you're beginning to look more like Oscar Berquist than a prominent Hibbing businessman."

"How can you blame me?" Kevin gave a sweeping gesture with his arm. "This is as close to heaven as anyone can get. And, old Oscar—well, he's quite an interesting guy as you already know."

"It's beautiful out here, all right...and the woodsman is quite a character for sure, but I can think of three places that are a lot closer to heaven than out here."

Kevin puzzled over *three places*, "Where in the world could they possibly be?"

"You get me a cup of coffee, Kev, and I'll tell you exactly where you will find them—and, each is just waiting for you to appreciate them."

Kevin understood the subtlety.

The two men sat on the porch sipping from their cups for a few minutes without speaking. Kevin could read a trace of grief in Tony's furrowed expression. The man he respected and loved more than any other had just driven out to talk to him, and Kevin had a sinking feeling that a deserved lecture was in the offing.

Kevin broke the silent chasm yawning between them, "I've spent more than a few hours visiting with Oscar Berquist. I think he's got more stories than you and I put together. He knew Grampa Daly years back and he's added some branches to the Moran family tree for me." Kevin would circumvent Tony's intended reproach, "I guess he didn't care much for my father, though. Oscar doesn't hold back any punches—called my Dad an 'arrogant sonofabitch—!" Laughing at the hermit's reference, Kevin added, "I'm using his exact words, Tony. He said that Peter was too rich and full of himself for his own good, and that my dad thought his money could get him anything in life he wanted. Even said that Peter learned otherwise, but a little too late to do him any good."

Yet, Kevin remembered another comment he'd overheard in North Hibbing's old Mesabi Park months before. That memory was a contradiction of sorts which troubled him even more than Berquist's condemnation of his father, and added to the conflict of his self-searching. Two men were standing near a deteriorated gazebo which had been donated to the city by his father—a quiet site Kevin often visited by himself. The old man said to his companion, "A helluva guy that Pete Moran—a real go-getter, that man was. Never let nothing stand in his way of building this here town, that's for sure. Now, if that son of his had half the mustard his pa had…"

That memory stung. Regarding Tony, Kevin reframed his earlier thought, "Most people believed much the same as Oscar, I guess—that my dad's money betrayed him. But not everybody judged him badly. Some even saw a greatness. Too bad his world had to end the way it did."

Tony considered the irony of Kevin's insight. He and Angela had talked about the same things the night before. He chose, however, not to comment on Peter's tragedy at this moment. Despite the promise to his daughter, Tony would let his perceptions of how Peter's wealth had destroyed him wait until a later time. His concerns over Kevin's relationship with Angie, and her painful disclosure, were matters of greater importance right now.

"Oscar though Daly was the salt-of-the-earth," Kevin continued his diversionary rambling, feeling uncomfortable over Tony's apparent disinterest in Oscar's stories and his unusual silence. "Okay, Dad, enough Moran family history. You were talking about three places that were closer to heaven than out here at the lake?"

Tony knew that Kevin had been avoiding an issue he wasn't comfortable talking about. He considered the initiative offered by Kevin's question-framed reminder: "Maybe what I meant to say was...*one place* and three people who live there. I think you know what I'm about to say."

"You're not very subtle, Dad. I deserve a reprimand for shirking my family responsibilities—I can't argue that with you. Did Angie ask you to come and get me straightened out?" Looking away from Tony's eyes, Kevin sat back in his chair, focused his gaze on the placid lake, and swallowed hard on his words. "Sometimes I wish Angie knew what was going on with me. The searching I'm going through all the time...Tony, we try to talk about things, but for some reason—" He shrugged his shoulders and opened his hands in a helpless gesture.

Tony could not blame Kevin entirely for the strained communication between his son-in-law and Angela, nor could he blame Kevin for his daughter's blackout problems. He forced a smile and placed a hand on Kevin's knee. He would be careful to avoid any "If you don'ts" or "What you should do's", and allow Kevin to do the problem solving for himself.

Tony's concept of 'being a man' in these difficult times was an insight best conveyed through his love and encouragement. He believed that men were cursed by an upbringing that stressed being strong at all times and keeping their emotions hidden from sight. The social expectations for men placed rigid constraints on being open, or vulnerable, or expressing their true feelings. To his way of thinking, if a man could never cry—then he could never be honest: If he couldn't be weak, he could never know strength.

"Kevin, I believe that the most important and challenging things in this life are really the simplest...like being a good husband and father. Everything else, however meaningful and well-intended it may seem—be it helping the less fortunate, building a better community, even going to church for worship on Sunday...all of these things, and a hundred others, that we place such importance on really pale in comparison to our commitment to family."

Kevin sat rigidly, feeling the swells of emotion warm in his chest.

Tony curbed the beginnings of a lecture, "Kevin, I know that you love my daughter with all your heart. Probably as much as I once loved Angie's mother and now love Becca. I know that. And, Angie's love for you—well, I don't have the words. When two people love each other as much as the two of you do…they should open every door and window of themselves to each other. Nothing should ever be closed—no pain or fear or guilt or shame—their trust becomes unconditional. And their forgiveness absolute."

Kevin could only nod at the depth of wisdom in Tony's words. Nobody knew more about love and pain than this wonderful man. He met Tony's eyes without responding.

"There's much more of course, Kev." Tony drew a long swallow of his now tepid coffee. "Sometimes, I think that being a good father is even more important than being a good husband. Too many men these days believe that raising the kids is a mother's role in life. 'Let mom do it' is the way most men think—and it's the worst possible attitude! Children need an involved Dad, a listening Dad, a Dad that's there for them all the time. Patrick and Maribec need you to be that kind of Dad, and…the rewards…" He gave Kevin's knee another squeeze, "The rewards are greater than gold."

"God, I know that…I wouldn't ever do anything to disappoint my children, Tony. I think I've been a great dad—until lately, I guess." Lately, he would have to admit, he hadn't found enough time for them. In recent months, Kevin had only found time for himself. A fleeting thought passed through his mind. Not long ago he and Angie had talked about their children and wondered how much influence their parenting might have on the kind of persons they might one day become. Both had wondered at the time if the personalities of Patrick and Maribec were somehow predetermined—perhaps, that view was a rationalization on their part and far too fatalistic as well. Kevin resolved to make a better effort, "God, sometimes I feel like such a failure."

"You are no such thing! We always learn more from our mistakes—big and small—than our successes. I think it was you who told me that once. Back in your 'political days', if I remember correctly."

"I've surely made my share. I should be a lot smarter than I seem to be," Kevin tried to laugh through his tight emotions.

"We all should be a lot smarter!" Tony met Kevin's eyes directly, "Now, I'm going to get to what I've probably been beating around the bush about for the past hour. When you get home this afternoon, I'd like you to do me a big favor—or, rather do yourself a favor. Ask Angela to tell you how she's feeling. That's all. I think—no, I know—she's got some important matters to share with you. Hers are pretty scary, Kev. But you've got to know about them." Tony paused, ran his fingers through his thick dark hair. He didn't want to alarm Kevin, nor did he want to divulge Angie's health problem. "She's kept some serious things to herself for quite a while."

Kevin regarded Tony closely but said nothing. "Anyhow, take the opportunity to share whatever issues you have with Angie. Tell her honestly everything that she needs to know about what you're going through. That will open some shut doors for both of you."

Although Kevin worried about what Tony had told him—'scary and serious things' that she had 'kept to herself', he would respect Angie's right to tell him what he should know.

"Will you do that, Kev? It'll be like unloading a sack of rocks that you've both been carrying around for much too long." he laughed. "I'm even going to pick up my grandchildren when I get back to Hibbing so the two of you can talk things out."

"Then you better get going, Dad." Kevin's voice strained, "Because I'm not even going to take time to shave or change clothes." He stood from the chair, "Thanks, Dad...thanks is a small word, I know—but it weighs a ton! I really needed a wake-up call." He fought back tears, "I've got some things—terrible things, inside me. I'm going to open all those doors and windows, like you said. And what comes out is not going to be very easy for Angie to handle."

Tony smiled, stood and put his arm around Kevin's shoulders, "She's got Zoretek blood, son. Don't worry about Angie handling anything you've got for her." Reconsidering his boast, Tony leveled his gaze, "On second thought, I think you should be worried about Angie—what she's going to tell you."

Kevin puzzled again at Tony's caution. "We've both got enough issues..."

Both men heard the car racing up the driveway, then the screech of brakes. Kevin lost his thought. Within seconds, Melvin Alto raced around the corner of the house. "Kevin, I called Angie and she told me you were out here," Melvin was panting, out of breath. "Governor Olson's dead! Died unexpectedly in Rochester yesterday. I don't know any of the details, but...he's gone!"

Kevin's jaw dropped. Floyd Olson had been a personal friend of his years before when he worked in St. Paul. "Oh, my God!" was all he could say at the news.

"I'm planning to drive down there tonight, Kevin. It would be great if you could come along, the funeral's probably going to be on Wednesday, but there are so many loose ends in St. Paul right now. I think we've both got to help in any way we can."

"Count on it, Mel. I'll be ready to travel whenever you decide to go."

Listening to the evolving plans, Tony stood speechless. Sensing that everything he had accomplished over the past hour was going up in a smoke of futility, he appealed to Kevin. "Couldn't this trip wait until tomorrow, Kev?"

Preoccupied with his torment of the moment, Kevin looked helplessly at his father-in-law, "I worked for the Governor, Tony...he even came up to Hibbing for my campaign."

"I understand, Kevin," Tony lied in a faint voice.

"I won't forget to talk with Angie before I go. Promise, Dad."

Tony believed that a critical opportunity would be lost in Kevin's apparently warped sense of priority.

A Place Near a Pond

Upon returning home from Sturgeon Lake on Sunday afternoon, he found Angie weeding her flower beds in the backyard gardens. For long minutes he watched his wife as she pulled stubborn weeds from the black soil and carefully deadheaded some of the spent blooms. Her dark hair was tied back with a kerchief exposing her delicate ears and suntanned neck. Through his eyes, Angie was the most beautiful woman in the world. Kevin was close enough to where she worked to hear her softly humming a familiar melody to herself. Within those unseen and fleeting moments, Kevin had fallen in love again!

Raising her head, Angie sensed that she was not alone in the yard. For reasons she would never completely understand, she could always feel Kevin's presence. Without turning from the purple dahlias and lupine, she called out his name "…Kevin?"

Then she felt his warm kiss on her neck, heard his hushed voice...
"I love you, Angie Moran. Dropping her trowel, Angie felt a swell of emotion that sent a wave of heat through her body. Turning her head, she met Kevin's deep-set green eyes, "And, I love you Kevin Moran. With all my heart I do."

"I've missed you terribly, Angie." Kevin swallowed hard on his next words, "…For a long time—I've missed you, sweetheart. Much too long.
I'm sorry for allowing us to drift apart."

Angie knew the meaning behind Kevin's apology. "It has been a long time. A long time since I've really felt the 'I love you'—and…I'm sorry, too." Tears began to escape her eyes, "Look at me—crying over my happiness." She rubbed at the streak of tears on her cheek making a smudge of dirt on her face.

Taking out his handkerchief, Kevin smiled as he dabbed away the smear of moist soil. "My beautiful Angie," was all he could say.

Angie laughed, "We're both a sight, aren't we? Me in my garden grubs with a dirty face and you…" She regarded her husband's stubbled face, tousled hair, and torn plaid shirt. "And you my handsome man are a sight for sore eyes!"

"I think we could both use a bath," Kevin winked suggestively.

Angie's father had stopped by the house minutes before and taken the children for the evening. Tony had informed her that Kevin would be traveling to St. Paul with Melvin Alto for the Governor's funeral later that afternoon and that she was invited to the Zoretek's for supper.

Angie frowned, "You'll have to get cleaned up and packed, won't you? When are you planning to leave?"

"Leave?"

"Dad told me about Governor Olson's death. I'm so sorry, Kevin. I know how much—"

"Floyd was a dear friend, Angie. But, I'm not going to the funeral."

Angie looked surprised, "Dad just said you were going with Mel."

"And Dad said some things to me, too. Far more important things. Yes, the Guv and I *were* close once: You and I *were* close once!" He deliberately used the past tense. "But, he's gone now…and you're here, Angie. Getting that closeness with you back is far more important than anything else in my life right now. I mean that! And getting the two of us back to where we should be—well it's probably going to take some time. It's going to take some opening ourselves up about lots of things."

Angie sighed, "We both have lots of issues, don't we?"

"We're going to start working on our problems; and there's no time like the present."

Angie could no longer hold her emotions in check, clutching his shirt and pulling him close, she began to sob uncontrollably into his chest.

"We've got to do that, Kevin."

Kevin read about the Floyd B. Olson funeral preparations in the Hibbing and Duluth newspapers, and listened to the public services held at the Minneapolis Auditorium on radio. The floral arrangement he had delivered to the State Capitol building was displayed alongside the palm-decked bier in the Capitol's ornate rotunda where thousands of mourners somberly paraded while paying their last respects. His personal note to the Governor's widow expressed not only his condolences, but a promise to visit with her when her bereavement was more tolerable.

The reason for Kevin's absence from all of the events surrounding the Olson funeral was a simple one: Tony's words had rung deep and true—Kevin had properly measured his priorities in life!

Later that afternoon the two of them went horseback riding across the lower stretches of the vast Maple Hill property. A warm breeze tousled their hair as they skirted a row of white birch hedged with orange Indian paintbrush sprouts, and headed into the tawny waves of tall meadow grass. A frightened grouse fluttered out in front of the riders and a red-tailed hawk swooped for quarry far ahead. The pungent fragrances of minty blue hyssops, and basil-scented harebells piqued their nostrils; clusters of swaying goldenrod assailed their wind-burned eyes. Their world on this glorious Northern Minnesota day virtually shouted its flourishing splendor toward the cloudless blue heavens above.

Angie's black Arabian, Flare, had lost a step over the years but still responded easily to his rider. Kevin rode alongside, "Let's head over to *our* special place." He reined in his gray gelding and turned behind his wife toward the southwest.

Angie drew ahead, prodded Flare and raced at full gallop out in front of Kevin. "First one there...!"

'*Our place*', as Kevin called the grassy band along a narrow creek which wound into a small, pine ridged pond, was where he and Angie had first made love. The memory of that afternoon, nearly five years ago, was never far from Angie's thoughts. Dismounting her horse, Angie asked, "Do you often think of that day, Kevin?"

"Probably in some way every time I touch you."

She smiled, "A perfect answer, my love. But can you remember the exact date? I know I can."

Kevin, spreading a blanket under the shady pine, took her hand and pulled Angie beside him. "Well, I know it was in October—early October, a Saturday. Is that good enough?"

"Not quite, Mr. Moran. I'm looking for a specific date. If my memory serves me, our son was conceived on that October afternoon."

Kevin smiled at the memory, "Or, later that night? Angie, guys don't remember dates very well—you know that."

"October tenth! 1931," she blurted proudly. Looking toward her tethered horse, she added, "It was on that same day you surprised me with Flare. And we told each other of our love for the first time. Remember?"

"How could I ever forget? I was so nervous and fumbling." Meeting her eyes, Kevin recalled, "And later you surprised me with the painting I've got hanging in the library. What a fantastic day that was!"

"Then plug it in your memory, Kevin. We should celebrate October tenth for the rest of our lives."

Kevin pulled her close to his chest, "I want to celebrate *you—every day*, for the rest of my life. How about that?"

Angie felt another swell of emotion, much the same as the one that overwhelmed her in the garden hours before. They hadn't really talked yet. Making love on the puddled bathroom floor had been erotically satisfying, and both experienced a closeness that had been missing for a long time…But if *that* October afternoon was wonderful history in their lives together; *this* afternoon might be a boding for their future!

Angie believed that life offered few perfect opportunities to empty one's soul—and, this was certainly one of them. Kevin's profession of moments before welled like the promise of a spring morning in her breast, sparked her wide eyes, and brought a lump to her throat. "We need to talk. More than ever before, and with an honesty that has eluded us both for…for years. Not months, I'm afraid to admit…but years! I've loved you through it all—that's never been an issue for me. The problem has been that I've had to love you from a distance, even when you're lying beside me in our bed. I can't live that way any longer, Kevin. I need so much more than I'm getting. Do you understand what I'm trying to say?"

Kevin lay back on the blanket, resting on his elbow as he looked into Angie's moist eyes. This *was* the moment in time, the place, the opportunity he often feared might already have been lost. How would he begin telling her about things that he didn't really understand himself? "You told me once that I couldn't find what I was looking for by probing down inside myself, no matter how hard I tried. That I needed to reach out to find the answers. You told me to reach out to you."

She remembered that occasion of nearly two years before—it had been in their bedroom as they were packing for the trip to Duluth; Father Foley's wake. She also remembered another time when she had tried in vain to break down Kevin's walls. Without commenting, Angie's eyes communicated that she wanted Kevin to continue with what he was saying.

Kevin could read her pause like a page in a familiar book. But how might he share his torment? He wished he had rehearsed his first words while they were riding aimlessly. "Angie, you have come to learn that I'm not the same person you fell in love with—on that October tenth, five years ago, in this special place near our pond. Neither of us is, I guess, nor will we ever be again.

"That young man had just finished law school and was brimming with confidence—a millionaire with a mansion on the hillside, ready to take on the world and all its challenges. Strangely, I only vaguely remember him. Then, that young man dragged you off to his 'dream job' working for the Mayor of St. Paul—then the Governor of Minnesota, and entering Iron Range politics as soon as we got back to Hibbing…"

"And seemed to be headed back to St. Paul as this area's new representative," Angie finished Kevin's recall.

"Maybe that's when I fell off my high horse. Maybe that's when I got in touch with something I'd never experienced before. Failure!"

Angie wanted to interrupt and reassure Kevin that he hadn't failed. Instead, she chose only to squeeze his hand. He was beginning to open himself…

"What I'm going to tell you, Angie, will be more difficult for you to know than it will be for me to confess. I did something so terrible back then that I've covered it up with lies and half-truths ever since." He closed his eyes at the memory, "It was on that morning when I went into the library after deciding to quit the campaign. Do you remember?"

Angie only nodded. Kevin was unmasking himself, his stress was undisguised, his voice tight.

"I closed the door to shut myself in…I was so depressed at the time, so disconnected, and so filled with self-pity that I took that pistol out of the drawer. I didn't know exactly what crazy notion was going through my mind, honestly I didn't. Maybe…maybe I was thinking of my father, maybe of you and all the people I'd disappointed."

"You pulled the trigger, didn't you, Kevin?" A quick pain split through her temples, a nausea settled in her stomach. "I think there was a loud crack and shattering glass…but I can't remember anything else."

Kevin nodded, "Then I panicked, ran into the kitchen and found you on the floor…Patrick was screaming. After you came to, I lied about what happened in there—in the library. Some foolish fabrication that didn't even make much sense at the time. I'm sorry, Angie—I was so ashamed of myself at the time, so scared!"

Long moments of silence followed Kevin's admission.

"That single experience changed me. It started a long process of trying to understand what I was all about. My weaknesses more than anything else, I guess. I believed that my father's demons were raging in my blood, tearing apart the person I thought I was. I'm still struggling with all that.

"Then the Evelyn Hayes tragedy blew up in my face. No, even before that—my brooding, searching, isolating myself, all of that had been going on for quite a while—running away from myself, I guess. Evelyn's murder only aggravated everything, including my self-resentment. I started keeping things from you, Angie. Little things and big ones—I began pushing you away from what I defined as my own issues. Yes, I defined everything by myself—the captain of my forlorn ship, I suppose. I felt a compulsion to guard myself against anybody seeing the weaknesses in me. The wealthy and successful Kevin Moran had everything. Right? A beautiful wife and kids, a mansion, a fancy hotel...really stupid and conceited stuff—the stuff my walls were being built from!"

Kevin searched for something more tangible to explain his self-consuming introversion. Gary Zench had to remind him the other morning of a whole list of hotel matters that were log-jammed on Kevin's desk. His friend had observed a growing dysfunction and commented that Kevin had become more like a visitor to his hotel than the man in charge of everything. Gary's offer to help him resolve things had been arbitrarily dismissed.

"Kevin..." Angie shook his shoulder almost playfully considering the stress of the moment.

"What?" Kevin realized he had slipped into a private reverie in the middle of what he had been trying to explain.

"I think I lost you for a few minutes, that's all. You were talking about pushing me away."

Kevin was at a loss for how he might pick up the loose thread of their conversation. Had he just pushed her away without even realizing that he was doing so? Self thoughts again...his own torment...how could he release the tight grip they held? A random thought passed through his mind.

"Angie, remember the other day when we met that ragged little lad on the street? Well, just to try and explain how pathetic I've become, let me be honest about *why* I did what might have seemed like a noble gesture. I bought those groceries for myself! Yes, I really did. I knew the boy's mother would think I was someone really special for what I'd done." Kevin shook his head dejectedly, "Isn't that sick, Angie?"

Angie wanted to shake him, jolt him out of his self reproach. "You're no different than anybody else. Believe that, Kevin. We all do lots of things to make us feel good about ourselves. I know I do that all the time. Maybe it's a quirk of human nature. What you did *was* wonderful—you could just as well have given him a dollar and walked away. The motivation for going out of your way to do more than that doesn't make any difference." Angie pondered the veracity of what she'd just said, "We think about ourselves all the time." For emphasis, she repeated her last three words—"All the time!"

"Maybe, but I don't believe that's how it's supposed to be. We've got to be better than that, Angie." Kevin met her eyes and considered his next words, "Especially when you love someone. Love should be selfless."

Angie leaned over and kissed him lightly on the lips. "We've got to love ourselves before we can give our love to another. I struggle with that as much as you do. I love you with all my heart, Kevin…and still—still I'm as self-absorbed as you are. Maybe I just don't punish myself as much as you do about it."

Kevin's smile was befuddled, "Tell me what you think about and struggle with, Angie. What's going on that I can't see from over my walls? I've done all the talking so far. I think we started with the idea about pushing away from each other. Pull me into your life."

Scared and shameful, Angie would attempt to open herself and share her own torments as Kevin had done. In her mind she turned where she always had in difficult moments like this one, and whispered an appeal to the Blessed Virgin, "Mary, Mother of God, pray for us sinners…"

Angie's tears, as she explained her anxieties surrounding a condition which she could not understand, were tears of relief. When she finished with the recent episode of Maribec's falling down the stairs, she apologized, "Now you know how terribly I've shut *you* out of *my* life. Please don't ever let me get away from you again, Kevin."

The August sun had passed its zenith and sunk more deeply into the western sky. The cool shade offered by overhanging pine boughs was gone. Only the snickers of tethered horses, the gurgle of creek water over mossy rocks, and the distant caws of a raven brood in a nearby tree marred the enveloping silence. *Their place* was an Eden belonging to only the two of them at the moment—a sanctuary isolated from every occurrence in the world beyond. Only the smiling eyes of God were upon them, and only His ears could hear the promises they made to each other that Sunday afternoon. Vows which were more meaningful than those of their marriage...they pledged to become *one* again, and to break down the walls each had made.

A gust of wind whisked through the tall pond reeds and sent a tress of Angela's dark hair across her forehead and eyes. Kevin brushed the curl aside and cupped her face in his strong hands, "*I will never let you get away from me again ...my dearest...my everything!*"

The love they made that afternoon was far different than that of five years before. No longer inspired with the same youthful passion, its splendor held a more profound bonding of spirits—a union far more compelling than at any time before.

~

When Gary Zench opened his office door on Monday morning he found Kevin sitting behind his desk. A smile of amusement animated his dark features, "What in hell...?"

Kevin stepped forward and embraced his friend before Gary could put down his briefcase or remove his stylish felt hat, "I'm back on the job, Gary. Back in our little world of hotel operations again—that's all! I've missed you, my friend."

Gary, who was Kevin's height but several pounds lighter, wore a well-trimmed goatee, and was, as always, nattily dressed. "I've missed you, too...but don't break my bones about it!"

"Go ahead and say it, 'or wrinkle my suit' about it, either." Kevin released his hug of the slender man and placed his hands on Gary's shoulders. The two of them had always enjoyed a unique closeness and humor, "Did I forget your last birthday, Gary—like everything else these past months?"

Gary rolled his eyes and gave his friend an expression of confusion. Where had Kevin's birthday question come from? "No. You've never forgotten...say, what's all this sudden affection about, anyway?" Gary said as he put his briefcase on the desk.

Kevin considered his friend's surprised look, "It's about opening my eyes, Gary. As corny as it may sound, I've finally realized that I've been lost for a while. And some very important people in my life have suffered because of it. How's that for an answer?"

"Just fine, boss—I guess?" He always used the 'boss' reference congenially, "Whatever woke you up this morning is long overdo—I'm glad to have you back."

Kevin smiled, choked out his next words, "I'm going to stay back, Gary. Forgive me for shutting you out and abandoning our ship."

Gary knew the pain behind Kevin's expression. The two of them went back to childhood together, "Apology dully acknowledged and accepted, Kevin." The hotel manager knew his boss didn't need to give him any deep, philosophical or spiritual discourse on the matter. Rather than assure his friend that he had been keenly aware of Kevin's estrangement, he chose a lighter track. "So, now that you've got that off your chest, and are feeling back at the helm again—let's talk about a raise in salary. Nora has been nagging me about giving our son a new little sister and I keep telling her we can't afford it."

Kevin's eyes sparked at the diversion, "Consider it done—but with one stipulation, Gary. Angie and I will have to be the godparents. Have we got a deal or not?"

∼

Inspector Carver Blake pushed the bulky stack of papers toward the corner of his desk. As much as it pained him to do so, the murder of Evelyn Hayes would have to be filed in the 'cold case' drawer of his cabinet. The Hibbing woman's body had been recovered from the reedy banks of a St. Louis River bay two yeas ago this month. Blake could remember several cases which were far more complex than this one in his twenty-three years on the Duluth force. Even some that went unresolved. But none had ever frustrated him more than the Hayes case.

"It's a damn shame, Freddy," Blake said across the expanse of his mahogany desktop to his assistant investigator. "If that woman had been some rich guy's wife, the case would have been given priority one. The mayor would have been on me like fleas on a dog."

"I'd have to agree with you on that, Carver. Once Moran's name was cleared, even the Hibbing department didn't give much of a shit about what happened to her."

"Sadly, nobody down here did either," Blake lamented. "So, what's your gut feeling? What really happened? Who murdered Hayes, anyhow?" Freddy Robinson had only been working with Blake for the past nine months and wasn't highly familiar with the case.

"Well, the murderer wasn't Kevin Moran if that's what you're thinking. He was as clean as a whistle—even if his involvement looked pretty suspicious for a few weeks. Moran had a pretty clever frame-job hung on him; that's my theory."

"What makes you believe that?"

Carver Blake explained how Kevin Moran's whereabouts on two different occasions had been corroborated, "An old woodsman, colorful fella I'd have to say—I interviewed him myself…anyhow, he'd seen Moran out on his property the night Evelyn was allegedly raped. Then that red-headed attorney, McIntosh, located a Mrs. Barker out in West Duluth. Seems the old woman recognized a young man she remembered as Kevin Schmitz, sitting up on the hillside on the afternoon of Foley's funeral. Credible witnesses—both of them. So, the time gaps were filled. And, Moran: I spent a couple of hours talking with him up in Hibbing. The poor guy had been put through a ringer by a few promotion-hungry cops up there, and by some local newspaper reporter who didn't know his ass from a two dollar bill. As I remember, though, Chief McGinnis never seriously doubted Moran's innocence and treated him pretty well through it all."

Robinson nodded, the Hibbing businessman, however, remained an enigma. "I remember reading somewhere that Moran was loaded with money—that true, Carver?"

"No doubt about that. But he wasn't the kind of guy who flaunted it; know what I mean? Pretty much a regular fella to my way of thinking. Does a lot of good things up there in Hibbing." Blake pushed away from his desk, leaned back in his chair, crossed his long legs at the ankles "…I've got a knack for reading people's eyes, Freddy. Always have. Eyes are the windows to a person's soul, you know. Kevin Moran might have made some foolish decisions, but a murderer? Hell, I could tell in two minutes that the man was telling me the truth."

"What about that Depelo character?" Freddy perused a page on top of the paper stack. "His name came up quite often, didn't it?"

"Depelo's a snake. I have no doubt that he raped the Hayes woman, and…" Carver Blake chose his next few words carefully, "He had what I call 'the eyes'. The eyes of a psychopath." Blake lit a Pall Mall cigarette, inhaled deeply, "That sleazy sonofabitch had alibis for every minute of the ten-day timeframe we were working with. I never believed a word he said, but—" Blake's lips rounded, sending a ring of smoke into the air, "But I couldn't nail him, Freddy. It came out during the investigation that Depelo was probably the father of the Hayes boy, Johnny…and, Evelyn's mother? Hell, she must have been living in a closet most of her life. She believed her daughter was cleaner than Ivory soap. No, Esther Hayes didn't have a clue..."

"That connection with Lavalle never panned out either, did it? Depelo was seen in Duluth that week, wasn't he?"

"We did have two witness accounts to that fact, but it didn't take us anywhere. Those two hoodlums knew how to cover their asses pretty well. Nope, that proved to be just another of several dead-end streets."

"What ever happened to Depelo?"

"Nothing as far as I know. His wife divorced him. He worked for a while as a real estate broker for some Hibbing big shot, but since—maybe a year ago—I really don't know. Lost track." Blake put out his cigarette, brushed ashes from his dark suit coat, and reached for the stack of papers, "He beat the rap, though. The lucky fuck. I'll wager this Hayes file never sees the light of day again, Freddy."

With his fatal prediction, Blake stuffed the papers in a large envelope and tucked them in the bottom drawer of the file cabinet behind his desk. "Nope, not unless Evelyn Hayes comes back to earth. Even then, that scumbag Depelo would probably slip through our fingers again. Just like he eluded the Feds for years during Prohibition. Some guys just don't belong on our streets..." His thought trailed off with the smoke from another Pall Mall.

~

In a small office at the St. Paul police precinct, another cop was contemplating a stack of papers strewn across his desk top. Keirnan McGinnis wore a sergeant's badge on his crisp blue uniform and a smile on his narrow face. The handlebar mustache was gone, along with the deep furrows his face had worn for years. Today was the first anniversary of his return to the capitol city where he had grown up and had served law enforcement with distinction.

Leaving St. Paul and taking the Hibbing Police Chief position years before had been a hellacious mistake on his part. Small town politics mirrored small town thinking—he'd learned that lesson painfully. Keirnan had been an 'outsider' from his first day on the job, and the cold shoulder of that Mesabi community matched its typical January weather. The issue that motivated his leaving the Hibbing department wasn't simply his failure to resolve the Hayes case—it was more about his fellow officers, and the people he tried to serve. Keirnan smiled at the photograph of his wife, Margaret, and their three children set near the phone on his desk. Margaret had never been able to make friends in Hibbing either, but being a dutiful wife, she never once complained about her lonely time on the Iron Range.

Among the papers in his top desk drawer was a letter he'd received several months before. Kevin Moran had written a thank you and apology message to him. The sergeant could quote a line from that letter, so deeply imbedded in his memory were those few words, *"Hibbing has lost a man of profound integrity because of its myopic vision and its cold heart."*

Maybe, Keirnan thought, his God had sent him to Hibbing to learn one of life's most valuable lessons, "One must walk in the valley in order to appreciate the mountaintop."

∼

Armando Depelo's bleary eyes opened on a gloomy Wednesday morning. Who was the blond-haired woman sleeping beside him? He pressed his memory of the night before...Francine or Florence? His head pounded the beat of a hangover.

Depelo had been living in a small upstairs apartment on North Chestnut Street in Virginia for the past year. His nightshift bartending job hardly earned him enough money to make the monthly alimony payments to his former wife, Carol. Yet, there were times when he considered himself damn lucky. He might have been working in the Stillwater State Penitentiary print shop and sleeping in a small cell for a conviction on rape...or murder charges. As it was, Carol had divorced him during the Hayes investigation which alluded to his paternity of the orphaned Hayes boy. And Alphonse Gerard ("You and your horseshit reputation better get out of this town") had fired him from the lucrative real estate management job he had going in Hibbing.

As was most often the case, mornings opened the door for more of the constant drudgery which characterized Depelo's fallen life. Of the two people who had ruined the prosperous circumstances of his former life, one had been permanently removed—the other...Kevin Moran—well, Mando could only hope that his nemesis would get the medicine he deserved some day. His consuming hatred of the Hibbing businessman was never at rest.

Getting out of bed, he pulled on his rumpled trousers and walked to the bathroom sink. Looking in the mirror, Depelo read the lines of age and liquor abuse that marked his face like a roadmap. The once handsome Italian's thick hair had thinned to a premature gray, his complexion was furrowed and ruddy, and his eyes were deep pools dwelling in puffy folds. Splashing cold water on his face and rinsing his dry, acrid mouth, Depelo decided not to shave or bathe until later in the day. From the mirror he could see the woman stirring, the sheet slipping away from her round bottom. He felt the growing hardness in his groin and ambled back to the bed. He might be flat-ass broke and look like hell—but he could still get it up…and that fact was the only positive aspect of his miserable life on this gray August day.

~

A heavy October morning fog lingered along the Lake Superior shore line. No trace of breeze stirred so much as a wrinkle across the blue-green expanse of water. The lazy ball of sun rising from the east, however, would burn the haze away like a candle flame on paper. Colleen McIntosh had a marvelous view of the great lake from the upstairs office window of her London Road home. Sipping at her cup of coffee, she perused the Saturday morning *Duluth News Tribune*, looking for a furniture sale. She had been redecorating her dining room for weeks and hoped to find a good price for an oak table and chair set.

A familiar name on the Society Page caused a start: "Renowned Regional Artist in Duluth' was the banner over the single column article. Colleen read the story.

> *Award winning artist Angela Moran of Hibbing will be the featured guest of the London Road Women's annual 'Art Exposition' to be held at the Duluth Armory this afternoon. Moran's awaited oil painting, 'Birch Ice' will be displayed and the artist will speak on "utilizing simple elements of landscape themes in expressing natural concepts". Following Moran's presentation there will be a coffee social and auction. Tickets are available at the Glass Block or at the door with all proceeds going toward the London Road Women's Club charity fund. The public and new members are cordially invited to attend the afternoon affair.*

Colleen smiled to herself. What a lovely way to spend a weekend afternoon. "I might just join a women's club today," she mumbled to herself. "And find a painting for the dining room wall at the same time."

Colleen's thoughts wandered back in time to the Evelyn Hayes murder investigation and her conversations with Angela Moran's husband. Although she had never met the Hibbing attorney in person, she had seen him at the Foley funeral nearly two years ago. In her uncharacteristic whim of rushing to the St. James reception, Colleen had been able to put a face to the telephone voice—a face that was easily conjured in her memory again. That reality both puzzled and disturbed her.

"That time must have been hell for Kevin." Colleen was talking to herself again while contemplating the afternoon reception. After his first call to her office, it became strangely more comfortable to refer to him as Kevin than as Mr. Moran. She recalled how swiftly the Hayes case had disappeared from the news after she located the West Duluth witness and the woodsman had given his statement to the police. Once Kevin's name had been cleared, Armando Depelo became a prime suspect. But, for reasons she never quite understood, Depelo was never charged with any wrongdoing. After her work had been completed, Colleen had only followed the investigation from a distance. A few weeks after the case was closed, she received a bouquet of flowers along with a thank you card and personal check for her services. She hadn't heard from Kevin since.

Colleen wondered if Kevin would be with his wife at the art show. If he was there, would she have the courage to introduce herself? Would he remember her face from the many at the funeral reception? Somehow, she knew that Kevin had seen her there. Was the brief locking of his eyes something she only imagined? With thoughts of Kevin came an inevitable curiosity, what did his wife look like? What kind of woman was she—a rich, artsy, self-centered…? But what difference did it all make? Did Colleen really want to know? Did she ever want to see Kevin Moran again?

The armory gathering seemed small in such a large convention venue. Angela Moran's informative speech was well-received by the crowd of mostly women. And, Colleen was certain, Kevin was not in the audience to share in his wife's deserved acclaim.

Following the thirty minute address, Angela Moran walked among her displayed works speaking briefly about some of the more celebrated paintings exhibited on easels near the makeshift platform at the front of the armory.

"Mrs. Moran, is this one for sale?" Colleen McIntosh inquired of the canvas titled 'Whitecaps'. "I live on Lake Superior and these waves—well, they look exactly like those that splash over the rocks on my lake shore. Your work is incredibly realistic, almost photographic."

Angela laughed easily at the attractive woman's well-intended compliment. In a whispered aside, she leaned toward the taller woman's ear, "It's supposed to be offensive to tell a painter that their portrait is like a photo, but I'm flattered anyhow."

Colleen smiled, "Then let me correct myself...no photograph I can imagine would come close to the feeling that your painting evokes, Mrs. Moran. It's almost surreal!"

"Now I'm totally flattered!" Angie looked from the woman to the picture on the display easel, "I hadn't intended to sell 'Whitecaps' today—but if you really like it...certainly, I'd consider an offer...Miss?"

"Just Colleen, Mrs. Moran. But, I'm afraid I have no idea of what to offer you?"

Angela knew that, if placed in an auction, this painting would probably receive a bid of two hundred dollars—a sizable sum of money. Before she could offer any suggestion, the striking woman, Colleen, had withdrawn a billfold from her handbag. (She chose to use her furniture money rather than write a personal check for the art work). "I'd like to offer you five hundred dollars in cash, Mrs. Moran. Unless, that's...?"

"That's too much, Colleen. Two hundred would be about what I'd hope to get...does that sound reasonable to you?" Then Angela had another thought, "With the understanding that I be allowed to borrow the painting back from you if I should have the good fortune of a showing in next year's Chicago Exposition."

Colleen McIntosh left the London Road Women's Club art show with a new membership in the charitable organization, and a beautiful painting for her dining room wall. Also, she departed with an unmistakably warm impression of Kevin Moran's lovely wife. In the hubbub that followed her purchase, however, she had failed to give Angela an address where she could be reached.

~

Sister Anne de Poris sent Kevin Moran a brief note.

Dear Kevin,

I've been waiting for nearly two years to meet those two children of yours. Since Father Foley's funeral, I've had several wonderful letters from Angela and no more than two birthday cards from you. So, rather than wait for you to bring your family to visit with this old Benedictine in Duluth, I've decided that it is the Good Lord's wish to make things much simpler for everybody. As you know, God always answers my prayers, Kevin. I will be joining my beloved friend, Sister Bridgette, at the Blessed Sacrament Convent in Hibbing in November. Angela has already assured me that you will have two additional chairs at your table on Thanksgiving Day. I so look forward to being with you all. Give my best to your lovely wife, and God bless you, always.

Yours in Christ,
Sister Anne

BOOK TWO

Emma and Conrad Phelps

A Collector of Rare Books

August 1938

Conrad Phelps, Junior, was a loner. A circumstance he had come to embrace as his lot in life.

Those wishing to describe the man in a considerate manner might choose a word like eccentric—others were often wont to regard him as strange or antisocial. By whatever measure, however, the thirty-three year old man was conspicuously different from most of those he encountered in his seemingly nondescript wanderings. He was physically short, slight-framed, balding, and was a thick lensed myopic whose appearance belied the reality of his circumstances. Conrad often chose his clothing from the musty racks of local Salvation Army stores and usually wore a pair of shoes that curled up in front giving his feet an elfin appearance. In the Groveland neighborhood of East St. Paul where he lived much of the time, Conrad was generally passed by without a second thought about who he was or what he was up to. His relative anonymity was due in part to the fact that most of the time, Conrad himself had no particular agenda to pursue. Despite being ostensibly alone, the man was never rude or obnoxious in any manner. Some people naturally give the impression that they prefer a solitary lifestyle to that of being gregarious. Conrad had become one of those people. Not necessarily by choice, but more because nobody had ever seemed to care.

Anyone seeing him enter the spacious Tudor home at the corner of Lincoln and Cambridge Streets would imagine him to be a boarder in the impressive residence only blocks from Macalaster College. Fewer still would ever notice that he was the only person, other than a maid, ever to enter or exit the exquisite house. The drapes were always closed to the streets beyond.

The library at Macalaster, and a book shop on Grand Avenue, were Conrad's favorite places and where he spent most of his time. However, if anybody paid any attention to him they would observe that the head librarian and the book shop owner always addressed the small, unkempt man, as *Mr. Phelps*. Both of these men knew who Conrad was, and treated him with the utmost dignity and respect, while the nameless others in Conrad's world passed him daily with little notice or acknowledgment.

On Monday mornings, however, Conrad dressed in a finely tailored black suit, solid black tie, and expensive Florsheim shoes when leaving the side door of the mansion to enter a chauffer-driven limousine. For two hours each week, Mr. Phelps had business to take care of in the executive suites of a downtown St. Paul office building. Monday's corporate meetings were a routine drudgery that Conrad felt obligated to attend.

Conrad Phelps, few would ever realize, was one of the richest men in Minnesota!

Being the sole heir of Conrad Phelps, Senior, the son had inherited a veritable fortune when his father died unexpectedly in March of 1932—more than six years ago. The late entrepreneur had amassed a business empire that stretched from grain elevators in Fargo, to flour mills in Minneapolis, and Mississippi barge transportation operations headquartered in Winona. At the time of his death, Phelps Senior's enterprises were valued in excess of twenty million dollars.

Conrad Junior learned of his father's fatal heart attack from a philosophy instructor at Macalaster College while he was reading Machiavelli's *The Prince* in the campus library. His response to the professor's expression of sympathy—without looking up from the text—was "Oh, my..." Then with a faint smile, Conrad posed a question: "Machiavelli was a fatalist, don't you think, Dr. Foss?"

The astonished professor who once had Conrad in class, watched as the slight man collected his notebooks, then heard him mumble, "I'll probably not be at the library for some time, Doctor." With that comment, Conrad politely excused himself. From the campus he returned home, packed some clothing and took the first train leaving for California where the Phelps' owned an estate. Conrad had no desire to attend his father's funeral or to get himself tangled up in all of the inevitable legal ramifications in St. Paul.

Conrad despised his father. And worse, he knew those feelings to be mutual. When a junior in high school at Durham Hall, his history teacher had given him the standard notification for semester parent conferences to be held the following week. Conrad crumpled the page and told the instructor "I have no parents, sir—my mother died years ago."

Only the week before that incident, while finishing the last of his dinner vegetables at the kitchen table, Conrad had overheard his father talking in hushed tones on the foyer telephone. (He and his father were going to attend a symphony orchestra fundraiser together later that evening). In that Conrad loved classical music, he almost looked forward to the event. As he was pushing away from the table he heard the gruff, but hushed, tone of his father's voice—"I'm almost embarrassed to take that homely runt out in public with me, Cal..."

Young Conrad pushed his fingers down his throat and purposely vomited his dinner onto the tile floor. His sudden 'illness' saved both of them any public embarrassment that night.

Conrad didn't enjoy being seen anywhere with his large, obnoxious, father either— but he kept his feelings to himself. In fact, Conrad had learned to keep almost every thought and feeling locked inside himself. His chosen privacy established rigid walls against his father's world of commerce and elitist society— a world he had come to despise. Never had the hands of human friendship attempted to knock down those walls and know the person hiding behind them. No one—except his long deceased Gramma Emma—ever really cared.

~

The immense Phelps' ocean shore mansion (Sunset Shores) north of Santa Monica was Conrad's residence for nearly a year following his hasty departure from St. Paul. While in California, he spent endless hours of soul-searching while wandering for miles along the wide beaches. More than ever before, the young man obsessed over his loneliness and estrangement. One rainy afternoon, Conrad, desperate for human companionship, decided to take a risk. For the first time in memory, he would attempt to share his solitary feelings with someone he thought worthy of trust. As he sat under a canopy on the villa's wide deck watching the drizzle beading swollen droplets upon the freshly painted railing, Conrad's contemplative mood was interrupted. "Tea, Mr. Phelps?" The tall, gangly estate manager placed a tray with carafe and single cup on the table top, "A most unpleasant afternoon, sir. Perhaps some lemon tea will take away the chill."

"Darold, would you kindly fetch yourself a cup and join me?" Conrad invited, closing the half opened book resting in his lap. "Your company would be most appreciated."

Darold Hurley, a graying and distinguished looking man in his middle fifties, had been the Sunset estate manager for as many years as Conrad could remember. From a previous conversation, Conrad had discerned that, like himself, Darold harbored little remorse over the recent passing of the Senior Phelps. "If you will forgive my saying so—a most self-absorbed and pompous man, your father," a candid Mr. Hurley had once observed. "The staff found it most difficult to please Mr. Phelps."

After sitting down across from Conrad and nodding politely, Darold said, "A pleasant gesture to invite me to join you, sir. I'm quite caught up on my agenda for the day and welcome the opportunity for a brief respite." Darold Hurley was an educated man and voracious reader.

Conrad shrugged with an engaging smile. For a long moment nothing was said, both men sensing an awkwardness. "Have you read Fitzgerald, Mr. Hurley? I'm enjoying his Gatsby story immensely."

"A most troubled man, sir…Gatsby. And, from what I understand, Fitzgerald as well. Yes, I've read most of his books."

"Aren't we all, Mr. Hurley? Troubled?"

The question perplexed the older man. For inexplicable reasons, Darold held a distant affection for his young employer. Conrad's discontent had been obvious to the servant for some time. "Some of us far more than others," he agreed.

Meeting Hurley's hazel eyes, Conrad asked: "Are you happy, Mr. Hurley? I mean, do you enjoy your life?" Conrad's heartfelt question hung in the air for several moments.

Darold offered a smile of amusement, "I might choose the word *content*, Mr. Phelps. Perhaps true happiness is an elusive ambition—a fool's gambit, if you will."

Conrad enjoyed the man's perspective. "You may be right about that." He considered the thought, "Contentment? That would suit me fine, I think."

Darold Hurley measured the small man's pained admission, decided to chance a most personal observation. Conrad Phelps, he believed, was searching for something far deeper than casual conversation.

"May I be candid with you, sir?" Hurley said in a sincere voice over the soft swell of the ocean a hundred yards below.

"By all means, Mr. Hurley."

"Sir, it is certainly not my place to question anything you might choose to do with your time…but I cannot help but wonder why for the past six weeks you have not left the property. And I'd venture to guess that your chosen isolation has little to do with any sorrow about the recent passing of your father."

Conrad considered that reality, "In all honesty, I despised the man. There's no mourning his death at all." Conrad took off his spectacles, rubbed his eyes with the back of his delicate hands, "What might you suggest I do, Darold. Do you mind if I call you that, Darold, I mean?" The prospect of having a meaningful conversation enlivened his spirits.

"I am pleased to have you do so…"

"Then call me Conrad, Darold. I would be pleased as well."

Hurley flushed at the idea, "Very well, sir—Conrad it shall be."

"Where would you suggest I go, Darold? And, do what?"

"Santa Monica is a lovely city, sir. Have you ever been out on the pier? It's become quite the lively place these past few years. A carnival of activity—amusing things are going on there all the time. I'd recommend that with confidence. And, I would be happy to drive you into Los Angeles whenever you wish. The city has been growing in every direction—almost beyond belief, you realize. To my observation, it's become almost like the entire world converging in a single city."

Conrad knew that to be true. He considered his employee's kind offer, "Would you…just show me around, Darold? Park the car somewhere and find some interesting things to do?"

Darold had grown up in Culver City not far from Loyola Marymount University and had previously worked at both a Beverly Hills estate and the prestigious Alameda Hotel downtown. "I'd enjoy that very much, sir—Conrad. I believe I could take you to almost any place you might like to see."

Conrad's eyes sparked for the first time in weeks. He had read nearly every book in the Sunset Shores library, "Bookstores? Do you know of any bookstores, Darold? Perhaps some shops with rare books, collector books?"

"I know of several, sir. Some of which are nearly as undiscovered as the books they sell."

"And colleges? I so enjoy college libraries."

Conrad and Darold talked for a long while about Loyola Marymount, books they had both read, and places to visit while on excursion. Then, to the surprise of both, Conrad posed a question from the depths of his pent-up depression, "Would you be willing to be my friend, Darold?" As soon as the words escaped his mouth, Conrad wondered about the propriety of such an unexpected, and equally unusual, inquiry. "I don't have any friends, you see. And..." And, what? Conrad wondered.

Darold's narrow face opened into a wide smile, "I would quite enjoy that, Conrad Phelps."

For another hour, Conrad opened his soul to the man. Pent-up feelings of loneliness, doubt, self-consciousness, and hatred spewed as if a dam had split and a reservoir drained. "My father hated me, Darold. And his hatred was contagious, I'm afraid. I hate to admit...but I was happy to see him go."

"Don't feel badly about your feelings toward him, Conrad, most people disliked the man. May God have mercy on him...and me as well, because—I'm ashamed to admit to you—I was one of them."

Conrad nodded without reply.

"And loneliness? Well, I believe you've probably chosen that course for yourself. So, if you find it depressing or disagreeable, you can change directions any time. I believe you are doing just that in befriending me this morning."

The following Monday, with Conrad choosing to drive the limousine for a few miles (much to the amusement of both), the two men ventured their expectations for a great day into the city. Conrad confided to his new friend that he had $18,000 in his bank account at the moment and several hundred more in his wallet, "I'm going to find a collector book or two before we get back to Sunset tonight, Darold. I've always dreamed about having my own collection."

"Then we must work on your dream today. What else might you suggest?"

"Whatever comes up, Darold!" Conrad laughed in pleasant anticipation. A small laugh, perhaps—but, one that came from his heart. The release was almost heady. "And, when we're finished with our shopping, Darold, the two of us are going to find the best steaks in Los Angeles for dinner."

The manservant chucked inwardly without comment.

Darold Hurley knew the ethnic neighborhoods and back streets, "Let's park over there and do some walking down Figueroa Street", he gestured. "I know where some interesting shops are located."

By mid-afternoon, Conrad had taken the first crucial steps in becoming a legitimate collector. In a Russian shop he made his first discoveries and purchased two books: Ivan Turgenev's *Fathers and Sons* (an 1862 first edition written in Russian), Anton Chekhov's *The Cherry Orchard*, and an original first copy in English of *Anna Karenina* by Leo Tolstoy. In another shop he found a biography on Turgenev. After an exquisite dinner at Sardi's, the two foot-weary shoppers headed up Highway 1 to Santa Monica where they spent the early evening hours on the historic Pier.

"What do you think of this, Darold?" Conrad's excitement could not be contained as he read a passage from the biography while the two of them sipped from their beer steins at a table on the Pier. "Turgenev is quoted as saying 'we sit in the mud and reach for the stars...' I'll have to remember that line."

Darold Hurley smiled at the younger man, "Truthfully? I find it far too pessimistic—even unimaginative, Conrad."

Conrad warmed to the intelligent man's dispute, "Maybe so, but I can honestly relate to what he's suggesting. I seem to have lived for as long as I can remember up to my knees in mud."

Darold took a long moment before responding. "That may be how things have been in your life, Conrad. But...I think you're going to change all that. Today was a good beginning for you." Looking up at the wide black, star-blazoned sky across the ocean, Darold added, "Reach for them. They are yours for the taking, my friend."

Conrad spent nearly a year in Southern California before returning to pressing business issues back in Minnesota. Young Phelps had maintained weekly communication with his corporate managers. In those conversations he had instructed his board of directors not to make any decisions that would change the status quo of Phelps Enterprises.

Back in St. Paul, Conrad held a series of meetings with operations chief, Calvin Hodge, and with Irving Gravling, the chairman of the corporate board of directors. Over the next four years, Conrad sequentially liquidated more than three-fourths of the Phelps' enterprises, selling the Fargo elevators and Minneapolis milling plants to the Luddington Company through a series of dealings. Ultimately, Phelps would only continue his ownership of the barge operations which were located in the Mississippi port city of Winona, sixty miles south of the Twin Cities.

Conrad's retrenchment strategy was premised upon unfavorable economic conditions and his "lack of interest" in getting rich of off his late father's holdings. (Throughout the tense months of corporate negotiations, Irving Gravling and most of the board of directors had resigned. Calvin Hodge stayed on board what he perceived to be a 'sinking ship' only because the longtime Phelps Senior crony had no place else to go).

The Junior Phelps retained his ownership of the Winona barge operations mainly because he liked Stewart Beatty, his operations manager there. Stu was one of the few childhood friends Conrad could remember, and had a large family to support. Also, Conrad enjoyed the laid-back pace of life in the Hiawatha Valley community.

Shedding his business suits for a tweed jacket and wrinkled cotton slacks, Conrad spent countless months in his old St. Paul neighborhood—visiting the Macalaster College library almost every morning, and searching for rare books in various city shops most afternoons. His Monday meetings downtown had been pared down to once-a-month but remained stressful necessities, and he looked forward to a day when he would be completely rid of the vestiges of his father's legacy.

Once again, old patterns began to define his life in St. Paul. Friendless and disaffected, his months became years, all of them lived in what seemed like the perpetual gray of a Minnesota winter. Conrad spent his Januarys at Sunset Shores enjoying a brief respite from the cold and the pleasant company of Darold Hurley. Despite Conrad's persistent appeals that his California friend join him in Minnesota, Darold was most *content* to remain at Sunset year around. (In the years since Darold's suggestion that Conrad 'reach for the stars', the young man had failed miserably to make even a modicum of change).

For reasons he never quite understood, St. Paul retained an alluring magnetism—drawing him back to the old routines of his melancholy existence. In that Winona was only a two-hour trip by train, Conrad frequently traveled to the quiet river city for a week or two. While there he would divide his time between the Phelps' Barge office on East Front Street and the St. Mary's college library situated on the steep western hillsides above the Mississippi. At the office, Conrad enjoyed the companionship of Stew Beatty. The portly operations manager, as homely as Conrad himself—with large ears and a small chin—had a wonderful sense of humor and was easy to small talk with. "If I had all your money, Mr. Phelps, I'd be the happiest man in the world," Stew said one morning over coffee. "I'd buy me a huge house, take the wife and kids on vacations…and never work another day as long as I lived."

"The American dream, isn't it, Stew? Well, consider yourself fortunate that you don't have all my money. It might make you more miserable than you can possibly imagine."

Stewart Beatty would never understand his boss's perspective.

In Winona, Conrad lived in the Phelps' large Victorian era mansion off Windom Park. The elegant four-storied house was one of four majestic properties Conrad had inherited from the Phelps' estate. In addition to the English Tudor home in St. Paul, the Spanish Villa mansion in Santa Monica, and the Winona Victorian, Conrad's father had owned a small chateau in Sorrento, Italy, which the son had not visited since his freshman year in high school nearly twenty years before. Conrad had often considered selling the Mediterranean property, but chose to avoid what would probably be a complicated real estate matter. And, with all the turmoil in Europe these days…?

~

Conrad scanned the front page of the Winona newspaper (the August 10, 1938 edition) as he sat in his simply-furnished but spacious living room: 'New Offensive in Spain' the headline read. He perused the article informing that government forces had driven a wedge between insurgent strongholds in the area of Catalonia. Nearby was a similar story: 'Japanese Troops Repel Russian Charge'. Disputed territory along the Siberia-Manchuria border was at issue.

Frustrated, Conrad mumbled to himself, "What is this world coming to?" A pacifist by nature, he had not kept abreast of the tumultuous world events, choosing rather to concentrate his attention on 'higher intellectual pursuits'. He had recently finished a Bertrand Russell book which denounced war in powerfully eloquent language. Conrad opened the newspaper to an inside page, found the crossword puzzle and an escape from the distressing front page stories. After dinner he would return to his upstairs study and continue his research project on Martin Luther.

Although raised a Lutheran in the predominantly Catholic community of Winona, Conrad was not a religious man in terms of practicing his faith. But theology was a fascination which brought him to the St. Mary's College library most afternoons. Studying the life of Martin Luther was his latest infatuation. Conrad had purchased nine of Luther's sixteenth century published manuscripts (in German)—some of them simple liturgies on various Biblical concepts, while others were little-known stanzas of poetry along with sermons and religious hymns. The Conrad Phelps collection of rare books and manuscripts, although not widely publicized, had grown in recent years to an almost inestimable value.

Conrad heard the telephone ring. "I get it Mizter Pelpz," Mrs. Galinski, the housekeeper, called as she rushed from the kitchen to the living room. "Fer you, sir," the squarely-built Polish woman said as she handed him the receiver. "Dinneriz ready whenever you are."

Conrad cradled the phone on his shoulder as he linked the word 'nullify' vertically with 'callous' on his puzzle. "Howard, I hope you've got good news for me!" Conrad pushed the puzzle aside and sat up on the sofa. "Did you locate the book I'm looking for?"

Howard Gross owned a bookstore near Macalaster on Grand Avenue in St. Paul. A collector himself, Gross had been commissioned by Conrad to locate an original edition (1754) of Puritan theologian Jonathan Edward's' classic, *Freedom of Will*. "There's a copy in Boston, Mr. Phelps—I've placed the order and should have it next week."

Conrad mentally visualized his schedule, today was the tenth of August, "I'll get up to St. Paul the week after next—probably on Friday…and stop by the shop the next morning—that would be Saturday, the twenty-seventh. How would that be, Howard?"

"Just fine, sir. It will be here when you arrive." But, Gross had more good news, "I can also get you a first edition of *Uncle Tom's Cabin* if you're interested. It's quite expensive, eighteen hundred, as you might imagine."

"Get them both, Howard. I'll have the bank deliver a check to you in the morning."

Hanging up the phone, and striding with swollen chest toward the kitchen, Conrad was almost euphoric. "I'm going to open a bottle of wine to go with your pot roast, Gretta. Will you join me in a toast to my good fortune?"

Dumbfounded, Gretta Galinski almost burned herself on the cookie sheet of dinner rolls she was taking from the oven, "I dunno, sir? Can I do that with you?"

Conrad put a hand on the matronly woman's square shoulder, smiled his amusement over the awkward circumstance he'd suggested: "Youz certainly can, Gretta," he said facetiously. "And, I'd like you to pull up another chair to the table, too. We're celebrating tonight!"

In all her years as the Phelps family housekeeper, Gretta Galinski had never before eaten at the kitchen table with her employer.

Later that evening, Mrs. Galinski would reflect that she had never seen any Phelps family member express such emotion. Mrs. Phelps, a morose alcoholic, had died when Conrad was in elementary school. The young man's father had been away on business most of the time and wore a perpetual scowl whenever he visited his Winona family.

AMNESIA

August 26, 1938

The elegant St. Paul Hotel hosted a Friday evening reception for the annual W.P.A. Artist's Conference which was to be held at St. Catherine's College the following day. More than one hundred artists from throughout the Midwest had gathered in Minnesota's capitol city for this evening's prelude to Saturday's workshops. In many respects, this evening's reception would be the highlight of the weekend's activities. Widely esteemed surrealist, Georgia O'Keefe, would be the featured speaker for the gala Friday event.

O'Keefe, a Wisconsin native, had gained national acclaim for her vivid paintings—as well as for her controversial feminist viewpoints. The hotel's ornate Palm Room was filled to capacity when she strode to the dais and took her place behind the podium. KSTP radio would carry a live broadcast of the distinguished woman's presentation.

After a thunderous ovation, O'Keefe gestured a hush to the predominantly female audience. "According to the program, I'm supposed to talk, or lecture, about 'Simplicity and the Surrealistic Dynamic'—now that sounds rather intimidating to me." Laughter mixed with applause at her opening comment. "But that's what my workshop at St. Kate's tomorrow is going to be covering…so, I'm going to depart from your published program and give you ladies—do I see a few men out there, too…?" More laughter. "Anyhow, most of you know by now that I've been raising more than a few issues about what the press likes to label 'Women's Rights'—just to be provocative, I'm sure—over the past few years. So as not to disappoint all of you and our radio audience, *tonight* I will be Georgia the woman, not Georgia the artist.

"When I was still a little girl, I used to think that since I couldn't do what I wanted to...at least I could paint as I wanted to, and say what I wanted to when I painted. Thus, painting opened my doors to womanhood at an early age."

Georgia O'Keefe spoke for nearly forty-five minutes inspiring several boisterous interruptions from the receptive audience. Among those in attendance were two of the following day's presenters: St. Paul's Gertrude Shibley and Henrietta Shore from Toronto. Georgia recognized both ladies, asking each to stand for acknowledgment Following O'Keefe's keynote speech the three women mingled among the throng of invited guests until nearly midnight.

~

The dark-haired woman, dressed in a lightweight lavender linen suit with a finely tailored fingertip length jacket and matching plumed hat, stood at the Market Street trolley stand. A colored hotel doorman had instructed her to take the Randolph Street trolley down Seventh and directly to St. Catherine's College earlier that Saturday morning. Because she was both nervous and excited about the workshops and tired from the late night before, she became confused: Which trolley had she been told to take? As a streetcar approached the corner, the woman asked a well-dressed gentleman waiting nearby, "Will this car take me to St. Catherine's?"

"Surely will, ma'am. Just transfer to the car going south on Snelling Avenue at the end of the line."

Perplexed by the mention of a transfer, she entered the streetcar anyhow. The front seat, across from the operator, was available. Sitting across the aisle from the attractive woman was a young mother with a small, bunting-clad child asleep in her lap. The Grand Avenue line slowly wound up the steep northwestern hillside while passing impressive mansions on either side of the street. From her window, the woman gazed upon the intriguing urban landscape as it passed by—mansions eventually gave way to shops with impressive displays of colorful merchandise. Crossing Lexington Avenue, then Hamline—the trolley continued on its route, stopping every two blocks to exchange passengers.

Glancing away from her gaze out the side window, the woman saw the automobile speeding into the Pascal Street intersection. She tensed, and then gasped! Too late... The screech of brakes was followed by the deafening crunch of metal! Lurching from the rails at the sudden impact, the top-heavy streetcar tottered, nearly rolling over on its side.

The woman, jolted from her seat, smashed her head against a guard railing—sending her plumed hat flying against the trolley's windshield. As she hit the metal bar her head turned…her eyes widening as the loosely held infant was thrown violently to the floor…first she heard an eerie scream…then saw a trickle of blood from the tiny nose… The baby's mother, jarred by the stunning smash slumped awkwardly forward…seemingly unconscious. Passengers shrieked at the top of their lungs!

"Oh my God!" The startled operator shouted through the growing din of startlement.

Shock-numbed, she absently contemplated walking away—down unfamiliar Grand Avenue—distancing herself from the gathering mayhem in the street. A crowd was beginning to collect around the cluster of stunned passengers and the horrible wreckage. Something catastrophic had just happened. But…what? The woman wasn't sure. Mumbling incoherently to herself, she aimlessly limped away, clutching her purple, pearl-fringed, handbag like a baby in her arms. The heel on one shoe had been broken.

~

Conrad Phelps looked up from Jonathan Edward's leather-bound book resting on the countertop of Howard Gross' Grand Avenue shop. Through the street-facing window he noticed the lovely woman—hobbling, her dark hair disheveled, as she passed by the front of the shop, shaking her head as if in disbelief of something. It occurred to Conrad that she was talking to herself.

Closing the cover of the book, Conrad seemed suddenly anxious. "Wrap them up for me please, Howard. To say that these books are exquisite is an obvious understatement. I must get home and look them over more carefully."

On the sidewalk outside the shop, an intrigued Conrad saw the woman again. She was sitting by herself on the wooden bench on the corner of Snelling and Grand. A streetcar had just departed. Watching, he waited several minutes. Another trolley came and went—still she sat. Conrad could see that she was still mumbling to herself by the gentle bobbing of her head. Curious, he walked over and sat down at the end of the bench. "Can I be of any assistance, ma'am?"

When she turned his way, Conrad was almost overcome with her beauty—dark ovaline eyes, full mouth, perfect features. He asked again if he might help.

"You might as well call my father and tell him about what happened." In a voice tinged with reproach she added, "I've really done it this time."

Confused, Conrad inquired further, "What have you done ma'am?"

"The car! Didn't you see? If people just put up fences around their property the deer wouldn't be running all over the place."

Her voice struck Conrad as that of a much younger woman than she appeared to be—almost like that of a teenage girl. "Maybe I can help. Would you like me to telephone your father, then?"

"He's probably asleep, you know. That's why I stole the car and ran away. So foolish of me…but I've learned my lesson this time." She shook her head, dark tresses falling across her forehead.

Conrad noticed a bruise above her right eye. "What is your father's name? Perhaps I can talk to him. There's a phone in the bookstore around the corner."

Without reply, she gave him a blank expression.

"Your father? Does he live in this neighborhood?"

She began to sob softly, shaking her head as she did so. "I don't know. That's just it. I hit the deer and smashed into the tree… and now I can't find it—the car or the deer. I'm sure I've killed the poor deer, there was blood."

Conrad considered that the lovely lady had become tragically disoriented. Some kind of trauma seemed to be confusing her thoughts of the moment. He regarded her delicate hands. She wore a wedding ring but had said nothing about contacting her husband. "Perhaps you could tell me your name, and then I can look up your father's number in the book."

"My name?" Her brow wrinkled, "My name?" she repeated with an enigmatic expression washing over her pale face.

The woman focused vacantly at the approaching streetcar without making any move to rise up from the bench. "This is the strangest place I've ever seen. Where did all these people come from? They weren't here a little while ago when it was dark out. That's one thing I'm sure about."

It was apparent to Conrad that the woman could not remember her name and seemed totally confused about where she was. Conrad chanced another tack, "Perhaps you could tell me your husband's name?"

"Don't be silly!" she laughed girlishly, "I'm far too young to be married. Goodness, I'd be the talk of the school if I were married."

"I'm not being silly at all. You are married young lady—just look at the lovely rings on your finger. And you're not too young at all."

The woman regarded her rings. "I don't understand. Nobody at school ever said anything about it. And, my father...how would he ever allow...?" She shook her head in disbelief, "I guess you're right, though."

Conrad brightened at the disclosure of her status, "You're a student then." Macalaster College was just across busy Snelling Avenue a short distance away. "Macalaster?"

"What's a Macalaster? I said 'school'—not that...what—?"

"Macalaster is the school over there," he gestured beyond the busy street. "What school were you talking about then?"

The young woman only shook her head, "That's just it, don't you see—I can't remember. I can't seem to remember anything! It makes me angry. First I destroyed my father's automobile and now this—this strange place." She pouted her displeasure, "Darn it, anyhow! You must think I'm crazy. Am I right about that—all mixed-up?"

"Some things are confusing you right now, for sure...a little mixed-up maybe —but certainly not crazy, my dear." Conrad was becoming intoxicated by the lilt of the woman's voice, her animated facial expressions, and the whimsical manner in which she expressed her frustration. "We've got a little problem here, don't we?" He took her hand in his own, "I would like to help you, if I can."

She gave him a puzzled look. "Could you tell me..." her nose wrinkled as if she were about to laugh in embarrassment, "...What my name is, sir? Do you have any idea...could you ask someone who knows me?"

Conrad was overwhelmed by what was happening, his feelings were running amok—impairing his usual good judgment. She had given his hand a gentle squeeze when asking him who she was—her searching eyes melted him. A lifetime of self-imposed estrangement from women seemed almost to melt in the moment. Women, Conrad had always believed, could only be interested in his money. He hadn't been blessed with good looks or the stature most women perceived as important in their 'tall, dark, and handsome' absurdity. But this woman, so innocent and vulnerable, might accept him for the caring and compassionate man Conrad believed he had always been. Perhaps...if given a chance, she might see him for himself, uncontaminated by any predispositions about his wealth. He swallowed hard and risked a foolish fabrication—one he might withdraw at the slightest incomprehension: "Your name is Emma!"

The woman nodded. Conrad searched her wide eyes for reaction. "Emma?" She almost looked pleased. "Thank you! Now perhaps we're getting somewhere.

Her coy smile lifted the corners of her full mouth, "And may I ask, sir…who are you?"

Years of empty existence were swelling inside Conrad Phelps at that fateful moment: His lifetime of self-denial slipping beyond his grasp. Any unconventional behavior on his part—be it even the slightest deceit or untoward act—had always been rejected on the basis of his carefully defined code of righteousness. "Don't do what you're thinking, Conrad"—a voice screamed from the depths of his soul. Every fiber of his being seemed in culpable protest… But—

Conrad's illogical contemplations prevailed. He was a bright man about to do something foolish, dangerous. The woman was vulnerable and obviously in need of help: Fate had made this moment!

She was staring at him, "You didn't answer my question."

"Oh, yes—who am I?" Conrad's words tumbled from his dry mouth, "Now it's you who's being silly, my pretty one. Just look again at your rings— I'm your husband… Conrad." His eyes squinted at the insanity of his illogical gambit; his stomach knotted with apprehension. In her present state of disorientation, however, anything he might tell her would seem plausible. If she could accept the notion of being Emma so naturally—why not Emma Phelps? Conrad was more conflicted than he could ever remember being—were his thoughts of the moment as irrational and convoluted as hers? Yet, if she laughed at the notion of being his wife, he could still offer a light "just kidding" retraction. He and Emma had already established an almost teasing banter between themselves.

A trace of blush appeared on Emma's pale cheeks, her eyes sparked as if a veil had been lifted, "Why didn't I know that?"

"Well, you just admitted a moment ago that you were very confused, didn't you?"

"Yes, I did—and I still am." She searched his magnified brown eyes behind the thick lens of his glasses, "I'm sorry…Conrad, I didn't remember. How terrible of me. I thought I was too young, you know…Oh, my—what a terrible day I've been having. My head is throbbing so bad I can't make sense of anything. You'll just have to forgive me, Conrad."

Conrad exhaled a sigh of relief. "I know that, my dear." He rubbed the back of her hand with his thumb. "But everything is going to be all right—just you wait and see." He knew then—at that precise moment that he would take Emma 'home' with him that morning. Conveniently, the housemaid was off for the weekend. Later, perhaps, he would call a doctor, the Ramsey Hospital…or the St. Paul police. Would she remember this bizarre conversation later? How long might her apparent blackout last? Could his 'story' be altered, unraveled? His head pulsed at the evolving deception, at that inner voice demanding he make things right before—before it was too late! "You must be exhausted, Emma. Let me take you home where you can have some coffee then…maybe rest for a while."

"Coffee? Conrad, you're teasing me. You must remember I don't like coffee—maybe when I'm older…" Emma puzzled over what she had just said. "But, I am older than I first believed, aren't I?"

Conrad Phelps had never been in love. Could such an incredible feeling consume one so suddenly, so totally, he wondered? And so unexpectedly?

Over a hastily prepared luncheon of sandwiches (Emma sliced the bread and found cheese in the ice box) and tomato soup, the two of them had talked for nearly an hour. Conrad, listening carefully to Emma's recount of her convoluted rural accident story, thought he had put some critical pieces of her puzzle together. The woman must have had an automobile collision years before, probably as a teen-ager: Striking a deer on some deserted country road, loosing control and crashing into some trees. That episode must have been traumatic. His Emma's memory processes had shut down somehow, reverting her back to—and locking her into a place in time many years before. Everything since that episode seemed to have been erased, or lost from consciousness.

Later, sitting in a nearby chair, he watched his Emma as she fitfully slept, his every emotion in chaotic disarray. Insidiously, Conrad had discovered who this beautiful woman was—and where she came from. When she retired for a nap in this upstairs guest bedroom only minutes ago, Conrad had found some old receipts while rifling through the pearl-fringed purse she left behind in the living room. He also found a yellowed photograph of the woman and a handsome man; presumably her husband. (He burned the photo and papers in the kitchen sink).

What had happened to cause her amnesic blackout? Why was she here in St. Paul—so far from home, and by herself? Who might be looking for her at this very moment? Had anybody seen them talking at the streetcar stop, or walking together across the campus, or entering the house? What might trigger a recall of who she really was, he wondered? How long would her amnesia last?

What kind of trouble had Conrad brought on himself? The woman was married, and he was certain, from the sizable amount of cash in her handbag and by her expensive clothing, of wealthy circumstance.

He wept softly as the questions pounded in his head. Feeling as if an unforeseen darkness had gripped his heart, Conrad searched his tormented thoughts for some explanation. What he was doing was so terribly wrong, so dangerous. He remembered reading a biography about Saint Augustine (a grave sinner before his conversion)...'people were sinful by nature...no mortal could ever hope to be innocent'. Conrad, like the revered saint, might only pray for God's incredible forgiveness. Might God Almighty condemn his soul for *one* grievous sin? Yet, he knew in his heart and mind, that his *first* sin would require a thousand others to sustain it. Prayer, however, proved impossible in his guilt of the moment.

Conrad was coming to grips with a dreadful reality: There was no turning back now! No way in which he could correct the terrible mistake he was making. His fate was already sealed. The timeframe for notifying a hospital or the police had already been stretched much too far. Emma was going to be his secret from the world. Conrad's obsession had already consumed rational thought. He would begin weaving the tapestry of deceit—do anything (and everything) within his power to preserve the treasure he had found. Conrad had decided that this woman—Emma—would be his own!

Strangely, his motivations were not sexual. Even now, as she slept only feet away from him covered with an old bathrobe from Conrad's closet—the ankles, of what he imagined to be her long and shapely legs—were exposed. There was no stirring in his loins. No, Conrad was positive he would never violate her in any manner. To even attempt anything sexual would taint both he and Emma, and be the most unforgivable of sins. At that moment, Conrad made a solemn *vow* —"I will never violate you in any way." He was convinced that his desire for Emma was the far more powerful attraction of companionship. She could fill the chasm of his loneliness—a void which had been carved into his depraved psyche over the course and curse of an empty lifetime.

If his thoughts of the moment were irrational, and most would believe they were, surely there were many people out there who had lived with desolation similar to what Conrad had experienced. They would understand! As he sat, watching her slumber...long curls of her dark hair splayed across the satin sheet, her arm caressing the pillow as child would a teddy bear, and Conrad was already conceiving a plan. An insidious scheme, so unlike anything he had ever imagined doing before, made him wonder if some demon had taken possession of all his logical discernment. Throughout his life, Conrad Phelps had lived by the rules. Scrupulously conforming behavior had been the sustaining pattern of his morality for all of his years—up until this cataclysmic day!

"If there is a God in heaven…forgive me," Conrad sobbed. "All I've ever wanted in this life is to be happy."

Downstairs, Conrad's devious plot began unfolding in carefully considered detail. Emma would need a wardrobe, a dramatic makeover of some kind, and a new history. Tomorrow, the two of them would have to escape St. Paul. In the next twenty-four hours, any mistake Conrad might make would be fatal. Nothing could be left to chance.

Helen Bates had never, in her twenty-three years as the women's fashion department manager at Dayton's Department Store, had a more bizarre telephone conversation. A man by the name of Adam Johnson had called Dayton's placing an order for women's clothing and accessories in an amount of more than six hundred dollars!

"Nothing cheap—I must be emphatic about that!" Johnson had stressed at the onset, "Only the very best that you have."

The caller told Helen that his sister from Des Moines had lost all her luggage and needed to replace her wardrobe immediately, several social engagements were on their agenda for the following week. "She will need everything—do you understand?"

It was odd, but not unheard of, for a man to be placing such a comprehensive order of women's clothing. But why wasn't the man's sister making this call?

Helen ventured a suggestion, "Dayton's offers a preferred customer service where we will come directly to your home with a variety of samples, styles and sizes—which your sister could try on and select only those..." Conrad curtly interrupted, "My sister is simply too overcome by this misfortune and has taken to her bed. Are you capable of taking my order or not?"

Rather than risk further upsetting Mr. Johnson, or worse yet, having him call a competitor like Donaldson's, Helen determined she would make some preliminary wardrobe inquiries. Before getting into details, she assured the potential customer, "We will do our very best to resolve your sister's problem, Mr. Johnson."

Satisfied, Conrad checked his notepad, "Oh yes, you'll need to know before I begin that every outfit should be a size six." Conrad had checked Emma's dress label before calling.

While keeping him on the phone, Helen asked specific apparel questions while writing everything down as her assistant, Louise Pritchard, rummaged through the racks of dresses. "He wants something purple, Louise...and a variety...nothing autumn weight...yes, definitely some of the *Hattie* stuff over there." Helen called from the counter. (*Hattie Carnegie* fashions were top-of-the-line apparel).

"Would you like me to select some accessories, Mr. Johnson?"

"Yes, of course...some nice jewelry to go with the outfits would be fine. A few necklaces...earrings, I suppose."

Helen continued writing everything down, "Cosmetics? Did your sister lose her toiletries as well, sir?"

"Yes...make up an assortment—a box full of things, she can decide what she wants when she gets the order."

Helen puzzled to herself, "...a box full?"

Louise Pritchard, standing nearby, whispered in Helen's ear, "Does he want underwear and bras, too?"

Using her utmost discretion with the gentleman, Helen offered the personal inquiry, "Shall I select some undergarments, sir?"

"Yes...by all means." There was a long pause, "Whatever you think appropriate. She likes fancy things...nothing too...suggestive though...I think you know what I mean. But maybe lacey?"

Helen considered a 'size six' woman, pondered her next discrete question: "Is she large busted, would you say...or..." Helen would allow Mr. Johnson to explain.

Conrad didn't think so...but strained for a reply, "Not really. She's resting now and I dare not awaken her with such a question. Send a few items—we'll just return anything that doesn't fit. Will that be an acceptable arrangement?"

Helen could almost feel the man's blush, "Very well, Mr. Johnson. We'll do our very best in that regard. How about sleep wear?"

"Everything! I've already told you she lost all her things." Apparently stressed by all the questions, Johnson's voice had noticeable raised again.

"Yes, sir...now let me see, my associate has placed some dresses here on the counter—let me tell you what she's chosen. Then you can tell me what...I know it must be hard without seeing them, but—" In the colorful pile were a *Hattie* plum suit with pearl beaded pockets; a pale powder blue felt jacket with rolled edges over an aubergine crepe sheath by *Schiaparelli*; two *Lanvin* broadcloth dinner outfits (one in navy chalk stripes the other in cocoa brown); and a blue gray caballero bolero jacket trimmed with crepe shawl collar over a flared crepe skirt by *Marcel Rochas*. "And we have a lovely *Altman* purple Zepher-knit culotte dress with a white felt belt...Everything I have out is of the latest fashion, and certainly the very best we have, Mr. Johnson," she assured.

"She'll need six dresses, and if you think they're pretty, ma'am, I'm sure she'll be more than satisfied. Also...three, no make that four pairs of shoes to go with everything—size six." (He had found the size on Emma's broken shoe). Was that everything? Conrad raked his mind as he looked at the scribbled list of purchases, "Find my sister a nice leather purse, too."

Helen puzzled again, but made the notation: Losing one's luggage was one thing...but—a purse? Why didn't she have had her handbag with her while traveling?

For more than half an hour the two women frantically filled the order, Helen leaving the phone at times to run and get something else.

Helen's unprecedented experience was stressful but great fun, too. "Six hundred and forty-eight dollars, sir." The manager informed Mr. Johnson when all the items had been assembled.

Mr. Johnson wanted everything delivered to his St. Paul address, and said he would pay for the order in cash, "I'll give the delivery man seven hundred—you and your associate can divide the change."

After offering a profuse thank you, Helen was given another strange request. "My sister will need her hair fixed tomorrow morning. A styling I guess you'd call it...and a coloring as well. Can you make any arrangements for me? Somewhere in the Groveland neighborhood? I'll pay fifty dollars."

Helen's sister-in-law, Beatrice Holcomb, had a small shop near Snelling and University and would probably drool at an opportunity to make fifty dollars on a Sunday morning! Helen gave the man an address and promised him a nine o'clock appointment.

SUNSHINE AND OCEAN AIR

An insidious scheme born of psychotic loneliness was now in motion. Any hopes of rescuing right from wrong were passing like ships in the night.

Conrad was perspiring, the wardrobe project had taken much longer than he had expected. But, he was certain, Emma would be both surprised and pleased. "An early Christmas," he might tell her. On his notepad by the telephone, Conrad checked the next item on his list, lifted the phone from its cradle again, and asked the operator to connect him with the Northern Pacific Railroad ticket office.

In five minutes, arrangements had been made for private Pullman berths on the two-thirty Sunday afternoon train to Seattle. The tickets would be held at the window for Adam Johnson. After arriving in Seattle, Conrad planned to make connections to Los Angeles under different passenger names.

The next call he made was long distance. "Darold…I've got some wonderful news!" Conrad explained that he had gotten married the previous week and that he and Emma would be arriving in California sometime the following Friday afternoon.

"She's beautiful! Darold, I know you'll just love my Emma."

Darold Hurley was excited and puzzled in near equal measure. Conrad, in all the years he had known the younger man, had never shown the slightest interest in women. It was Darold's guarded suspicion that his employer was—perhaps, asexual or, even more likely, attracted to men. The manservant was ashamed of himself at that moment. "Conrad," he said with all the sincerity his confounded thoughts could muster, "Your good news simply overwhelms me. I will have everything in superb readiness for you and your bride."

Emma had been sleeping for nearly two hours—the wall clock hands were at one fifty-eight. Conrad turned on the living room Zenith radio, found KSTP on the dial, and listened for the local news.

As fate would have it, another question unraveled quickly: A Grand Avenue streetcar had been derailed in a terrible collision at Pascal Street that morning. There were two fatalities; a child believed to be about seven months old, and the driver of the automobile. "Names will not be released until family and relatives have been informed," the newsman reported. "Veteran operator, Virgil Hespert, claimed that 'he had never seen such tragedy'. Further details of the eight-forty accident in St. Paul this morning, will be provided on the comprehensive five o'clock news program."

"Conrad?" He heard Emma's call from upstairs. "I still have a terrible headache."

Emma was sitting up in bed when Conrad entered the guest bedroom with a glass of water and two aspirin tablets. He had noticed the small bruise on Emma's forehead when he first met her—only hours before. It seemed to him, however, like a lifetime ago! "Here, maybe these will help."

"Where am I, Conrad? Everything still seems so strange—like I've never been in this room before. And this bathrobe? I seem to have put it on over all my clothes. Was I that tired?" Shaking her head and rubbing sleep from her eyes, she placed the white tablets in her mouth and swallowed the full glass of water. "I feel as though I've slept for days," she said yawning deeply and rubbing her eyes.

"You were that tired, my dear. Remember we were talking about your accident, and how upset your father was going to be—before going up to bed? Well…you needn't worry about that any longer. I've talked to your father and he's just happy to learn that you're okay."

"But, I'm not okay, Conrad. I feel queasy and achy. Worse than I did before taking a nap. Maybe I should see a doctor."

"I don't think that will be necessary, Emma. At least not right now. What you need after your ordeal is a little vacation—that's all."

"Did daddy say I was going to be punished for taking his car?"

"Oh, no." Conrad forced a laugh, "In fact, it was he who suggested the vacation idea." He would be patient regarding this woman's amnesic condition. Despite her apparent acceptance of being old enough to be his wife, she remained locked into an age pattern Conrad believed to be about sixteen. Moreover,

Emma's youthful charm was more consuming to him than if she spoke and behaved as a woman of more appropriate age—twenty-five or so, he guessed.

Emma rubbed her forehead, "I hope those pills work. It's just splitting up here, all the way to the back of my head."

"You wouldn't believe what some sunshine and fresh ocean air can do for your health, Emma. Better medicine than any doctor in the world might prescribe."

"Ocean air? That would be a long ways from here, Conrad, don't you think? We learned about the oceans in grade school geography lessons. Where are we going for this vacation?"

"California, Emma. We're going to California—tomorrow, in fact. Out to our lovely home on the ocean."

"We have another home?"

"Yes, we do. Oh, Emma, I have so many things to tell you about. Marvelous things. I know you can't remember any of them now, but just wait—by the time we get to California everything will be clear in your mind again. I'm sure of it."

Emma regarded her husband, his thinning brown hair slicked back from a high forehead, the thick glasses magnifying his large brown eyes, the narrow nose. He wasn't a good-looking man, but had straight white teeth, a pleasantly engaging smile, and a masculine voice. More than anything, her husband seemed to be a gentle, understanding, and kindly soul. "I sure hope so, Conrad. I've got lots of remembering to do. Even about you…you and me both. When you came in the room a few minutes ago…" Emma lowered her head, "I'm almost ashamed to admit it; but…it was almost like you were a stranger."

Conrad tried to make light of Emma's observation. Sitting down beside her on the bed he said, "When we get on the train tomorrow, I'll begin telling you everything, Emma. When we met…all the fun things we did together before we got married…our plans and hopes and dreams—everything!"

~

"Are you sure about this, Conrad?" Emma asked appraisingly from the beautician's swivel salon chair as she regarded herself in the hand held mirror. "I can hardly recognize myself."

After the blonde coloring treatment, the hair stylist, a woman in her thirties named Beatrice, had created an upswept *queue-de-cochon* rather than doing a permanent wave. "You certainly do look like a different woman, Miss—?" The question hung for a moment, "A most attractive woman, I might add."

"Mrs. Phelps," Emma blurted absently while running fingers through her hair.

Conrad cleared his throat, paling noticeably at Emma's innocent admission. Hopefully the stylist would forget the name. Appraising Emma's dramatic change, Conrad was perfectly satisfied. With the new hairdo, and fashionable new *Altman* purple dress, his Emma was exactly what he'd hoped for—an almost unrecognizably changed woman! "Thank you, Miss Holcomb, my wife looks simply stunning." He gave the stylist a fifty dollar bill and whisked Emma out the door.

When everything was packed, Conrad made a quick survey of his house to make certain nothing was left behind. All of Emma's old clothing, her purse, shoes—everything was collected and stuffed into an oversized pillow case. Stepping out the back door without Emma's notice, he hurried to the garage and threw the sack up into the rafters where it would be out of sight until he could better dispose of it later.

On the way to the station, Conrad asked the Minneapolis taxi driver to stop at a familiar book store on Hennepin Avenue. "I'll only be a few minutes, Emma. Just wait in the cab." Knowing exactly what he was looking for, Conrad found a section of psychology books near the back of the store. Quickly scanning the titles, he selected a book by Sigmund Freud, another by Alfred Adler, and a third by Carl Jung. At the counter, Conrad picked up the Sunday issue of the *Minneapolis Star Tribune*. Armed with ample reading material, he was out the door in less than five minutes—with plenty of time to make the train's scheduled departure. He didn't want to spend any unnecessary time hanging around at the busy depot. Conrad had worn a light topcoat, turned the collar up around his lower face, and pulled his wide brimmed felt hat down over his eyes. And blurry eyes they were—he'd placed his spectacles in the inside pocket of his coat.

Once seated in the Pullman on board the express and heading West toward Fargo, Conrad gradually began to relax. He hadn't slept the night before and seemed to be functioning on nerves alone. Emma's growing excitement, however, was contagious. Passing through miles of nondescript Western Minnesota landscape, she had a barrage of questions. "You told me yesterday that once we were on the train you'd tell me about when we first met and everything that has happened since."

"I'll do even better than that, my dear…because I can remember you from way back when you were just a little girl."

Emma giggled delightedly.

By the time the Northern Pacific Express had passed into the foothills of Western Montana the following day, Conrad had contrived a personal history for his new bride. His fabrications, having withstood a thousand questions, were almost as real to him as they were to Emma. While she slept, Conrad scribbled notes about the imaginative story (and the stories within the larger story) so that he might review, or remind Emma of specific details, at any future time. When informed of her mother's untimely death (pneumonia) and her father's debilitating health conditions, Emma cried openly. "I had no idea, Conrad," she would say in wide-eyed incredulity on countless occasions. "Will I ever be able to see my father again?"

"I hate to say this, Emma…" Conrad swallowed hard, "But when I talked with his nurse last Saturday she informed me that his disease had become highly contagious and told me he was going to be transferred to some hospital in New York—I think it was. So, it could be a few years before…"

"He must be so alone out there," Emma lamented.

"Quite the contrary. He gets the best attention money can afford. He wants you to know how much he loves you…but, hopes you will understand it's best that you allow the professionals to treat his condition." Conrad realized that this fabrication strained the limits of believability, but he could always come up with something more credible later. Most importantly, his objective was to gradually push Emma's father out of her thoughts.

Emma, she had been told, like her husband, had been born and raised in Winona, lived in a neat little two-story home only a few blocks from Conrad's house near Windom Park, and went to the same elementary school as he did. The two of them were classmates in both first and third grades (he even gave her some authentic Washington School teacher's names) and later—both attended Winona Cotter High School—class of 1923. Emma, he informed, was Catholic and he a Lutheran—"But my dear father valued a Christian education and insisted I attend the parochial high school." At times she puzzled and probed with questions. "Yes, we are both thirty-three years old, my dear," he assured over her doubt. "Even though you look much younger, and are far better looking, than I am. Your husband is not what most women would consider a handsome man."

Emma blushed, then laughed at the notion, "You have the nicest brown eyes when you take off your glasses, Conrad." Then she added with a noticeable pout. "Thirty-three? Maybe I should learn to drink coffee—don't you agree?"

Both laughed at the notion.

Conrad's fantasy about their chance meeting years after graduating from Cotter High School, when both had relocated in Ohio, was something out of popular pulp fiction magazines. "When we saw each other again both of us knew immediately, Emma"..."We had a small church wedding with just our friends because of your mother's passing only months before"..."Your friend Sandy Jones—came all the way from Winona to be your maid of honor"... "Not having a reception was your idea, Emma. I agreed, of course"..."In the Pocono's of Pennsylvania. We had the greatest honeymoon any two people could ever hope to have"...And on went the colorful stories.

Although Conrad had made this Western trip in the past, never had he enjoyed his travel more wondrously. Seeing the varied landscape—especially the majestic Rocky Mountains—through Emma's eyes was unlike anything he'd experienced before. The breathtaking woman at his side was becoming the companion of Conrad's most unbelievable dreams; she was enthralled with everything she saw and full of questions for him to answer. It was like writing a novel and creating all the sets in advance of the film that would follow.

"My father was right, Conrad," Emma blurted as the train sped through the desolated countryside of Eastern Washington. "A vacation is what I needed more than anything. My headache hasn't bothered me at all for these past three days. Maybe having you restore my memory is all that I needed to make me feel well again. Thank you being so patient with me."

Conrad smiled, lightly kissing her cheek. His happiness was overflowing the dam which had been blocking the river of his existence for all these years.

"And maybe it's your soothing voice. Have I ever told you how dearly I love the tone of your voice...and the fine words you use when explaining things to me."

Never before had Conrad's heart been so warmed by a compliment: Nor his spirit so enlivened by another's companionship! He contemplated an observation by Robert Lewis Stevenson that he had read somewhere long ago..."To travel hopefully is a better thing than to arrive..."

Yet Conrad constantly wondered about the perils and pitfalls awaiting their new life together in California. And behind his wondering was a well of worry, shame, and even guilt. When might Emma awaken? Or, would she? What might happen if she did? Would she hate him? Could this heinous crime ever be forgiven? There seemed to Conrad's warped thinking, a helpless aspect to this abduction that nobody might ever be able to comprehend. All he could do now was placate himself with the wondrous enjoyment of these stolen moments. If there were going to be dire consequences at some unknown point in the future—it would all have been worth the price he would pay. These few days had given him more joy than he ever imagined possible: He would willingly pay the consequences if, or when, the time came.

Yet…maybe, maybe this woman would always be Emma. Conrad lit another cigarette, finished the last aspirins from his bottle. Maybe…

At night, while Emma slept, Conrad would watch her for hours. Once he gently stroked her soft blonde hair, breathed in her scent. When his tired eyes were not glued upon his wife, Conrad absorbed himself in the psychology books he'd purchased before leaving St. Paul. Freud was fascinating. Why had so many critics misjudged and maligned the pioneer psychoanalyst all these years? Freud's analysis of the subconscious mind and repressed memories were revolutionary. Yet, despite the profound insights, Freud's theoretical constructs did not mesh with Conrad's own perception of what had probably happened to Emma.

Adler, formerly a colleague of Freud's, wrote about 'post traumatic stress disorder' but in this particular book, was far too vague on amnesia to shed any light on Emma's condition. Carl Jung's elaborate theories were tedious reading and the psychologists conceptual framework of 'archetypes' seemed more spiritually based than empirically scientific to Conrad's manner of thinking.

In Seattle, after purchasing tickets to Los Angeles for Mr. and Mrs. John Anderson, Conrad perused every major paper he could find in the depot's newsstand for any reports of a missing woman in St. Paul. Although no Twin Cities papers were available in the station, at least the disappearance had not become national news in these first four days.

On the Portland-Pacific Zephyr, Emma became noticeably restless, agitated. For long minutes she had nothing to say, which was unusual for her. Conrad, ever attentive to any mood swing, inquired gently, "Are you feeling well, Emma?"

Emma nodded without reply.

"Perhaps the long journey is wearing you down, my dear. Can I get you anything?"

"Nothing right now. I was thinking of my father, that's all."

Conrad allowed the matter to rest.

The green landscape of Oregon was behind them and the blighting front of gray ocean weather had passed. Early morning sun and blue sky seemed to perk Emma's spirits. "Where are we now, Conrad?"

Conrad enjoyed explaining the changing geographic settings. "We've been in California for more than an hour I think. Look up ahead."

The gigantic Sequoia trees north of Mendicino strained her neck as she stared from the window, "You must tell me more about California, Conrad— are there sharks in the ocean? Is our home too large for me to manage? And the people…will your dear friend Darold like me?" Emma frowned, "I'm getting nervous, Conrad. My headache has returned—not as bad as it was before, but…"

"Don't worry, my dear. Everything's going to be just fine." Conrad reviewed the spurt of questions; "Don't worry about sharks…it's the sea lions we must be wary of."

Emma frowned, "What?"

"I'm only kidding," he laughed at his attempted humor. Maybe tomorrow we can find some sea lions. They're only big seals, you know—harmless creatures. We can feed them fish from a rock outcropping not far from our home."

Emma reveled in the thought. "Oh, Conrad, we must do that."

Taking her hand, Conrad continued, "As I've told you many times, Emma, you will be a queen and our home will be your castle. Don't worry your pretty little head about any housekeeping chores. And Darold, my goodness, Darold will simply love you!"

During the brief San Francisco morning layover, Conrad called ahead to Darold Hurley at Sunset Shores. Darold, anxious to meet them at Union Station in Los Angeles, admitted "I'll probably be an hour early. You cannot imagine my excitement, Conrad. I've got a wonderful surprise for the two of you when you arrive," he said. But Darold would not tell his employer what the surprise was.

"Darold, you know that I'm not one for surprises. And don't forget that Emma will be exhausted."

"Conrad...remember that night we first talked—years ago? When I told you to 'reach for the stars'? Well, somehow, I have the feeling that you're doing that. It makes me so very...*proud*. Yes, Conrad—proud is the best word."

"I'm feeling proud of myself, Darold," he lied. Although happier than he could ever remember being, proud was the last word Conrad might choose to describe his feelings. "Now, Darold...I must ask you, is this surprise something I should tell Emma about? Everything out here is new to her, you know, and I couldn't bear anything upsetting."

Darold considered Conrad's legitimate concern, "Only a reception, sir...our staff is so happy you understand. And, it's scheduled for tomorrow evening so the two of you will have plenty of time to recuperate from your travels."

The news was mildly disturbing, but Conrad did not have the heart to squelch Darold's well intended plans. "Just so long as it's nothing too festive."

Darold paused, "Very well. Is there anything I can take care of before I leave for the station?"

Conrad's thoughts had become centered on Emma's well being. Considering that she might be delighted with a new dress for Darold's little party he suggested, "Perhaps you could arrange for a seamstress. Emma's wardrobe is limited and she'll probably need a lightweight outfit."

"Conrad!"

Conrad was dozing after too many nights with only a few hours of sleep and Emma's appeal startled him. "What is it, my dear?" Almost every minute of his life these past days held the fear that Emma might awaken from her amnesia. "What?" He became rigid in his seat, met her eyes..."Is something the matter?"

"Palm trees, Conrad! I see hundreds of palm trees."

THE BELLE OF THE BALL

California's early September sunshine bestowed the Friday afternoon with a radiance that Emma could hardly believe was real. A smile of anticipation shown in her wide eyes as her gaze flashed across the landscape of rolling brown mountains, orchards, and ravines as they approached Los Angeles. Her headache was gone…"It's like a picture book, Conrad," she exclaimed, her nose pressing against the window. "Now I can't wait to meet Darold and your friends, see the ocean and beaches, your big house. I'm not even nervous any more. I think I'm living a dream of some kind. How much longer?"

"It's *our* house, my dear. And, we're almost to Los Angeles. Only another hour or so before we arrive. Aren't you exhausted from five days on the train?" In the back of her thoughts she wondered why she slept alone while Conrad read his books or simply watched the passing scenery. At times she considered her husband's occasionally detached behavior, as well as his lack of affection almost, brotherly. Perhaps he would explain why he dozed at the window rather than slept in their bed later.

"Oh—not any more." Turning from her window gaze, Emma met his eyes, "You've hardly had a wink of sleep in days, Conrad. You're the one who must be tired."

Conrad had not slept more than a few sketchy hours since leaving St. Paul. Instead, he read books and newspapers, worked crosswords, smoked one cigarette after another (since purchasing a carton of Camels in Seattle), and had drunk countless cups of coffee. When Emma was sleeping he watched her toss and turn fitfully, and wondered about her dreams. Sometimes he wept over what he was doing: Tears of shame and tears of happiness were in equal measure. All the while, Conrad feared that Emma might awaken from her amnesia and bring his fantasy to a catastrophic end. Yet, the further from Minnesota they traveled, the safer he felt. None of the Western newspapers he had scanned along the way carried any reports of a missing Minnesota woman.

"What's the matter, Conrad? You're not looking well." Emma took his clammy hand in her own. "Perhaps it's all those cigarettes?" She smiled at the statement-question, and added, "When did you begin smoking? I can't remember seeing you smoke until—where was it that we stopped? Was it in Seattle?"

Conrad removed his spectacles, "You're quite perceptive, my dear Emma; it was in Seattle. I've only recently returned to smoking, and with all the coffee—well, it is probably a bad combination for my health."

As the Portland-Pacific Zephyr approached the huge Los Angeles Union station, Conrad's face betrayed an apprehension that had dogged him since his conversation with Darold Hurley from San Francisco hours before. He should have pressed Darold for more details about the surprise reception but didn't want to spoil his manager's fun. Perhaps his friend had invited a few of the neighbors and planned a small banquet in the spacious dining room.

Conrad decided to prepare Emma for what might eventuate, "Oh…I almost forgot, we are going to have a little homecoming party tomorrow evening at Sunset. Some of my neighbors are going to be there to meet you, Emma. Wonderful people, you'll see for yourself." The fact that his neighbors were only vaguely familiar was just as well—nobody would have questions or doubts about his recent 'marriage'. "I'm not quite sure what Darold's got up his sleeve, Emma."

"I'll be able to meet some of your friends, then," her eyes sparked in anticipation.

"I'm sure it will be a small affair with only a few old friends from Santa Monica, Darold is quite excited about all this you know." Conrad almost choked on the word 'friends'— nobody ever visited the Phelps estate.

"That would be wonderful. I think I like parties…don't I, Conrad? You told me that I enjoyed being around people—at least, much more than you do."

Conrad had a feeling that Emma would light up a room of strangers and charm them off their feet. He surprised himself with his response. "That's all in the past, my dear. I mean my discomfort with people. Being that we're married now, I'm going to make some changes."

Emma gave Conrad a puzzled expression, "I'm sorry, I haven't thought to ask—but how long have we been married? Maybe you've already told me, but—"

Would he have to conjure another bit of history? But Conrad was certain he'd already explained the details of their wedding. Was Emma beginning to forget *their* story? His notebook was under a stack of reading materials. "Only two weeks, my dear. Back in Ohio. Remember, it was a small wedding at the church and you didn't want to have a reception at the time?"

"Before the accident? I still get so confused."

"Yes, my dear." He gave her hand a gentle squeeze, "In no time at all it will be as if nothing happened. All you need is some quiet time to relax and enjoy yourself. Anyhow, the little party that Darold has planned will make up for the one we didn't have in Ohio."

Emma nodded absently without comment. Conrad had been so helpful and patient since...? At times it seemed like years since the accident and at others, only days ago. Conrad had assured her many times that once in California everything would come back to her. All the memories of her family and childhood, along with a recall of their wonderful years of courtship. Still, it all seemed so very strange—muddled in her thoughts like an endless fog.

Darold Hurley nervously paced the Union Station platform. He was indeed an hour early. Conrad had reminded him that he was leery of surprises and hoped the affair was "nothing too festive." What Darold had planned, however, was far more extravagant than anything he'd ever arranged at Sunset. He bit at his lip trying to recall exactly what he'd told Conrad in their earlier conversation. Darold had been deliberately vague about details but had mentioned that this was going to be the "happiest occasion in years!"

Watching the sleek Zephyr locomotive crawl to a stop, Darold mumbled a consoling reminder to himself, "My heart was in the right place...even if I might have erred in judgment." Nothing that had been planned could be undone now. Darold Hurley was prepared to face the consequences if his employer was disappointed. But Darold had a way of consoling Conrad, of making him see things from a more positive perspective. It was Mrs. Phelps, and her reactions, that troubled him the most. He tried to smile though his growing torment. What would she be like? What kind of woman would find Conrad attractive enough to marry?

He vaguely remembered his friend saying that Emma was beautiful. Puzzled, his mind could not help conjuring an image of someone more matronly, domineering—even severe.

As the passengers stepped out onto the massive platform, Darold spotted the two travelers, waved from beside the luggage cart and smiled.

His sense of protocol suggested he first greet Conrad's new bride first. Stepping forward as they approached, he hailed: "Welcome to California, Mrs. Phelps! I'm Darold Hurley, ma'am—" Darold's jaw had noticeablely dropped only halfway through his brief introduction, "...So very delighted to make your acquaintance." He extended his large hand graciously, hoping to conceal his surprise. Mrs. Phelps was beautiful! Incredibly so. How gravely he had misjudged in forming his mental picture of this woman. With that realization, however, an inevitable and painful suspicion rushed into his thoughts. A 'gold digger'—what else could possibly explain the unlikely match? His deep-set gray eyes turned from Mrs. Phelps to Conrad, quickly offering a hand shake, "So good to see you again, sir."

"Darold, I've told Emma so much about you," Conrad offered weakly, while noting that his friend's eyebrows wore the strangest expression. It almost seemed to him that Darold were brooding over something. Conrad chose not to inquire if anything was wrong.

Brusquely, it appeared to Conrad, Darold stepped a few feet back and nodded, "If you will excuse me for a very few minutes, sir, I'll have the car loaded and we can be off to Sunset. I've reserved a table and beverages in the lounge while you and Mrs. Phelps wait, sir." Before taking his absence, Darold added, "And, the seamstress you requested is expecting Mrs. Phelps' arrival as we speak, sir."

Emma regarded the tall, distinguished looking man dressed meticulously in a formal black suit and wearing a bow tie. "Excuse me, Mr. Hurley, did you say a seamstress...waiting for me?"

"Yes, ma'am, just as your husband instructed earlier. He suggested you could use a California party gown." Darold looked from her to Conrad, and back to the woman not quite certain what else to say.

"What forever for? I already have a trunk full of new dresses." Emma turned her befuddled attention to Conrad standing awkwardly with his hands thrust deeply into his trouser pockets. Her tone was almost indignant, "How can we possibly afford any more clothing?"

Darold's mouth dropped ever so slightly at the woman's spirited question. Her pouted expression, however, was deadly serious—her voice almost girlish.

Trying to justify himself, Conrad stammered almost apologetically, "Just something new for the party, my dear. I want you to look your very best, and be comfortable, of course."

Emma shook her head, "I just cannot allow you to spend any more money on my wardrobe. I have a lovely new dress still in the Dayton's wrappings, Conrad."

Conrad, hoping to avoid a scene acquiesced with a wan smile, "Whatever you wish, Emma."

Turning toward an embarrassed Darold Hurley, Emma said, "Wouldn't you agree with me, Mr. Hurley? Spending money unnecessarily is foolish."

Caught in what he realized to be a thorny situation, Darold shrugged his shoulders and offered Mr. Phelps an ambiguous smile, "Perhaps Mrs. Phelps is right, sir?" Conrad would be upset enough when he learned of Darold's reception arrangements, so perhaps this woman might be a needed ally when the time came. "I mean, sir…we can always send the seamstress home."

"You're right, of course, Darold. Emma will be just fine. She will look lovely in any one of her dresses. I was just being impulsive, I guess."

Gently clasping her husband's elbow, Emma humored, "If you don't mind, I shall ask the seamstress to sew me a new bathing suit, Conrad. I can't wait to swim in the ocean!"

Relieved at the simple resolution, Darold excused himself a second time. "Very good, ma'am. I'll have you both at Sunset in time to enjoy the late afternoon on the beach. It's truly the most beautiful part of the day on the ocean front, Mrs. Phelps."

"Will you join us for a swim, then, Mr. Hurley?"

Feeling cornered once more by the spirited woman, Darold turned again to Mr. Phelps for some cue as to how he might respond to the innocent but grossly inappropriate invitation.

Conrad attempted to spare his manager any further embarrassment, "I'm sure Darold has a hundred chores to do when we get home, my dear. Maybe another time, when Mr. Hurley is not so busy."

Obviously relieved, Darold nodded respectfully, dabbing his white handkerchief at his forehead.

But…

Emma winked at the tall, perspiring man, "I'll help you with the chores so you can join us, Mr. Hurley. I know that you're one of Conrad's dearest friends…I so want you to be one of mine as well."

As he walked to the train's luggage car, Darold could not help but shake his head in disbelief. Mrs. Phelps was like no other woman he had ever met. And, most certainly, she was not the gold digger of his first impression. What a breath of fresh air Emma Phelps was going bring to Sunset Shores. His amusement could not be contained...swimming? The three of them? Darold nearly laughed out loud, "How in creation did Conrad Phelps ever find this incredible woman?"

Yet, Darold was perplexed—and wasn't quite certain why. There was something most unusual about Emma Phelps—something even more baffling about this unlikely union of opposites.

~

While arranging the reception on less than one week's advance notice, Darold Hurley had, nevertheless, given impeccable attention to every detail. The Phelps mansion had not hosted a party of any kind in nearly a decade, and was becoming regarded by many in the oceanfront community as the 'Sunscorned Shores' estate. The massive gates off the Pacific Coastal Highway were always locked and signs of any human activity about the verdant property were rarely seen. To some local observers, the house was regarded as haunted by some Phelps family ghost. Yet, its Santa Monica neighbors were aware that the huge Spanish-style villa was meticulously maintained and staffed year round.

So, when invitations were hand-delivered to nearly one hundred guests, news of the Saturday evening affair began to spread rapidly throughout celebrity conscious Los Angeles, and was even briefly mentioned on the *Times* 'Society' page. Most of those invited were strangers to Darold Hurley—but, people reputed (he'd read most issues of *Variety*) to be avid Hollywood party-goers. For the first time in recent memory, the massive wrought iron gates to Sunset Shores would be unlocked to carefully-chosen neighbors and celebrated visitors.

Darold used every connection he had developed over the years. Saturday's final preparations would be supervised by the professional house staff of Samuel Goldwyn (Goldwyn's manservant was an old friend of Darold's) who were well accustomed to lavishly entertaining California's social dignitaries.

Darold had employed Richarde Valeri, a celebrated Los Angeles chef, to prepare the menu and manage the expanded kitchen staff. Valeri's entrees would include Pacific Ocean salmon from Alaska, filet mignon from select Texas beef cattle, and Montana pheasant. Among the choice seafood hors d'oeuvres would be imported Volga River caviar, Sardi's famous shrimp cocktails, and New

England clam relishes. Buckets of chilled French vintage L'Bossier champagne were to be strategically placed throughout the living and dining rooms and a completely stocked wet bar established on the large wraparound deck overlooking the ocean below. All of the special arrangements were accomplished in four days time and at a cost of nearly twenty thousand dollars. Darold's justification of the lavish expenditure could be simply justified: The sizable Phelps annual entertainment budget had remained untouched in seven years!

After Mrs. Phelps had retired to her room, Darold explained the arrangements to Conrad over a bottle of wine while the two men relaxed in the living room. "I know this all sounds quite extravagant, Conrad, but having now met your charming wife, I almost feel a sense of vindication. I'll admit to being quite worried that I had gone too far when we talked this morning."

"I have no doubt Emma will have a wonderful time, Darold. It's me that I'm worried about. All these people I don't know. I don't want my wife to get the impression that I'm some manner of social misfit. What will I find to talk with these people about?"

"I understand your concerns, Conrad. But, I'm sure you will manage just fine. You're highly intelligent, an expert on books, and have some corporate experiences...you're every bit the equal to anyone I've invited to the party."

"Nice of you to say, but I don't have much social experience. I've been so reclusive all these years." Conrad forced a weak smile, "I'll need some coaching, Darold. You're experienced in these things."

Darold laughed at the admission, "You're going to be with total strangers. Just stretch your imagination, that's all. And if you choose to acknowledge being a recluse...that might even have some mysterious appeal to these gregarious folks."

Conrad had an idea, "Pretend you don't know me, Darold, and I'll introduce myself." Both men stood for the spontaneous enactment, "Con Phelps, glad you could join us tonight..." Conrad attempted to project a confident voice, but found himself laughing at himself.

Straight-faced, Darold offered advice, "I would discourage using 'Con'—people may well have a negative perception of cons!" Both men laughed at the possibility. "And the handshake is so critical, Conrad...not so limp—now, give me a firmer grip."

Darold smiled approvingly, "Much better. I think your tone of voice and your demeanor worked quite well... Let's try your introduction once more."

"You will be making many of the introductions for me, won't you, Darold?"

"Quite right—I will. But much of the time you will be on your own."

Conrad nodded, "Very well, then, I'll go through this again."

For nearly an hour they practiced scenarios.

"I think I can pull this off, Darold," Conrad acknowledged.

"You're ready," Darold lifted his glass in toast, "To your *new life*, Conrad. Now that I've met Emma, I cannot help but believe nothing will ever be the same for you—nor the same around here, either." Darold laughed deeply over changes already experienced, "I hate to admit it…but before this afternoon, I haven't had a swim in years. Who would have thought it possible—the three of us playing like children on the beach? Emma is almost magical—perhaps you've found yourself a leprechaun without even realizing it, Conrad my friend!"

Emma Phelps slept late into the Saturday morning. Having spent two hours on the beach with Conrad and Darold the afternoon before, the new bride had become extremely exhausted and had retired soon after dinner. When she awoke, Emma found her husband sitting in the chair near her bed. "I'm so excited to meet your California friends, Conrad. Darold told me that he expects a house full of people tonight."

Conrad hadn't slept for more than an hour in the adjacent bedroom the night before. He and Darold had stayed up until after midnight reviewing the details of the elaborate reception. Conrad was nervous despite Darold's every assurance that the event would unfold flawlessly. The more he thought about it, the more Conrad realized he was actually warming to the occasion. His new life would have to be different, he well realized, and the reclusive patterns of old would no longer work satisfactorily. "As I've told you, Emma, don't be surprised if very few of the guests remember me. California society is that way—people are so fickle and self-absorbed. Everybody lives in their own little world out here. And, I've been away for a long time."

In fact, the only familiar face in the crowd might be that of Gerald Sweeney—a former Minnesotan and friend of his late father. Sweeney, nearly seventy, lived up the coast from the Phelps estate and was somewhat of a recluse himself.

"That's okay, Conrad. I enjoy meeting new people." Darold had told her the day before that she would "charm the daylights out of every one" and be the "belle of the ball" (which she didn't really understand and had forgotten to ask Darold to explain). "I'm going to be the belle of the ball tonight, Conrad," she blurted exuberantly from the prop of pillows behind her head.

Conrad could not contain his laugh, "Where did you get that notion, Emma?"

"Darold told me so."

"I'm sure he's right about that, my dear. You will turn every head in the room, I'm sure." That reality, however, troubled him. What would people think? Conrad was a small and uncomely man whose only claim to notoriety was his incredible wealth. Inherited wealth. Nobody at the party would know what he did for a living, where he spent his long absences, or who he was as a human being. Everybody there would have their familiar 'label' attachments—business, politics, entertainment—while the host, in their 'status judgmental' eyes, would be somewhat of an enigma. How would he answer all their inevitable questions? "Shipping", he would confidently tell them when introducing himself while remaining as vague as possible while doing so. He would be cautious not to mention Minnesota any more than absolutely necessary. And, how many of those present would be old friends of his father? What might they know of Conrad Senior's diverse enterprises? Conrad's thoughts had been tormented by 'what if's' for days. By far the scariest 'what if' of them all being…What if his Emma suddenly awakened? What if something dramatically unforeseen happened in the midst of all these people?

"What does that mean?"

"What's that, sweetheart?" The affectionate reference slipped from his mouth for the first time as he started from his momentary reverie.

Emma gave him a puzzled look. 'Sweetheart?' Conrad had never used that word before. Yet, there was a familiarity about it. Had her father called her sweetheart…or—? For a long minute she said nothing.

"I'm sorry, what does *what* mean, Emma? I was daydreaming"

"Oh. Belle of the ball. Is that something important, Conrad?"

"It means that you will undoubtedly be the loveliest woman at the party tonight. Darold's prediction will certainly come true."

And, Emma was just that!

The guests began arriving shortly after seven to the 'black tie' affair. A sit-down banquet had been scheduled for nine o'clock and by that time nearly a hundred guests swarmed about the mansion. Darold's efforts to provide all possible comfort and convenience to the overflow crowd had not gone unnoticed.

"I'll never understand how you managed to pull this off, Darold," Conrad complimented his friend. "I never realized that Sunset could accommodate so many people—and so comfortably at that."

"Everybody seems to be enthralled with your home, Conrad," he smiled his own satisfaction. "Perhaps we can do something like this again. Are you having a good time?"

"I think I'm actually surprising myself, Darold," Conrad said with a measure of pride in his voice. "And isn't Emma splendid?"

Darold had noticed that Conrad's eyes never left his lovely wife.

Vivacious and charming, Emma met everybody with a cheerful and unpretentious warmth that most guests had rarely experienced in the Los Angeles party circuit. Conrad had spent some time that afternoon explaining how she might answer questions posed by their guests. She was from Ohio (where they had been married), educated at Oberlin College (probably nobody would have heard of the small Catholic institution), and had been employed as an interior decorator in Shaker Heights near Cleveland. "But Conrad, I don't remember having done any of these things," she protested.

"In California everybody is whatever they want to be, Emma," he explained. "Darold told me that we simply pretend at being whomever or whatever we want; that's the real enjoyment of it all." When she understood what Conrad was suggesting, Emma laughed, "That sounds like great fun for both of us! Who and what at are you going to be?"

And, fun it was! Emma (having had some additional coaching from Darold that afternoon) behaved admirably, presenting herself without any California tainted airs as a genuine, if not whimsical, young Midwestern woman. Even Conrad was admirable, at times becoming almost boastfully full of himself. In one gathering he was a shipping magnate, at another an import-exports franchiser, still others left their conversations with Conrad having the distinct impression that real estate was his forte. To a Hollywood film editor named Danford Mitchell, Conrad suggested that he was back in California to consider bankrolling some movies and was hoping to find some intriguing scripts. "When in Rome…" he said on more than one occasion. While being introduced to California's popular U.S. Senator, Gilbert Stavnes, Conrad even offered to make a generous contribution to the politician's next campaign. "We've needed a strong voice out in Washington for a long time, and you've given us that, Gil." Conrad used the Senator's first name as if they were old friends.

Never far from the host, Darold tugged at Conrad's elbow and whispered in his ear, "Take it easy, Conrad. Excuse my vulgarity but you're getting over your ankles in…bull droppings!"

Full of himself at the moment, Conrad laughed almost heartily, and then cupped his hand near Darold's ear, "What if I actually did all the things I've been talking about? Wouldn't that be something?"

Emma, dressed in her new plum colored *Schiaperelli* crepe dress from Dayton's with pearl accessories, looked strikingly sophisticated. In that she was rarely asked about where she was from or where she had been educated, she made her own conversational initiatives with the guests she encountered while mingling widely throughout the house. When asked by Governor Stavnes' wife about her future plans, she said, "First, I'm going to find some hungry sea lions, then help my friend Darold rearrange the house, and do my best to become a Californian, that's all." Her unexpected candor came out of nowhere and brought laughs to all those gathered around her.

"Have you ever thought of becoming an actress, Mrs. Phelps?" A slender woman with diamonds on several fingers, asked. "Movies have become Southern California's greatest attraction, you realize."

"Not at all. That's for beautiful and talented people, I think. I'm just going to hike along the ocean and swim most of the time. And Conrad says that we must do some more traveling when time allows."

"Don't sell yourself short, my dear. I'd simply love to introduce you to some of the Hollywood people—like Sam Goldwyn or Frank Capra. You're gorgeous Emma, and spirited, too."

"We'll just have to have lunch one of these days soon," said Mrs. Gilbert Stavnes. "You simply must meet some of my women friends."

Conrad smiled approvingly at everything his wife had to say—and the wistful manner in which she expressed herself. There was little doubt in his, or anybody's mind, that Emma was truly the 'belle of the ball'. At one point, after their scrumptious meal had been served, she whispered in his ear, "This is so delightful, Conrad. I can remember being at a big party before…somewhere? Later you'll have to tell me about when that might have been."

Conrad's face drained of color. "Some other time, my dear," was all he could say. What memories still lurked at the edges of her awareness, he wondered? What happenstance might trigger a return?

As the ornate pendulum clock near the foyer swept into the early morning hours, and several of the guests were beginning to offer their 'thank yous' and repeating their 'congratulations' to the hosts, a sudden hush engulfed the living room. Two men, one of them obviously intoxicated, had apparently crashed the Phelps' party. The astonishment, however, quickly became a hubbub of conversation which spread like fire through the crowded room.

A heavyset, toothy man standing at Conrad's elbow stood on his toes to see what was happening; "God damn, Phelps, you sure know how to throw a party," he exclaimed with a poke to the ribs of his host. Slurring his delight he added, "How in the hell did you pull this off?"

"I'm as surprised as you are," Conrad replied in a stunned disbelief of his own.

Standing with his arm draped over the shoulder of his companion near the center of the Phelps' living room, was the most familiar celebrity in American movies. The handsome star had obviously been celebrating something himself that night and wanted to do some boasting, "We'll start the actual filming in January. And, let me tell you all that it's going to be the biggest production Hollywood's ever seen." Then with the smile that had charmed the hearts of millions of movie-goers, he added, "Even bigger than my friend Vic's *Wizard of Oz*!" Vic was Victor Fleming, one of filmdom's most celebrated directors. Fleming stood beside the disheveled actor, reveling in the attention the two of them were getting.

"Selznick's going to spend millions and the sets are going to be like a rebuilding of Atlanta right in the middle of MGM's studios. And when they shoot the fire...hell, you'll see the flames all the way up here!"

From a distance, Conrad looked on in near paralysis. What was he supposed to do under these bizarre and totally unexpected circumstances? His eyes scanned the room for Darold Hurley. Before he could react to the developing commotion his visitors were creating, Conrad saw the throng begin to part as Emma, her dress pulled above her ankles to prevent her tripping, strode toward the movie star. "Who are you—and what do you think you're doing by making a spectacle of yourself in my house?"

Conrad, recognizing the actor from newspaper photographs, felt his knees begin to buckle at the immediate uproar of laughter. How could Emma not know...? It was almost unthinkable!

Confused, Emma wondered what she had said that seemed so funny to everybody in the room. Perhaps the intoxicated ruffian's boasting about some fire was humorous to those who knew him, but not to Emma. "You've had far too much to drink."

The handsome man was clearly as amused as everybody else in the room. "Too much to drink?" He reached for a half emptied bottle of champagne resting on the coffee table, put the neck in his mouth and guzzled the remaining contents to the wild amusement of all. Then, turning to his companion and squinting his world renowned grin, he pronounced, "Victor, I think we've just met our perfect Scarlett!"

Everybody roared!

Emma, startled over the boisterous commotion, took the bottle dangling loosely from the man's hand, "That will be just about enough! Please tell me what you're doing here…and, what this fire business is all about before I have my husband and Darold escort you out that door!" Emma gave a sweeping gesture toward the wide entry foyer.

By now, the toothy man at Conrad's side was nearly doubled over in his laughter, "You staged this, didn't you, Phelps? I've never—in all my life…seen such a performance. Never!"

Before Conrad could begin making his way through the growing circle surrounding his wife and the movie star—Emma repeated her threat, "This minute!"

Trying to contain his own hilarity, the movie icon offered his hand to the distraught Emma Phelps, "My friends call me Clark, ma'am. And your friends call you—?"

Emma only glowered as the room erupted in more laughter.

"I'm sorry if my behavior has unsettled you, ma'am. But Victor and I saw all the cars lining your driveway and had to stop in to say hello to you folks. That's all."

The actor covered his eyes at the quick camera flash from somewhere in the room. Annoyed, he shouted "…What the hell's…"

"And the fire, Clark? Tell Emma about Selznick's movie." Shouted a bulbous nosed man nearby. We've all heard that you're playing Rhett, but who's doing Scarlett?"

"And who's directing?" Implored a red haired woman from the front of the tightly forming circle.

"Yes, tell us Clark! Everybody's dying to know what's going on with the production." The diamond fingered woman, almost giddy over the scene, shouted from somewhere in the middle of the crowd.

Conrad's hoarse voice shouted over the din, "Get that man!"

Unnoticed, a *Variety* gossip columnist who had been following the two celebrities all evening had entered through the open front door with his camera hidden under a loose jacket. Jessup Bray was witnessing what might become the story of this season unfold before his eyes. For a few minutes he lingered at the edges of the crowd (committing the incredible dialogue between the actor and hostess to memory) before slipping into the perfect position for his career photo. When Clark Gable took the lovely blonde woman's hand and introduced himself, his quick flash and pop caught everybody's attention—while noticeably irritating the actor. With catlike instinct, Jessup Bray moved back away from the crowd and slithered out the open door, racing all the way to his car parked nearly a hundred yards up the winding entry drive.

His photo and scoop story would be referred to as the 'shot heard around Hollywood' the following week!

"Oh, no...!" Conrad Phelps' moan could almost be heard above the din. Heads turned in his direction, "Where did that flash come from? Find that man with the camera!" But his appeal was to no apparent avail. "I'll pay a thousand dollars for that picture of my wife and Clark Gable," Conrad was heard to tell some people nearby. "Get him...anybody..." Conrad was beginning to panic. Darold...Darold Hurley—wherever you are. Stop him before he gets away!"

Hurley, more amused than most, had been watching the episode from an alcove off the living room several feet away. Being taller than most, he had seen the entire episode and had caught a quick glimpse of the stranger with the camera as the reporter pushed forcefully toward the door. Too many people stood between Darold and the outside entry for him to make a quick pursuit.

The reporter had already reached the front porch when Darold heard Conrad calling his name. Not certain what he should do, Hurley pursued the reporter, running as fast as his long strides would take him toward the highway. But by the time he approached the open gate, all he could see were the taillights of a dark sedan speeding away.

(Roland Ashe and Martin Crumbley, the two gate security personnel hired for the evening's party, were playing poker for matchsticks in the stone entry building).

~

At three in the morning, a distraught Conrad quietly opened the door to Emma's bedroom, and quietly found his chair near her bed. He would rather watch her sleep than sleep himself. The evening's reception rolled through his thoughts like a horror movie in slow motion. Everything has been so perfect until…that egotistical actor arrived. How could he have ever prepared for something so unexpected? He couldn't have—the milk had been spilled and damage control seemed all that he and Darold would be able to do.

One of the party guests had informed Conrad that the man with the camera had a *Variety* card tucked into the band of his felt hat. Conrad and Darold would follow up on the lead the next morning—or Monday at the latest. In the meantime, Conrad would hope against hope that newspaper publicity of any kind could still be avoided.

Emma's naivety that evening had been far more charming than demeaning. People might wonder why such an apparently 'worldly' woman had not recognized the Hollywood movie star, but the fact that she didn't made her all the more endearing. Even Mr. Gable admitted there might not be a better suited person in all of Hollywood to portray Scarlett O'Hara than Emma Phelps!

As he watched Emma turn from her side to her stomach, hugging her pillow in her typically childlike embrace, Conrad felt an overwhelming swell of emotion. He loved this woman as he had never imagined he was capable of loving another human being. In just one week his life had changed more than it had in his entire lifetime. That pleasant thought brought a faint smile; followed by an upsetting swell of disbelief. How could anything so dreadfully wrong feel so right?

As she slept, Conrad wept. Along with his torrent of tears came a quiet murmuring of desperate prayers. Prayers for her family and loved ones, petitions to God for his own continued happiness, professions of remorse over the pain he had caused. "Please, God…don't ever take Emma away from me."

~

In the back of Conrad's thoughts, however, another scheme was already evolving. He and his wife would have to go away—far away, perhaps to Europe. Further, they might even leave the following week. His new life with Emma was destined to become one of fugitive survival.

'WHERE'S SCARLETT?'

While Emma lay tanning on the beach below the sprawling mansion, Conrad and Darold shared a decanter of coffee. "Everything was going so well, Darold," Conrad recalled, "and I was having the time of my life hobnobbing with all those people...while Emma was, as you predicted—the absolute belle of the ball."

Darold nodded, smiled at Conrad's lingering stress; "Despite the bizarre circumstances, Mr. Gable was charmed by Emma. He told me so after the ruckus over the *Variety* reporter. He even apologized, offering to help us locate the photographer," Darold said with his gray eyes focused far out to the sea. The man-servant was repeating information he had shared with Conrad during the hours after the party, and still puzzling over his friend's overreaction. Was Conrad too overprotective?

Distraught, Conrad remained unforgiving. "Gable ruined the party. If he hadn't crashed our party none of this would have happened. Obnoxious Hollywood celebrities—that's what they were. And, if I had a gun..." Conrad shook his head at the absurdity, "I was about to say that I'd shoot those two security people at the gate. If we could have stopped that photographer and confiscated his camera, I wouldn't be nearly as upset as I am. As it is..."

Darold appeased, "We'll find the culprit and get the picture he took, Conrad. Money talks louder around here than anyplace in the world." Yet Darold remained confused by his friend's consuming obsession to get the photo before it appeared in any newspaper. Emma hadn't expressed any upset over the episode, she even laughed along with Mr. Gable at their humorous encounter. The actor's charm had won her over. Darold recalled Emma telling Gable afterwards that she would ask her husband to take her to all of the actor's films. "And you must come over and go swimming with us one of these days when you're not so busy in Hollywood."

For long minutes nothing was said between the two men. Conrad had left his "as it is" hanging in the air without hope of resolution.

"I'll make some calls this afternoon and locate the *Variety* office tomorrow morning. If your offer of a substantial reward isn't enough, perhaps the threat of a lawsuit will be what it takes to make those people think twice about publishing the photograph."

Conrad snuffed out another cigarette, got up from his chair and walked to the railing. With his back to Darold, he finished the thought which had been lingering in his mind throughout his sleepless night. "Darold, I haven't told you this before, and do so now in the strictest confidence…but—" He paused a long moment almost as if to catch his breath. "Emma has a health issue. Some time ago she was in an automobile accident and she still gets terrible headaches. We've seen some specialists at the Mayo Clinic in Minnesota," he lied, "And they've suggested we see a Doctor Helling in London. He's some kind of neurological expert. It's affected her memory to some extent and we're both quite concerned about it."

Darold stepped to Conrad's side, placed a large hand on the much smaller man's shoulder. He had not acknowledged his suspicion that something wasn't quite right with the woman who had so charmed him during their brief acquaintance. There had been moments when Darold regarded Emma's behavior as that of a teen age girl—her naivety, pure innocence, and uninhibited spirit. "I'm sorry to hear that, Conrad. Have you made any arrangements with this doctor?"

"Yes, only last week, Darold. But I haven't told Emma yet. Already she's fallen in love with this place far more than I imagined she would, and I don't know how she'll react to taking another trip so soon."

"She does love the ocean, there's no doubting that. Just look at her, Conrad," Darold gestured outward. Emma was delightfully splashing in the rolling waves—almost like a little girl.

Conrad's sympathetic smile at the sight evidenced his torment, "As much as I dread doing so; I'm going to have to make travel arrangements tomorrow. Our appointment in London is a month from this Tuesday." His head ached worse than it had the night before. As he had expected, his gravest sin would spawn the commission of thousands more. His life could well become a pattern of running and hiding, covering his—and Emma's—tracks along the way. Conrad's inexorable future was fraught with both the dangers of being discovered for his crime, and Emma's awakening from her bondage of amnesia.

As Conrad watched his playful bride diving into an onrushing wave, a lump swelled in his throat: "I'll give her the news this afternoon, Darold." His eyes met those of his friend, "I might need your help with this, Darold. If you could encourage her to leave Sunset for a while."

"I understand completely, sir," Darold rarely used the formal reference any longer, "whatever I can do in Emma's behalf—"

Emma waved from the beach and called over the swell of the white breakers, "You must get your swim suits…I think I've spotted a sea lion near the rocks over there," her arm swept in wide gesture up the shore.

∼

Conrad had some good fortune in booking a voyage to Europe. A Long Beach company had a liner departing on Tuesday morning for New York City. Upon arrival there, after eighteen days at sea, the transfer to a Cunard liner destined for London was easily arranged.

Conrad consulted his hastily written notes. He and Emma were registered as Mr. and Mrs. Phelps out of Long Beach so that there would be no problems with getting their passports in New York. While there for the stopover, photos would be taken and visa documents arranged for several European countries. His deceptive travel plan was complicated. Many details could be taken care of during the lengthy voyage. He and Emma would clear customs in London as the Phelps', but from there, the false trail he had improvised would become difficult for anyone to follow. Tickets from London to Amsterdam would be purchased in advance, as would tickets from London to Stockholm, and London to Geneva. Hotel reservations in London would be under the name of Mr. and Mrs. John Clarke. They would remain 'Clarke's' until they arrived in Paris where Conrad would use the name Phelps again. He would arrange accommodations at the luxurious Ritz while at sea or from London. Railroad transportation from Paris to Naples under another assumed name would be taken care of later.

Conrad would travel with more than six thousand dollars in cash, and would be careful to avoid using any personal checks. Later, he gave Darold a false itinerary from London, "We'll travel to Stockholm after Emma's appointment, and from there, who knows? Perhaps Oslo or Helsinki."

The final deception was expeditiously arranged by telephone. Conrad called the Phelps Enterprises office in St. Paul and talked briefly with Calvin Hodge. "I'm going to be spending the next few weeks in Texas, Calvin. So, I won't be in touch with you for a while. Just keep an eye on things up there as always." Conrad would add a dose of flattery for the pompous manager, "I'm lucky to have you, Cal. We'll have to talk about the company…and a raise in salary, when I get back."

~

The Panama Atlantic steamship, *Sebastian*, afforded a simple luxury that Emma reluctantly settled into after earlier protests over the idea of leaving California. When told of Conrad's travel plans, Emma displayed a defiant temperament for the first time: "I'll not go anywhere until I've seen all of Clark's movies! I told him I would do so at our party. And you haven't even taken me to see Hollywood yet, Conrad."

Without divulging anything about Emma's getting medical attention, Conrad had promised her "more than you can ever imagine" at their destination. "We will see places like London and Paris; then Florence in Italy, before arriving at our villa in Sorrento. Who knows, we may even find some Clark Gable movies playing in Europe." Conrad worried to himself, however: Europe's current unrest might complicate his Italian destination. Travel arrangements from France might prove challenging, and he had not visited the Sorrento property in nearly twenty years.

Before their departure from California, Darold's pledge to the couple softened Emma's spirited disapproval. Using her first name, he cleverly supported Conrad's plan while promising—"I am going to have a small theater built downstairs, Emma, and further—I'll purchase all of Clark Gable's movies directly from the MGM studios. So when you return, we're all going to watch each and every one of them as many times as you wish. I'll even invite Mr. Gable to join us if you would like."

When asked about feeding the sea lions, Darold informed her, "September is the worst time of the year, Emma. But by next summer we should be able to find hundreds of them just up the beach."

On a busy Monday of shopping and packing, Darold drove Conrad and Emma through Hollywood and showed them the MGM studio buildings where *Gone*

With The Wind was going to be filmed. "When you return, we'll all tour the neighborhood and see the celebrities' mansions," Darold promised.

∼

"I'm sorry about how everything turned out, Emma," Conrad said from the deck chair beside his wife. His apologies had been as profuse as his promises. They had been at sea for eleven days and were now on the Atlantic, heading for the trans-ocean port of New York City. "Once we return, you'll have every opportunity to become a Californian." (Another of Emma's protests had been centered upon her ardent wish to become "every bit the Californian" as the other women at their gala party).

"I'm going to do just that, Conrad. And I'm going to have lunch with Hollywood people, too. Just like the ladies said I could."

In his efforts to refocus his wife from her California disappointment, Conrad always reverted to their travel itinerary. "The day after tomorrow you will see the Statue of Liberty with your very own eyes—the pictures in our brochures don't come close to the real thing. Can you imagine that?"

Mollified for the moment, Emma inquired, "And don't forget we're going to see real castles when we get to Europe—aren't we?"

The cruise had been mostly relaxing for Conrad and afforded an opportunity for him to catch up on the long deprived patterns of sleep he'd been accustomed to before leaving Minnesota—already nearly three weeks ago. If Conrad was unwinding, however, Emma was becoming moody, tense, and noticeably agitated. Perhaps, the main reason for her discomfiture was too much time without roots. It was also possible that the unusual nature of their relationship was beginning to stress his wife. Once when he asked her "What's wrong?" Emma responded defensively: "I might ask you the very same question, Conrad."

Conrad understood both the insinuation and the reason for her provocative tone of voice. Throughout their countless hours of conversation, all matters relating to intimacy had been carefully avoided by both of them. The issue was understandably sensitive and undermined every primal concept of marriage. Emma was not completely naive and Conrad had failed to figure out any reasonable way of approaching the disturbing 'separate bed syndrome' to his wife. One evening he considered a light, even humorous explanation of their issue; "I know it's been like having an elephant in our bedroom and ignoring it's there," but he dispelled that superficial notion as inappropriate under the circumstances. Instead, Conrad was compelled to conjure a medical excuse which he hoped might get him through another discomforting moment.

In a voice tight with emotion, Conrad said—"I'm aware that these past few weeks have been so stressful for both of us, my dear. But, with the rest I'm getting now, my health is gradually returning. That hernia problem I had this summer really hasn't quite resolved itself yet, and the insomnia I've had along with it…you've been so patient with me, Emma." Conrad's forehead wrinkled at the outlandish excuse he had fabricated. Like so many others, this explanation was flawed—but borderline believable to Emma.

Emma's forehead wrinkled. Hernia? Insomnia? Perhaps this was another part of their past that she had forgotten about. Rather than probe, Emma allowed the intimate matter to drop for now. "I understand, my dear," she said weakly. "Things will settle down soon, and you'll be feeling much better won't you?"

"When we're settled, Emma…I'll begin feeling like a new man—I'm sure of it."

In New York, while filling the three hour layover void for baggage transfers, Conrad purchased an armful of newspapers at an International shop while Emma browsed in the adjacent souvenir section. Awaiting him in the Cunard office, with his travel visas and assortment of tickets, was a bundle containing several copies of *Variety* which Conrad had advance ordered shortly after leaving Long Beach. (A twenty dollar tip to the Sebastian's communication specialist enabled Conrad to cable instructions ahead of the ship whenever he wanted). Also included in his 'special order' was a copy of the *Minneapolis Star Tribune* from the two Sunday's previous.

Back on board the ship, Conrad stuffed his trove of papers in his steamer trunk while Emma changed into her pajamas and robe in the bathroom. He would read the issues later that evening while Emma slept. "You'll have to show me the souvenirs you found," Conrad said through the closed door. A paper bag rested upon Emma's bed. It would be more enjoyable for her to surprise him with her purchases so he resisted the temptation to snoop.

Earlier he had explained that his efforts to locate the hospital where her father was being treated had proven fruitless. If Conrad had it to do over again, he would have conjured a much better story about her father's 'contagious illness', but—so far—every aspect of his elaborate fabrications seemed to be holding up.

Emma still talked often about her father and made Conrad promise that, when they returned from their voyage, the two of them would pay him a visit.

Returning refreshed from a relaxing bath, Emma sat on her bed and opened the shopping bag. Among her purchases were three fifty cent replicas of 'Lady Liberty', a 'movie star' magazine, and a nickel chocolate bar. "They're the same," Emma pronounced with a sense of pride as she fondled the small statuettes, "but this one's for daddy."

Smiling at her obvious delight, Conrad inquired, "And the other two?"

"This one's for Darold…and this one for Kevin—whenever I see him."

Conrad paled with sinking heart! Two nights before, Emma had been sleeping fitfully and he heard her cry out the name 'Kevin'. Trying to conceal his emotion of the moment, Conrad forced a smile, "They will be delighted that you thought of them, Emma."

"I'm not done yet, Conrad." Reaching again into the bag she said, "Close your eyes. I didn't forget you." Emma had found a hard-cover book that said Pulitzer Prize Winner on the cover, "You can open your eyes now…I hope you like it—it cost more than the statues."

Conrad felt the tug in his heart as he took the book from Emma. He wanted to cry his happiness of the moment. "It's a perfect gift, my dear—what more can I say?" Emma had chosen *The Colonial Period of American History* by Charles McLean Andrews. "You remembered how much I love history…I shall treasure this always, my dear."

His elation, however, brought a sadness he could not speak about. In the rigamarole of all the paper work, he had forgotten to get something for Emma.

The front page photograph and story in Tuesday's (9/06/'38) *Variety* virtually leaped from the paper. Conrad's hands shook as he read below the picture of Emma taking Gable's hand:

RHETT MEETS HIS SCARLETT!

> *Just days after the MGM's momentous announcement that Clark Gable had been cast in David O. Selznick's 'Gone With The Wind' production, the Hollywood screen star exclaimed, 'We've found our Scarlett' to director friend, Victor Fleming. Their bizarre meeting could have been a hit movie—part drama and part comedy.*

> At the Conrad Phelps Santa Monica mansion reception attended by a 'Who's Who in Los Angeles' (with a guest list including Senator and Mrs. Gil Stavnes) Gable and Fleming crashed the party shortly after midnight. The two stragglers had spent a bar-hopping night on the town and were reportedly heading to Fleming's Malibu residence.
>
> Once inside the Phelps' lavish living room, Gable was accosted by the hostess, Emma Phelps. "Who are you...and what are you doing here?" the lovely blond woman shouted at Gable. Much to the amusement of the guests, it appeared that the naive Ohio woman actually did not know who Clark Gable was! "This is being staged," one onlooker suggested when the confrontation began. But, in moments, it was obvious to all—Emma Phelps was in the dark; not only about Gable's identity; but adding to the preposterous—she had no apparent clue as to what the GWTW project was about!
>
> "You've had far too much to drink" the spirited hostess told Gable, and threatened to have her husband (political activist, Conrad Phelps) kick him out of the house. Visibly surprised by the fiery-tempered beauty, Gable told Fleming, "Victor, I think we've just met our Scarlett!" (Neither Selsnick nor MGM has yet to announce who will be cast to play Scarlett O'Hara in the upcoming blockbuster).
>
> Ever charming, Gable introduced himself: "My friends call me Clark" and apologized for his intrusion to the delight of more than one hundred astonished guests. Loretta Cohen, wife of international retailer Jacob Randolph Cohen, commented: "Keep an eye on that woman; Emma Phelps is going to be the next Bette Davis—mark my words!" Who knows, stranger things have happened! And, if Clark Gable is any judge of talent, Mrs. Phelps has star written all over her lovely face. This Variety reporter will keep his eyes open.

"Oh my God!" Conrad mumbled under his breath. Ruffling through the papers he found the following Saturday's *Variety*. Once again, on the front page under the byline of gossip columnist, Jessup Bray, was a follow up article:

WHERE'S SCARLETT?

The Hollywood watch is on! Since Tuesday's Clark Gable scoop in Variety, all eyes have been searching for the next Bette Davis. The knockout blond (of 'We've just met our Scarlett' fame) wife of shipping magnate, Conrad Phelps, has not been seen since Saturday's gala Santa Monica party. According to neighbors, Emma Phelps is as mysterious to them as she is to this reporter. "We had never met either of them," (Conrad or Emma) claimed nearby resident of twenty years, Louise Kasner. "We only went over to the Phelps' place to be courteous—but, I'd be less than honest if I didn't add, 'curious' as well." Curious is the buzz word. Allegedly, the recently married Ohio couple arrived in Santa Monica only the day before the reception. "Nobody's ever seen them before," said another neighbor, Katherine Knox. When asked if she was 'curious' as well, Mrs. Knox exclaimed, "You can bet your life on that, young man. Lots of folks around here wondered if the Phelps' place was actually haunted."

The plot thickens: Mysterious couple, haunted house, sudden disappearances! And, this reporter has been informed that Conrad Phelps offered Variety two thousand dollars for the photograph of his wife, and threatened legal action if it were published. "We'd invite a law suit," said Variety executive, Martin Speigle. "Anything that might flush out Hollywood's 'mystery woman' of 1938.

Phelps' property manager, Darold Hurley, refused any comment beyond, "The couple is off on their honeymoon and will be returning in a few weeks."

Oscar-winning director, John Ford, claiming to be enamored by the flood of rumors, has offered to audition Emma Phelps for his upcoming, multi-million adaptation of John Steinbeck's classic, 'The Grapes of Wrath'.

So Hollywood will be watching for you Emma—wherever you are!

Disturbing news did not end with the *Variety* articles. In the *Minneapolis Star Tribune* Conrad discovered details about the missing Minnesota woman. Conrad studied the recent photograph of the dark-haired subject of a citywide search. Although relieved that the picture was of poor quality and Emma's makeover had made her unrecognizable, the story was never-the-less unsettling. A St. Paul police sergeant, Keirnan McGinnis was frequently quoted throughout the story. "No new leads"…"…She was in St. Paul for the 'W.P.A. Artist's Seminar' at St. Katherine's College"…"An apparent history of mild amnesia"…"Now believed to have been a passenger on the fatal Grand Avenue trolley last Saturday" …"…A purple hat which might have belonged to —"…"Police are asking that anybody who might have information…"

The article mentioned a reward, along with an appeal from the husband and family members, and "a growing concern that she might have left the Twin Cities." Although Conrad found no specific reference to a possible abduction, McGinnis was quoted as speculating, "Somebody, probably in St. Paul, knows where the missing woman is—we implore that party, or those parties, to come forward immediately."

Lingering in the back of his thoughts these past weeks was Conrad's contingency plan. As he carefully tore the Minneapolis paper to small bits, the dreadful reality of a failing charade struck him like a punch to the stomach. At some point, Conrad's trail would be discovered—and he was going to get caught! The 'what then?' scenario required a contingency even better than his post-abduction planning had been. *Abduction!* The very word—with its evil connotations—sent stabs of remorse into the very marrow of Conrad's being. He had cruelly, and willfully, violated this vulnerable woman by taking her away.

Conrad's self reproach of the moment was two-fold: He despised every deceit which embellished his depraved scheme, and he loathed what might become his equally pathetic recourse. He might be forced at some point to refine his version of what had happened with an *"I had no idea"* explication. After all the roles he'd already played, ignorance would be relatively easy. *"She swept me off my feet."* The woman's beauty and charm would make this assertion believable to anybody. *"She never told me anything,"* and, *"How was I to know?"* would be evidenced by her amnesia. *"She wasn't wearing any rings."* The wedding ring! Why had he saved her rings? If or when they returned to St. Paul, Conrad would take them from the stocking stuffed in an old shoe in the closet where he hastily hid them. *"She wanted me to take her to California."* Thus, his hasty departure. *"She insisted we tell people that we were married—came from Ohio."* Plausible, under the circumstances of traveling together. *"All the time I had doubts, of course…but this Emma (that was the name she gave me) just wanted to have a good time."*

Characterizing her as a loose woman might cast aspersions on his own morality. Conrad would reconsider this point. *"She must have known before hand that I was wealthy."* Such a 'defense' would take careful detailing, and ultimately perhaps, some careful collaboration on the part of his friend Darold Hurley.

"No!" Conrad cursed these treacherous thoughts under his breath. "I could never do anything like that" —never disparage Emma's reputation, never implicate Darold…never let myself sink to such despicable depths. "No, one mortal sin is enough!"

For the first time, Conrad pushed his thoughts back in time—to the St. Paul street corner where the foreshadowing of calamity had all begun. Anybody with an ounce of sanity would have recognized the woman's dysfunction and called the police. If he had done that *one and only*, rational action…Conrad could have gained the respect of everybody who loved and cherished this remarkable woman. In all likelihood, his assistance in her amnesic circumstance, might also have won him her friendship for life. 'Conrad Phelps the decent man who helped a troubled soul in a time of her gravest distress!'

But, instead of doing what was right and honorable—Conrad wept quietly into his handkerchief, "Will I ever be able to forgive myself? Will Emma ever forgive…? Conflicted with angst, shame and remorse; memories of these past weeks rushed through his thoughts. These treacherous days had been the most wondrous of his life! However demented this episode might appear to everybody else: Conrad had found a precious jewel in the rock pile of his world, and the only genuine happiness he had ever experienced. Tears streaked his cheeks, given another day, another week—perhaps a month or two; Conrad would fill whatever time remained with an impassioned devotion. He would provide his Emma, his princess, with every material luxury his fortune could provide.

And, while lavishing her—Conrad would wait for the inevitable.

He paced the large space of the private berth, dabbing at the tears that welled in his tired eyes. Staring for a long moment at the crumpled and shredded papers on his bed, Conrad's thoughts were drawn back to the present reality. He was a wanted man! A felon! As he stood in this very room so far from Minnesota, people—maybe hundreds of trained professionals—were searching for his trail. How long before 'Adam Johnson' would be connected to the woman's disappearance? Dayton's? …the beauty salon on Snelling? …then, the Phelps house in St. Paul? …the Northern Pacific passenger list?—A trail that would lead to Sunset Shores in Santa Monica. The party and the *Variety* photograph? Conrad and Emma's *Panama Atlantic* passage to New York and *Cunard* voyage to London? Was finding his convoluted trail inevitable?

In his back pocket was the small notepad which outlined his stories and schemes. Would anybody be able to follow the Clarke's from London to Paris? Or, the Phelps' to Sorrento, Italy, where his family owned a Mediterranean villa. How far behind were they at this very moment?

~

While staying at the luxurious King Edward's Hotel in the bustling Kensington District of London, Conrad and Emma filled their days with sight-seeing excursions (Buckingham Palace, Hyde Park, Piccadilly Circus, and the Tower Bridge) in addition to shopping at world renowned Harrods Department Store.

Emma delighted as a new world opened before her eyes. Together, they enjoyed the most exquisite dining and entertainment the historic city had to offer the wealthy Americans. Conrad replaced the rings Emma had 'lost' with a twenty carat diamond in a Florentine gold setting and purchased a matching necklace and brooch. "You're spoiling me too much," Emma protested. But, Conrad's checking account (which he used only sparingly) was bottomless. "I don't need any more jewelry or clothes, Conrad…I already have everything imaginable!"

At times, Conrad wondered if his extravagance was reckless. But, he rationalized, travel records already evidenced his presence in London—and, his checks would take weeks to clear the bank.

While touring and shopping, Conrad found bookstores. Explaining his hobby to Emma, Conrad suggested: "It will be a legacy for our children when we have them. Some of the books in my collection will be worth tens of thousands of dollars years from now."

To Conrad's astonishment (in a small shop near Trafalgar Square) he discovered the most valuable manuscript his eyes had ever beheld: An original, hand-written Saint Thomas More essay. The eleven-page essay had been discovered by a young accountant in his late father's attic weeks before, and the store owner was planning to sell the treasure at a Sotheby's auction the following month. Then, the timely visit of a wealthy American collector named Conrad Phelps changed his mind.

The following morning, Conrad telephoned Howard Gross at his friend's bookstore in St. Paul. The content of his call was carefully rehearsed. After a length of time, the connection was made. As expected, the trans-Atlantic operator identified London over annoying static which made reception difficult.

"Yes…I'm in London, Howard. After leaving your shop—when was that, nearly a month ago already? I booked a passage—a fellow I've dealt with before had just called and said 'You've got to come to London before the manuscript gets to auction'—so, as you might imagine, I dropped everything."

"I've wondered where you've been, Mr. Phelps. What were you looking for in London?"

Gross was hardly audible, but Conrad continued:

"You won't believe it, Howard…"

"I've just purchased an original Thomas More manuscript..."

"I'm having trouble hearing you, Howard…"

"Yes…after hearing about the More manuscript I caught the first train to New York…

"So, what's new in St. Paul these days?" Anxious to get to the crux of his call, Conrad blurted the question.

Howard Gross was as excited as his long-time customer over the great news. Ignoring the question: "You must have paid thousands, Mr. Phelps—I can't even imagine."

"I did…" Conrad pressed again, "I can't find a Twin Cities newspaper anywhere over here. Can you hear me, Howard?"

"Quite well, sir."

"Good. Before leaving St. Paul, I heard something about a streetcar accident just down Grand Avenue from your store—was anyone killed?"

"Just terrible! But that's not the half of it, Mr. Phelps." Howard Gross explained events developing in the aftermath of the collision. "The other day some detective was in the shop. Not only mine, but every business on Grand Avenue, mind you. Wanted to know the names of people who had stopped by on that Saturday morning. Went through all the receipts, about sixteen of them—and, do you realize?—we forgot to write a receipt for your transaction, Mr. Phelps.

Conrad breathed a sigh of relief, "We've never needed them, Howard—business between friends, you know."

"It wasn't until the guy was leaving that I remembered."

Conrad's mouth went instantly dry, "So, you gave him my name?"

"Of course. I don't know if he wrote it down with all the others in his notebook, though—seemed like he was in a hurry. But, there's this missing woman they're looking for. Quite a manhunt—I mean, well you know…talk is that she was probably abducted. Terrible! Just think—a kidnapping in our neighborhood."

"Her family must be miserable."

Conrad had heard about all he wanted, "I'm going up to Amsterdam tomorrow…and will probably finish up my travels in Stockholm. (Should anyone inquire as to his whereabouts, this information would correspond with his travel tickets and visas, and lead pursuers far from his meticulously planned trail).

"Sometime near the end of the month, or early October, I should imagine…No, Howard, that won't be necessary…I'll call you…"

Next, Conrad contemplated calling Darold Hurley. Darold was the only person in the world who might be able to conjecture on he and Emma's Sorrento destination. Despite the phony itinerary he'd given Darold before leaving, he had confided that Emma's accident and memory loss would require the attention of a London neurologist. Should he ask Darold to cover for him? Might Conrad remind his friend that Emma's condition must be kept in the strictest confidence? Or that further treatment in Vienna would be necessary. Would Darold be willing to lie if necessary for his employer? Conrad mused about his dilemma. When would Scotland Yard be knocking at his door…or the Serrate when he and Emma arrived in Paris? Conrad would be looking over his shoulder every step of the way.

No. Darold would be discrete if anyone came searching for he and Emma. Yet, if there appeared to be any suggestion of trouble, would Darold be able to get word to Conrad—through Conrad's Italian manservant (What was his name, anyhow?) in Sorrento? Conrad would call his Italian estate that afternoon, introduce himself, and inform whomever was managing the property of his travel plans. He would then establish a necessary link to forward any messages.

Yet, on the other hand, Darold Hurley, being an absolutely righteous man, would not be inclined to lie about Conrad's whereabouts. Especially if Darold learned the truth about Emma. Had his manager been taken in by Conrad's many deceptions before leaving California? He almost regretted telling Darold about Emma's health issues. Would Darold be as cooperative as possible with authorities under the circumstances of helping them to locate Emma? His friend had been smitten by his wife's spirited charm.

No, Conrad would not contact Darold now.

"I knew this would happen!"

Emma's words almost paralyzed him, "What would happen?" he dropped the book Emma had given him onto his lap, and regarded his wife sitting in her nightgown and robe at the vanity and brushing her hair.

"The roots!"

Conrad was confused. 'The roots of his deception?', 'the roots of her amnesia?'—the roots of what? "I'm sorry, my dear. What on earth…?"

"My hair, Conrad. The dark roots are showing."

Conrad sighed his relief, "We'll take care of that tomorrow, my dear. There's a beauty shop on the mezzanine downstairs."

Emma pouted. "No…I'm getting tired of this blond hair. Didn't you like the way I looked before?"

"You are beautiful either way. I just prefer…"

Emma turned to face him.

Conrad could not discern her expression: was it shame, or hurt, or guilt in her dark eyes?

"But it's not natural," Emma said. Ever since their first night together, Emma had repressed her concerns about Conrad's *unnatural* behavior toward her. She was his wife and yet…"Conrad, do you really love me?" Her question was laden with doubt. She knew their relationship was as unnatural as her hair coloring.

Conrad's mouth sagged, "Why, of course, my dear. How could you ever doubt…?"

Standing up from her chair and facing him she exclaimed, "Isn't it obvious? We're married and still sleep in separate beds. You never touch me…I might as well say it—you never touch my breasts, or…between my legs." She began to sob her anguish, "You've never watched me undress or seen me naked. Conrad, you don't even know that my hair down here is dark," Emma said, pressing a hand to her groin. "Is there something undesirable about me…?" She sobbed from the depths of her spirit. "Don't you want to…to do what married people are supposed to do—?"

Conrad felt a self-loathing over her justified distress. From the very beginning of his charade he knew that the sensitive issue of intimacy was going to be a problem the two of them would have to resolve. But he had vowed to himself from the onset that he would never violate Emma in any respect: a promise which would remain inviolable!

Since their first night together, Conrad had kept his most audacious fabrication in reserve. Conrad recalled their earlier conversation on the *Sebastian* voyage. His excuse at that time was an alleged hernia surgery and insomniac fatigue. He'd promised Emma that his sexual dysfunction would resolve itself with a little rest. But now his wife seemed to have reached the edge of her frustration. Her eyes were imploring him to say something—to explain what was wrong between them!

Rising from his chair, Conrad stepped to his wife and embraced her more tightly than he'd ever done before. The feeling of her body against his was disconcerting—he felt clumsy, inept, and artless as his hands rested limply in the hollow of her lower back. Fighting back tears, Conrad's words came in a voice hoarse with emotion. "We've been over this before, my dear—on our cruise, and before we were married. I'm sorry...sometimes I forget about your memory issue." He patted her back lightly, brushed a kiss against her cheek. "I'm going to see a specialist about my condition. You've been so patient with me these past weeks, Emma. I've not wanted us to sleep together because, you know...I wouldn't be able to consummate..." Conrad mouth was dry. "It would only be painful for you—for both of us. And I don't want either of us to have our feelings hurt. Please don't ever think that I don't find you desirable, Emma. Please—Emma, you're beautiful!"

Despite his tearful assurance, Emma was confused, the throb of a headache pierced her temples—a blinding sensation! For an instant her mind flashed back to...there was a tree overhead shading the sun, the gurgle of a stream, the scent of wild grasses and pungent pine—an exhilaration swept her: "Am I really beautiful, Kevin?" Emma breathed her question into Conrad's ear. Her eyes closed tightly over the memory of a time and place locked within a past she couldn't grasp.

"Emma! What's happened? Are you all right?" Conrad shook her shoulders.

"W—h—a—?" Her eyes opened widely. "Conrad, what's the matter with you? You're shaking me!"

"I thought I lost you for a moment, Emma. Another headache?"

"No. A sharp pain! A terrible one. Did something happen? You look as white as a ghost."

"Can't you remember?"

"Remember?" She looked absently around the elegantly appointed hotel room; then met Conrad's eyes. "Where are we?"

Conrad's heart was pounding. It was over now—finally! Emma had awakened. All was lost and Conrad was speechless with a paralysis that gripped like a vice. The beginnings of a confession came rushing like a swollen river flooding into his thoughts—

"Conrad?" Emma gasped. "You're crying, my dear. What have I done?"

Clinging to a hope, Conrad's voice was choked, desperate: "Don't you know where we are, Emma?"

Shaking her head, she tried to console her distraught husband. "What a silly question! We're in London, of course. Why do you ask?"

"I thought for a moment…"

Then their conversation came back to her, Emma flushed: "I'm sorry I upset you, my dear. It's that memory thing. You were explaining about your condition and something strange came over me—I don't think I even allowed you to finish what you were saying."

Conrad sighed noticeably, "You asked if I loved you, Emma. Then— you wondered why we weren't sleeping together."

Emma's eyes cast downward, "I know. It all started with my hair, didn't it? My natural color? And I spoke about being naked. Sometimes your behavior really bothers me, Conrad."

"And it bothers me, too. More than I've been able to properly explain, Emma." He took her hand and gently led her to his bed, "Sit beside me for a while. Regardless of any personal embarrassment on my part, it's imperative that I tell you about my condition again; you need to understand." Conrad fabricated about what he termed his 'male impotence', using words like hormones and male sexuality which he imagined might be appropriate medical terminologies for the alleged condition. The truth, however, would have been even more painful for Conrad. He was not impotent in the slightest measure. There were times while Emma slept when he saw her breasts (and had to forcefully squelch his powerful impulse to touch and kiss her pink nipples) and had, on two occasions, seen the swell of Emma's mons with its narrow band of dark, pubic hair. And there were other occasions when his pulsing erection required the relief of secretive and shameful masturbation.

"I promised to see Doctor Giovanni when we get to Sorrento, Emma—and, I will! He's written many papers on the subject of male impotence and is considered to be a world expert."

Emma squeezed his fragile hand, "I so very much want to please you in every way a wife should please her husband, Conrad. I do care so much for you." With her desperate profession of love, however, came a swell of doubt. What were her true feelings for this man—her husband? Wanting to please Conrad was an honest sentiment, and Emma truly felt a measure of affection. But at times she thought him a stranger.

Conrad, still smarting from the mention of 'Kevin' said, "Now that you know, perhaps we can sleep together."

"I think that's how it should be, Conrad."

That Friday afternoon, while Emma napped, Conrad tried to contact his villa in Sorrento. After a frustrating hour trying to locate an operator who spoke English (finally one was found in the distant Naples communications department), he learned that the Phelps' estate no longer had telephone service. "I am not certain of my facts, Mr. Phelps...but it is quite possible that your property has been, how can I say...taken over by the government? And, as I'm certain you realize, all foreign travel to Italy is strongly discouraged at this time."

Conrad tormented while Emma slept. What if political problems prevented their travel to Sorrento? What if the Phelps' property had been seized by Mussolini's damned Fascists? Where would he and Emma go then? Customs presented the greatest hurdles in that all of his official documents were in the Phelps' name. Conrad tried to calm himself. Consulting his notebook, he reconsidered his strategy. The 'Clarke's' would check out of the hotel tomorrow morning—two days earlier than originally planned. He would tell the desk to hold the room while he and Mrs. Phelps toured the English countryside for a few days. Tickets to Calais, France (on Tuesday) were already booked in the name of Phelps. Another subterfuge came to his thoughts—a Mr. and Mrs. Lawrence Greene would leave Dover, England, the next morning! Conrad smiled at the notion. He would surprise Emma with a promise to begin looking for medieval castles on the European mainland.

Scratching his head, Conrad considered another ploy. His next call was to Cunard Lines. Conrad booked a return passage (as Conrad and Emma Phelps) to New York for the following Wednesday. He would be certain to tell the front desk that after touring England, he and Mrs. Clarke would be returning to the States. As convoluted as everything seemed on paper—he would make it work. If anyone was looking for him and Emma, they would have a nightmarish experience.

The Phelps' left London on Saturday morning. To some they were the Clarke's—heading up to Stratford and touring northern England, to others they were the Greene's traveling to France. Still others would find the Johnson's registered on a Nor-Europe train to Amsterdam. Lastly, Cunard officials would have record of Conrad and Emma Phelps returning to New York next week. Despite having no clear touring agenda after their arrival in Calais, Conrad was buying time. He would be careful to make certain that his footprints would not lead anybody to the Ritz Hotel in Paris.

'Rooftops Under Snow'

Their first few days in the 'City of Lights' enthralled Emma far more than the four days they had spent in London's overcast and congestion. Upon arriving in France, Emma surprised Conrad, "Please call me *mon cherie*, it means 'my dear' in French you know." His wife had been in an unusually reflective mood of late and it made Conrad edgy whenever Emma wasn't quite herself.

"*Mon cherie* it is, my dear," he said lightly. But, wherever did you pick that up?"

"I just can't explain it, Conrad. Hearing the people here talk seems so familiar, though. Do we know anybody who speaks French?"

"Not to my knowledge. While we're in Paris though, you'll surely pick up some common French expressions—"

"*Tres bien!*" Emma smiled, "Now, isn't that just something! It means that 'I'm pleased' or 'very well'…I think, or something like that anyhow. Surely somebody taught me the expression before."

Conrad puzzled, almost everything about his wife's past was of his own creation. He should have told her that she had taken a French class in high school—maybe he'd tell her that later. "You probably picked it up in the little tourism booklet we purchased in Dover before boarding the ferry," he suggested.

"I haven't even opened the cover yet." Exasperated, Emma sighed, "Oh well, I'll figure it out one of these days."

Guillaume LaBlanc was employed by Conrad as a guide while the Phelps' toured the magnificent city taking in many of the historic and tourist sights. "As you realize," Guillaume told them one morning, "We are all quite nervous over here these days. All around us—in Spain and Germany…and Italy—there are many *problemes.* Of course, Hitler and his Reich are most *affreux*—or, frightening?—you might say in your English."

The Frenchman was tall, solidly built, auburn-haired and ruggedly good looking. Emma was almost ashamed of her growing attraction to the handsome man—an inscrutable chemistry that seemed almost familiar to her. If the man's physical appearance seemed vaguely memorable, his resonantly accented *Hitler* reminded her of someone else entirely. "Have you ever been to Ohio or Winona, Guillaume?" Emma, determined to figure out the *why* of familiarity, asked the Frenchman on their third day of touring.

Guillaume, about twenty-five, was an art and literature student at the Sorbonne, and a part-time employee of the luxurious Hotel Ritz where the Phelps' were residing. "Winona? I've never heard of the place, Mademoiselle," he laughed. "Is that an American city or something?"

"Oh, yes, it is—in Minnesota. I was born there."

"Minnesota! The capital city of Minnesota is St. Paul on the Mississippi River," Guillaume said proudly.

Emma startled…"St. Paul!" A flood of emotion flushed her face. Looking at Conrad standing only feet away while focusing his new camera, Emma reached for her husband's elbow. "Did you hear what Guillaume said, Conrad? St. Paul. I remember going to St. Paul…"

Conrad almost dropped his camera. Searching her eyes for any sign of recall, he took her hand in his. Her flashbacks were occurring every few days now. Thinking quickly, "Yes, my dear. We have a home in St. Paul. Surely, you remember. Sometimes these lapses of yours can be almost embarrassing?" Conrad forced a weak smile, but his rebuke was unusually sharp. "All this travel has confused your thinking," he said, glancing from Emma toward their guide and shrugging his shoulders.

Guillaume was perplexed by the exchange but said nothing.

Emma frowned, "I'm sorry. We lived there before leaving for California—didn't we, Conrad? I'm just so…so, absent minded all the time."

"Well, *mon ami's*, where to next?" Guillaume asked. The three of them were resting on a bench in the exquisite *Jardin des Tuileries* off busy Rue de Rivoli, enjoying a break from their touring in the early afternoon sun. That morning they had wandered the shops along the historic *Champs-Elysees* and enjoyed an elegant luncheon at the avant guarde *Cafe Laduree*. "Might I suggest the Louvre, our former Royal Palace?" Guillaume gestured down the street toward what was now an historic museum. "Nobody can say they've experienced Gay Paree until they've visited the world's finest art museum… *oui*?"

"We must do just that, Guillaume," Conrad agreed. "Emma you can't imagine all the art treasures in the Louvre over there," His eyes went from his wife down the wide boulevard.

"Museums are so stuffy, Conrad. You promised we'd get some ice cream and take a river tour this afternoon." Not wanting to be completely disagreeable, however, Emma compromised, "All right, if we don't spend too much time looking at statues and pictures. And don't forget the castles you promised!"

While touring the immense *Musee du Louvre*, Guillaume allowed the American couple to wander through the Gothic exhibits of the Denon wing by themselves. When in the building's Renaissance area, the French guide offered, "If you have any questions, just ask me, *sil vous plait*…I am studying literature and art at university."

Passing through the Baroque section, Emma remarked; "All these portraits are painted with such dark colors…so depressing; and I have no interest in the sculptures or artifacts, I'm afraid. I'd almost rather walk through a cemetery where there's fresh air and natural light."

Sensitive to Emma's apparent boredom (even De Vinci's *Mona Lisa* had failed to inspire anything more than a passing glance) Conrad was about to suggest they leave the museum for now. It appeared they would be touring in Paris for a while and maybe there would be a better time for the Louvre—perhaps, a rainy autumn day. An ice cream might save the afternoon for all of them.

Before Conrad could offer an alternative, Guillaume spoke: "Madame, I absolutely agree about the depressingly dark colors of what we've seen so far. Just allow me to take you and Mr. Phelps upstairs to the *Sully* Wing for a few minutes. I'll show you some colorful paintings that will make your heart leap and your eyes water—I promise!" His appeal, like his smile, was irresistible.

"What's upstairs, Guillaume?" Emma's expression offered a hint of optimism for the first time in nearly an hour.

"The great French Impressionists!"

Emma puzzled.

Conrad, feeling outside their conversation, offered his insight, "That would be…Renoir, Monet…and, Degas; am I correct, Guillaume?"

"*Tres bien*, Mr. Phelps! And, Eduarde Manet—he's my favorite—and Cézanne. There are so many of them to see…to experience; their colors and forms are *magnifique*!"

Emma started at the word, *magnifique*. Like so many other French words she'd heard these past days, this one struck her as almost hauntingly familiar. *Who* had used *magnifique* before? She pressed her memory to no avail. Whenever she tried hard to remember some seemingly trivial detail, her head ached. It was beginning to pain her now. "I don't know…why don't the two of you go upstairs. I'll sit outside in the fresh air."

"We can see the Impressionists another time if you like, Emma," Conrad took her elbow.

Although Guillaume was disappointed and recognized that Emma had probably had enough, he offered a last appeal: "Fifteen minutes—please, that's all I ask—fifteen minutes?"

Emma pouted at the suggestion. But she knew Guillaume's heart was set on showing them the exhibits, "A few minutes" she compromised.

Once upstairs, Emma found herself lingering at a Mary Cassatt painting, *'Margot in Bleu'* for a long moment. The colorful portrait sparked her eyes, "This truly is *magnifique*, Guillaume. It was worth coming up here if only to see this lovely painting. The painter's colors are absolutely exquisite."

Inspired, Guillaume suggested they view some Manet works, "Allow me to take you over there," he gestured toward the far corner opposite of where they were standing. "Manet has become most popular with my fellow art students these past few years."

Conrad, pleased by Emma's sudden interest, commented "If you see something you like, Emma, I'll purchase a quality reproduction for you."

On their way toward the Manet exhibit, Emma suddenly stopped. On the wall to her right was a painting that riveted her attention. Stepping closer, Emma's eyes widened at a painting by Gustave Caillebotte titled *'Rooftops Under Snow'*. "This one, Conrad!" she exclaimed. Emma's heart leaped—the snowy white landscape brought an immediate flashback! Emma remembered watching snowfall from a window…from somewhere upstairs. Then an image fixed in her thoughts, a white tree with icicles dangling from leafless branches. She wanted to tell Conrad and Guillaume…but swallowed the notion in her dry mouth. Closing her eyes she imagined a winter scene awash in white. In her mind's eye she was peering at the snowscape and brushing a canvas in her own favorite colors—

whites: various shades of white. She was happy in this room of her imagination, a studio with all the trappings of an artist—a room that felt as real as this ornate museum space where she stood.

"Emma?" Conrad interrupted her reverie. "You like this…?" he stepped closer to read the artist's name on the brass plate below the painting, "this Caillebotte?"

Emma nodded speechlessly—there were no words to describe the feelings she had just experienced. Her sensation of the moment was something to be treasured in the private recesses of her mind. Closing her eyes against the throb in her head, Emma imagined a portrait of her own—from her studio window somewhere…the memory flashed a vivid image behind her eyes. A sloping hillside lined with huge pine trees and clusters of birch, a pasture… a barn in the distance, horses. "*Flare!*"

"What's that, Emma?" Conrad, aware that something had overcome Emma, repeated her last word, "*Flair?*" But Emma only looked confused.

Guillaume was equally puzzled, "*Tres bien*, 'flair'. Caillebotte has an interesting style, or *flair*, as you put it so *exactement*—I can actually feel winter when I study this painting. Can you as well, Madame?"

Both men had misunderstood her observation, but Emma would not tell either of them that *Flare* was the name of a horse. *Her horse!* Turning to Conrad, she spoke almost dramatically in a voice that her husband hardly recognized—*the voice of a woman!* "I must paint! I was born to paint and that's what has been missing in my life… Conrad, that must be the block! And the snow… How long has it been since I've seen snow?"

More perceptive at this moment than she could ever remember being, Emma sensed something was wrong. A fragment of her past, like a puzzle piece, was back in place and Conrad somehow didn't fit into her picture. A strange feeling engulfed her like an ominous cloud. She felt estranged from everything around her, lost in some unfamiliar place. Who was she? Where was she? What had just happened? The questions pulsed at her temples—"I don't feel well, Conrad." His name seemed unusually awkward in her mouth when she spoke it…Conrad even looked different—older?

"Let's go back to the hotel where you can rest, my dear?" Emma's face seemed drained of color to him. "Another headache? Should I call a doctor?"

Emma recouped her composure as if some vague force compelled that she do something. But what she needed to do was becoming lost in a heavy drape of foggy doubt which she could neither see through nor lift from her eyes. A doctor? No. For reasons she could not explain, she did not trust the idea of seeing a doctor. Worse, at that moment, she could not trust Conrad! Whatever was wrong with her had something to do with her husband. Why did she sense that? What could she do about it? Looking vacantly at Guillaume standing nearby, a premonition overwhelmed her. The tall man seemed as confused and distracted as she. Their eyes locked for a brief moment ...

Guillaume saw something in Emma Phelps' eyes at that instant which touched him almost spiritually. For whatever reason, the lovely woman was seeking an empathy from him—or some nature of reinforcement which seemed beyond his comprehension of the moment. She appeared to him as helplessly suffering some inner pent torment. Emma needed him—not her husband! What should he say? Without prethought or rationale, the strangest words came from his mouth: "I will purchase some painting supplies for you, Mrs. Phelps. I can feel your desire to paint!"

"Thank you—*Merci beaucoup*—Guillaume. You must have been reading my thoughts," Emma said with an enigmatic smile. "Would you kindly deliver them to the hotel for me?" As Emma opened her beige leather purse for some currency, she felt faint. This was not her purse! Her mind swept back to a purple, pearl-fringed purse clutched in her arms. She was walking...no, limping on a broken shoe, down a strange street. She was in St. Paul...looking for...St. Katherine's College. Artist workshops were scheduled at the campus that morning. Although only a fragment of something larger that still eluded her, that morning street scene in St. Paul was real! She looked up at Conrad, "Where's my pearl purse?"

Conrad recognized that Emma was going through another flashback. These episodes were occurring whenever she became stressed. "Which one, my dear?— you have several of them back at the hotel."

"The purple one..." Emma caught herself before ending her comment with "Conrad". Even her husband's name seemed too strange to mention. She seemed certain now...that she had first learned Conrad's name after the accident. But which accident? There had been more than one of them! She was positive..."the purse I had with me in St. Paul."

Conrad turned to the bewildered Frenchman and handed him a wad of paper money without even counting out the amount, "We'd both appreciate the favor, Guillaume. Emma needs some rest right now. Perhaps you might bring some art supplies...this weekend," Conrad smiled weakly.

"Yes, Messieur...this weekend." Guillaume looked at the substantial wad of money, "I won't need this much, Mr. Phelps."

"Keep whatever's left over," Conrad said almost too desperately. "You've been wonderfully helpful to Emma and me these past days."

Emma approached Guillaume, stood on her toes and placed a soft kiss on his cheek, "You are an angel, Guillaume."

Back at the hotel, Emma slept fitfully through fragmented dreams more frightening and real than any she had experienced before. One of them woke her:

A man was standing on something, a dune of sand or an outcropping above. He was looking for her but couldn't see her on the open beach below. She was screaming "I'm here...find me...take me home..." But he only looked beyond her and then, turned away. The man was not Guillaume...but—someone else who reminded her of Guillaume!

Conrad heard the scream, "Kevin!" from the bedroom of their suite.

Rushing into the room he found Emma sitting up in bed, "What's wrong, Emma?" His wife was ashen, her forehead wet with perspiration. "Another nightmare? I heard you call for *me*."

Emma looked absently about the strange room. Not long before, she remembered awakening from her sleep in a different bedroom. Disoriented, she regarded the man sitting beside her and holding her hands. Shaking her head, all that Emma could say was; "A terrible dream—I was lost."

Conrad fought against tears beginning to well in his eyes. Emma knew she was lost! One-by-one the scattered puzzle pieces were coming together in her thoughts. Her cry for Kevin moments before was the third in the past eight days. Something bizarre had happened to Emma at the museum that afternoon. It was the snow in the picture, Conrad was certain of that. Then that embarrassing episode about Emma's purse and her being in St. Paul. What could he do about it? Who could he turn to? Might there be a doctor...someone who could sort all this out for him—for Emma? Would such a precarious step ruin everything? Maybe...but maybe not. There was a chance that a trained doctor could provide some important insight—like, how long this amnesic condition might last, but Conrad knew he wouldn't take that risk.

His next words had to be perfectly chosen. "Emma, it's time for us to talk about some things that are tormenting you. You have not been well these past few weeks. Since that accident you have had many serious lapses of memory." Tears escaped to his cheeks. "I talked with Darold about your condition before we left California, Emma. I told him I wanted you to see the best doctors in the world. You see, that's our main reason for traveling to Europe." Conrad dabbed at his eyes with a corner of the loosened sheet at Emma's side.

"What accident?" Emma's eyes searched to the depths of the weeping man's soul.

Desperately conflicted, Conrad considered two options for answering Emma's profound question. Fabrication had been the foundation of their relationship since the first moments, and that foundation was eroding. It was possible that his clever deceptions were only making everything worse for both of them. Perhaps, the time had come for Conrad to open Emma's eyes to a small measure of reality. Doing so may have catastrophic ramifications, but...

"Emma, on your way home from downtown St. Paul, you were in a terrible streetcar accident. When I found you, you didn't even remember my name. It was that confusing, troubling...I didn't quite know what to do. You talked about hitting a deer and how angry your father would be about the damage to his automobile. I thought that a trip to California might be the right solution—a little vacation in the sun. But I'm afraid things have only gotten worse for you."

Emma pulled her hand away, covering her mouth in horror, "A baby was hurt! I remember. He was bleeding on the floor and his mother...the baby's mother was unconscious. And...I walked away from it all." Emma fought back her own tears, "...that was not the same thing—I mean, that was a different accident. I was fifteen when I crashed my father's car and was running away from home."

Conrad nodded. He would allow Emma to purge her memory without interrupting her train of thought.

Emma looked away for a long moment. She vaguely remembered the morning streetcar accident in St. Paul, and the snowy night crash years before as separate episodes. It was the wide gap in between which had become a demonic void in her life. With her realization came a flood of memories (meeting Conrad while sitting on a bench, streetcars coming and going, walking across the space of a campus) and a torrent of confusion. How had all these things come together? What did Conrad really know about her—about their meeting in St. Paul? Had *she lied to him* about who she was and about where she came from? She had to find out: "Did I tell you my name was Emma? And that I grew up in Winona?"

Conrad could feel the lump in his stomach rise into his throat, "You have *always been* Emma. We grew up together in Winona. We both know that, my dear."

Emma knew at that precise moment—everything between them was wrong! *Seriously wrong!*

Throughout that Thursday evening and the following day, Emma Phelps behaved much as she had for weeks—playing the role of Conrad's devoted wife, going through the motions of being enthralled with Paris as if nothing had happened. Inspired by a new confidence that she was soon going to remember who she *really* was, Emma would conjure a plan of her own. When Conrad had lied to her saying "...You have always been Emma," she resolved to uncover the truth. How long Conrad had been deceiving her remained a mystery she would somehow untangle. (Her response to Conrad at that critical moment was simply, "I thought so. Forgive me for being so absent minded all the time.)"

Conrad had seemed mollified by her apparent recollection. "Now, tell me about that terrible dream of being lost, Emma."

"It was something really foolish, I was a little girl in Winona and my father was looking for me under the front porch, that's all."

Conrad didn't believe her dream was something so trivial, but not wishing to pry more deeply, he let the matter drop.

Later, Conrad asked Emma about her willingness to see a doctor. "There is a specialist in something called psychoanalysis in Vienna, my dear. It's only a short trip from Paris."

Emma would remain coy and be ever so careful not to overplay her weak hand. If Conrad's perception of her remained uncompromised she would continue to behave in the security of that mode. "Don't be silly, we have too many other things to do. If the headaches get really, really bad—maybe then we can see a doctor, okay?"

Before noon on Saturday, Guillaume stopped by the Phelps' suite with an armful of packages. A bellboy accompanied him carrying a collapsible wooden easel. Guillaume smiled widely, his white, even teeth flashed his satisfaction, "With all these supplies you'll be able to set up your own studio right here in the hotel." He had purchased assorted tubes of oils and watercolors, brushes, palates and several canvasses; along with etching charcoals and tablets. The young French art student knew exactly what materials to buy and where to find them.

After helping Emma set up her easel near the curtained window where the lighting was ideal, Guillaume joined Conrad for a cup of creamy cafe au lait. Traces of concern lined his handsome face. Mr. Phelps had given him far too much money for the purchases and he was uncomfortable about keeping nearly one hundred extra American dollars.

"She certainly seems pleased, doesn't she, Guillaume?" Conrad commented as he watched his wife unwrap a package of oil paints.

"*Oui*, Mr. Phelps." Guillaume agreed absently, taking some currency from his shirt pocket and placing it on the table. "It was my great pleasure to do this shopping for you and your wife...I cannot, in good conscience, take a gratuity of such extravagance, Mr. Phelps. Please take this extra money back."

"I wouldn't think of it, Guillaume. A young student like yourself can use the money far more than Emma and I. Besides, just seeing Emma so excited about painting means more than any amount of money."

Guillaume would not argue the point. Mr. Phelps was obviously wealthy and he had back rent to pay on his flat in Montmartre. "*Merci beaucoup*," he thanked Conrad and returned the money to his pocket.

"Where did you find the supplies, Guillaume? We may need to find the shop on our own one of these days."

"Near my flat, sir. In the Montmartre neighborhood. An uncle of my friend is the proprietor...and he was most pleased by your purchase. Like everybody else, Mr. Grojean struggles to make ends meet these days."

Conrad inquired about book shops in the Montmartre neighborhood and was delighted to learn that there were several. "I'm a collector of rare editions, Guillaume. Especially theology manuscripts."

Guillaume smiled enthusiastically, "I didn't know that, Mr. Phelps; but, yes there are several shops in Montmartre."

While the two men talked about books they had read and Conrad further explained his hobby, Emma unwrapped her packages. A printed name on the brown bag she was holding sparked another memory from her past. Emma repressed a sudden urge to shout. An image of a small Frenchman virtually burned through the drape of fog over her past. Why hadn't she thought of him before? Every nuance of this intriguing language had been floating around the edges of her memory since their arrival in France. Jacque was the wellspring for the unconscious recall of the French expressions that puzzled her. *Jacque Grojean!* Emma had a name and a mental picture of a face with a voice to go with it...but still the most vital connection had not been made. Jacque was an artist—a friend—somewhere from her past...but—where? It almost seemed as if Emma was adding an assortment of valuable keys to her ring, but couldn't find any keyholes—couldn't open the necessary doors.

Emma glanced over her shoulder at the two men talking at the table. Guillaume would know! Just as Guillaume had been the key—the angel?—at the Louvre only days before, Emma knew that her friend was going to be her light from darkness. "Please, Mary Mother of God, help me find my way!" Emma mumbled the prayer under her breath. She wondered, "Where did that come from? The petition to Mary?" The words of her brief supplication came so easily; sounded so very familiar on her tongue. Closing her eyes, Emma spoke with the Virgin Mother for a long moment.

Conrad, ever attentive to Emma's moods, noticed her reverie: "Emma, is something the matter?"

Conrad's voice was like a stab in her heart. "I was just saying a prayer." For two days, Emma had not used Conrad's name in their conversations. There had been an inexplicable block to any recognition of who he was. "Why haven't we been going to church?"

Conrad, puzzling at her mention of praying and her unexpected question, rejoined: "We visited Notre Dame just the other day, Emma. You didn't say anything then. Would you like to...? "

"Yes. I *need* to...not just to look at everything like a tourist—but to pray. To light a vigil candle."

"Of course, my dear. We can go any time; this afternoon if you wish."

Guillaume recognized a growing rift in the relationship between this unusual American couple. Emma's winsome beauty and unbridled spirit almost seemed a contradiction to Conrad's uncomely appearance and doleful demeanor. Although confused by their obvious differences, and attracted to Emma's refreshing élan, Guillaume felt something inside that disconcerted him even more. A voice in his mind which he'd never heard before was compelling him to be an *instrument* of some kind. He was supposed to be doing something for Emma—but what...?

Rising unusually early on that Saturday morning, Guillaume had left his flat and walked the several blocks to *Sacre-Coeur Basilica*. The majestic church with its golden interior mosaics on the Montmartre hillside overlooking the city of Paris was a landmark he passed every day without regard. But on this bright October morning he was curiously inspired to attend mass. While in church, he became lost in prayers of his own—prayers to Maria. Was his impulse wildly coincidental? Or…? How could he explain his compulsion? Turning to Conrad, Guillaume suggested, "Perhaps the two of you would like to go to *Sacre-Coeur*. You would say in English, *Sacred Heart*, I believe. It is *tres magnifique*—there is no more splendid church in all of Paris."

On Sunday morning, Conrad read an English edition of a Paris newspaper. The headlines were a portent of doom: At a conference in Munich, Britain and France had agreed to the cession of Czechoslovakia's Sudetenland to Hitler's Germany! Only two weeks before, British Prime Minister Neville Chamberlain had returned from Germany with an historic proclamation, "There will be peace in our time." The gates to the cancerous spread of Nazi influence had now been opened. Conrad, like so many others who followed the tumultuous political-military events, was beginning to see the writing on the wall—Hitler and Mussolini could form an alliance with a potential to dominate all of Europe.

"We must go to the American Embassy again tomorrow, Emma. Everybody there seems to be dragging their feet on resolving our problems with the property in Sorrento," Conrad said over his newspaper as Emma painted contentedly in a shaft of light from the window.

Emma did not respond.

Putting aside his paper, Conrad pushed away from the table and wandered over to where Emma sat at her easel. His mouth dropped at the painting; Emma had captured the fury of a Minnesota blizzard on her canvas! The bold brushstrokes of manifold hues of white lashed before a backdrop of steel gray sky. Emma *was* an accomplished artist!—of that there could be no doubt in his mind. "My goodness, Emma, that is an impressive picture," Conrad complimented as an icy chill crawled up his spine. "It must be some place you remember very vividly."

"Yes, it is—everything just flowed from a picture in my mind."

'CHERIE'

Impatiently, Conrad paced the carpeted Ritz Hotel suite, adjusting his tie knot and tucking his dress shirt into his trousers: "Emma, my dear, our appointment is in thirty minutes," he called toward her closed bedroom door. "We mustn't keep the ambassador waiting." Conrad had become determined to resolve the complicated Italian property issue that Monday morning so that he and Emma could continue with their travel to Sorrento, post haste. Emma's unpredictable behavior since arriving in Paris days ago continued to make him nervous.

When Emma's door opened, Conrad gasped, "You haven't even gotten dressed!" Emma, hair tousled, was still in her nightgown.

"I can't go. I have another terrible headache. Maybe we should see that doctor you suggested…"

Frustrated and ignoring Emma's comment about seeing a doctor, Conrad raised his voice in an unusually agitated manner, "I can't leave you here, Emma—and our meeting is very important. Won't you dress yourself quickly… take some aspirin?"

"I must sleep. I had nightmares again and I'm exhausted."

Torn by indecision, Conrad regarded Emma's pale complexion. Perhaps the embassy matter could be taken care of by himself in a couple of hours. He had never left her alone before and worried over the prospect. "Are you sure you don't mind if I leave you by yourself for a short time, Emma?" In order to lift her spirits, Conrad reminded her that they had opera tickets for that evening. "Don't forget we're going to see *Swan Lake* tonight." The *Opera Garnier* was the most opulent theater in the world, and this evening's performance of *Swan Lake* by the renowned Bolshoi Ballet Company of Moscow would be spectacular. Such an incentive might inspire a quick recovery for whatever was ailing her at the moment. "Are you as excited about that as I am, Emma?"

Emma forced a weak smile, "Yes...that will be wonderful."

The instant Conrad closed the door behind him, Emma hurriedly began to dress. All night she had planned what she would attempt to do that morning. Ten minutes later, Emma was downstairs in the posh lobby of the *Ritz* Hotel and speaking with a clerk at the front desk: "Parle vous l'Englais?"

The uniformed man nodded.

"Guillaume LaBlanc's phone number, *sil vous plait.*"

Emma learned that Guillaume had never given his employer a telephone number and the clerk was reluctant to give her the tour guide's address. Frustrated, she reached in her purse for some currency. She had an American twenty dollar bill, a five, and an assortment of Francs. Emma handed the clerk her five, "I must locate Mr. LaBlanc."

Outside the hotel, Emma found a waiting taxi and gave the driver a scribbled address; 42 Rue St-Vincent. As the taxi sped north, the majestic *Sacre-Coeur* (which Guillaume had told her about on Saturday) loomed like a white ghost across the hilltop. In twenty minutes, the cab was winding past a cemetery and passing through narrow streets before stopping in front of an old three story brick building. Offering a handful of francs to the driver, she thanked him and got out onto the deserted sidewalk.

Emma drew a deep breath as she entered the decrepit structure. Number three was at the top of a long flight of stairs. Saying a quick prayer, she knocked lightly.

The young woman who opened the door was strikingly beautiful, "I am Guillaume's friend," Emma blurted, offering her hand. "May I see him?"

The petite, dark-haired woman smiled, "*Mais non,* I'm sorry." In broken passages of English, the woman explained to Emma that Guillaume had classes until noon and then would probably be going to the hotel.

Not knowing what to do, Emma scribbled a note on a pad from her purse. "Will you give this to Guillaume when he returns? It's very important that I talk to him."

Emma left the building and walked toward the towering Roman Byzantine domes of *Sacre-Coeur* only blocks away where her note to Guillaume said she would wait for him. It might be hours, she realized, but once inside the walls of the enormous Basilica she would feel safe…and have time to pray. Emma's hastily conceived plan was simply to hide from Conrad and hope she could win the confidence and support of Guillaume—the one person in all the world who could help her now. Emma had considered trying to find the Montmartre art shop, where Guillaume had purchased her supplies on her own, but chose rather to remain off the streets where she would be less conspicuous to pedestrian eyes. With Guillaume's help, Emma might be able to make the connection she believed could link her with the distant past which lingered at the edges of her memory. The name *Grojean* seemed her greatest hope of eventually breaking the grip of the amnesia that kept her from knowing who she really was. She prayed to the Virgin Mother that Guillaume would be God's special angel and light her way out of her consuming darkness.

~

Guillaume LaBlanc was the son of Madeline Myre LaPointe, an ardent agitator, outspoken social reformer, and a strong voice in the growing pacifism movement in Paris. The widow had published several papers on her social and political views, and was widely considered to be a 'persona non grata' by the unpopular Villard government. After her husband's death in the Great War, Madeline changed her month old son's name from LaPointe to her maiden name, LaBlanc. The change was never registered with the authorities in Thoiry (thirty miles east of Paris) where the family resided. After moving to an apartment in Paris, Guillaume's birth certificate was destroyed, and the boy enrolled in elementary school as LaBlanc. Madeline was determined that her son never be conscripted into the military—neither the authorities in Thoiry or Paris had any record of a Guillaume Henri LaBlanc.

When Guillaume was twelve, his mother explained what she had done—and why. Since then, the young man had flourished under the pseudonym, excelled in academics, but continued to maintain a low profile which kept him relatively distant from his beloved mother. On occasional weekends and for holidays, the two of them spent precious time together at the small cottage in Thoiry where Madeline still spent much of her time. Only a few trusted family members and friends knew about the mother-son relationship.

~

Monday morning found Guillaume LaBlanc in the Sorbonne campus library. Distracted, he looked up from the book he was reading. He hadn't slept well the night before; still unable to dismiss his confused feelings of the previous Saturday. There was something in Emma Phelps' eyes that haunted, pleaded, compelled…but what that obscure *something* might be remained a mystery. In fifteen minutes he had an Italian Renaissance lecture to attend. Guillaume pushed his chair away from the table, collected his books and headed for the door; but instead of turning toward the campus classroom buildings, he found himself walking away. This would be his first missed lecture of the semester.

Gabrielle was towel drying her long, dark hair when Guillaume rushed into the small room. "Aren't you supposed to be in class?" At first surprised, she considered the earlier visitor to their flat, "Is something the matter, Guillaume? Your American friend was here only an hour ago." Gabrielle, having worked the weekend, had this Monday off from her waitressing job at the Savoy Hotel in the Latin Quarter of Paris.

"I thought she would try to reach me—somehow…?" Guillaume read the scribbled note his girlfriend handed him.

"Gabrielle, I must go to the church right now. Emma needs me."

"The American woman seemed very frightened about something, Guillaume. Is she in some kind of trouble?"

"I don't think so, sweetheart. But she's frightened?—my instincts tell me she is very much disturbed by something. I must help if I can."

Conrad left the embassy frustrated. His negotiations had failed to provide travel papers to Sorrento for he and Emma, and information on the status of the Phelps' property there was impossible to track down. "When they stonewall us like this, Mr. Phelps, it usually means they are withholding information. Foreign owned lands, especially in Southern Italy, have been expropriated by Mussolini's Fascists in the guise of 'national security'," Ambassador Kline informed him. "I can arrange a meeting for you with the American ambassador in Rome if you'd like. Graham Williams is much closer to the issue than I am."

Conrad shrugged his narrow shoulders, "I'll let you know, Mr. Kline. Maybe I'll end up taking care of matters for myself."

Conrad entered the hotel lobby looking as if the weight of the world were on his shoulders. How would he tell Emma that they were probably stuck in Paris longer than planned? He'd promised her castles and beaches, told her stories of Pompeii and nearby volcanic Mount Vesuvius. Would she be disappointed in him? How was Emma feeling? His concerns about Emma always dwarfed those of his own well-being. Her happiness was more important than anything else, and…her mood had been noticeably changing these past few days.

His chagrin, however, turned quickly to a black frown. On a settee table, Conrad spotted a bulky, well read copy of the *London Times* that someone had left behind. What first caught his attention was that the Sunday issue was an English translation. On the lower right front page was a banner that sent Conrad's head spinning: *American Woman Believed Abducted.* Quickly scanning the story, Conrad swallowed against an onset of panic. The story contained accurate descriptions of them both and stated that Scotland Yard was searching the English countryside. The names Clarke and Johnson were mentioned along with Phelps in the single columned article.

Tucking the paper under his arm, Conrad raced up the stairs, down the second floor hallway, and swept into the room breathing heavily—"Emma…! We've got to make some arrangements…Emma? Emma… I'm back. Emma?"

The rooms were silent. Where could she be?

Overwhelmed with a sickening panic, Conrad searched the suite. She was gone! Nauseous and shaken, he called the front desk clerk. A young man named Berthume, explained what had occurred earlier that morning, "She caught a taxi, sir."

"Guillaume's address…in Montmartre? A taxi? How long ago?" Conrad tried to digest the information the clerk had provided. Emma had taken a taxi to Guillaume LaBlanc's flat nearly three hours before. In an attempt to conceal his alarm, Conrad told the clerk in a controlled voice, "No, that won't be necessary. Our guide has probably taken her shopping for the day."

What was going on? Conrad's first confused thoughts focused on an affair. That Emma might have become attracted to the handsome Frenchman would be no surprise, but: So openly? Surely if there were some kind of tryst, both would be more secretive about arranging a meeting. Would Guillaume even consider such a risky entanglement? No. It was something far more unnerving. Emma's behavior of late had been bizarre, unpredictable. Fragments of memory were coming back to her—Kevin, snow, being lost in St. Paul: And the incredible painting of yesterday! Conrad sensed that Emma was beginning to keep things from him. Distancing herself, closing up. Was her earlier excuse about being ill a lie? Had Emma planned to run at her first opportunity? Conrad reproached himself for leaving his wife alone while he went to the embassy. "How absolutely stupid of me," he mumbled to himself.

Conrad considered his options of the moment. His gut instinct was to get a taxi and begin searching for Emma in Montmartre on his own. He had Guillaume's address, but what if she returned while he was gone and didn't find him at the hotel?

Should he contact the police and make a report? Another no! Making no decision, Conrad reasoned, was probably the best decision. He decided to wait until he heard something from her, or from Guillaume. Conrad checked the clock—it was 11:15; Emma had left the hotel at about 8:45. Sitting on the edge of Emma's bed he lit a cigarette. From what he could discern, Emma had not taken any clothing, and all of their suitcases remained stored in the large closet. Perhaps it was nothing more than an impulsive shopping excursion—or going to the Montmartre church. Guillaume had told her about the Sacre-Coeur Basilica the previous Saturday, and Emma seemed interested in visiting it with him. Yes, it had to be that church in Montmartre. Or...where else might she have gone? Yet, behind his conjecture were his darkest fears: Did Emma knows? Was she on the run?

Conrad tried to shake his apprehensions and think positively. Emma could be spontaneous and impulsive. She had used almost all of her tubes of white oil paint the day before, and mentioned to him that she would need more supplies soon. Guillaume knew where the art shops were. He cursed himself for throwing away all the wrapping papers—there might have been an address for the shop.

Swimming with his torment was the even darker specter of Emma's fidelity. "No...God, don't even let me think that Emma could ever...!" he said into the empty room. He began to pace. "Not my Emma." He had to cling to that weak thread of conviction: Emma would never risk any sexual involvement with another man; especially a virtual stranger to both of them.

But, Guillaume...? What did he really know about the young, endearing, Frenchman? Tall, handsome, smooth talking LaBlanc—was he a seducer of vulnerable women?

Agonizing, Conrad scrunched his cigarette into the ashtray. He would wait for an hour or two. Then...he would go looking. The police would have to remain his very last resort. No, the punishing reality struck him like a bolt—the police could not be involved! The *London Times* article flashed in his memory as he focused on the paper he'd thrown on the sofa. A missing American woman would raise too many questions in too many places. The Sûreté must already know that Scotland Yard is investigating the abduction of an American woman. And what about the U.S. embassy? How long before Ambassador Kline learned...?

In a worst case scenario, Conrad might have to begin running by himself— away from Paris; where no one could find him. How much time did the ticking clock allow? Another day...or hours? He fought against his fears and his tears; the prospect of being alone again was terrifying!

Sit tight. Don't panic. Perhaps he was blowing everything out of proportion? Conrad regarded the clock—11:35, then the black phone. It had only been a few hours—Emma would call. Or, maybe, Guillaume?

"Emma, there you are," Guillaume approached the huddled figure kneeling with a scarf draped over her head and face. His American friend was praying the rosary before a side altar near the front of the huge basilica. "Gabrielle gave me your note. What is the matter, Emma?"

Emma rose from the kneeler and clung to the tall man. "Oh, Guillaume, I need your help. Desperately! I cannot go back to Conrad."

Perplexed, Guillaume gave her time to explain. "There, there...don't cry, *mon cherie*." Sitting down beside her on the wooden pew he took her hand, "Tell me what's happened. What can I do?"

For the next twenty minutes, Emma explained her predicament between deep sobs, "So...I'm not sure who I am, Guillaume. As I told you, there was an accident and my memory somehow disappeared. Conrad must have..." Tears were streaking her face now. Trying to regain a semblance of composure, she finished..."abducted me. It's all so confusing, but I'm not Emma Phelps! I'm positive of that, Guillaume. I'm not Conrad's wife."

Startled, Guillaume asked, "Do you have any idea who you are, Em—"
He bit off the name. Her story was almost unbelievable, but—"What do you want me to do for you? I'll do anything...Take you to the police?"

"No—not yet, Guillaume. But you can take me to that art shop where you found the supplies. Somehow, as bizarre at it seems, I think there is a connection.

The name, Grojean—I know that name. Somewhere in my past there was a man named Jacque Grojean," Emma said recalling the name. "He was an artist..." She sobbed, "A dear man, a friend. He will know, Guillaume, I can almost feel his...his intervention in all of this. Jacque and others as well. It's almost like invisible hands are somehow guiding me—sending me to you, Guillaume."

Guillaume contemplated the spiritual essence of her appeal. He had been feeling a similar compulsion. As surreal as it seemed: Could there be divine forces at work, drawing them together in this sacred place? Giving her hand a squeeze, he repeated the name: "Jacque Grojean?" shaking his head. "The shop owner is Pierre, not Jacque. Grojean is a common name here in Paris, Emm—I'm sorry." He tried to laugh, "What am I going to call you now, *mon cherie*? We'll need another name for a while, won't we?"

The woman reciprocated Guillaume's awkward attempt to laugh at her confusing situation. While dabbing at her tears, she blurted—"Just that...*Cherie*."

"There it is, up ahead, Cherie—Pierre's shop." Guillaume gestured with one hand while taking her elbow with the other. "Trust my translations as I explain your predicament; Mr. Grojean speaks very little English, I'm afraid."

The distinctive smells wafting throughout the small shop piqued her memory—closing her eyes, the woman tried to stretch her recollection. She could picture a similar place in her mind—but where that might have been remained lost in her fog.

After Guillaume's introduction, Pierre extended his small hand and spoke an affectionate greeting in French. With typical animation, Guillaume began explaining the purpose of their visit to the proprietor and got an occasional nod in response. "*Oui...Oui...*" the mustached artist acknowledged, his dark eyes shifting from Guillaume to her as he listened. "*Mais oui...Jacque.*"

After a few minutes, Guillaume turned to the expectant woman anxiously awaiting his translation, "Jacque Grojean was Pierre's older brother. An American citizen, Pierre says..." Guillaume took her hands, "He has passed, *mon cherie*—nearly two years ago, I'm afraid."

A pang of emotion caught in her throat, "Tell Mr. Grojean...I'm so very sorry about his brother." She lowered her head in a silent prayer for her deceased friend, feeling an overwhelming sense of defeat. What seemed like a promising connection to her past was suddenly lost.

"*Merci*, Cherie," Pierre nodded at the woman's condolences, then began explaining something in French.

"That's it!" She interrupted Pierre's discourse with a spark in her eyes, "That is the place, Guillaume! I heard him say it…!"

An hour later, while having a sandwich at a back table in a nearby bistro, they tried to tie the tangled story together. A chilly drizzle was in the air and the couple found an intimate refuge in the cozy restaurant. A pair of wax-dripping candles rested on the checkered tablecloth between them offering a glowing warmth to her hands cupped about them. Guillaume shook his head, "What do we do now, Cherie? Our police can make a contact with that place in Minnesota…and let them know where you are, your *predicament*. Then—"

"But who do we tell them—the police, I mean—is lost in Paris? Surely not Emma Phelps. I need my real name."

"Don't you think the police can figure that out?"

"I don't know, Guillaume. But somehow the police frighten me." For the first time in hours, she wondered about Conrad. A strange tinge of sadness behind her relief and optimism of the moment. What was he doing? Had he contacted the police himself? Were the gendarmes looking for her now? Would she be arrested? How might she explain what was happening? Her thoughts became muddled in a growing confusion. If Conrad had somehow convinced the authorities that she was his wife—what then? Conrad was far more clever than she. What if he fooled the police and took her away again. To Italy—or to some doctor he'd talked about in Vienna? She was in a quandary!

"*Cherie*? What are you thinking about?"

"Not the police. Not yet, anyhow."

Guillaume understood her fears—of the police, and perhaps of Conrad. "What can we do?"

"You must hide me, Guillaume. I fear that the Paris police are already looking for me. We need time…time to better figure out what to do next. Where can we go?"

Cherie's conclusion, however, was unsettling to Guillaume. He had always promised his mother that he would avoid any and all situations that might place either of them under unnecessary scrutiny. If the police were already looking Montmartre was not safe. Mr. Phelps had lots of money…and his story might be far more believable than Emma's. Perhaps she was right about needing more time. If the Sûreté had been contacted about Mrs. Phelps, Guillaume's apartment would be the first place they would go. And, Gabrielle could confirm that Emma had been at his flat that morning. Guillaume's girlfriend knew that he was going to meet her at the *Sacre Coeur*. Montmartre might be swarming with police even at this moment. Perhaps the only safe place would be in his mother's house in Thoiry—thirty miles east of Paris. But getting out of the city without detection could prove difficult.

"Cherie, are you prepared for another abduction?" Guillaume said lightly, a smile creasing his handsome face. "I'll have to take you some distance away from Montmartre if we're going to hide."

She nodded, smiled, "Anyplace you think is safe. I trust you with all my heart, Guillaume. You're my angel." Searching her handbag, she withdrew her money, "All I have is this to take care of us." She placed the American twenty and several francs on the table.

Guillaume laughed to himself. In his pocket he still had the extravagant tip from Conrad Phelps. "Money will not be any problem. It's getting out of Montmartre without being seen that worries me, Cherie." Rising and taking her hand, Guillaume said, "Let's go right now. I have a friend only a few blocks from here—he owns an automobile."

OUT OF THE FOG

The Paris police were not looking for Emma Phelps.

Conrad, on the edges of shock over Emma's disappearance, consulted a telephone directory he found in a drawer by the phone and found an advertisement (printed in both French and English) under the 'Private Investigation' section of the thick book. It was midafternoon and the past three hours had been a private hell. He could no longer wait and do nothing.

André Bouchard answered the telephone himself, "Quite fluently, Messieur," he responded to Conrad's first question. And to the second inquiry, "Yes, I locate missing people all the time, Mr. Phelps."

"My wife has done this before, Mr. Bouchard...taken some money from my wallet and gone off on a shopping spree. It's embarrassing to me, and frustrates her family back in Cleveland...you understand. So, none of us would want anything to appear in the papers." Conrad carefully elaborated another fabrication, "Emma's quite a storyteller—she often claims to have amnesia or some outlandish condition, you know. Sometimes, she even fools people into believing that she can't remember her name or where she's from. We're in Paris to see a doctor about this."

After explaining where and when he believed Emma had gone from the hotel, and giving a careful physical description of both Emma and Guillaume, Conrad answered a few other basic investigative questions. "This Guillaume mentioned taking Emma to *Sacre-Coeur* just the other day," he added as a footnote to all the previous information.

"I'll find your wife, Mr. Phelps. I was born and raised up there. If she's anywhere in the Montmartre neighborhood..." Bouchard licked at the corner of his thick mouth. The thousand dollar (American) 'finder's fee' was more money than he'd seen in six months.

By late afternoon, André Bouchard's leads brought him from LaBlanc's apartment to the Pierre Grojean art studio. A well dressed, blond, American woman in Montmartre left a trail that even the Paris police could follow.

During the chilly afternoon, Bouchard had talked to dozens of people along the Montmartre streets including the attractive waitress at the bistro where he was sipping a cup of cafe au lait while catching glances at her shapely hips as she moved from table to table. It was nearly six and he'd promised Mr. Phelps an update on his activities. Borrowing the bistro phone, Bouchard had called the Ritz. "I've got a short list of some of LaBlanc's friends, Mr. Phelps. I'm positive that when I offer these deadbeat artists fifty francs, some tongues will start wagging."

"And this Guillaume LaBlanc is a familiar face in he neighborhood," the detective reported from his phone at a Montmartre bistro. "Your wife and this LaBlanc fellow were at *Sacre-Coeur*—just as you thought, Mr. Phelps. Then the two of them visited an art shop up here. I've talked with both LaBlanc's girlfriend and the shop owner, Pierre Grojean—neither one of them would tell me much more than they'd seen the couple." Bouchard's trail had gone suddenly cold at the art shop.

"Please, keep me posted on anything you find, Mr. Bouchard. I'm worried for Emma's safety—this LaBlanc might be some kind of…crazed pervert, you know. I don't trust him at all."

"I'll find your wife by tomorrow, Mr. Phelps—I'm sure of it. I'll be pounding on doors all night if that's what it takes."

Tomorrow? Conrad's patience had worn thin, "Call me back about nine, Bouchard. I can't stand the thought of my wife spending the night with another man, especially a dangerous one."

Conrad opened a new package of cigarettes, stared out at the early evening street below. The past seven hours had been the longest of his life. What was he going to do? Even if he were to find Emma…? His greatest dread was that she had gone to the police. But if she had done so, surely the Sûreté would have contacted Conrad by now. No, Guillaume must be hiding her somewhere in Montmartre.

The waiting was eating away at Conrad's insides. Should he go to Grojean's art shop himself? Or, to Guillaume's address where he might watch the comings and goings? He cursed himself for feeling so inept and helpless. And—he felt betrayed. How long had Emma and Guillaume conspired? Where would they hide? Clinging to his fragile thread of hope, he wondered: Was there some other explanation that had escaped him these past hours? Could Emma have gotten lost somehow? No, she and the Frenchman had already been seen together. Would Guillaume take the risk of sheltering, abetting, or—*abducting* his confused wife? The word stung his muddled thoughts. Abducting? No, despite his transient fears to the contrary, he knew Guillaume was a decent man. He would not harm Emma. Maybe the young Frenchman, realizing Emma's confusion, would telephone Conrad at some point—or, even better, bring her back to the hotel.

Conrad's troubled thoughts ranged from one extreme to another and ran through a gauntlet of possibilities—most of them increasingly negative. As it had so many times that day, the notion of sexual motivations cut back into his mind. Emma was young and attractive—so was her new friend. Yet, Conrad could not dismiss his feelings of affiliation with the Frenchman; his trust in the man's moral righteousness. Shaking the notion of an illicit affair, Conrad forced himself to focus on something more tangible and positive. Sooner or later, Emma would be found. With that thought, however, came another flood of contradictory concerns. Paris was an enormous city—so inviting of anonymity. Guillaume, although seemingly a loyal sort, was far more attached to Emma than to Conrad. And Guillaume was smart—probably perceptive enough to both understand and sympathize with Emma's condition. More likely than not, Guillaume would help her escape, if that was what Emma was trying to do.

Conrad was playing from a weak hand. Guillaume was a decent man motivated by a desire to help Emma, while Bouchard, on the other hand, was motivated solely by Conrad's handsome reward.

The phone rang. Conrad, feeling a chill of apprehension, stood paralyzed for a long moment. News from Bouchard already? Guillaume? Emma?

"This is Conrad Phelps," he spoke in quivering voice.

The woman's words on the other end of the line were heavily accented, her English difficult to understand... "I am reading to you from a note, monsieur:

> *Cherie is safe. Don't go to the police. We will contact you when we know all the facts.*

"That is all, monsieur, *bon soir*." The phone went dead.

Conrad's hand was shaking as he returned the receiver. The caller, he was certain, was a confidante of Guillaume's. He replayed the few words in his mind. *'Cherie?'* Had Emma already changed her name? *'Don't tell the police?'*...Or, was it —'involve the police'? Whatever, it seemed clear that Emma had not yet gone to the authorities. That was good news. But, *'when we know all the facts?'* —Conrad could conjecture about the meaning of that segment of the message: The facts referred to Emma's true identity!

He sighed and mumbled to himself while lighting another cigarette, "At least she's safe for now." But somehow, Conrad had never had any doubt about that. It was already nearing seven o'clock. Looking over the busy street below his second floor window, Conrad dolefully watched the pedestrian traffic. So many couples, affectionately holding hands—happy, carefree, and in love. Just the way he imagined it would always be with he and Emma: The two of them—with all the money in the world to spend. Traveling the world, enjoying each other's companionship as they toured ancient castles and wandered isolated beaches. As he remembered his promises to do these things with Emma, his thoughts returned from marvelous fantasy to harsh reality—

On the table nearby were the Bolshoi ballet tickets for tonight's performance. Like everything else he might ever imagine, the two empty theater seats seemed a harbinger of what lie ahead.

Leaning against a lamppost below the window was a woeful soul in unkempt clothing, his floppy tam pulled down over his ears. A small man. Alone. Unresponsive to passers by—someone nobody seemed to recognize or care about. Conrad saw himself in the derelict. His reflection shook him back to his former life, his loneliness, and the dull, empty patterns of anonymous daily routines. Visages of Conrad's sad, and pathetic former life brought tears to his eyes. How dramatically Emma had changed everything! A picture of his Emma peering from the train at the majestic range of Rocky Mountains formed in his thoughts, then another of her splashing in the waves on the California beach, and then an image of his lovely wife mingling with guests at their gala reception—such vivid memories. Would there ever be more...?

Turning away from the window and the solitary man across the street, Conrad sat in a nearby chair, elbows on his knees, his delicate hands cupping his drawn face, and sobbed. A prayer wormed into his torment of the moment..."God forgive me...In all Your mercy—forgive what I have done." With the petition came an unexpected resolve. He contemplated undoing the wrongs he had done.

Should he go to the police and turn himself in? Perhaps it wasn't too late. A heartfelt confession might mitigate the severity of the punishment he deserved. Someone might understand—be sympathetic, even have a positive regard for Conrad's remorse and contrition. Were he to throw himself to the mercy of a court, might his heinous misdeeds find the slightest measure of pardon? If only he could talk to Emma—right now! Tell her the truth before anybody else, plead for her forgiveness—promise to take her home. Yes, he could do that.

~

Madeline LaPointe was nearly as tall as her son, but her frame scarcely carried a hundred pounds. After Guillaume's late afternoon phone call, she took the first available train from Paris to Thoiry where she would meet them that evening. Madeline, although wary, sensed an urgency in her son's tone more than in his few words. Repressing her concerns, she chose not to ask him any questions until later.

In precise English, the intelligent, gray-haired woman regarded the woman called Cherie, "I have read about amnesia in psychology journals, my child, but have always been—I must admit—somewhat of a skeptic. How tragic this must be for you—and for your family and loved ones in the States."

The young woman nodded without reply. Her family? Since discovering where she was from that afternoon, she had forced her mind to process the connection as fully as possible. Jacque Grojean had been her mentor, his little studio her refuge. A vague picture of the place had begun to form—banks of snow along the winter streets…a castle-like school building only a short distance away…a majestic hotel. The hotel was something significant, she believed. A man, tall and handsome, with the brightest smile seemed a part of her emerging picture.

"What was that, Cherie?" Guillaume asked.

"What?"

Guillaume met her eyes, "*Kevin!* You just said, *Kevin*. Don't you remember?"

"No…I was daydreaming, I guess." But hearing the name from Guillaume's mouth triggered a sudden memory. A confusing memory. She mulled the name over in her thoughts. "I think I'm finding my way out of the dark, Guillaume. Things are coming back to me…in small waves!"

"Cherie—are you feeling okay?" His voice laden with concern. The woman was as white as her linen blouse.

She nodded with the trace of a spark in her dark eyes.

While having a late dinner, Guillaume and his tormented friend had explained all that had happened that day to an attentive Madeline LaPointe. The more she spoke of her recollection, the better Cherie understood them. Guillaume's timely insights added another dimension.

"When I talked with Gabrielle, she told me that a Mr. Bouchard had been by my flat looking for Emma Phelps," Guillaume informed, "She believed the man was a private detective despite his denial when she inquired. "I don't have any idea about what the police know or what, if anything, they are doing right now." Guillaume then told his mother about the note he'd asked Gabrielle to write down and relay to Mr. Phelps at the hotel. "Surely, she has contacted Mr. Phelps by now."

Madeline pondered the sequence of events that day and as far back as the young woman could remember. Her bizarre account of an accident in St. Paul, Minnesota, fleeing to California, and then halfway around the world was something out of fiction. Even more strange, however, was the behavior of the apparent abductor, Conrad Phelps. What kind of person would do such a thing? In it's every detail the story strained Madeline's imagination. Yet, she believed what the troubled young woman was telling her. And her son Guillaume was no fool.

Madeline contemplated what needed to be done. From her years of outspoken criticism of the French establishment, she ruled out any contact with the Sûreté authorities. Watching the clock hands sweep toward nine o'clock, Madeline made her decision: "There is only one logical thing for us to do right now."

Madeline LaPointe stood up from the sofa where she had been sitting and picked up the telephone. "Will you please connect me to an overseas line please, operator...*le Etates Unis*." Almost dropping the phone, Madeline was dumbstruck by an expression of unbridled joy flashing across the young woman's pretty face—.

"*Kevin...Kevin Moran!*" Emma Phelps blurted. "Guillaume...Madeline...I know who I am!"

~

Listening to a pessimistic nine o'clock report from André Bouchard (phoning from a Latin Quarter hotel) discouraged Conrad even more than he already was. "Nobody's telling me anything, Mr. Phelps. It's possible that your wife and her lover have fled Montmartre." The detective winced at his uncalled-for reference to LaBlanc, and considered making an apology. Rather, he offered weakly; "I still have a few names…"

Offended, Conrad snapped, "I don't appreciate that remark, Bouchard." Yet, inside he was resigned to the impression others might have of his wife's disappearance. "Don't make those kinds of assumptions again, Bouchard!"

"Sorry, Mr. Phelps—I didn't mean to say that," he said contritely as he imagined losing a lot of money. "Like I said, I've still got some people to check with."

Conrad had already dismissed the notion of turning himself in to authorities as being too unrealistic. Throughout his befuddled analysis of the situation he had been weighing his diminishing options in the likelihood of the investigator's failure to locate Emma within a few hours. Remaining in Paris any longer did not seem to be one of them. Bouchard could continue his search without Conrad's involvement.

Yet, Conrad worried—how might he learn of any new developments if he were not in frequent communication with the investigator? And what if Emma returned to the hotel to find him gone? Dumping a heaping tray of cigarette buts into the trash and pouring another cup of coffee, he cursed his predicament under his breath.

"Do you have any idea where your wife might have fled—I mean, if she isn't in Montmartre?"

"Absolutely none. She doesn't know the city. You're the investigator." Conrad's next contention was uncharacteristically profane and intended to strike a nerve in the detective, "It's not where Emma might go, for chrissakes, it's where LaBlanc might take her."

Bouchard chose not to comment at the obvious.

Conrad was rethinking his next steps. Throughout the past several hours, a sketchy plan had been taking shape. It now seemed clear to him that his only recourse was to run—and get going before it was too late. "Keep looking, Bouchard," he instructed in a sinking voice, "I'll leave half of the money I promised you at the front desk. When you find out anything important contact me—get out your pen and write down where I'll be…"

In the lobby downstairs, Conrad paced for a few minutes. Feeling the eyes of the desk clerk, he picked up a train schedule brochure from a nearby table. He approached the clerk and slid the envelope with Bouchard's name across the countertop, "Ask for identification when the man picks this up."

As he crossed the street, Conrad could hear the approaching wail of sirens splitting the chilly Paris night.

BOOK THREE

Searching for Angela

MISSING IN ST. PAUL

August, 1938

The annual Chamber of Commerce fishing trip to Lake Namakan was only a two day expedition, but Kevin Moran had packed enough gear to outfit him through a month.

"Can I throw in the kitchen sink?" Angie chided facetiously as her husband tightened the cords around a bulky sleeping bag. "Are you bringing provisions for all twenty guys, Kevin?"

Tony Zoretek and Marc Atkinson would be picking him up in another twenty minutes, "Too much, huh? I do this every year, don't I? What should I leave behind?" Kevin shook his head without looking up.

Angie critically surveyed the pile on the foyer floor. "I might suggest a few things. Let me see... One wool jacket will do for an overnight in the woods. Extra boots? The ones you're wearing should be enough. All that rain gear? And three tackle boxes? Should I go on...?" She pushed the extra pair of leather boots off to the side with her slippered foot.

"You're right, of course." Kevin said, opening the tackle boxes and rummaging through the assortment of lures, leaders, hooks and bobbers of every sort. "I can probably get everything I need in this one big box."

Angie laughed to herself. She and Becca were also leaving for the weekend and Angie had packed all her clothing in one suitcase. "If men think women overpack, they sure miss the boat."

Although preoccupied, Kevin caught the pun, "You're comparing apples and oranges, Angie. We're camping out in the wilderness, not staying at a fancy hotel overnight." Closing the lid on his tackle box, Kevin stood up and met her eyes. "I wish I were going with you to St. Paul, sweetheart." Despite not wanting to overreact, his concern could not be repressed, "I'm going to worry about you."

Angie was registered to attend a Midwest Artists symposium at St. Catherine's College in St. Paul over the weekend. Becca Zoretek had agreed to be her traveling companion, and so while Angie was attending workshops, Becca would be visiting her mother, Josie Kaner, in nearby Highland Park. The two women were booked on the nine o'clock train to the capitol city, and after their arrival, Angie would take a cab to the St. Paul Hotel while Becca traveled to her mother's house. They planned to get together early Saturday evening at Mrs. Kaner's house for dinner. Angie would stay overnight there and the two Hibbing women would return home on Sunday's train. "If you want to worry; worry about catching fish, Kevin—I'll be just fine."

Kevin stepped toward his wife, cupped her face in his hands, "I know you will. But, if Becca weren't going with you...I'd cancel out of the Chamber trip and tag along to your woman's thing—you know that."

Angie had not had a blackout episode in two years, but Kevin still harbored apprehensions. He'd almost changed his plans about joining the other fishermen. Though he wouldn't admit it to Angie, it was only the day before that he made his commitment to join the Namakan Lake expedition. Angie gave him a kiss, "I'm so excited—just think, I'll be meeting Georgia O'Keefe at the hotel reception in St. Paul tonight."

Kevin saw the spark of excitement in her dark, ovaline eyes, "And she will be meeting you. The honor will be mutual, sweetheart. Don't sell yourself short, you've made quite a name for yourself in art circles—I'd be very surprised if this O'Keefe woman doesn't already know that."

Angie smiled at the compliment. She had, in fact, received a hand-written letter from Miss O'Keefe some weeks before mentioning that the renowned artist was looking forward to meeting her. "It's going to be a great time, Kevin. Who knows, I might even stay an extra day or two and visit the museums down there. Could you get along without me for—"

Both were interrupted by the familiar beep of Tony's new '38 Packard from the driveway outside. "Will you help me get this stuff loaded, honey? Your dad's anxious to get rolling. I don't think he's even coming up to the door to lend a hand."

Watching the car drive down the long Maple Hill driveway, Angie waved. It was seven and she had to get herself ready and pick up Becca before eight-thirty.

Clara Motter, the housekeeper, was already giving the two children their breakfast. This would be the first time in years that she and Kevin would both be away from the kids for a weekend. A weekend seemed like a long time to Angie.

∼

"A great time, Dad." Kevin said giving Tony a quick hug. It was getting dark and the two men were unloading the car after the long drive back to Hibbing from the Canadian border lake. "Angie won't believe all the walleye I caught—"

"Mr. Moran!" Clara Motter was at the door, "Doctor Becca's been trying to get you for three hours…wants you to call her back as soon as you get in the door."

"Something wrong?" Kevin dropped the canvas bag of gear and hurried into the foyer with Tony at his heels. "Did Becca say what she wanted?"

Kevin's mind raced. He had promised Angie that he'd call her at the Kaner house when he returned from the fishing trip. "Something's happened to Angie," he mumbled under his breath.

"Thank God you've finally called, Kevin! I've been beside myself…" Becca's voice strained.

"Settle down, Becca. Tony's here with me—what's the matter?"

Tony watched as Kevin's face contorted in unmitigated anguish. Whatever had happened was taking considerable time to explain.

"You called the college…and the police…and the hotel!" Kevin reiterated what Becca had reported. "I'll be on my down there in five minutes, Becca. Stay by your phone. I'll call and check in with you at every opportunity along the way." Looking at the pendulum clock nearby, Kevin noticed it was just after nine; "I'll be getting to your mom's house late—I mean early in the morning. Should take about six hours."

Before hanging up the phone, Kevin bit at his lip but said nothing for long moments. Finally, in a raspy tone, he assured Becca, "Everything's going to be okay—we'll find her. "Say hello to Tony, I'll fill him in along the way. He doesn't know it yet, but he's coming with me."

After giving unnecessary instructions to Clara, who knew as much about taking care of the children as he did, Kevin and Tony threw their bags back into the trunk of the Packard and headed off to St. Paul. Kevin would drive the initial leg to Floodwood where they would make their first call back to Becca. From there, they would call from Moose Lake, Hinckley, and other coffee stops along Highway 61 to St. Paul.

"I had the strangest feeling before we left on our fishing trip, Tony. I shouldn't have let her go to that art thing in St. Paul alone."

"Don't blame yourself, Kev. She was traveling with her doctor for heaven's sake!" Without saying so, Tony knew that Kevin's concerns were related to Angie's history of blackouts. "And try not to be an alarmist—like you told Becca, we're going to find her."

Taking turns at the wheel and exceeding every posted speed limit, the two men were making every effort to keep each other awake and trying not to dwell too long on the exigency of the moment. The two-day fishing trip was rehashed, baseball pennant races analyzed, and world tensions discussed at length. Yet, despite every effort at diversion, their conversation inevitably turned to the dark possibility: "What if she's been abducted?" Kevin blurted the thought that kept cropping into his mind but had been too long repressed. "Maybe she's not lost at all. Maybe…?" But Kevin could not utter his deepest fear.

Tony, checking the speedometer while Kevin gazed absently at the blurred tree-lined roadside, did not comment on the sinister theory. He had imagined the same tragedy countless times himself.

"The Twin Cities are so huge—so full of riffraff."

"Don't even think about it. Worry is wasted thought. I'd bet anything that she's had a *little* episode and gotten herself lost." Tony emphasized *little* so as not to add to Kevin's apprehension. "There are a lot more decent people in St. Paul than there are perverts. Someone's going to report Angie to the police before we get to Becca's place." Tony said optimistically, reaching over and giving Kevin's knee a squeeze.

It was nearly two in the morning and the two travelers were passing through White Bear Lake, within forty minutes of Highland Park. They had made four calls along the way only to find that nothing had changed—Angie had not been heard from.

∼

After getting Kevin Moran's call at five in the morning, Keirnan McGinnis attended early mass at the St. Paul Cathedral, then drove over to the prestigious St. Paul Hotel to confer with his old Hibbing friend. An impromptu meeting had been arranged for seven. The police sergeant would brief the group on the status of his department's 'missing person' investigation of the past several hours.

"Thanks for joining us, Keirnan." Kevin stood as the policeman entered the plush office of Terry Whelan, the hotel's manager and a close acquaintance of Kevin's from years before.

"Sorry it has to be under these circumstances, Mr. Moran," the lanky, red-haired Irishman said.

Kevin introduced Terry and Keirnan, "Just Kevin, please. You remember Tony Zoretek from your Hibbing days, don't you, Keirnan?"

The out-of-uniform officer nodded, "Good to see you again, Tony."

"Without the mustache, I might have had to take a long look," Tony said as he accepted Keirnan's strong handshake. "Hard to picture you without that handlebar under your nose."

Terry Whelan, a short and stocky man, looked up at Kevin and Tony. The two strapping Hibbing men looked like football linemen—rawboned Zoretek was well over six feet and Moran only an inch or two shorter. He offered Keirnan a chair, "What have the police learned so far, officer? Keirnan grimaced, "Nothing more than you three probably already know, I'm afraid. Mrs. Moran left your hotel, Mr. Whelan—at about eight-thirty yesterday morning. She talked with your doorman, Darby Poole, briefly—asked directions to St. Kate's. Poole told her to take the Randolph line streetcar from the corner of Market Street."

Whelan lit a cigarette, then added, "And her luggage was tagged at the desk for taxi delivery to Mrs. Kaner's address in Highland Park."

"I guess that's about the extent of what we know at this point. Angie never showed up at the art workshops at St. Catherine's—nor at the Kaner's where she was expected in late afternoon." Kevin said in an exasperated tone.

"I checked with the desk sergeant at the department before coming here," Keirnan said. "They've been looking all over the neighborhoods between here and the campus—have been doing so since Tony's wife called the station last night about five."

"What now, Keirnan?" Whelan asked. "Keep looking?"

Keirnan shrugged. "Captain Duane Locher's heading the department investigation right now. He called the Randolph streetcar operator, a man named Virgil Hespert—actually got him out of bed last night. Seems that Hespert cannot recall a passenger of Mrs. Moran's description getting on his trolley yesterday morning. Claimed he had only two fares at the Rice Park stop—an elderly man and a regular named Plum—Gretchen Plum. Locher located the Plum woman and she said the same thing; only she and an old man got on at Market Street by the park." McGinnis informed.

"I'd be inclined to believe what this Hespert fella said, it's often said that those trolley operators have incredible memories of their fares," suggested Whelan, leaning away from his desk and tossing the cigarette into a brass spittoon near his feet.

"I hope your right about that," McGinnis said, "The police are also interviewing that operator on the Grand Avenue line who had the accident yesterday. He's been badly traumatized so it might take some time."

"What accident?" Kevin almost leaped from his chair.

Keirnan explained the fatal collision between the streetcar and an automobile at Pascal Street that had derailed the trolley and killed a one year old child as well as the driver of the car. "Worst accident in years. Lots of folks got banged up and had to be hospitalized—including the child's mother who is in critical condition as we speak."

Whelan had a copy of the *Pioneer Press* newspaper near his attaché case on the floor. "There's a front page story on the accident right here." He passed the bulky paper to Kevin.

Scanning the article, Kevin wondered. Was it possible that Angie had been a passenger on the Grand Avenue line? Looking toward McGinnis, he raised the question.

Keirnan shrugged his shoulders, "That's a possibility I've considered. If we don't develop any leads on Randolph—Grand will likely be the next focus of our investigation. In fact, maybe we can do both areas at the same time. Let me run the idea by Locher—he's calling the shots."

Tony, who had mostly listened to the three way conversation, met Keirnan's eyes, "What can Kevin and I do? We're not leaving St. Paul until we find my daughter."

Keirnan rubbed his face with long fingers, "Don't suppose you've got any photographs of Mrs. Moran along with you? We could use something recent to get into the newspapers…to pass around the streets."

Tony looked with futility at Kevin who returned a similar expression. That was something neither of them had thought of before leaving Hibbing the night before. "We'll have something for you before the end of the day. Can I use your telephone to call Hibbing, Terry?" Tony regarded the black phone on Whelan's desktop; he had several photographs of Angie at home and Marco could bring them down."

Kevin was on the same thought track, "Tony, I've got a framed picture of Angie on my desk at the hotel—it was taken only months ago. Can you contact Marco or Rudy?—Even Marc Atkinson would be willing to drive down right now if you ask."

"Taken care of. Excuse me for a minute." Tony made the long distance call from a chair next to Whelan while the other men listened to the brief conversation. Hanging up the phone Tony announced, "Marco's out the door right now. He'll get your photograph at the hotel, Kev. Should be in St. Paul by later this afternoon."

Terry Whelan stood, "Gentlemen, you have my hopes and prayers. I'm going to let you use my office for anything you need to do—for as long as you want. Kevin, Tony...I'll put you up here at the hotel if you'd like, as well as any of your Hibbing friends who come down. Rooms and meals—everything—I want to take care of it for you."

Kevin hugged the smaller, graying man, "That's wonderful of you to do, Terry. I think we'd like to take a few minutes to figure out what we're going to do next, make some phone calls—you know. Thanks, my friend."

Whelan shook hands all around and excused himself.

"I'm going to head over to the station down the street if there's nothing else for the moment. I might be able to round up a few extra cops to help us do some looking," Keirnan said. "Where can I meet you two—say just after noon?" He offered a small, tight smile, "We're going to turn this town upside down, Kevin...Tony. We've got some fine investigators on our police force...and I'm one of them!"

"I believe that, Keirnan," Kevin said. "Maybe we can meet at Saint Katherine's and work backwards along Randolph Street—what do you think?"

~

It was eight-thirty on Sunday morning. Kevin noted the time on the wall clock. Just twenty-four hours ago—this exact minute, Angie had left this hotel. The irony was painful!

Tony made a call to Becca. "We're going to wrap things up here shortly, then..." He looked toward Kevin who was staring at the clock, and cupped his hand over the phone, "Kevin will you go up to the Cathedral with me. I'd like to say some prayers before we try to figure out what to do next. Becca's mom would like us to stop by and have a quick lunch before..."

Getting a nod from Kevin, Tony told Becca they would be coming over somewhere around ten.

"Oh, Gary Zench called only minutes ago, Tony," Becca remembered, her thoughts were still in shambles, "He's driving down with the picture you wanted. Marco's going to travel along for company. Gary said that before the end of the week, half of Hibbing would be in St. Paul looking for Angie if she isn't found pretty soon."

After hanging up the phone, Tony shared Becca's information. "So, by later today we're going to have Gary and Marco to help us out."

Kevin smiled at a reality he often took for granted: He and Angie had many friends. "I'll give Clara Motter a call before we head up the hill to the church. I'll let her know what's going on down here. I know I won't have to worry about the children, they absolutely worship their nanny." Kevin asked Clara to let Sister Anne know, "And give Rudy and Claude a call as well."

Kevin paced the office floor, rubbing his stubbled face in frustration. "I don't have a clue what the two of us are going to accomplish by ourselves, Tony. I guess you're right, some prayers might be helpful, then something to eat—before we meet Keirnan at St. Kate's around noon."

The St. Paul Cathedral dominated a hillside overlooking the city's river-edged downtown. Only a few blocks to the east was Minnesota's majestic Capitol building. Kevin was familiar with both awesome edifices from years before when he and Angie lived for a brief time on Summit Avenue. Their son, Patrick, was baptized in the enormous Renaissance style cathedral seven years before.

Inside the granite walled church, sun filtered through enormous rose windows. "I'd forgotten how magnificent this Cathedral is," Tony whispered to Kevin as the two men walked toward the imposing gold gilded altar. Six chapels surrounded the massive sanctuary, "I'm going to light a vigil candle over there," Tony gestured toward the St. Cyril chapel.

Kevin smiled knowingly, Cyril was a patron of Slavic people, "And I'll do the same at Saint Patrick's chapel."

Kneeling before the Irish saint, Kevin wept quietly. He hadn't prayed for anything in so long that he felt a pang of guilt over his spiritual void. Closing his eyes, petitioning words were the first to cross his lips, "Please, don't let God take my Angela from me, Saint Patrick." Dabbing at his tears, Kevin looked upward, "And Father Foley, I know you're up there too, Pat—pray for your old friend. Ask the Lord you served so devoutly to lead Angie back to me." In his final strained appeal, Kevin offered, "Jesus, if you keep her from harm's way… I'll come back to you."

∼

By mid afternoon, much of Hibbing had learned of the disappearance of Angela Moran. Clara Motter had dutifully called the Sister at the Blessed Sacrament convent, then informed Claude Atkinson who made calls of his own, including one to Hitchcock at the *Hibbing Tribune*.

Sister Anne explained the situation to Father Potocnik who, in turn, asked his congregation to "Keep Angela Moran in your thoughts and prayers" at the eleven o'clock Mass. In that a vast majority of Hibbing residents were Catholic, word spread rapidly in the community.

By four o'clock, a small contingent of Hibbingites was already gathered at the Kaner residence in Highland Park. Tony's brother Rudy drove down with Marc Atkinson; Gary Zench and Marco Zoretek joined Kevin, Tony, and Becca. For three hours that afternoon, Kevin and Tony (with Keirnan McGinnis and two officer friends of Keirnan's who volunteered their day off to help) had wandered along West Seventh toward Randolph Street from downtown St. Paul to St. Katherine's college. People at every streetcar stop were questioned as well as everybody else they encountered along the busy route. A photographer friend of Josie Kaner promised to reproduce a negative from Angela's photograph and have fifty copies available by later that evening.

For the most part, however, their search was fruitless. Kevin, in his zeal to 'be totally informed' interviewed Virgil Hespert, the streetcar operator, and later found Mrs. Gretchen Plum's address on South Snelling Avenue. Both remained positive that no one fitting Angela Moran's description had been on the trolley the previous morning.

Another passenger on Hespert's trolley was located. After pressing her memory, Plum recalled the name of someone who might know the 'old man' who had boarded at Market Street along with her on Saturday morning. Cedric Klancher, Kevin learned, was that old man. "No sir, I'm sure as snow in January there was no good-lookin' women ridin' in the car. I still got a keen eye fer a pretty girl."

Keirnan had to agree with Kevin's conclusion, "Your wife didn't take the Randolph line! We're going to have to go through this same process of asking folks who rode the Grand Avenue line yesterday morning—from Market Street downtown to Pascal where the accident happened."

Where else was there to look? Kevin agonized to himself as he raked his brain for some insight that might have been overlooked. Could she have taken some other line—in some other direction? From Market Street, trolleys traveled both east and south over the Mississippi River. Pressing his thoughts, he had a flash. Angie had said…yes, before he left the house on Friday morning—"Maybe …I'll stay an extra day and visit some museums while I'm down there…"

SISTER ANNE'S VISIONS

Sister Anne de Poris spent the afternoon praying before the Virgin Mary's side altar in Blessed Sacrament church. As always, she began with petitions of mercy for the souls of her parents (and protection for brother, Jed), followed by devout expressions of thanksgiving for her many blessings in life. On this Sunday, however, the nun asked her omnipotent God to *give* her another vision. Such requests were rarely made by the humble woman kneeling before the bank of vigil candles. Anne's spiritual insights, as she considered them to be, always happened without any petition on her part. When she asked God (as she often had asked Him to show her where her brother, Jed, was...) only vague perceptions resulted. But, for reasons she did not fully comprehend, the sister found herself asking to be blessed with another miraculous insight. "Help me, Heavenly Father, to see where your child, Angela is..."

Sister Anne was born Laura Keene on a small farmstead south of Fargo on the North Dakota prairie. Her first vision occurred when she was only a girl of seven. That vision was as memorable as it was tragic. In her mind that day was an obscure picture of her father hanging from a tree near the Red River only two miles from the family's ramshackle house. Her vision, however, would not allow Laura to understand the reason for Wesley Keene's suicide—would never unfold an awareness that her father had found his naked wife in the horse barn with a drifter only hours before a broken-hearted Wesley wandered off to kill himself.

When she was twelve, another dreadful vision occurred while she was saying her bedtime prayers. Laura was not surprised to find the note in her mother's familiar handwriting on the kitchen table the following morning. 'Take Jed to Ante Mildred's hose in towne'. Her mother never returned, and her aunt died three years later leaving Laura and Jed Keene orphans. Again, the girl's vision did not reveal the reason behind the tragedy. Thelma Keene had abandoned her two children to leave the farm with a pair of men and a traveling carnival troupe.

Two orphanages, and three years later, the siblings were separated—Laura going to Saint Cloud, Minnesota and Jed?—she never knew. Another vision led nineteen year old Laura to a Benedictine convent in St. Paul where, in six years, she became Sister Anne de Poris.

Of the Catholic Sister's seventy years, more than forty had been devoted to her students at the St. James parochial school in West Duluth. Over those four decades there had been other visions: some of which were ominously dark, while others held delightful promises.

Her prayer before Mary on this August afternoon was voiced, as always, with an expectant faith. After saying her second rosary, Sister Anne had the beginnings of the vision for which she had prayed: There was water, perhaps an ocean…and Angela Moran was almost unrecognizable. While in her trance, the nun experienced a feeling of safekeeping for the lovely woman. It seemed to Anne that Angela was under some mystical spell—but that she was being cared for.

As always, the deep sensory experience exhausted the frail woman. But, this episode had been worse than any other in her past. Anne was gripped with confusion over what to do about the vague discernment. Only two people had ever been told of her transcendental powers: Father Pat Foley, her confessor; and Sister Bridgette, her dearest friend.

When her mind cleared, Sister Anne again prayed to Mary: "Protect her from all harm while she is away from us. And, give her loved ones, especially Kevin, forbearance in their trial."

Knowing that Angela was safe, Anne would wait patiently for her spiritual insight to bring fruits before sharing anything with Kevin.

∼

The first tangible breakthroughs in the search for Angela Moran occurred on Monday afternoon. First, George Sartori at the Twin Cities Transit Authority garage reported finding a woman's purple hat on the streetcar which had been disabled in the Grand Avenue collision. "It's got a feather on it," he reported to Captain Duane Locher who had been placed in charge of the investigation.

Locher picked up the hat at the service garage and located Kevin who was knocking on doors along the south side of Grand Avenue near Lexington. The

Hibbing contingent had been canvassing the neighborhood since early that morning.

"It's Angie's—I remember it well," Kevin acknowledged somberly. "She would have been wearing something purple with her suit—I'm sure of it. Didn't the doorman at the hotel—what's his name...?"

"Poole," Locher reminded, "Darby Poole."

"Yes, I think Poole's description of the woman he talked to on Saturday morning mentioned she wore a feathered hat."

"It did, Mr. Moran."

"That means Angie was on the trolley that..."

"Was in Saturday's accident," Locher completed Kevin's thought. "We're quite certain that she was not among the injured passengers because the police got a complete list. So..." The police veteran ventured a theory, "She must have walked away from the accident scene." Knowing that Angela Moran had been at Pascal Street was a critical revelation. Locker scratched his head, "Your wife could have gone in any one of four directions from there."

Gary Zench had arrived from across the street where he had been knocking on doors, "Then we're probably wasting our time in this neighborhood, aren't we?"

Kevin looked into the western afternoon sun and gestured, "Let's drive down to Pascal right now, and work our way to Snelling, and then up toward University Avenue. We can get Becca and the others to help—maybe split ourselves up into four groups and go in every direction."

Keirnan McGinnis's police team was looking for possible witnesses in the Grand Avenue neighborhood east of Snelling Avenue and was unaware of Locher's recent discovery.

"Yes, officer, I did." Florence Watterson, a house maid with an accent, informed Keirnan as she looked at the photograph McGinnis handed her. "Woman that looked just like this one here, was walkin'...maybe I should say limpin' along, down that sidewalk there—right past our front yard. Woulda been around nine, I think."

McGinnis scribbled Watterson's name and address on his note pad. "What else can you tell me, ma'am?"

"Well, I said 'g'mornin', pleasant-like, ya know. But she wasn't paying no attention. Seemed to me like she was talking to herself—that's what she was doing—just a-talking to herself." Standing in the open doorway, the heavy woman swatted at a fly with the photo in her hand, "I watched her for a minute or two, clutching that lil purse of hers like a doll or sumpthing. Heading over toward Snelling she was."

Anxious to get his new lead back to Captain Locher and Kevin Moran, Keirnan tipped his hat, "Much obliged, Mrs. Watterson. If you think of anything else please let me know."

"Lemme see, she din't look much too good. I cud tell right away that she, pretty lady—let me tell ya that; anyhow, she seemed kinda…all messed up is the only way I kin describe her. Messed up, somehow."

The *St. Paul Pioneer Press* carried the Angela Moran disappearance story with a photograph on the front page of the Monday issue.

After leaving her job in the Dayton's women's apparel department, Helen Bates scanned the article while her husband drove their Plymouth sedan across the Mississippi bridge toward the Bates' South St. Paul home. "A woman from Hibbing is missing, Homer," she said casually. Homer Bates had relatives in neighboring Keewatin, "Her name's Moran. That name familiar?"

Homer had worked for two years in the Mahoning Mine near Hibbing as a young man. "Moran…? Ya. He built that big hotel up in Hibbing back in '07, or around then. But he's been dead for years. Folks claimed it was a suicide. Must be some relative of Pete Moran's, though. Everybody up on the Range is related somehow."

"Says here she's the wife of a Kevin Moran—says he owns the Androy Hotel up there."

"Must be in the new city of Hibbing. Moran's hotel burned to the ground just after it opened. Big story back then." Homer turned off onto Concord Street, "Cubs win yesterday, Helen? Check the sports page for me."

Helen's sister-in-law, Beatrice Holcomb, rarely paid any attention to the front page of the Pioneer Press—"All the news is so depressing these days" she would tell her customers. At her small Snelling Avenue beauty shop, the women usually talked about movies and fashions and local gossip anyhow. Beatrice did not pay any attention to the photograph of the dark-haired missing woman from Hibbing. After browsing the Hollywood rumor's column, she went to the comics, and then to the daily crossword puzzle.

On Monday evening, Keirnan McGinnis met with Kevin, Tony, and Gary Zench in a small Irish tavern on South Snelling Avenue. The other Hibbingites were having supper at Josie Kaner's house before meeting the three men later at the Grand Avenue corner of the Macalaster campus to resume their search.

"I'd say we've done pretty well today, fellas," Keirnan said optimistically over a mug of Schmidt beer. "We've pretty well established that Mrs. Moran was in this very neighborhood on Saturday morning."

Kevin forced a weak smile, "But from what that Watterson woman said, Angie must have been injured in the accident. What was it she told you again?"

"Said she seemed kinda 'messed up' were the exact words she used."

Kevin's greatest worry was that Angie had experienced another blackout. "My wife has a history of…" Painfully, Kevin explained Angela's health issue to Keirnan.

Gary Zench listened intently, "Why didn't you ever tell me about that, Kevin? I had no idea."

Tony, drinking the only glass of milk the barman had served in days, laid his hand on Gary's shoulder. "Angie wouldn't allow it, Gary. She even kept it from her family until only a couple of years ago. I guess we all thought the condition had gone away."

Gary set down his mug, "Shoulda said something about the blackouts yesterday, Kevin." Then looking at McGinnis, he added, "The police have probably only been talking to the doctors at Ramsey Hospital where most of the injured passengers were taken. Maybe somebody took Angela to some other hospital…or some private doctor?" He was sensitive about not mentioning a mental doctor or psychologist.

"Good thinking, Gary!" Kevin's eyes widened as his eyes moved from Zench to McGinnis. "Can you get your people on that right away? I've been so out of sorts that it didn't cross my mind until Gary brought it up. Maybe—maybe…?"

Keirnan didn't want to squelch Kevin's inspired hope of the moment, but the policeman knew it was highly unlikely that Angie Moran had gone to a doctor. "It's been my experience that the docs report that kind of thing to the police right away. They'd be in trouble with us if they didn't."

Kevin could not help thinking of darker possibilities. "You must have more than a hundred doctors down here, Keirnan—maybe twice that. Who's to say that one of them isn't…I hate to say it, but I've got to—one of them isn't a sex pervert of some sort?"

Keirnan nodded knowingly; that sinister possibility was something to consider. Angela Moran was a strikingly beautiful woman. St. Paul was a big city, and even larger Minneapolis was only a stone's throw away— "We'll get on that, Kevin. And, while were at it, our department's got a pretty good list of people you call *perverts*! We call it our 'crud column'."

~

The next three days were unproductive. Kevin was both exhausted and despairing. Everybody was doing everything they possibly could, but to no apparent avail. Names—hundreds of names from shopkeepers, local residents, streetcar passengers in wide concentric circles from the accident scene outward— had all failed to develop any new leads.

The only break from the rigorous search routine that Kevin and Tony had allowed themselves to do was some shopping for clothing and personal items. In forty minutes, both men purchased enough to last them for another week or two. Although mostly light weight shirts and slacks and other casual items that could be easily laundered, each of them bought a new suit. Captain Locher had scheduled another major news conference for the coming weekend. The disappearance of Angela Moran had been receiving front page coverage in both the *Pioneer Press* and *Minneapolis Star-Tribune*, and airings on all the local radio stations.

Senia Arola and Claude Atkinson had organized a Greyhound busload of Hibbing's concerned citizens. A contingent of nearly forty people had arrived on Wednesday morning to offer any possible assistance.

"I can't thank you all enough for coming down to help," was all Kevin could say when he greeted the crowd. Among those in the Iron Range contingent who had traveled to St. Paul was the small Gustavson boy whom Kevin had bought groceries for two years before. "When I told him about your wife… Jeffrey just wanted to do something," the eleven year olds mother said proudly. "I couldn't say no to that."

The youngster looked up at Kevin, "I'll talk to the kids down here, Mr. Moran. They know more about some things than grownups do," he expressed knowingly.

Kevin placed a hand on Jeffrey's blond head, "You're right about that young man. I really appreciate your helping out." Reaching in his pants pocket, Kevin found a five dollar bill. "This is for you, Jeffrey, and I don't want it going for groceries—understand!"

Senia had made lodging arrangements with Terry Whelan at the St. Paul Hotel on Monday morning. From the moment she heard about Angela's disappearance, her total energy became focused on mobilizing the community. After the group had unboarded from the bus and gathered around Captain Locher for an impromptu briefing, Senia slipped away for a few private moments with Kevin. "We could have rounded up a thousand people, Kevin. The whole town has come together, you wouldn't believe all the calls I've gotten since Sunday. The two of you have given so much…" She choked on her emotion, tears streaking her face, "I'm sorry. But Angela is so precious, Kevin."

Kevin had never seen Senia cry. The reserved Finnish woman was one of the strongest people he knew. "We're going to find her, Senia, and she's going to be fine," he consoled.

In addition to being iron-willed, and stalwart, Senia was a masterful organizer. On the trip down to St. Paul she had studied a city map and almost committed the grid layout to memory. Regaining her composure, she pointed her finger to an area she had circled on the large paper, "Tony and Gary have informed me of where all of you have already been. Angie might have walked north on Snelling here, and up to University Avenue. Being that's the main artery between St. Paul and Minneapolis there's a lot of ground to cover. What do you think about several of our group covering that territory today?"

"Anything you folks can do will be most helpful. Keirnan, over there," he gestured toward the uniformed officer talking with Claude Atkinson, "Is coordinating those things. Let's see what he thinks."

Senia stepped closer to Kevin, embraced him warmly, "You know I'd walk to China and back for you, Kevin." She might have added, "And for your father," but kept that sentiment inside. "You are the son I never had."

Late on Thursday night, Kevin received a phone call.

"Sister Anne, so good to hear from you," Kevin was fighting back tears. "I know you've been praying for all of us."

After a few minutes of getting caught up on the progress of the search, Anne's voice dropped an octave to a hoarse whisper, "Kevin, I must tell you something that will have to remain between the two of us." Anne explained her gift of discernment: "Whenever I *ask*…my visions are difficult to interpret. I would not be calling tonight if what I *must* tell you was not a certainty. Angela is safe! I can assure you she's protected by an angel of God." The nun swallowed hard on her next words, "But I'm afraid, she is no longer where you've been looking these past days. She's gone far away—as far as the oceans. I've prayed for further insights, but so far I have nothing really clear."

Kevin could hardly believe what Sister Anne was telling him. "How can you be...?" But he caught his doubt of the spiritual woman's veracity. She had given him her assurance that she was never wrong! "Is there anything else, Sister? Even those things that still aren't clear to you—please tell me!"

After a long pause, Anne said, "She is with a man, Kevin. But...she is safe in his company. I have no picture of the man in my mind."

Kevin's pervert theory was never far from his thoughts, "You're absolutely certain of that, Sister? She's with another man and not in St. Paul?"

"Absolutely!"

Both Twin Cities departments had posted pictures and checked departure depots (both bus and train) trying to identify any names from the St. Paul neighborhoods—especially Groveland surrounding Macalaster. If Anne's vision was correct, and he had placed his faltering faith on that, the investigation would have to be expanded across the country. "We'll concentrate our attention on what you've told me...and I'll keep your confidence between us, Sister."

"Kevin, I feel that finding Angela will take some time. You need time to rest and pray." Anne paused, "When you return to Hibbing we will visit, Kevin—there is something else, but ...not on the phone. It's about you... I must say good-bye now."

After a sleepless night, Kevin joined Tony and Gary at the Kaner breakfast table. Becca was making pancakes and scrambling eggs— fresh coffee was perking on the gas range.

"You look like death warmed over, boss" Gary said facetiously.

Kevin only nodded with a weak smile creasing his unshaven face. Outside, gray sheets of rain beaded on the window pane. Kevin looked absently at the bleak morning.

"Heard you on the phone last night, Kev. Any news?" Tony asked.

"Yes and no, Tony. Sister Anne called from Hibbing."

Tony waited for an elaboration...but Kevin said nothing more about the late conversation other than "she's praying for us all".

Bleary eyed, Marc Atkinson was the next to arrive in the kitchen, followed by Marco Zoretek. Young Marco didn't wait for an invitation to eat. Before sitting down with the older men, he filled his plate and began his first helping of pancakes.

"What's up for today, fellas," Marc asked while sipping a glass of orange juice. "Back to the Macalaster neighborhood?"

"I think that's what's on our Friday agenda, Marc," Gary said.

"We'll have a meeting with Captain Locher and Keirnan at seven-thirty before getting started," Tony informed.

The search headquarters had been established at Old Main on the Macalaster campus. Although none at the table would admit to their growing frustration, a fifth day of searching was not a pleasant prospect— especially on this inclement morning. The contingent had knocked on more than a thousand doors by this time. Weariness was setting in!

Gary Zench swallowed hard on what he was about to say. "The Hibbing bus is heading back late this afternoon. How about you guys? Are you going to stay down here over the weekend?"

Tony met Kevin's eyes, "If nothing breaks today or Saturday…maybe we should consider heading back to Hibbing for a few days. We could all use some rest. What do you think, Kev?"

Kevin's thoughts were preoccupied with Anne's revelation of the night before. Angie was not in St. Paul—that reality burned in his stomach.

Although he had promised the nun not to say anything about her vision, Kevin was torn. He needed to talk with Tony…and Keirnan McGinnis. The search would have to be expanded from coast to coast!

After Captain Locher's dismal update on progress, the search teams left Macalaster with their photos of Angela Moran along with neighborhood assignment maps. More than forty Hibbing volunteers and twelve St. Paul policemen headed out into the rainy morning. Kevin promised Senia and Claude Atkinson that he would make every effort to meet the bus at four that afternoon to personally thank the Hibbingites for their devoted assistance.

Outside Old Main, on the manicured Macalaster campus, Kevin summoned Tony and Keirnan to join him under a tall elm, out of the wind blown drizzle.

Knowing that both Tony and Keirnan were devout Roman Catholics made what Kevin had to explain that much easier. "Keirnan, I have a dear friend, a nun up in Hibbing…she called me last night."

Tony nodded his awareness of the call which Kevin hadn't said much about.

Careful not to betray his promised confidence, he went on to explain, "Sister Anne is a very *special person*. Gifted is the best word I can use to describe her. Anyhow, as bizarre as all this may sound, I'm positive that Angie has been abducted by some man and is no longer anywhere in St. Paul. The search needs to refocus…somewhere—out East or West."

∼

Officer Michael Sullivan and his search team spent most of the week compiling a list of people who had visited the various shops in the Grand and Snelling commercial district. Business owners were asked to press their memories and check all receipts for Saturday morning, August twenty-seventh. Clarke's Dry Cleaners had twenty-four customer receipts between ten and noon, Grand Tire Sales had nineteen, Howard Gross's book store had sixteen, Milan's Bakery proprietor Milan Barcotti could recall from memory nearly twenty customers, and six receipted orders. Sullivan's list had grown to over three hundred names in two days. Each name on his list, which meant traveling to all corners of the sprawling two cities, had been dutifully followed up.

On Friday morning, a dispirited Michael Sullivan knocked on the door of a large Tudor style home on the corner of Lincoln and Cambridge Streets in the Groveland neighborhood. Sullivan inquired for a Mr. Conrad Phelps. The housekeeper, a tall, slight woman named Loretta Flynn told him that Mr. Phelps was not in. Sullivan showed the picture of Angela Moran, "Never seen her, officer," was Flynn's curt reply.

Sullivan made a note, *Phelps not at home—check back later.*

'Blessed Are the Sorrowing'

It was already dark on Sunday night when Tony's Packard pulled up next to the Moran's Maple Hill residence. On the long journey back from St. Paul; Tony, Becca, and Kevin had been preoccupied with their own private thoughts. The long week had worn them down and conversation had been minimal.

Before leaving the Capitol city, Captain Locher and Keirnan McGinnis had engaged Kevin in a lengthy conversation about which he had shared nothing with Tony and Becca during the six hour trip. His stomach was still sour over the dialogue.

"I've got some difficult matters to go over with you, Kevin," Locher said. "But before you go home, they need to be discussed. Keirnan is convinced that your wife has been abducted—and that well may be the case. I, on the other hand, must play the *devil's advocate*. If Mrs. Moran was not abducted, then…"

Locher had written down a series of questions which began with, "Describe your relationship with your wife. Were you happily married?"

Kevin was unprepared for any personal interrogation. "The past two years have been wonderful," he began what would be a painful ordeal.

After fifteen minutes, Kevin was exasperated. "Angie would never leave me for another man!" he said explosively. "I resent your implications, Locher. Every couple has some rocky times, but any notion that Angela has…" He shook his head, "No. Angie's been kidnapped."

Locher explained that if that were the case, "There will be some mistakes made by the kidnapper or kidnappers. I hate to say I hope you're right, Kevin…but if whatever happened was something *mutual*—between your wife and the abductor—well, that's going to make our job damn tough!"

The Captain noted Kevin's dismissive head shake at the word *mutual*, but probed further. "Let's face it, you're a wealthy man. From the beginning I've been more than curious why you haven't been contacted. From my past experiences, when a wife or child is abducted, the perpetrator is after money. Yet…there's been no ransom notes that I'm *aware of*." The last three words of his statement held the tone of a question and were conveyed with narrowed eyes.

"Is there an implication in what you've just said, Locher?"

"None whatsoever."

"There better not be. My housekeeper and my secretary at the hotel have made note of all my incoming phone calls and checked the mail daily."

"That's good," was Locher's only comment.

Although he wouldn't admit it, Locher was also skeptical of Keirnan's theory that Angela Moran was no longer in the Cities area. The 'feelings' of some nun in Hibbing held little sway with the veteran officer who had been misled by a psychic back in the Dillinger days. Nor would Locher tell Kevin that his commitment of fifteen officers assigned to the case would be pared by two-thirds. "The FBI has a picture of your wife and a physical description. They're willing to have their agents make inquiries in port cities on both seaboards."

After unloading the car, Kevin embraced Tony, then Becca. "I don't have the words…" his voice choked.

"Rest up, Kevin. It's going to be strange going in there…" Becca regarded the huge house, "Just take every comfort in those two wonderful kids."

It was agreed among them that they would wait for word from McGinnis as to *if* and *when* they were needed again in St. Paul.

"This is going to be hard, Kev." Tony stressed the obvious, "But all we can do right now is wait."

The children were a comfort, but a small consolation. Kevin spent long hours and days at home, withdrawing from the hotel and civic activities in Hibbing. The waiting was not only difficult, it was killing his spirit!

On the Friday of his first week home, Sister Anne called from the convent. The two of them had visited on several occasions, but Anne had not experienced any new revelations. "Will you join me at the church this evening, Kevin? I'd like to talk with you some more."

Strangely, all sacred adornments and religious connotations of the ornate Blessed Sacrament Church only served to depress Kevin even more than he had been. Arriving early, he tried to pray. But there was an underlying anger, and the church seemed an enormous tomb from which his supplications rang hallow.

Anne found Kevin sitting in a pew near the front altar and sat down beside him. "Will you pray the rosary with me, Kevin, before we talk?"

He tensed, "Sister…I can't do that right now. I'm sorry."

Anne gave him a long and knowing look. "You've been in a spiritual desert for some time, haven't you? I've felt it, Kevin—almost profoundly."

Kevin tried to be light, "You told us in sixth grade, Sister —about the lost sheep. Well, yes…I've had some troubles with God."

"There is no greater joy in heaven than when a lost sheep is found. That was the message of my story."

Kevin nodded without reply.

Anne clutched the dark beads of her rosary for strength in what she had to say. "As hard as I try to pray, I'm not getting a clear picture of Angela, Kevin. I'm sensing that there is a block…a barrier to seeing what I'm asking God to show me."

"What is it, Sister? What is He telling you? Tell me and I'll pass it along to everybody who's out there looking for her."

"Everybody out there doesn't need to know, Kevin. Only you do." Her delicate fingers slipped over the beads, *"You are the block!"*

Kevin met her sad and tearing eyes, "I am the block? For heaven's sake, Sister, I've done everything…"

"Kevin, you must get to confession and communion. When you do that…*I know*, yes I know, that God will let me see more. Promise me you will."

Kevin's eyes went from Anne to the massive stained glass window beyond her. Anne was asking him to do something he wasn't ready to do. A small tear formed in the corner of his eye. "I will." His promise was a lie and Anne sensed it.

Anne touched a finger to Kevin's escaping tear: *"Blest are the sorrowing, they shall be consoled."* She smiled. "I must pray by myself now, may God go with you."

Kevin walked out from the church feeling emptier than he could ever remember. Tears streaked his face—"God! Where are you? He called into the night sky.

The depth of Kevin's despair was beyond definition. Days passed in endless succession. On his library desk he had placed an X on every day since Angela's disappearance. From August 26 ran a string of twenty-two black X's—! This Saturday, September 17, seemed the worst day of his life. Sitting alone in the dark of his library he contemplated another depressing Saturday—years before. His thoughts drifted painfully back to the desolation which had pushed him to the brink that morning—and then to memories of his deceased father. If there was a weakness in his Moran bloodlines, there was a strength as well. Kevin pushed away from the desk and cursed, "You could never do it! I can never do it either. Never!" With that profound realization locked in his resolve, he left the library and quietly walked up the stairs to where his children were sleeping. Careful not to awaken his son, he spent minutes sitting on the corner of Patrick's bed watching his seven year old sleep. "Your mommy will be back," he whispered. "Until she returns, you're daddy will be strong for you." In Maribec's room across the hallway, he made the same promise.

In the kitchen, Clara Motter was playing solitaire. His housekeeper had been a heaven sent presence throughout these past trying weeks. So had his many friends. Not a day passed without an invitation to join a family for dinner. Maple Hill had experienced a stream of visitors bringing baked goods, hot dishes, toys for the children—or just to visit, console, encourage. Claude Atkinson even stayed overnight at times and the two men chatted endlessly while playing chess until the early hours of the morning. Tony and Becca, Gary and Nora, Senia and Steven...along with people Kevin hardly knew, were in contact daily.

And every night at precisely nine o'clock, Kevin received a call from Keirnan McGinnis. In the twelve days since he'd left St. Paul the report had always been the same—the police in the Cities were doing everything they could, the Feds were also doing everything they could—nothing was happening!

Keirnan dreaded making the daily calls as much as Kevin dreaded receiving them. "Something's going to break, Kevin," his friend said for the hundredth time trying to disguise his waning optimism. "There's not a day goes by that I haven't called New York and Boston, or Los Angeles and Miami. I keep asking Locher to send me out to LA or Miami to do my own looking around."

"Send both of us, Keirnan. We've got to get out of our rut and do something—anything!" Kevin knew how hard this ordeal was on his friend. "God bless you, Keirnan," he said before hanging up the phone.

Struck by his last words, Kevin sat back on the sofa. *God bless you!* A feeling—like a dam had suddenly exploded inside him—swept like a wave over his morose contemplations. Anne's earlier admonition struck a strident chord—*"you are the block!"* Was pride his block? Was he so deeply into himself that he couldn't acknowledge God's powers? Or...was it something even worse? Did he believe that his unconfessed sins of past months and years were unforgivable? Whatever the block, contrition was necessary. There might not be anything Kevin could do from Hibbing right now—nothing Keirnan could do in St. Paul, and nothing all the police in the world could do—But it wasn't hopeless. His Angela was every bit the lost sheep that he had allowed himself to become.

Kevin called Father Potocnik at the Catholic Church and asked the priest, "Will you hear my confession tonight, Father?"

On Sunday morning, Kevin gave Clara Motter a fifty dollar bill and told her to take a couple days off. "Help me get the kids ready for church, and I'll drive you in to your sister's house in town."

Clara wasn't told where Mr. Moran had gone at nine-thirty the night before, but wherever that might have been, it certainly seemed to have perked him up. "Kids, after church, were going to pick up Grampa and Gramma and go to Bennett Park for a picnic. What do you think about that?" Kevin said brightly. "And, somewhere along the way, we're going to find you some ice cream cones."

A late September afternoon in Northern Minnesota with a cloudless sky and temperatures in the sixties can be more gorgeous than anywhere else on earth. This Sunday afternoon was that kind of day. Bennett Park offered acres of green grass, magnificent trees, and a playground with slides, teeters, and monkey bars that spelled heaven to kids. A favorite visit for all of them was the park's popular zoo. The children fed popcorn to the monkeys, carrots to the deer, and hung over the railings to watch the brown bears splash in the den's pool.

Becca's picnic basket brimmed with roast beef sandwiches, potato salad, plump sliced tomatoes, and chocolate chip cookies that melted in one's mouth. Two pitchers of sweetened lemonade helped everything go down pleasantly.

Kevin, the children, and their grandparents spent a marvelous afternoon unwinding from stresses too long held inside. This was a day to recover and relax and enjoy the manifold gifts of life. Kevin napped in the shade while Becca played with Maribec and Tony played catch with his grandson.

"Where do you think mom is, Grampa?" Patrick asked as he tossed an arcing baseball across the space between them.

Tony considered the question, mindful of how Kevin had answered the same inquiry many times. "Let's sit down for a few minutes and talk, Patrick."

The lad tossed his glove toward the trunk of an oak tree. The two of them sat down without speaking for a long moment. "Where do you think your mom is, Patrick Anthony?" (It was Tony's pet name for the boy named Patrick Anthony Claude—after Father Foley, himself, and Claude Atkinson).

"Dad says she got lost in the big city."

"Well, that's exactly what we think has happened." But Tony saw doubt in his grandson's eyes. "Why do you ask your grampa?"

"Someone at school said she got kidnapped."

"Have you talked to your father about that?"

Patrick looked away, "Nah…whenever I bring up mommy, well, I think it hurts him, Grampa. He doesn't say so…but, his voice kinda changes, you know." Patrick got some tears in his eyes, "Grampa, I heard him crying in his bedroom the other night."

All too often, feelings of well-being are ephemeral. Such was the case with their marvelous Sunday picnic in the park. Despite his resolve and good intentions, by Wednesday Kevin's emotions were in turmoil again. He and Tony were sitting on the back deck of Kevin's Maple Hill mansion watching the late afternoon sun fade in the west. Kevin pointed toward Angie's flower garden which was long past its bloom of weeks before. "Everything's dying, Tony. Days are getting shorter…"

Tony placed his hand on Kevin's knee, "Nothing I can say is going to change reality, Kev. I'm hurting, too. There are times when I just have to wander out to the workshop by myself and cry."

Kevin nodded knowingly. "Patrick told me about your conversation in the park last Sunday. I tried to tell him I had been crying for myself—not for his mom—and, that sometimes I get really lonely. I hated that he had to hear me…but I think he understood."

"I think it's good for a boy to know his father can cry."

Kevin nodded, "Maribec seems to hold everything inside. I've tried to talk to her about her feelings."

Tony laughed softly, "She's her mother's daughter, that's for sure. I remember when Mary died. Angie needed to cope with her mother's passing by herself, in her own private way, and I couldn't get through to her for the longest time."

For long moments nothing was said. The memory of Tony's beloved wife and Angie's mother needed time to settle.

Kevin got up, began to pace across the wooden deck, hands thrust deeply into his pockets, shoulders bent. "Tony, I've got to go back down to St. Paul for a few days. Just sitting here and waiting—I just can't handle the torment of doing nothing anymore."

Tony understood the frustrations of impatience. He had expressed those very same feelings to Becca on more than one occasion. "I know what you're saying, believe me I do!"

That night Kevin placed the twenty-sixth X on his desk calendar.

The following Thursday morning, Kevin and Tony were driving back to St. Paul. There was no plan or purpose that either could explain, but just doing something other than waiting was justification enough. Becca's mother, Josie Kaner, would be expecting the two men for supper. Keirnan McGinnis would take them to breakfast the next morning.

It felt good to be moving even thought they traveled with little hope.

~

Colleen McIntosh loved stylish clothes and could afford to buy the finest fashions. As the Duluth attorney rummaged through her fall wardrobe she made up her mind: A shopping trip would be scheduled. For Colleen, nearly everything she did required precise planning. Whenever she made a decision, she would attempt to maximize her desired outcomes. A shopping trip would be combined with something professionally related, or vice versa. As she contemplated the new colors for autumn, a blueprint began to take shape in her thoughts—she was resolved 'kill two birds with one stone'—perhaps three.

A business trip to St. Paul had been delayed long enough; Colleen would make the long drive and personally interview two female witnesses in an automobile insurance claim a Cloquet client had filed. While in the Capitol city, she would find time to visit Dayton's. The large department store carried all the latest lines, including her favorite fashions—*Hattie Carnegie*.

The third possibility concerned Kevin Moran. Since reading about Angela Moran's disappearance (which had been major news for three weeks) she had stewed over calling Kevin. Instead, she mailed him a note expressing her deep concerns, prayers, and sympathy. Swimming in the back of her mind was what else she might be able to offer her former client in terms of help? In that Colleen had developed wide contacts in the professional woman's community in the Twin Cities over the years, she raked her brain for any contact that might be able to provide an insight as to what might have happened to Kevin's wife. It seemed clear to her that one of two things had occurred: Either Angela had left her husband, or she had been abducted as some news stories were suggesting. Being 'lost' for more than three weeks just didn't make any sense to her.

Eva Bentley, one of the few female attorneys in St. Paul and a good friend of Colleen's, had a grapevine. So did Professor Arlys Higgins at the University. Maybe one of them had heard something she might pass on to Kevin after she arrived? Colleen called the Lowrey Hotel in St. Paul and made reservations for Friday and Saturday nights.

~

On Friday morning (the day would be the 27th X on Kevin's calendar) he and Tony met in the office of Keirnan McGinnis at police headquarters in downtown St. Paul.

"I'm sorry to admit that we're down to just five of us still working the case. Locher's put me in charge of things for now, but says he wants me to be available for anything else that comes up," the police sergeant said ruefully. "Locher's finally come around to our way of thinking and seems positive now that Angela is not in the Twin Cities any longer. He insists that the Feds are in the best position to pick up any leads."

Kevin nodded somberly, "It's a big country, Keirnan. Where—?"

"We have a theory, for whatever good that does us right now, but if your wife was abducted by…let's say by someone with lots of money; then…maybe he took her to Miami. I only say this because that's where most of the rich folks from up here prefer to go."

"But if it's someone from your crud list, Keirnan…what then?" Kevin said in a tone of frustration.

Keirnan shrugged without comment.

"Who's working on the investigation outside of St. Paul, I mean for the Feds? Is there any one person in charge?"

"Matter of fact, Kevin, there is this fella in Miami that I've talked with a few times, names Miles—Gunther Miles, he's about as close as I can think to being a lead agent. Here, let me get him on the phone right now. You can talk to Miles yourself."

A veteran investigator who worked on the Lindbergh case years before, Miles couched his pessimism, "We've got Mrs. Moran's picture posted up and down the East Coast, sir. If she's out here—we're going to locate her."

Kevin asked if there was anything—anything at all… "I'm going crazy doing nothing." He swallowed, "Will you be candid with me, Mr. Miles? What do you think?"

In previous conversations, Miles had told both Keirnan and Locher that the lack of any ransom demands undermined their abduction theory, "I'll be as frank as I can. In cases like this, time always works against us, Mr. Moran. But it only takes one small lead, you know. One break."

Keirnan took the afternoon off, and invited his Hibbing friends to join him for a round of golf at the Keller Golf Club: "Sometimes we get our best ideas when we're relaxed and least expect them," he conjectured.

"Relaxed? When playing golf?" Tony laughed for the first time that day, "Keirnan, the only golfers who can relax while chasing pars are the very good ones, or the very bad ones. I'm stuck somewhere in the middle of both types!"

On Saturday, Kevin, Tony, and Keirnan reviewed lists of names—people from the St. Paul police 'crud column', people who had been in the Snelling and Grand area on the Saturday of Angela's disappearance, people who "might have seen someone" who looked like Angela Moran's photograph, people who had left town unexpectedly. As he reviewed names, Kevin raked his brains. Someone knew something…but who? Each page was identified with the name of the officer who had done the field work or conducted an interview. On one page a name jumped to his attention. "Who is this?" Kevin asked Officer Sullivan who was meeting with the group at the time.

Sullivan had been working on the case since the first day, "Vincent Depelo? He's the cop who filed the report—why do you ask, Mr. Moran?"

Kevin explained the vendetta from years past. "A man named Armando Depelo from Hibbing once swore he was going to get me some day, 'Knock me off my high horse', is how he put it."

Vince Depelo, however, was one of the most respected officers in the department, and willing to drive over to the police station on his day off. "No relatives on the Range that I've ever known about," he informed them pleasantly. Vince knew every Depelo family in the Twin Cities, and called all five from the office. None had knowledge of a man by the name of Armando Depelo.

On the drive back to Josie Kaner's house, Kevin said defeatedly, "Dead end streets everywhere, Tony. Coming down here was probably a big waste of time."

Tony tried to uplift Kevin's sagging spirits, "I disagree completely. If nothing else, we've met some truly fine policemen who are doing everything they can...if you had any doubts that the folks down here were sitting on their hands—well, that notion's been dispelled. They're a committed group."

Kevin nodded, forcing a weak smile, "Sorry, Tony. You're right, of course. My God, Vince offered to track down every Depelo who ever set foot in America for us. Can you believe that?"

Although neither said as much, both knew that if Mando Depelo was seeking revenge, he'd hire someone to do the dirty work for him. Armando was a coward.

∼

Late Saturday night, after Tony and Josie Kaner had retired, Kevin contemplated taking a walk in the Highland Park neighborhood. He was too tired to sleep. Too depressed. The evening was light jacket cool and starless; a feeling of rain hung in the air. As he quietly opened the front door, Kevin heard the telephone ring.

"Colleen! Colleen McIntosh..." Kevin recognized the voice from two years before. "No, you didn't wake me..."

"... I haven't been sleeping very well for weeks..."

"...Yes, stress isn't the word for it—I've been a nervous wreck...I was just thinking of taking a walk before it rains..."

"...Oh, and thank you for the thoughtful note you sent me..."

Colleen explained that she was in the city on business and calling from the Lowrey Hotel in downtown St. Paul. "Actually, I exaggerate the business aspect of my trip, I wanted to visit some friends and do some shopping. I'm sorry to call you so late, but something has come up. I tried to reach you in Hibbing. Mrs.

Motter told me you were down here for the weekend. She gave me the Kaner phone number."

"Yes. Tony and I have spent a couple of days trying to be useful, but we're going back tomorrow without much to show for our being here." Behind his words, Kevin was curious about a sense of urgency in Colleen's words. He would let her explain.

Colleen could sense the dispirited edge in Kevin's voice, and tried to be light, "You never know what a woman might find when shopping, Kevin." She explained her most unusual experience at Dayton's that afternoon. "I was looking for something in the *Hattie Carnegie* line…" She recounted her conversation with a saleslady named Helen Bates, "It may be nothing at all, but my gut instinct tells me that something worth checking out happened on the Saturday of your wife's disappearance." Colleen went on to tell about the unusual order which had been placed by a man named Adam Johnson. "Helen said he bought Dayton's last three *Hattie* dresses over the phone—along with hundreds of dollars worth of other clothes and female accessories. Over the phone, mind you! Wanted everything delivered… claimed it was for his sister from out of town."

Kevin found Colleen's voice almost too mesmerizing to concentrate on the details of her story. In imagining the face that went with the voice his attention to the details she described lapsed. At first, the significance of a man buying hundreds of dollars worth of clothing over the phone did not strike him as anything to be so excited about. Then it hit him like a slap in the face…"Colleen, is it too late for me to buy you a drink?"

GROVELANDNEIGHBORHOOD

At the Kaner breakfast table early Sunday morning, Kevin seemed unusually quiet, almost agitated. Tony's eyes tried to connect with his friend who was staring absently out the kitchen window at gray sheets of rain beading on the pane, "I heard you leave the house last night, Kevin," he commented with an open-ended expectation that Kevin might say something. Somewhere around eleven Tony had heard the telephone ring and Kevin answer.

Kevin nodded without reply.

"Something come up?"

"No, I just couldn't sleep—decided to take a walk," Kevin winced imperceptibly at the lie.

Tony frowned, "A walk?" Within a few minutes after the call, he had heard the Packard engine start. It had begun raining outside. Tony swallowed his next question; deciding to let Kevin explain where he had really gone at another time. "Did your walk do you any good?"

Kevin did not respond for a long minute. His thoughts were back at the Lowrey bar and his meeting with Colleen McIntosh. At first sight, Kevin recognized the strikingly lovely face and long cinnamon hair from years ago. Taking her hand and smiling, "Where have I seen you before?" was his first question.

After a slight flush, Colleen readily admitted having been at the Foley funeral reception at St. James for a few brief moments. "I must confess that I wanted to put a face with the voice of the man who I might be representing in the Hayes episode. When I saw you…I left immediately. That was all—I'm an impulsive person, Kevin—always have been." She laughed easily without mentioning either

her embarrassment or her awareness that Kevin's eyes had locked momentarily with hers back then.

"Why didn't you introduce yourself, Colleen?" he had asked over their glasses of chablis, but he was too taken in by her loveliness and the playful lilt of her voice to remember her response. Moments later, Colleen told him about having met Angela at an art show in Duluth. "Beautiful, gifted, and extraordinarily nice…" is how Colleen described her impression of Angie Moran. "I have one of her marvelous paintings, you know."

"What's that, Tony…?" Recovering from the brief reverie, Kevin remembered, "…Yes, the walk…it must have done some good—I slept better than I have in days." The hint of redness in his eyes, however, belied the truth.

One lie requires another and another to sustain any semblance of viability. "I got a call from a woman named *Bates* last night. She might have something worth checking out. I'm going to meet her downtown at nine," Kevin announced. There was a germ of truth in what he said. He and Colleen would meet at nine and then go over to Dayton's to interview the ladies apparel employee.

"What did this Bates woman tell you, Kevin?" Josie Kaner asked as she refilled his coffee cup. "You seem so offish this morning; are you sure you slept well last night? And you haven't touched any of your breakfast."

Kevin could not acknowledge that he was saving his appetite for the possibility of a second breakfast at the Lowrey Hotel. "Can I borrow your car for a few hours, Mrs. Kaner?" His eyes turned away from Tony's mother-in-law, "I think I might stay down here for a couple more days, Tony." The two men had planned to travel back to Hibbing after breakfast and Sunday mass. "If this Bates lead has any substance, I'll want to follow up on it."

Tony frowned at "*I'll* want to…" Why was he being dismissed? Excluded? "I don't have to go back, Kev. You haven't said what the Bates conversation has to do with Angie."

In vague terms Kevin explained the bizarre clothing purchase by a man named Johnson more than three weeks ago. "So, maybe I've got another name to check out. Bates is going to find this Johnson's address."

For the second time, Kevin had used '*I*'—not '*we*'! Something strange was going on. Tony had sensed Kevin's estrangement since both had joined Josie in the kitchen only minutes before. "Would you like some help, Kev. Two of us can cover more ground than one?"

Kevin did not answer for a long minute. "No, that's okay. You've got plenty of things going on in Hibbing this week…and it's not fair to Becca." As soon as he said it, Kevin realized that his words rang hollow.

Rather than argue, Tony pushed away from the table without finishing his scrambled eggs. Apparently Kevin had lost sight of the fact that Angie was not only his wife—but also Tony's daughter. "If you'd rather I go…that's fine. I'm sure Becca will be pleased that I'm coming home." Giving Josie a light peck on the cheek and a thank you, he excused himself. "Before I go upstairs and pack, Kevin…don't forget that Angie is my daughter. That's why I'm down here. If you think I should step out of the way for a while—have it your way. But something strange seems to be going on here…" Tony left the kitchen without completing his thought and with a terrible knot in his stomach.

Sunday morning traffic on Randolph Street was quiet. Heading east toward downtown St. Paul, Kevin's stomach churned with anger and guilt in near equal measure. Behind the flicking wiper blades, he mumbled angrily under his breath, "Damn it anyhow, Angie, why didn't you get on the right streetcar! You'd be home now—where you belong—if only…" Passing a trolley stopped at a street corner, his thoughts wandered from his wife to where he was going on this dismal morning. With that reflection came consuming guilt. Not only had he been thinking more about Colleen McIntosh than his missing wife these past twelve hours —he was anxious to see the lawyer again!

As Randolph sloped down the hillside toward West Seventh and into the city, he remembered the brief conversation at the Kaner breakfast table. He knew that Tony read him too well and was angry about his suggestion that Tony go back to Hibbing. The only real father he had known in his life was a perceptive man. Kevin's guilt was complicated by the rancid lie about where he had been last night. As soon as he told Tony that he'd only gone for a walk, he knew Tony believed otherwise.

Kevin met Colleen McIntosh near the elevators in the posh Lowrey reception area. Due to the time, Colleen suggested they skip breakfast and hurry to the Bates meeting. Outside the massive hotel, Kevin took her elbow with one hand while holding an umbrella he had purchased in the hotel shop in the other. Colleen leaned against his arm as they walked along the wide sidewalk. It was only a few blocks to Dayton's and the rain was becoming a thick gray drizzle. Colleen was tall, slender, and (beneath her light raincoat) wore an exquisite outfit that perfectly accentuated her deep green eyes. Kevin, shaven for the first time in three days, wore a dark suit and tie.

"Mrs. Bates will be expecting us. I called her at home earlier this morning," Colleen informed, stepping lightly over a puddle of water on the sidewalk. "She thought of something else that might shed some light on this Mr. Johnson matter, but I was rushing to get dressed and suggested we talk about it when the three of us got together. I hope she didn't think it rude of me."

Kevin was unusually quiet this morning and looked tired, Colleen thought to herself. His stress was far more apparent now than it had been last night. "Helen did sound excited, though."

"I hope this all pans out. I've more or less abandoned Tony to meet this Bates woman."

Colleen wondered at Kevin's comment. Despite his every effort to front his confidence in their conversation last night, he was off his game this Sunday morning. Colleen McIntosh made her living by intuiting things below the ostensible surface. Although she did not know Kevin Moran very well yet, she was certain that his being with her was disturbing him. When her shoulder rubbed against him she could almost feel a flinch in the muscles of his strong arm. And his deep green eyes held something she had trained herself to recognize—guilt! She wanted to ask him if he had mentioned to Tony who he would be with this morning, but she chose not to. Better not to invite a falsehood. Instead, Colleen smiled a confidence she hoped Kevin would reciprocate.

"As I told you, Kevin, I've got a gut feeling about this, and my instincts are usually correct. What Helen told me yesterday is so extraordinary—and this 'something else' she mentioned, who knows what that's about?"

Heads down against the drizzle, they stepped from the curb. A yellow cab rounded the corner sharply, horn blaring…the man behind the wheel shot her an irate expression, as his cab almost clipped Colleen's knee.

Seeing what was happening in the nick of time, Kevin quickly pulled her close to his side, "My God, are you okay, Colleen?"

"My fault. Not paying attention. If that cabby's looks could kill —" She tried to make light of the incident, "I'd be a dead lady!"

Kevin laughed tightly without reply.

Helen Bates was in her fifties, stylishly attired, and wore her gray hair in a tight bun. The saleslady led her well dressed visitors to the third floor office of her supervisor, "A much better place to carry on a conversation," she said. It was obvious to both Kevin and Colleen that the full figured woman was anxious about something. It was Helen's day off, but she had gone to the trouble of coming downtown to meet with them.

Colleen, slipping quickly into her attorney mode, found the nearest chair and opened her leather covered notebook. She cleared her throat—ready to begin her overview of what the two women had talked about the day before. Regarding Helen, who was still standing, Colleen smiled, "Please sit down and relax, Mrs. Bates. Kevin, you as well." Kevin was standing awkwardly until Helen seated herself. "Shall we pick up from yesterday, Mrs. Bates…?"

Helen forced a thin smile of her own, "I have the receipts and delivery address you asked for this morning right here," she handed Colleen several sheets of paper.

Colleen skimmed the numbers, then set the records atop the notebook on her lap, "Thank you, now you told me earlier—"

Impatient to share her revelation, Helen Bates blurted, "Miss McIntosh, what we covered yesterday doesn't seem to be very important in light of what I have to tell you now. I wanted to tell you on the phone this morning..." Her eyes darted to Kevin, who appeared to be brooding about something— "I know what happened to your wife, Mr. Moran!" Helen's voice pitched: "My sister-in-law gave Mrs. Moran a hair coloring and styling early on Sunday morning—the day after she disappeared!"

Kevin's jaw slacked, "What?"

Colleen dropped her pencil, "Forgive me, Helen—"

"That's okay," Helen Bates began her incredible recollection by explaining that this 'Mr. Johnson' had made an unusual request after placing the clothing order. "I didn't think of it until this morning, Mr. Moran—so I called my sister-in-law, Beatrice—actually got her out of bed. I told her to try and find a picture of Mrs. Moran in an old newspaper." In her excitement, Helen lost her train of thought for a moment, "Bea's been on vacation in Brainerd for two weeks, but never reads the paper even when she's home." The saleslady shook her head as if to imply that her sister-in-law was a scatterbrain of sorts. "Anyhow, she was able to find a picture—and sure enough, she recognized your wife as her customer. Bea was positive! 'How could I ever forget that appointment' she said to me. Then, she told me you'd never recognize that Mrs. Moran was the same woman anymore."

Helen paused to catch her breath, "The man was really pleased with the blond coloring and new style on his wife, Bea said. He gave Bea a fifty dollar bill when she was finished."

Helen's eyes darted from Kevin to Colleen and back again.

"Was this man's name, Johnson?" Kevin asked the critical question.

Colleen retrieved her pencil from the carpet near her heeled foot, leaned forward in her chair, then repeated—"Was it Johnson?"

Helen shook her head, "Bea said the man's name wasn't Johnson, I asked her that, of course. She'd remember Johnson because her husband's sister married a Johnson."

"Did she remember any name?" Kevin said breathlessly.

"No, I asked her that, too—twice. Bea thinks she remembers the woman, your wife, Mr. Moran—saying what her last name was. Bea wasn't really paying attention but said she might recognize it if she heard it again. She was positive that it wasn't Moran!"

Colleen looked from Helen Bates to Kevin, then regarded the receipt order that she had been given moments before. Soon they would be able to find out the real name of Mr. Johnson. "Is this the delivery address, Helen?"

"Yes, ma'am. We sent five good sized packages, and Mr. Johnson—or whoever he was, gave the delivery boy seven hundred dollars just like he said he would."

Below the name 'Beatrice Holcomb' on her note pad, Colleen wrote the address of Mr. Johnson and another name: Randy Burich was the delivery boy identified on the delivery orders.

Looking over her shoulder, Kevin watched Colleen's lightly freckled left hand neatly script 'corner of Lincoln and Cambridge Streets'. Shifting his gaze to the saleswoman, he asked, "Where's that address, Mrs. Bates?"

"Over in Groveland. Just a few blocks east of Macalaster College, I think. Randy could take you right there if you'd like him to."

"I'm sure we can find it, Mrs. Bates," Kevin was familiar with the neighborhood after spending so much time there these past weeks. "Can we talk with your sister-in-law?"

"Let me call her right now," Helen got Beatrice on the phone and talked hurriedly for a few minutes. "She says she'll meet you at her shop on Snelling."

Shaking her head as she had done earlier, she added, "Doesn't want you see her house right now; it's a mess."

After profusely thanking Helen Bates for her information, Kevin and Colleen stepped outside the small office into the awakening department store. Overwhelmed by the magnitude of the breakthrough, Kevin impulsively pulled Colleen to his chest. "You're an angel, Colleen. If it hadn't been for you…?" He felt the press of her small breasts against him and was momentarily distracted, "Now we've finally got some legitimate leads to follow." The scent of Colleen's long cinnamon hair was intoxicatingly feminine.

Colleen felt a twinge as well. Kevin Moran was a handsome man and his arms were strong. Lightly pushing away from his chest, she composed herself, "Let's do some follow-up with the delivery boy…and then with Helen's sister-in-law over on Snelling." Her voice was strained and her words came in a slight gasp. "We'll have to confirm everything Helen's told us, Kevin. The police will want to talk with the Holcomb woman, too. We ought to call Sergeant McGinnis before leaving the store."

Kevin met her green eyes, "Thanks to you, Keirnan and his guys will have a lot more to work with now." His head was swimming at the moment—with the new potentials, and with the lovely woman who met his gaze. Her features worked perfectly together—the delicate nose, high cheek bones, strong chin.

Her mouth pouted, "On second thought, maybe you should get together with the police right away, Kevin. I can interview Burich and Holcomb while you fellows check out the address Helen gave me."

Anxious to get over to the Groveland neighborhood, Kevin nodded his agreement with the suggestion. Maybe Captain Locher would want to join them. "You're right, it might save some valuable time if we split up for now, Colleen."

Colleen pulled a page from her notebook, "Let me write down the delivery address for you." As she wrote Lincoln Street her hand quivered ever so slightly.

"Where can I get in touch with you later, Colleen?"

On the notebook page below the Johnson address she'd written, Colleen added a footnote: *Room 642*.

Pushing Josie Kaner's Buick sedan through light traffic, Kevin accelerated to forty up the long Grand Avenue hillside in the direction of Macalaster. He'd made calls from Dayton's, and both Keirnan and Locher had agreed to meet him in half an hour at the Old Main building on the campus.

Locher, scanning a phone directory, was already seated in the small office that had been the search command post weeks before. The veteran cop could read the fever in Kevin's expression, "You look like you've seen a ghost," the policeman said. "Fill me in on what you've learned. I don't see any Johnson at the address you gave me over the phone."

"I'll give you my wallet if the guy were after is named Johnson."

After Keirnan's arrival, the three men drove Locher's squad car east from Old Main toward the Lincoln Street address only a few blocks away.

Arriving at the large Tudor styled home on the corner of Lincoln and Cambridge, Kevin announced, "This is the address Mrs. Bates gave me."

From the porch, it appeared as if the house was unoccupied but they knocked several times anyway. Heavy drapes covering the front windows prevented any view of the inside room. Walking around the house, no interior lights could be seen under the blinds and drawn shades. Locher was the first to comment on the obvious, "Nobody's at home. We'll have to inquire of the neighbor next door."

Matronly Virgie Drobnik answered the knock at the front door of the somewhat smaller, stucco fronted house, one door down from the corner. The white apron clad woman's jaw dropped at the sight of three men, two of them in police uniforms, and the other dressed in an expensive suit, standing on the front steps. Gripping the door frame with one hand and holding a feather duster in the other, Virgie stammered, "What do you want?"

"We're looking for a man named Johnson, ma'am." Locker said, "Your next door neighbor." He gestured an arm toward the Tudor.

"Johnson? I'm afraid you're on the wrong block, officer. No Johnson's living there. Other side of the street, down the block…there's some Johnson's."

Kevin, anxious to be involved, stepped to Locher's side and pointed to his left, "whose house is that, ma'am? We've been given this address," he waved the paper near the woman's face. "It says Johnson right here."

Squinting her narrow eyes at the tall man, Virgie became indignant. "I can read. What do you want to know for?"

Locher put a calming hand on Kevin's elbow, "Let me, Kevin." Then, smiling graciously, "Don't be alarmed, ma'am…we're only conducting an investigation this morning. If you don't mind, I'd like to start by getting your name."

Reluctantly, Virgie gave her name, "I'm the housekeeper for the Tillman's," she said in a defensive tone. "They're over in Wisconsin today visiting their daughter—that's why I'm working on a Sunday. Been employed by the Tillman's family for going on three years, sir. Three years in October."

"The Tillman's live here, okay…" Locher made a note of the name. "Who lives in the Tudor house next door, Miss Drobnik? You're certain it's nobody named Johnson?"

"Mostly nobody lives there."

Locher shrugged, "Can you explain, ma'am?"

"You should be talkin' to Loretta. She's the housekeeper over there. But she's lucky—always gets her weekends off."

"Loretta?"

"Loretta…don't know the last name. Only met her a few times."

Impatient over the round-about questioning, Kevin interrupted again, "Will you tell us who owns the house?"

Virgie glared for a long moment at Kevin before directing her answer to Locher. "Phelps family owns the house. I think the son, though I hardly ever see him, has his father's name—Conrad. But Mr. Phelps died years ago."

Confused by her answer, Locher asked, "Then the son—Conrad Phelps—lives there now? Did I hear that correctly?"

"I just told you that. He ain't never there, though. House has been like a morgue for a month or so. Even that Loretta woman skips a work day now and then. Who'd ever know?"

"You have seen this Mr. Phelps from time to time, though, haven't you, Miss Drobnik? You could give us a description?" McGinnis inquired.

Virgie shot a hard look, "I'm *Mrs.* Drobnik, got a husband. Make sure you got it written down right on your tablet there. Mrs.!" She scratched her head, "Before I say anything else, what's yer business with Mr. Phelps? He done somethin' wrong?"

Locher explained they were looking for information relative to a missing woman named Angela Moran. "We were hoping to talk with Mr. Phelps about her."

"Then why'd ya call him Johnson in the first place. Tell me that."

After five minutes of explanation, Virgie Drobnik relaxed and gave a superficial description, "About forty or so, I'd guess, maybe less. A small man, thinning hair—maybe brown, wears glasses. You'd never know he was rich by the way he dressed, let me tell you."

Both Locher and McGinnis were writing everything down. Feeling important, Mrs. Drobnik elaborated, "Loretta told me once that he was some kind of book collector. And I think he spends lots of time over at the college. Seen him there a few times when I was walking home in the afternoon. Pleasant enough fellow, says hello when we pass."

Fifteen minutes later, the three men left the Tillman's foyer, still drenched from standing too long on the porch in the rain. Mrs. Drobnik had not invited them inside until learning the nature of their investigation. "My heart goes out to you, Mr. Moran," she had said. "Read about it in the papers."

"What do we do now?" Kevin asked.

Locher checked his pocket watch. It was nearly eleven and he had family plans for the afternoon. "We can knock on a few doors and see if anybody knows who this 'Loretta' woman is…maybe pick up something on Phelps."

Kevin had an agenda of his own, "I'm going to run over to that beauty shop on Snelling. I'll try to get some kind of verification on the description Mrs. Drobnik just gave us."

"Let's meet for a quick lunch at O'Malley's in an hour or so." Locher suggested. "We can compare notes."

Kevin missed Colleen by five minutes but caught Beatrice Holcomb as she was locking the door to her shop. The hair stylist had long, stringy hair in need of brushing, and hadn't found time to apply any makeup this morning. Kevin introduced himself.

"Just finished telling the lawyer lady everything," Holcomb said in flat tone before catching herself. "I'm sorry, Mr. Moran. You must be having a shitty time with all this. Damn unfortunate, I'd say. And, I feel awful that I don't read the papers like I should. Customers talked about your wife, though. I just never had no idea. Hell, if'n I'da known..."

Kevin smiled, Beatrice Holcomb—although vulgar—was a talker, "I don't want to keep you, but does the name Phelps ring a bell, Mrs. Holcomb?"

"Damn, that's it! I knew I'd remember. Told Helen that this morning. Yes, that's the name the woman, your wife I mean, gave me. 'Mrs. Phelps", she said—clear as hell's bell."

Wincing, Kevin asked her to repeat, "*Mrs.*? She called herself Mrs.?"

"Sorry, sir. But that's what she said to me."

Beatrice explained events of that Sunday morning again, stressing how dramatically different his wife looked after the styling. "Like I told the lawyer just before you came, the pictures you got ain't no damn good any more. Lawyer lady said the picture could be fixed up by the police."

Kevin nodded, "Can you describe Phelps?"

"I got a keen eye for faces, Mr. Moran. Let me see. He was only an inch or so taller than his wife—your wife, I'm sorry—really. But his hair was really thinning—I notice people's hair right away. Wore thick glasses that kinda slipped down on his nose. Slight man, maybe even skinny—No more than a hundred forty. Damn expensive suit."

The description matched. "Anything else you can tell me?"

Bea searched her memory. "When he gave me the fifty, I noticed he had quite a wad of money."

At O'Malley's, Kevin shared his news with Locher who was sitting in a corner booth. Keirnan, he noticed when arriving, was on the telephone at the counter. "It was Phelps who took Angie to the beauty shop. The lady there said we'd never recognize my wife."

"Your attorney friend called the department an hour ago. Told the duty officer to get our sketch man over to Holcomb's place this afternoon and work on the photo. This McIntosh is really on the ball—I should have thought of that myself. Anyhow, our artist—guy named Grady—will be on it right away. I authorized the overtime."

"How long before…?"

"We'll have a new picture by tomorrow morning," Locher answered the anticipated question.

"Find out anything else in Groveland, Captain?"

Locher explained that the neighborhood didn't have much of any consequence to offer. "Guy across the street, a fella named Dorsher, said Phelps was hardly ever around here. He thought Phelps worked at the college or was a student there. Always carrying books around, he remembered. Had no idea Phelps owned the house across the street—thought he was probably a border."

Keirnan McGinnis joined the men. "Called every Phelps in the phone book. Not much. One woman said I must be looking for the Phelps that owns a business of some kind downtown. I checked. There is a Phelps Enterprises in the book, a Cedar Street address. Nobody answered the phone of course."

Locher shook his head, "Sunday's are the bane of investigators, Kevin. Always so much harder to find people at home and most businesses are closed besides. Tomorrow we can check out the college and local bookstores."

After a few moments of 'nothing much else to say', Locher bridged the void. "We're going into Monday with more leads to work with than we've had since we started. Let's get together at my office at seven in the morning. I'll have the new sketch of Mrs. Moran by then—then we'll go out and find this Loretta woman."

"Then we're going to go out and find Conrad Phelps, Captain," Kevin added with more enthusiasm than he shown in weeks. "Wherever he might be now, his days are numbered!"

FRIENDS OR LOVERS?

"You've got to be kidding, Kevin!" Colleen said over the linen draped table in the posh decor of the Lowrey Hotel's dining room. The late Sunday evening clientele were dressed formally, many having returned from the symphony performance at the Lyceum. "Conrad Phelps! Are you that isolated up in Hibbing?" She went on to explain the once formidable Phelps financial empire. "He's sold much of his father's holdings over the past few years. A sizable portion to Luddington, the corporation I had a dogfight with two years ago. Never met Conrad Senior's son—but I've been told he's…what's the best description, a recluse of sorts."

"That fits with what I've been told—no friends, a book collector— I knew he was wealthy, but from what you've said, multi-millions! It doesn't make any sense, Colleen. All that money…and—an abductor? A damned perverted abductor!"

"Careful, Kevin. Don't forget we're both attorneys, our 'presumption of innocence' code…despite all you've learned today, there are still lots of gaps to fill."

Kevin frowned, "I know that, but—'

"But, how can I say anything about presumed innocence after talking to Beatrice Holcomb today, right?"

"Yes, that and…Colleen, the guy's just disappeared somewhere—presumed innocent. Bull—? Maybe my legal ethics aren't up to snuff, but he's a weirdo, and the last any of us know he was with my wife."

Colleen avoided arguments she could not win, "Let's not quarrel, Kevin. All I'm saying is that we don't know for certain, that's all."

Kevin reached across the table, took her hand in his, "I'm sorry. We've come too far to get into any stupid arguments. Maybe you're right, and maybe I am—

we'll find out damn soon. Still, I'm going to be working on the premise that Phelps is some kind of sick deviant."

Colleen found Kevin's hand cold, pulled hers away and gestured for the waiter. "Let's order, and see if we can't come up with some kind of plan." Colleen would tell him later that she was returning to Duluth in the morning. She had to be in court at three the next afternoon.

Kevin ordered the prime rib and Colleen a shrimp salad. Loosening his tie, Kevin broke the lull in conversation, "Any plan we come up with has to start with unraveling the mystery of Conrad Phelps."

Colleen nodded, "And, the mystery of Angela Moran. Kevin, you've not said a word about your wife." Colleen was perceptive enough to realize that all his attention seemed focused on Phelps. Was their something dark about Angela, or their marriage that Kevin was hiding? Was what happened really an abduction? All she seemed reasonably certain about was that Angela Moran had gone to St. Paul for an art show, and then disappeared. If she was unhappily married…? She'd grilled Beatrice Holcomb thoroughly. The beautician said that Angela did not appear to be under any noticeable stress. And that the man who was with her didn't look like an abductor at all. "Kinda meek" she'd described. "Mousey, even. Not the kind of man that would intimidate a woman at all. If anything, he seemed a lot more nervous that she did."

"What do you mean, 'the mystery of Angela Moran'?"

"Just that, Kevin. Remember, I've met your wife. I told you how attractive and charming I found her to be. Vivacious and talented. You just nodded. Were the two of you close? Happily married?"

Kevin felt a pang of anger. What was Colleen suggesting? Did she think Angie might have left him for another man? He looked away to collect his thoughts, to repress his annoying indignance. Happily married? Swallowing a lump in his throat, "Yes, I mean…we had a rough spell a couple of years ago—but since then…everything's been wonderful between us."

Colleen was searching his eyes but let him continue without commenting on the 'rough spell'.

"Better than ever. Colleen. What makes you think…? " Suddenly, the reality hit Kevin like a stomach punch. "My God, Colleen…I just realized something—something I haven't told you. How stupid of me. Angie has a health problem—blackouts…" He went on to explain.

"That poor woman. What you've said puts a whole different slant on my perceptions, or misperceptions, Kevin." Despite her new insights, however, Colleen could not forget Kevin's earlier admission of marital problems. Were things between Angela and him really 'wonderful' or 'better than ever' as he had put it? She decided to leave that matter alone. "What else haven't you told me?"

Kevin met her green eyes for a long moment. He had already confided Sister Anne's vision to Keirnan and Tony. "There is something else, Colleen."

After ten minutes, Colleen smiled, "I'm Catholic, too, Kevin. Not nearly as devout as my dear father, but I grew up with saints and miracles. Visions? At a certain level, I can believe that."

Their meals were served on elegant Irish Beliek plates, with coffee in Waterford Crystal. While eating, Colleen tried to steer their conversation in lighter directions—even sharing a lawyer joke she'd heard recently. But Kevin was too obsessed with his banal perceptions of Conrad Phelps to recognize her leads. And he had switched from Chianti to scotch. She lost track of how many times Kevin had said "we're going to get him" and "when I get my hands on…" Her feelings were running from warm to cool the more his male swagger surfaced. Maybe it was the liquor? Maybe the consuming anger? Nagging in the back of her thoughts all day were her troubling "what if questions"…this was her last night in St. Paul. Room 642 was just an elevator away. What if Kevin wanted her? What if she wanted him? What if there was an opportunity?

After declining dessert, the table was cleared. Neither had eaten more than a few bites of their expensive and elegantly served entrees. Kevin ordered a double scotch—Colleen another cup of coffee. It was getting late and Colleen needed sleep. Pushing her chair slightly away from the table, she offered a wan smile, "Before we call it a night, I want to give you a name to follow up on tomorrow." Inside a matchbook cover, Colleen wrote the name Calvin Hodge. "He's the man to see at Phelps Enterprises. He goes way back to the early Conrad Senior years."

Kevin pushed his scotch glass aside, filled his dinner goblet with ice water, and pocketed the match book. "I'm sorry, Colleen. I've not been myself tonight. I can't remember the last time I've had four drinks." He was perceiving Colleen's cool demeanor and sensing her obvious intention to excuse herself in a few moments. "You've been gracious beyond belief to put up with all my false bravado—even arrogance, for the past hour. It's all stress in disguise. I don't sleep nights and I haven't eaten a decent meal in weeks."

Reaching for his hand, Colleen gave a light squeeze and nodded sympathetically, "I understand. No, I take that back—I can't really understand what you're going through." Then laughing lightly she added, "I've had worse dinner dates, Kevin. Much worse! Maybe under different circumstances..." She began to rise from her chair. "Good luck with your leads tomorrow." Almost as an afterthought, she added, "I've forgotten to mention that I must drive back to Duluth in the morning. You can give me a call at home if you like, and let me know what Hodge has to say. Chin up, my friend."

Kevin stood, "How can I thank you enough? If it were not for you, well...? He laughed for the first time that evening, "I've suddenly become a tongue-tied attorney—I truly don't know what to say, Colleen." "A distinguished member of the bar at a loss for words?" Her smile vanished as quickly as it had appeared. For a long moment she said nothing. "Maybe...what you ought to say is...'thanks' and then...'good night.'"

"The "thanks" is easy—the 'good night'?—" Kevin felt awkward, the pain of a thousand thoughts swirled in his head. Part of him wanted to try and take her upstairs to her room—another to let go of his unsettling lust. One voice told him to leave their table as *friends*, another to complete their evening as *lovers*. In his emotional tumult, the last thing he wanted to say was the first to escape from his suddenly dry mouth.

Colleen nodded and took his hand in hers.

∼

"I'm very sorry to hear about your wife," Calvin Hodge said after Kevin Moran had introduced himself and briefly explained the purpose of his visit to the Phelps Enterprises office the following morning. Hodge was a meticulously dressed man in his late sixties, heavy jowled and thick lipped. "But I find this all very hard to believe. Conrad?" He repeated with a belly laugh. "Someone's sold you a bill of goods, I think."

"Think what you might. Where is he right now, Mr. Hodge? If this is his company you must know," Kevin said bluntly. Hodge had shifty eyes and Kevin was put off by his the sarcasm in his laugh and the arrogance of his corporate status.

Hodge leaned back in his expensive leather chair, "What do you really know about my employer, Mr. Moran? He's an eccentric little man with no business sense and far too much money to spend. He's ruined the company his father worked a lifetime to develop. He goes where he pleases when he wants, and doesn't give a shit about what I do here. No interest whatsoever. Sometimes I'd like to kick his little ass, you know what I mean?"

"I didn't ask for a biography. Where is the man now?"

"I don't have a clue. Last I heard from young Conrad he said he was in Texas, or going to Texas. That was about a month ago—said he'd be back here in a couple of weeks. Still haven't heard from him." Hodge forced a weak laugh, "Even said we'd talk about a raise when he returned. Fat chance of that happening. Why he'd raise my salary I have no idea?"

Kevin could care less—"Texas? Where in Texas did he call from?"

"Didn't say. Could have been anywhere. I know it wasn't a business trip…probably looking for some rare books. That's what he wastes his fortune on—books!"

Kevin made a mental note to ask the FBI to focus their attention on rare edition book stores in Texas. Always lurking in the back of his thoughts was the concept of water from Sister Anne's vision—an ocean. Texas was huge mass of land…but also had a long coastline on the Gulf of Mexico. "Could it have been Galveston?"

"Your guess is as good as mine."

Keirnan McGinnis and Officer Sullivan knocked on the door of the Tudor home on Cambridge Street. The drapes were pulled back and the front door ajar. "I'm coming," said a voice from inside. Loretta Flynn's mouth dropped. Her son Larry must be in hot water again.

McGinnis made quick introductions, allayed her fear that Larry Flynn was in trouble with the police, and explained why they were looking for Mr. Phelps. "Mrs. Moran's husband will be joining us here any time now."

"That's preposterous, sir. Conrad Phelps buying all those women's clothes? Taking a woman to a beauty parlor? If that don't beat all—you don't know Mr. Phelps very well. Mr. Phelps has nothing to do with women…or anybody else for that matter." She scratched her head and invited the policemen inside. "Unless it was some kind of book deal."

Loretta Flynn could not identify the 'new' picture of Angela Moran. "Never seen her—here or anywhere else. She don't look nothing like the picture I seen in the paper, though."

While they discussed the matter of Mr. Phelps' whereabouts, Loretta confirmed Keirnan's description of Conrad, acknowledged that he had "some kind of business downtown", and that she "hadn't seen hide nor hair of him in more than a month."

"If he's not in St. Paul, Mrs. Flynn, where might he be?"

"Spends lots of time in Winona, officer. That's where he grew up you know; still has a nice house down there."

"May I use your phone for a minute, ma'am?"

Keirnan called Locher at headquarters and told the captain to get in touch with the Winona police. "Phelps has a house down there, Captain" Keirnan could not hide his excitement.

Locher made a note. "We've just heard from Kevin. He wants me to have the Feds to focus on book dealers all over Texas, for God's sake! A tall order to say the least. He told me that's where Phelps was last heard from. Checking out Winona will be easy, and I'll give that a priority. Things are really starting to pop, aren't they, Keirnan? We've got five hundred new pictures circulating already this morning. The papers will have front page stuff to run."

The knock on the front door was Kevin Moran. After quickly briefing McGinnis and Sullivan on his progress that morning, Kevin asked Mrs. Flynn if the police could look around the house for a few minutes. "We've got every reason to believe that Mr. Phelps and my wife were here for a short time—probably on the weekend of August 27th."

"I don't work weekends, Mr. Moran. But, I'd rather you didn't…" there was a nervous tinge in the lanky, gray headed woman's voice.

Keirnan puzzled, "What's the matter, Mrs. Flynn?"

"I haven't been too good at my housekeeping. With Mr. Phelps gone all the time, I just…well, mostly I spend my days reading or listening to the radio."

"We'll keep that between us, Mrs. Flynn," Keirnan smiled. "I'd probably do the same if I were you."

Feeling better, Loretta sighed weakly, "Well, go ahead then. Just don't put nothing in your notepad about my dusting and vacuuming."

Kevin visited with Loretta Flynn about Conrad's idiosyncrasies for a few minutes while McGinnis and Sullivan poked around downstairs. "I'd say you do a pretty good job, Mrs. Flynn," Sullivan said from the kitchen, "Everything's spic and span."

"Well…you haven't been upstairs yet," she tried to laugh. "I guess I haven't been up there in weeks either."

Mrs. Flynn was explaining to Kevin that Conrad spent most of his time at the Howard Gross Bookstore on Grand Avenue, or the Macalaster campus, when he was in St. Paul. "Except on Monday mornings. He gets dressed in a suit and gets picked up by someone in a black car outside. Told me once that he always had this business meeting…"

"Kevin, come up here for a minute," Keirnan summoned from the top of the stairs. Excusing himself, Kevin tucked his small notepad in his suit coat pocket.

Keirnan's eyes were downcast and his throat tight, "Brace yourself Kevin—this guest bed's been slept in!" He had pulled back the bedspread and sheet. In his fingers was a long strand of dark hair.

Kevin felt tears begin to well in his eyes as he took the strand in his hand. Leaning over the pillow, he smelled the fine linen, "Angie slept here, Keirnan. I'd recognize her scent anywhere."

∼

Curtis Miller worked at the ticket window for the Northern Pacific Railroad office at the downtown Minneapolis terminal. "Someone else skip town, officer?" he asked Sergeant Riley Wolfe of the St. Paul department.

Riley laughed, "Nope. But I got a new picture of Mrs. Moran to post. The old one over there needs to be changed," he waved his arm to the bulletin board. "Might as well ask a few questions while I'm here, Curt. Says in my notes from before that you were working on…let me see—the weekend of August 27th. That right?"

"Yep, I told you that weeks ago, officer."

Wolfe showed the ticket man the new photo reproduction and described Conrad Phelps. "Need to see your passenger lists again, Curt," the blue clad officer said. "Looking for the name Phelps…or maybe Johnson, in your departures ledger."

Curtis found the large leather log, scanned the names with his long finger. "I got a Johnson, here. The two-thirty out to Seattle. A Mr. and Mrs. Adam Johnson, Pullman car." He turned the book so Wolfe could see the names in the register.

"Can you remember them, Curt? Anything come to mind?"

Curtis Miller pressed his memory. "There was a guy…kinda stood out as I recall—wearing a long rain coat. Remember wondering why…seems to me it was warm and humid that Sunday. He was a short man, like you said this Phelps guy was. But he was wearing a felt hat—so I don't know if he was balding or not...but he didn't wear any glasses. No, he was squinting like the sun was in his eyes. Somehow I seem to remember that."

Within minutes Captain Locher had another curve ball thrown at him, "Seattle? Phelps and an unidentified woman, registered as the Adam Johnsons—Sunday the 27th? It fits with the Dayton's alias we have."

"Yes, Captain. Miller didn't get a good look at the woman but thinks he saw her from behind while she was walking with 'Johnson'. Says he's almost positive she was a blond. The man was about the same height as we have down for Phelps—the woman nearly as tall."

"We'll get on the Seattle connection right away. Thanks, Riley—good job."

~

When Kevin and Keirnan met Locher at the St. Paul headquarters. It was nearly noon. Kevin had picked up chicken salad sandwiches at a delicatessen outside the police building for lunch.

"We've given the Feds a headache this morning," Locher said. "Texas, Washington...and Gunther Miles, the agent down in Miami almost had a bird when I told him to get rid of all the old pictures. Hopefully, with the priority deliveries, the new sketches will be in their hands by Wednesday."

"And we've dispatched the sketch down to the Winona police. They will have it by mid-afternoon," Keirnan added. "We'll be kicking each other in the butt if Mrs. Moran has been less than ninety miles away all this time."

Kevin's first thought was of a spance of water. "Winona's on the Mississippi, and aren't their lakes there as well?"

"City's built along a lake on one side and the river on the other," Locher informed. "Pretty little town with the hills and all."

Keirnan knew what Kevin was thinking. "It's nothing like an ocean, but Winona's got lots of water."

The late September afternoon was autumnal brilliant, and the amber elms of Rice Park offered an ideal respite. Still overwhelmed by the flurry of new information and from racing back-and-forth across the city these past six hours, Kevin needed a few minutes to organize his thoughts. The adrenaline which had kept him charged was noticeably fading. Since childhood, Kevin had found that a solitary walk inspired his best thinking, and rejuvenated his spirit. He walked for nearly an hour, oblivious to the manifold sounds of the busy city surrounding him.

Finding a shaded wooden bench amidst the park's greenery was a perfect place to wind down and focus upon his next steps. Closing his eyes he allowed himself to slip into a meditative prayer. Asking the Almighty to listen to his words, Kevin thanked God for bringing him to this moment and reverently petitioned "Keep my Angela safe from any harm and bring us back together. Bless my every action in finding her…and bless all those who have been helping me…" In the back of Kevin's mind were some phone calls he needed to make in a few minutes. "And bless those with whom I speak this day."

~

Tony and Becca were having leftover pot roast for lunch. Tony brooded, "Still not a word from Kevin. I called your mother and she said he came in late last night or early this morning, and was gone before seven. Didn't tell Josie anything either—just out the door with a quick good-bye."

Becca could read her husband's stress like a book. Since arriving home yesterday afternoon, Tony had been unusually withdrawn. She waited for him to break the ice, but he said little more than "Kevin's staying down there by himself."

"What's bothering you so, sweetheart? Did you and Kevin have some kind of problem? You haven't told me why he stayed and you came back."

Tony met her deep-set, dark eyes. He had never kept anything from Becca before and couldn't do so now. "There is a problem with Kevin. I gave Kevin some strong words and left with a bad taste in my mouth. I don't quite know how to tell you this…and I may be completely wrong about my suspicions, but I'm positive that Kevin lied to me." Tony went on to explain the Saturday night 'walk'. "Not only was he evasive, but I got the impression he wanted me go home and leave him to himself." Tony swallowed hard on his next words, "He was planning to meet this Bates woman again yesterday. What do you think, Becca?"

~

Colleen McIntosh had a hard time concentrating on the hearing testimony being presented at the County Court House in Duluth. For the past many hours she had tormented herself over whether she had done the right thing the night before. Would she ever hear from Kevin again?

~

Kevin was back in Locher's office by late Monday afternoon. "Sorry, Kevin." Locher had just finished explaining that the Winona police had come up empty. "Phelps hasn't been seen down there in nearly a month. They interviewed his housekeeper, a Mrs. Galinski, and a guy named Beatty who manages the Phelps' barge operations down there."

Kevin slumped in his chair. "Damned frustrating. To have a name and all these new leads…Have you heard anything from Seattle or anyplace in Texas?"

"Nothing yet, Kevin. Maybe later tonight or tomorrow. Why don't you take a break—go home and get some rest?"

Back at Josie Kaner's, Kevin made a difficult phone call.

"Tony, I'm sorry for yesterday. I got too full of myself again. Too absorbed with my own agenda…" Kevin bit at his lip, "And I lied to you besides!" He went to explain all that had happened these past two days and how Colleen McIntosh had been so instrumental in finding the critical leads he'd been following.

Relieved, Tony apologized for not having been more forthright himself, "I wanted to shake you, Kev. To tell you to cut the bull and level with me." As the magnitude of Kevin's revelations settled in, however, Tony's became almost at a loss for what else to say. "It's all so unbelievable. You know who it was."

"We're all over the map right now, Tony. But I still can't help feeling like our car's stuck in the snow—wheels spinning, rocking back and forth, but we're still not able to get it out of the ditch."

Tony understood the analogy. "Do you want me to come down and help you fellas push."

Kevin forced a weak laugh. "I'm afraid we need a set of chains right now, Tony. No…I'm going to hang around St. Paul for a couple more days and then head north to spend some time with the kids. Give my love to everybody up there…and tell them we're getting closer."

~

Tuesday and Wednesday were the longest days of Kevin Moran's thirty one years. And the most painful. Officer Sullivan's team had discovered a pillow case in the rafters of the Phelps garage. Inside the bag were Angie's lavender linen suit and personal effects—but Kevin declined the invitation to come over and make a positive identification. "I know they're her things…I can't bear to see them." The well of optimism had gone dry. Conrad Phelps, and Angela, it seemed to him on this bleak day, had disappeared from the face of the earth.

Officer Ned Fearing should not have been working that week—much less been assigned to join the Phelps investigation. The veteran St. Paul cop was going through some stressful personal issues. His wife of seven years could no longer deal with his drinking, and had left home with their two children the previous Friday. Judy Fearing was living with her mother in Forest Lake. On Monday morning, Fearing interviewed the proprietor of a Grand Avenue bookstore named Howard Gross. The middle aged book dealer had never seen the attractive blond-haired woman in the sketch Fearing offered to him.

"Is the name Phelps familiar, Mr. Gross?"

"Probably my very best customer, Officer Fearing. A collector of some reputation, I might add."

Fearing asked Gross to verify the description he had been given.

"Yes, that would fit Mr. Phelps to a tee."

"When did you last see him?"

"About a month ago. Before he left for London and other parts of Europe. It's ironic you should ask about Conrad, he called me just last night. He's purchased a priceless Thomas More manuscript."

Fearing scribbled some notes on his pad. His thoughts were miles away at the moment. Should he drive up to Forest Lake that afternoon and apologize to Judy…promise to go on the wagon, get some help? The policeman was tormented, "Thank you, Mr. Gross." He tucked the notepad in his jacket pocket and left for Shady's Tavern to figure out what he should do about his crumbling marriage.

Hours later his notepad was stuffed in the pocket of a jacket he wouldn't wear again for two weeks. The Gross interview was totally forgotten.

Scotland Yard

Kevin was thinking in numbers this Thursday morning. He was planning to return to Hibbing and add a week—seven more X's—to the string on his desk calendar. In his disheartened thoughts he calculated the number of days since Angie's disappearance to be thirty-four. In two more days the month of September would become history!

And the number four throbbed within his nagging headache of the moment. It had been four nights since he'd last seen Colleen. He wanted to call and assure her that they had done the right thing—but he couldn't bring himself to do it. What had Colleen been thinking these four days? Would they ever have an opportunity talk about what they had chosen to do—and why? Could he continue to shut her out of his life?

Kevin easily found a parking place near Locher's downtown office. It was early (seven forty on his watch) but he wanted to be briefed on the latest developments before driving Josie Kaner's car up to Hibbing. Becca's mother had treated him like a son these past many days, and sent along a fresh batch of "baked with love" peanut butter cookies for the police officers on morning duty.

After settling into the familiar chair where he had spent countless hours seated next to Locher's cluttered desk, Kevin slid the aromatic paper bag across to the Captain who was talking on the phone when he sat down. Smiling, Locher stuffed his first cookie of the morning in his mouth, placed another in front of himself— "Let me call you back, Sully. "

Looking up from his second cookie, Locher said— "I got a call for you ten minutes ago. Hodge over at Phelps' offices wants you to call him back as soon as you can. He told me that our Mr. Phelps might be returning from Europe—coming back to California. Yes, I said coming back, and I said California! Wait until the FBI gets that bit of information—they'll be sending us a bill for travel expenses."

Kevin's hand was on the telephone so fast he almost tipped Locher's cup of coffee over the desktop. Pulling out the matchbook in his pocket, he flipped the cover to Colleen's note from Sunday night: "Operator—give me Phelps Enterprises at 18-3318, please.

"Moran returning your call...what's this about California?"

Calvin Hodge was in a surly mood. Before answering Kevin's first question he pleaded, "Will you remind Locher to get his cop's asses out of my offices? They have been turning this place upside down for two days. I've already told him that Phelps cleaned almost everything out of here long ago, and the only records worth a grain of salt are probably down in Winona with Beatty's little barge operations. That said, let me tell you what I've just picked up from a guy named Hurley..."

Hurley? "Yes, Mr. Hodge—please do just that...Locher told me you said Phelps was coming to California?"

After nearly ten minutes and a page of scribbled notes, Kevin hung up the phone. "Phelps and his wife..." he choked on the word *wife*, "should be returning to Santa Monica very soon. I've got a name here to call, but it seems..." Kevin explained that an estate manager named Darold Hurley had called the Phelps office on Tuesday. "Hurley claimed he was trying to locate Conrad and Emma Phelps—said they were vacationing in Europe, and asked if Hodge's office knew when they were expected back. Apparently Hurley told Hodge's secretary to forward any information...which she forgot to tell Hodge anything about. Apparently, Hurley's understanding was that the couple planned on returning to California any day now. Hodge claims he didn't get the secretary's message until just a few minutes ago. Apologized for not remembering the Phelps family still had a place out there. He thought Conrad Junior had sold it 'along with everything else' years ago."

"California...Europe? God, wait until I pass that along to the Feds." Locher nearly gagged on his third cookie.

Kevin pushed away from the desk, "If what this Hurley says checks out—I'm going to be heading to California this afternoon. I want to be there when Conrad Phelps and *my* wife get back from their..." He could not say the word *honeymoon*.

(Nor could he share that Hodge had used that very word in his report only moments before). "…when they get back from their travels."

Locher slapped the desk, "Kevin, even if I have to take vacation time and pay for it out of my own pocket—I'm going with you. And Keirnan, too! I want some St. Paul, Minnesota, police officers there when this asshole is arrested."

Still bewildered over the latest lead, Kevin only nodded absently.

"Let me get on the phone right now. We'll have the LA cops and the FBI all over Santa Monica within an hour," Locher said excitedly.

Kevin stood, "Can I borrow an office with a phone? I've got some calls of my own to make."

The room Locher offered was more like a storage closet than an office. Old cardboard boxes were stuffed on shelves from floor to ceiling. A single light bulb hung over a desk covered with layers of dust. Kevin regarded the California phone number that Hodge had given him, but decided to make another call before connecting with Mr. Hurley at Phelps' Pacific Ocean villa near Santa Monica. Sister Anne had told him that an ocean appeared in her first vision, but that her interpretations at the time had been vague. Kevin had not talked to the Sister since leaving Hibbing last week, but his gut instinct was to talk with her before any body else.

"Sister Anne. I need to talk with you," he blurted. "Listen to what I have to say and tell me if you think…" Before he could say anything about California the nun was speaking.

"Kevin!" Sister Anne's voice had a tone of relief. She believed that God had truly inspired his call at this precise moment. The nun had just been praying to hear from Kevin. "I have seen more— not much, but enough to believe that the *block I* told you about is disappearing. My images, however, still remain confusing." Clutching the scapular she wore about her neck, Anne continued. "First, Angela is safe—protected in some way by an angel—maybe more than one angel. I've seen a magnificent white church…on a hillside. The church is a refuge for her, I think."

Anne paused, "And I've seen you, Kevin. Standing on what seems a hill of sand—you are looking out over an ocean. I'm afraid, that from there—you will not find Angela. She must find you."

Kevin confused over the Sister's words. "I won't find Angela? What are you saying, Sister Anne? I feel so close right now." He briefly explained the information on California and his plans to get out there as soon as he could.

"Kevin, I can't tell you what to do. But I cannot see you finding Angela out there in California. I'm sorry. She is still far away, but…God's angels will help her find you. I'm certain of that."

"What am I to do, Sister? I can't just sit here in St. Paul if she's somewhere far away." He wanted to ask if Anne was perfectly clear about her visions but swallowed the question.

Anne was feeling something, and did not speak for a long minute.

"Sister? Are you still there?" Waiting, he repeated his question.

"Kevin, this Mr. Hurley you mentioned is a good man. An honest man who has been deceived. Talk to him yourself right now."

Anne was feeling suddenly drained and needed to pray some more, "I must leave you to the task at hand, Kevin. After you talk with this Hurley, please say a prayer—ask God to lift your burdens and give you peace of mind. Will you do that?"

Kevin promised.

∼

Kevin had outlined his questions in typical attorney manner. He checked the wall clock. It was six-thirty California time. Hopefully somebody would be up early out there.

"Mr. Hurley, my name is Kevin Moran and I'm calling from St. Paul. I'm sorry to be calling so early, but there is an urgency."

Hurley first tried to place the name Moran with Phelps Enterprises executives but couldn't do so. At least it wasn't Hodge calling. Calvin Hodge was an obnoxious man—much like Conrad Senior. "So good of you to return my call. Have you been in contact with Mr. and Mrs. Phelps, Mr. Moran?"

Kevin corrected, "I'm not calling from the Phelps' offices…let me explain, sir." Following his notes, Kevin began what became a nearly fifteen minute description of all the events since August 26 when Angela Moran left Hibbing for St. Paul.

Darold Hurley listened in stunned disbelief without interrupting by asking any questions. With every word the incredible story became something more out of fiction than reality. When Mr. Moran mentioned his wife's history of blackouts,

Hurley winced. He had noticed from the moment he met Emma Phelps at Union Station in Los Angeles that the woman had behaved as if she were more adolescent than adult. His first impression of Emma was that her speech and demeanor were that of a sixteen year old girl: Certainly not that of the twenty-seven year old woman as Mr. Moran had described his wife.

Darold felt a sense of total betrayal as he listened to the sincerely pained man from Minnesota. After Conrad's departure, he had tried to contact the London doctor whom Emma was scheduled to meet. He wanted to tell Emma that the movie theater he had improvised at Sunset Shores was nearly complete, and that his collection of Clark Gable films was growing. There was no Doctor Helling in London!

"As unbelievable as all this must seem to you, Mr. Hurley, Conrad Phelps abducted my wife in St. Paul a month ago."

It took Darold a moment to respond. "I believe you, Mr. Moran. What a tragic experience you have been suffering through. It may be small consolation to you, but I am terribly hurt myself right now. If you will indulge me, I will tell you everything I know from the moment your wife—I'm sorry if I call her Emma at times, sir—somehow she will always be Emma in my thoughts…" Darold found his morning cup of tea. His throat had suddenly gone dry. "Since your wife arrived in California on Friday, September second— somehow…I'll never forget that afternoon."

If Darold Hurley had been astounded by Kevin's story—Kevin was equally overwhelmed by what Hurley told him. Tears streaked his face as the stranger from California described the Emma Phelps he knew—she was Kevin's Angela Zoretek of years before. He pictured Angela romping on the ocean beach and stealing the evening at the gala Phelps reception. "The belle of the ball" were Hurley's words. Angie was that, Kevin knew. Listening in a patient pain to the deep voiced man, Kevin contemplated intimate and personal questions about the Phelps' relationship, but all of them remained stuck in the back of his throat.

"To say that Emma—Angela—was refreshing and charming would be a gross understatement of fact. We all fell in love with her immediately and our enchantment only grew in the short time she was with us." Darold Hurley was smiling at his fond memories. "A breath of fresh air that we've never experienced out here before, Mr. Moran."

Not knowing quite how to respond to Hurley's description, Kevin regarded his notes. The purpose of his call was to get any and all information this man had to give, "Mr. Hurley, you said that Phelps planned to go from London to Stockholm, is that correct?"

"Yes, and Amsterdam in between."

"And you haven't heard from him since he left California on the—did you say, Tuesday the sixth of this month?"

"Yes, sir. I have it all right here. According to the itinerary I was given...they would have arrived in London on the twenty-seventh."

Kevin considered the date Hurley had provided. That would have been two days ago—today was the twenty-ninth. Mr. Hurley seemed a very forthright and sincere man—a refined gentleman—just as Sister Anne had told him he would be. Kevin had many more questions but needed to get this critical new information to Locher right now. "Mr. Hurley, I have one last question for the moment; and a hundred more for later. But you seemed certain that your Mr. Phelps would be returning to California?"

"Oh, yes. Mrs....I mean, Angela, just loved it out here. If Mr. Phelps is on the run, as I suspect he might be right now, who can possibly know?" Darold Hurley's voice choked with emotion, "You must forgive me, Mr. Moran—this is all so overwhelming right now. I was actually beginning to like Conrad...and, your Angela—I'm quite certain..." The tightness in his throat hurt..."I became irresistibly infatuated with her."

Darold Hurley was an only child that had grown up under the stern eye and rigid thumb of a father who believed the world turned on one simple principle: The 'Golden Rule' was inviolable to John Hurley. Darold had many fine qualities, but foremost among them was his honesty. Therefore, whenever he had been victimized by another's deceit, the pain ran deep in his marrow. Darold felt numb when he hung up the phone that morning. His trust had been violated in a manner never to be repaired. He would write his letter of resignation—effective immediately—that day and mail it to the St. Paul office of Phelps Enterprises.

As Darold was walking out to the deck to enjoy the incredible Pacific Ocean vista—perhaps for the last time, the door chimes rang. Approaching the front entry foyer he cast a glance through the massive front window. Two police cars were parked at the top of the drive.

At nine o'clock, Kevin and Keirnan were sitting around Locher's desk. They had placed a call to an office at Scotland Yard fifteen minutes ago. It was now five o'clock London time. Three pairs of eyes watched the sweep of the hands on the wall clock without anyone breaking the silent vigil. An Inspector named Damian Halley would be calling them back "within the hour"—all they could do now is wait.

After telephoning an FBI agent in New York City seeking confirmation of the Phelps' customs clearance (on or about September twenty-second) the St. Paul police department kept the line to Locher's office open for the international call. Officer Sullivan manned another line to receive an anticipated call from New York.

New York called at nine-twelve. "It's kinda crazy, Captain," Sullivan reported to his boss. "Conrad and Emma Phelps picked up their passports in New York—along with various travel visas for...Netherlands, Sweden, and Switzerland! They were booked on the Cunard liner, *Norfolk* for London. The Feds are checking for London arrival confirmations right now."

At nine-fifty, Locher's phone rang. The captain listened intently to Damian Halley's five minute report. Locher's notes were precise. Both Kevin and Keirnan's eyes watched the words as they appeared on the white sheet of paper at Locher's elbow. It seemed as if the information from London corroborated Sullivan's earlier information. The Phelps had arrived at Southhampton on September twenty-seventh.

"The guy's clever," Locher said after hanging up the phone. "He pre-booked travel to Amsterdam and Geneva. He also booked passage to Stockholm with the Cunard Lines. Obviously, he's trying to cross us up. Scotland Yard is checking all three destinations right now, but it's going to take some time."

"What about London?" Kevin asked anxiously. "Are they looking in London?"

"Halley's checked all the major hotels for any Phelps registrations. That's what took him so long. No Phelps, yet. But there are several more hotels to check. At the same time, he's getting lists of all American guests at the London hotels. He told us to try and be patient—it's going to take a while. He needs photographs as soon as we can get them over there."

∼

Colleen McIntosh had taken Thursday off and planned to work on her litigation briefs at home rather than drive to her downtown office. From where she was sitting, Colleen could see the Angela Moran painting 'Whitecaps' which hung on the wall of her newly redecorated dining room.

Kevin was in her thoughts this morning as he had been for days. There had been no phone call.

She was attempting to be honest with her feelings, but failing miserably. Kevin was married. Happily married or not, that reality was an ache that would not go away. Try as she might, the memory of the previous Sunday night lingered painfully. "You did the right thing, Colleen" she told herself a thousand times. "Now, get on with your life."

Carver Blake had asked her out to dinner twice in recent weeks. The Duluth detective was handsome and bright—but Carver was no Kevin Moran. If Carver called again, however, Colleen would accept his invitation. Maybe she was growing tired of being by herself all the time? Maybe her independent lifestyle was highly overrated? Maybe a man in her life would give her more satisfaction than she was getting from the successes of her career.

But...there was always this same aggravating question: What if Angela Moran never returned?

Becca Zoretek and Senia Arola met each other for breakfast at the Androy on most Thursday mornings. The two women were continuing a five year tradition which had always included Angela Moran. It had been Angie who gave their little gathering the nickname 'femme la trois'—something she had picked up from Jacque Grojean. Seated at the same table they had always reserved, Becca and Senia were in low spirits this morning.

As always, Senia asked about Kevin. Becca, pleased that Kevin and Tony had patched up their little differences, said..."He called from my mother's last night to tell us he'd be returning to Hibbing today. It's been a long week for him—especially after having such optimism on Monday."

"Still nothing on this Conrad Phelps character, then. Claude told me last night that he had called Keirnan McGinnis for an update. Claude has been such a dear—he calls Steven almost every day to see how he's doing." Steven Skorich, Senia's friend of many years, had a heart condition along with several other physical ailments which kept him at his home most of the time.

The two women shared bits of second-hand information. "I wish there was something we could do, Senia—but, it seems we can only wait and pray for a miracle."

Senia, an accountant by training was not a prayerful woman, and miracles were an alien concept. Nor, was Senia a patient woman. The suggestion of 'waiting and praying' was not something she could find any consolation in doing. And, as much as she loved Angie, Kevin's welfare had always been her life's priority. "I'm glad Kevin's coming home, Becca, that poor man has been through absolute hell for weeks! What can we do to lift his spirits?"

Before leaving for their work places, Senia proposed a barbecue out at Maple Hill that evening. "Kevin loves a cookout, Becca."

Becca, however, was reluctant. Kevin would surely want time to be with his children. "Let me ask Tony what he thinks first, Senia."

Senia felt rebuffed. "I'm sure Tony will agree with my idea. He's been through a lot himself. Let me know what Tony thinks as soon as you get to the hospital so I can call Clara Motter and ask her to get started on things. And, I'll ask Claude to contact all of Kevin's friends," Senia volunteered with enthusiasm.

Becca stood up from the table, "If Tony likes the idea, I'll ask him to be sure to invite Sister Anne. I have the impression that Kevin and she are in touch with each other almost daily."

Senia puzzled over what Becca had just said. Sister Anne? Why hadn't she been aware of the connection? Behind her controlled exterior, Senia had a weak spot: When it came to Kevin, she needed to know everything! The fact that she did not know about the Catholic nun was troubling for her. The fact that Kevin had not called her since leaving for St. Paul a week ago was even more painful.

Upon hearing the proposed plan, Tony fumed, "I don't like the idea at all, Becca. Senia's just not being considerate of Kevin's grieving right now. I know her heart's in the right place—but I'd say no. Let Kevin have some time alone with the children." Although he would never say it, Tony was often disturbed by Senia's almost misguided 'mother's' fixation on Kevin and his well being. "Tell her no as gently as you can, Becca. Perhaps you could suggest that the four of us, and Steven if he's up to it, get together for dinner on Saturday or Sunday."

'DON'T PUSH THE RIVER'

The Friday morning report from Scotland Yard was discouraging. "The Phelps' seem to have vanished into thin air after arriving in London on Tuesday," Damian Halley acknowledged. "We've got a list of seventy-three American couples registered at various hotels and we're working as best we can to match the descriptions you've given us. We'll get back to you chaps in mid-afternoon—unless we discover something important sooner," the Inspector promised.

More waiting! Kevin called Tony from the closet office down the hall to apologize again for not making it back to Hibbing the day before. He had talked with Clara and the children last night, as well as Senia and Claude. Seven year old Patrick told his father that there was a girl named Patty in his second grade class who "kinda liked him". The boy had an issue he wanted to talk with his dad about when Kevin got back home. "I don't like being called 'Pat', Dad, can we change my name?"

Maribec sang an alphabet song she'd learned in kindergarten over the phone. "I can count to a hunnerd now, Dad," she boasted.

Kevin gave Tony the latest information, including his conversation with Darold Hurley in Santa Monica. "I'm keeping my chin up, Tony—you do the same. Scotland Yard's people are probably the best investigators in the world."

While Kevin was away, Locher had called the FBI agents in Seattle and Texas explaining that Phelps was "most likely in London" right now. The police captain asked the G-men to contact Customs and request that they check arriving passengers in the New York and Los Angeles port cities. "Distribute that new Angela Moran photo I've sent out to all of your customs people. It's a long shot, but we've got to cover all the bases." Locher was a Cubs fan and partial to baseball jargon.

At five-thirty that evening, London time, (nine-thirty in Minnesota) Damian Halley called Locher in St. Paul. "First, the good news. We've got an American couple who match Conrad and Emma Phelps—smallish man, attractive blond wife. They registered at the King Edward's Hotel last Tuesday night."

"And the bad news, Inspector Halley?" Locher asked, his smile fading as he regarded Kevin sitting rigidly across from him. Leaning forward in his chair, Kevin watched as Locher scribbled names and places on his notepad. "I can't believe it!" the captain said in exasperated voice. "Phelps is either very clever or he's running scared."

After ten long minutes, Locher hung up his phone. "Phelps and Angela might be passing themselves off as the Clarke's—allegedly from Ohio. They checked out of a London hotel this morning—told the hotel staff that they were going to be touring England for a few days. From here it all becomes, well—awfully damn confusing to say the least! An English Channel ferry company has a booking for Mr. and Mrs. Phelps—leaving Dover for Calais next Wednesday. Cunard Lines officials have the Phelps' booked for a return to New York on the same day. Are you following this convoluted story, Kevin?"

Kevin nodded, "You've got other notes there as well, what's the Amsterdam business about?"

"Well, that's where the Johnson name reappears again. Advance tickets to Amsterdam were purchased by an Adam Johnson while in New York last week. Departure for the Netherlands is scheduled for Monday morning. Naturally, Halley doesn't know if Johnson is Phelps or Clarke.'

Kevin mused. Darold Hurley had mentioned Amsterdam. "I'm guessing the Phelps tickets to France are a ruse. So are the arrangements he's made to return to New York. If he's running, he wouldn't be using 'Phelps' on any documents—don't you agree? He's used the Johnson name with some success before."

Locher scratched his head, "Your guess is as good as mine right now."
"From what Halley said, the Yard's covering all the bases."

As the wall clock swept toward ten, Kevin's restlessness resurfaced. He needed to walk, to think, to pray. "I'm getting a case of claustrophobia in here, Captain. When I feel like this I need some fresh air to revive myself. I'll see you in an hour or so."

Walking south on Cedar Street, Kevin's destination would be the green Mississippi River bank which buffered the city. A sharp wind swirling through the canyon-like streets rendered the morning air crisply autumnal. After crossing Kellogg Boulevard, he found a bench overlooking the river flowing majestically far below. Allowing himself to relax, Kevin pondered the wide band of blue water. Something Angie had told him years before came to his troubled thoughts… *'Don't push the river—it flows by itself…'* The wisdom of that obscure Far Eastern philosophy settled easily in his mind.

As his meditation deepened, Kevin closed his eyes, putting himself in a quiet and peaceful place, where everything dwelled in perfect harmony. In his imagining, Angie was lying on a blanket at his side, looking up into some overhanging pine boughs. A brook was gurgling melodiously, a meadowlark singing into the fresh smelling afternoon air. "Let me feel you, my sweetheart—your warmth, your spirit, your love." His words, muttered softly to himself, brought a smile to his haggard face, and ushered the beginnings of a quiet prayer. The Beatitudes which he'd memorized in grade school so long ago crossed his thoughts. He felt the gentle touch of Sister Anne dabbing a tear from his cheek in the church only days before… *'blessed are those who sorrow'*. Kevin was beginning to cry.

Without his awareness, an old woman had joined him on the bench.
"What is troubling you, young man?" a concerned voice inquired. From where the words came, Kevin had no perception. Was it an angel?

Kevin made no reply, but a smile returned to his face.

"Let God take your burden from you."

His eyes still closed, Kevin nodded. That, more than anything, was what he was trying to do—give up the pressing weight on his shoulders. After his prayers, he opened his eyes. The sun, shimmering its reflection upon the wide river, gave him the surreal impression of a golden pathway. At that moment he knew that Angela would return to him. Leaving the empty bench behind, he walked confidently back into the canyons of the city. The old woman was gone.

~

Edwin and Irma Johnson were detained at the Nor-Europe terminal. The Omaha couple was asked to answer some unexpected questions. Edwin, a small man in his forties and balding—Irma, a shapely blond several years younger than her husband—had been awaiting the train to Brussels and Amsterdam. It took nearly an hour for the American travelers to clear the misperceptions. It took another three hours for them to catch the next train.

Joe Clark was a college professor on sabbatical from Dartmouth College. He didn't know that he was being followed by two men. The short and spectacled English Literature teacher was touring Stratford on Avon. Standing with his camera focused on the replicated Globe Theater where Shakespeare's plays were performed, he felt a strong grip on his elbow.

"May I see some identification, sir?" A burley man inquired, ruining his perfectly framed shot of the theater.

After checking Joseph's passport, the second agent asked, "Where's your wife, Mr. Clark?"

When both men flashed their Scotland Yard badges Clark was petrified. "I'm not married," he stammered.

"Will you kindly come with us and answer a few questions?" said the first agent.

Joe Clark's day in Stratford was ruined by two hours of interrogation at the local constabulary's office.

Paul Phelps owned a Kensington flat only blocks from Harrods where he worked in the 'collectables' section of the world's largest department store. The thirty-two year old, Phelps, had lived in the London neighborhood for seven years. As he left for work on that Saturday morning he had no idea of what a hellish day it would become. He had no more than opened his umbrella against the drizzle when two much taller men were on either side.

Yard agents were combing London. The name Phelps raised a red flag. "Where you headed, Mr. Phelps?" was the first of more than a hundred questions he would answer before the morning's end.

To Scotland Yard, Wednesday, October Fifth, seemed the most critical day of their investigation so far. The agency had posted several agents at both the Cunard docks, and the Dover port where the Calais ferry passengers assembled for transport.

Halley's report was as dismal as the London day had been. His first word summarized everything else he had to say perfectly, "Nothing!"

Thursday and Friday passed uneventfully. Yard agents were posted in every English tourist attraction from Stonehenge to Bath. Travelers, regardless of nationality, were asked if they had encountered a couple fitting the descriptions of Conrad and Emma Phelps. Halley was in contact with police officials in Amsterdam, Stockholm, and Geneva. The Sunday *London Times* put the Moran story on its front page. Port locations were given special scrutiny. Under whatever name he was using, Conrad Phelps had become a ghost.

Jerry Madison had enjoyed his first week of vacation since joining the clerical staff at the United States Embassy in London. Madison and his redheaded Scottish girlfriend, Sadie Stewart, spent five days in Glasgow where he met Sadie's parents for the first time. Michael and Cathy Stewart were most impressed with the young American diplomat. "My job is not that awfully important," he confessed. "I just try to solve problems for U. S. citizens traveling in England." Jerry went on to explain some of the more 'important' problems he had resolved.

After returning from his trip on Saturday night, Jerry decided to spend Sunday morning catching up on the workload he'd sluffed before taking his vacation. Near the top of the stack of papers he found the photograph of a pretty blond woman from Hibbing, Minnesota. Jerry had grown up in the little town of Hayward, Wisconsin and remembered learning about Hibbing's massive Hull Rust Mine—the world's largest man-made hole—in his tenth grade geography class.

In the attached missing person ('possible abduction') report, the name Angela Moran did not register with the young clerk. But, the name Phelps virtually leaped from the page. Digging frantically through the drawers of his desk he located what he was looking for and placed an immediate call to Scotland Yard.

The Yard official who took Madison's call told the clerk to sit tight for a few minutes. "Inspector Halley will call you from his home."

Madison picked up the phone on the first ring. "A man named Conrad Phelps called here a week ago, on Friday…he was trying to verify ownership of some property he has in Sorrento, Italy." Jerry went on to explain to Halley that he had been on vacation for a week and had "no idea that he was leaving something important" behind on his desk.

Halley cursed the Sunday reality—nobody's around, everything's closed!

~

Making Sunday connections with officials in both Rome and Naples proved as difficult as Halley had imagined they would be. It took hours to get through the maze of Italian bureaucrats, none of whom were cooperative or encouraging in the slightest. One person after another transferred the sensitive property issue along to someone else down the line. Considerably complicating matters were the language barriers which required translators at both ends of the various conversations. Halley was becoming increasingly convinced that the Italians were stonewalling something—but had no clue as to what that something might be. In frustration, Halley told one official, "Look, sir…I don't think you are getting my point. Phelps was interested in his property—Scotland Yard is interested in Phelps himself. We need to locate him in a criminal investigation. What do you know about this man and his wife?"

By day's end, however, Halley had not learned anything about the Phelps' whereabouts, but was informed that the Italian government had "probably confiscated" the Phelps' property on some vague grounds of tax delinquency. The official who made that assumption promised to find out for certain, and let Scotland Yard know as soon as possible.

"This year or next?" was Halley's curt reply.

Halley was confronting the same frustrations on Monday. Rome validated their "probably" contention of the day before. The Phelps property now belonged to the government of Italy. Conrad Phelps, they assured the British Inspector, "Will not be allowed to travel in our country".

Late on Monday evening, however, something totally unexpected happened. An English speaking operator from the Naples telephone department called Scotland Yard. Lucille Torentello had translated some of the complicated, and often heated, communications of the day before. Frightened about possible government reprisals, the twenty year employee had not revealed information she believed might be most helpful to the British authorities. While following the dialogue between officials from both sides, Lucille's heart went out to a woman she knew nothing about— an abducted American named Emma Phelps. She felt compelled to take a risk and offer her help.

The Naples phone call caught Halley as he was gulping the last of his twentieth cup of tea that day and was about to turn off the lights in his office, "Scotland Yard, Inspector Halley here..."

"Conrad Phelps—he has called here." Lucille identified herself and whispered excitedly. "So has the American Embassy in Paris."

Recognizing the Italian woman's voice immediately, Halley spilled tea on his wrinkled white shirt, "Is it safe for you to explain further, Miss Torentello?"

"No, sir. A Mr. Kline..." the receiver went dead.

Kline? Halley quickly checked his directory. Wendell Kline was listed as the U.S. Ambassador in Paris.

In less than a minute, an operator had connected his call to the U.S. Embassy where he spoke with the Ambassador's after hours desk. Kline, he was informed, was unavailable. "This is Scotland Yard. It is imperative that I reach the Ambassador right now?" Kline, he was informed, was attending a banquet and choral program with a group of faculty and students from the Ambassador's alma mater, Emory University in Atlanta.

"Maybe you can help me, Mr. Boyer. I'm trying to locate an American citizen by the name of Conrad Phelps. I believe he has recently been in contact with your embassy..."

"Let me check our logs, Inspector. Yes, Mr. Phelps had an appointment with Mr. Kline this morning. I don't know the nature of his visit, of course."

"Listen, however you do it, get a message to Mr. Kline right now. Tell him to contact me immediately at this number." Halley gave his number, hung up the phone, and contacted the Sûreté in Paris, requesting that the French police begin searching for an American named Conrad Phelps—or Clarke, or Johnson. Then he waited and stewed and wanted to kick himself. His eyes scanned the large map hanging on the wall across from his desk where some twenty pins indicated tourist locations across England and in Brussels, Amsterdam, Stockholm, and Geneva. The single pin in France was stuck on Calais! Mumbling, Halley cursed, "Why and the hell didn't I focus on Paris?" Perhaps, though he would never admit it, he had an attitude problem—the Sûreté, he was convinced from past experience, couldn't find the Eiffel Tower on a clear day!

At nine o'clock, Wendell Kline returned his call. "Yes, I remember him well. An upset little man—wanted to get on the next train and head for Sorrento." Kline explained that Phelps claimed he had property in Italy and wanted the embassy to assure him that he could safely travel there with his wife. "I offered every assistance, but remember him saying he would "take care of things for himself" when he left my office in a huff this morning. Is he traveling illegally, Inspector?"

"To say the least! Where is he now? Do you have any idea?" Halley briefly described the investigation he was heading.

"I had no idea!" Kline said indignantly, "Why wasn't I told about this matter a week ago?"

Halley apologized, "We had every reason to believe he was in London, sir…or—" He elaborated on the complicated Phelps trail. "Now, back to my question of a few minutes ago, "Where might we find Phelps?"

"After what I told him about trying to travel in Italy, I would hope he has cooled off enough to think rationally." Kline realized after saying it, that Phelps had not been speaking nor behaving sensibly. "I'm quite certain that he and his wife are staying at the Ritz Hotel. My guess is that he's probably still there."

Halley's next call was to the night manager of the Ritz. "Yes, Inspector. Mr. and Mrs. Phelps have been our guests since last—last Wednesday." John Berthume's mouth went dry. Something very strange had been going on that day, and he now felt caught in the middle of an awkward situation. The Ritz policy of protecting the privacy of their patrons might have to be compromised. In all his years, Berthume had never had an inquiry from Scotland Yard.

"Are they in your hotel right now—at this moment?" Halley's voice suggested an urgency.

There was a significant pause.

"Are they there?"

"No, sir. Let me explain. Mr. Phelps left the hotel nearly an hour ago, Inspector. He seemed quite upset!—paced back and forth across the lobby for several minutes. I think he was looking at a train schedule brochure, but I'm not certain."

Berthume continued his report in well enunciated English. "Mrs. Phelps left the hotel without her husband early this morning. Our desk clerk gave her the address of one of our employees, a Mr. Guillaume LaBlanc. He's a college student and part-time tourist guide. Anyhow, Mr. Phelps seemed highly agitated when told of her departure later—about noon, I believe. He didn't leave the hotel all day. Then about an hour ago he came down to the lobby. And, as I said, he left—quite agitated I would say. According to our log, Mrs. Phelps has not returned to the hotel."

Haley wrote down the Montmartre address that Berthume had readily volunteered. The hotel manager verified the descriptions of both Conrad and Emma Phelps. "Is there anything else, Mr. Berthume?"

The manager was quick to respond, "Yes, Inspector. Mr. Phelps left an envelope at the front desk for an Andre Bouchard before leaving. Looks to me like there's money inside."

"Who's this Bouchard? Haley asked as he scribbled down the name.

"I have no idea, Inspector."

"Well, if Bouchard shows up to claim the envelope, call the Sûreté immediately—will you do that? They will have some questions for him."

Halley had worked with the French police before and was quick to think of an old friend, and the only member of the French force he trusted implicitly. His next call would be to Benjy Duvalle.

At ten-fifteen, Halley was briefing his inconvenienced Paris friend on the Phelps case. Benjy Duvalle and his naked wife had finished a bottle of wine and just climbed into bed. "I'll get over to Montmartre right now, Damian." After a suffered apology to his wife, Duvalle was at the 42 Rue St-Vincent address in thirty minutes awakening a lovely young woman named Gabrielle.

Benjy, out of uniform and wearing casual black slacks with an oversized matching turtleneck sweater, struck Gabrielle as sincere while the agent explained the reason for his late intrusion.

"I cannot tell you where she is—I have promised this to Guillaume." She explained that a man named Bouchard "a detective I think" was also looking for Emma Phelps. "I called Mr. Phelps at the Ritz Hotel earlier this evening and read him the note Guillaume left for me. I have it here." Gabrielle found the paper in an end table drawer near the worn sofa and passed it to Duvalle.

Cherie is safe. Don't go to the police. We will contact you when we know the facts.

"Who is this Cherie?" Duvalle asked as he handed back the note.

"Guillaume calls his American friend by that name. She is Mrs. Phelps."

"Is there anything else you can tell me?"

"*Mais non.* Be assured that the American woman is safe with Guillaume. He is a good man. You will not find him, Mr. Duvalle, nor will that creepy Bouchard. Not until Guillaume wants you to."

Duvalle knew who André Bouchard was. The private detective was a former Sûreté officer who had been fired for taking bribes, and now had a pariah's reputation among the police in Paris. If Bouchard was in Montmartre, Duvalle would find him—and follow him. He would call Halley first, and assure his friend that the woman named Angela Moran was safe—probably somewhere in Paris.

∼

Scotland Yard and the Sûreté did not know that a contact between two small cities, one in France and the other in Midwestern America, had been made only hours before.

When Halley got Duvalle out of bed for the second time, it was three-thirty on Tuesday morning—Paris time. He gave his friend careful instructions. "Angela Moran has been located. Word from the American FBI reached me at home minutes ago." Halley rubbed sleep from his tired eyes. "Mrs. Moran is resting comfortably in a small town east of Paris—Thoiry. I'll locate your chief inspector at the Sûreté and brief him that she is in French jurisdiction. I'm going to request that you be given the responsibility for providing Mrs. Moran with expeditious transport to London." Halley gave Duvalle the Thoiry address, "Hopefully, your supervisor can meet you at Thoiry in an hour. Keep in mind, Benjy, Mrs. Moran has been traumatized and that the LaPointe woman who's sheltering her seems very skeptical of the French police."

Duvalle was grateful for Halley's confidence, "I'll do my best to allay any apprehensions Madeline LaPointe may have. I've heard of the LaPointe woman, Damian, she's a well known agitator and pacifist around Paris. I'll call you when I've met the LaPointe's."

"When Mrs. Moran is safe, we're going to find her abductor, Benjy—no place on earth will safe for that fugitive!"

"...My Soul to the Devil"

Monday, October 10, 1938
9:00 P.M.
Thoiry, France

"Kevin...Kevin Moran!" the comely woman blurted the name. "Guillaume...Madeline... I know who I am!"

Madeline LaPointe had just connected with an overseas operator—
"Hold the line a moment, *sil vous plait...*" the old woman instructed in an excited voice while turning to Cherie.

"My name is Angela Moran! It's all coming back to me now," she looked from Madeline to Guillaume sitting at her side on the patterned sofa. "Ask for Hibbing, Minnesota, Mrs. LaPointe. Yes...they will know everything."

Angela's eyes, wide and clear, held a spark Guillaume LaBlanc had not seen before. "Ask for the Hibbing police, mother!" His hand found Angela's, his smile was radiant—"Angela...such a beautiful name, *mon cherie*. Angela!" he repeated.

∼

Officer Roy Olson listened to the richly accented voice through the static of nearly four thousand miles. The Hibbing desk sergeant's eyes widened upon hearing the name "Angela Moran".

"Yes, ma'am..." Olson stammered, "We have been looking for Mrs. Moran." Under his breath, however, he cursed..."What the hell am I supposed to do now?" It was twelve-twenty and Chief Rich Bernard was attending the Monday Chamber of Commerce meeting across the street at the Androy Hotel. Should he keep this woman, Madeline something, on the line? "Yes, ma'am," he answered the woman's question, "I am the police. Can you hold...for just a minute?"

Cupping the phone, Olson shouted across to fellow officer, Jerry Gregorich, "Get your ass over to the Androy and tell the Chief that Angela Moran has been found. Ask him to get over here right away—I don't know what to do!"

Gregorich was eating a sandwich at his desk, "Another crank call, Roy? Where the hell is Angela Moran this time?"

"How am I supposed to know? The operator gave me some place in France. Just go, damn it! Let Bernard take care of this."

"With whom am I speaking?" Angela asked, "This is Mrs. Moran. Can you reach Kevin for me?"

The voice on the line was clearly American, "Sergeant Olson...Mrs. Moran," the panicked officer said through the growing lump in his throat. "I think your husband is in St. Paul right now...but Chief Bernard will be here in just a few minutes. Can you stay on the line?"

Angie pondered, St. Paul? "Why is my husband in St. Paul, officer?"

Olson was explaining some sketchy details of the international search when the office door swung open. Olson quickly scribbled a note for the two men approaching his desk. As he expected, Tony Zoretek had been at the Chamber meeting with Bernard. Olson held up his notepad.

Tony, reading the large message Olson held—'Mrs. Moran's on the line'—beat Bernard to the phone, "Angela? Is that you, my dear? This is Dad!"

Through her sobbing, Tony recognized Angela's voice immediately. "Are you okay?"

Angela explained that she was fine, now. "I'm with dear friends, Daddy...Yes, I'm okay. I'm finally safe."

Sobbing along with his daughter, Tony didn't know quite what to say or do at the moment, "I can't tell you how...how happy...how thankful...Angie, are you sure that everything is okay?"

Angela, now in control of her emotions, explained where she was and who her friends were. "Can you and Kevin come and get me, Daddy? Take me home?"

"Absolutely," Tony assured in a confident voice. "Angie, will you tell Chief Bernard where you are? He's right here. Then...we will talk some more."

Bernard nodded to Tony, "Just sit down for a few minutes, Tony. We'll get going on this as soon as I have the information I need."

~

Kevin Moran was sitting on the same wooden bench overlooking the Mississippi River that he'd visited nearly every day since the previous Thursday. He'd left Locher's office at twelve-thirty on this sun drenched Monday to be by himself and meditate. Despite Scotland Yards discouraging weekend reports, Kevin continued to harbor an optimism—he had given Angie's fate to God. Each of the past three days had begun at morning mass in the hilltop basilica overlooking downtown St. Paul.

Closing his eyes, Kevin allowed himself to slip back into his special place near the pond on his Maple Hill property. It was within this vivid imagination that he found his strongest connection to Angela, and where his sustaining peace of mind was able to envelope him.

"Mr. Moran! Mr. Moran!" Officer Sullivan was gasping for breath after running several blocks as fast as he could. "Mr. Moran…your wife's been found. She's okay!"

Kevin was so absorbed in his meditation that neither the voice nor the message registered in his distant thoughts. His smile was peaceful and his world of the moment far away.

"Mr. Moran!" Sullivan stood panting beside the bench. Anxiously, he grabbed Kevin's shoulder, shook gently—"Angie's been found."

Kevin's eyes opened. For a brief moment he could not comprehend what the perspiring Sullivan was so worked up about. Then, it struck him!

Leaping from the bench he wrapped his arms around the policeman and sobbed his happiness. "Where is she, Sully? Where is Angie? Is she unharmed? Where?" The rush of questions came as if a dam had exploded and every emotion released. "Oh, thank you, God. Thank you!"

Kevin clung to Sullivan. Gradually the shock of Sully's news sunk in and his composure returned. "Tell me…what's happened?"

"Locher's got all the information, sir. He just told me find you—and bring you in. Let's go back to headquarters and find out when your wife is coming home."

~

Conrad Phelps paced the Ritz Hotel lobby browsing a train schedule. The desk clerk was watching. Without striking any unnecessary conversation he gave the clerk an envelope with the name Andre Bouchard scribbled across the front. "Ask for identification when the man picks this up," were his only words.

When he stepped out onto the street, Conrad knew his charade was over! The approaching shrill of sirens only confirmed this reality. From across the wide avenue moments later he watched the two Sûreté police cars pull to a screeching stop in front of the stately hotel building.

He ran.

Blocks away he stepped into a bistro and found a table toward the back of the crowded room. Conrad had nowhere else to go. Panicked, no logical plan came to mind. Collecting his thoughts he ordered a glass of wine, gave the *garcon* an American twenty, and asked the waiter to bring him a pencil and some paper. Of all the terrible things that might happen to him now—never seeing his Emma again seemed the worst. Without her, Conrad's life was meaningless. All the angry scorn in the world, coupled with his ruinous humiliation, and probably a life locked in some prison— no consequence compared with the consuming pain of his loss.

"I'm sorry, Emma," he mumbled to himself. "Forgive me…" His tears, however, had already been spent.

When the pencil and paper—along with a decanter of wine—were delivered to his table, Conrad asked for bread and a sharp knife.

Conrad began to write:

Dearest Emma

Thank you for the happiest weeks of my life. May whatever painful memories you have of our time together be tempered by the reality of my love for you. A love that inspired my every deceit and a love that conjured every goodness in me. Emma, I stole you from your loved ones and for that I cannot ever be forgiven. But, out of respect for you and for them, I never once violated the sanctity of your true vows of fidelity to Kevin. The lover of words that I am serves me in this dark hour of loneliness. These tragic lines are memorized from a man named Masefield—

'Love is a flame to burn out human wills,
Love is a flame to set the will on fire,

> *Love is a flame to cheat men into mire,*
> *One of the three, we make Love what we choose.'*

I chose to allow my Love to cheat you of days spent with your loved ones. I am willing to pay the price for doing that. Emma, the villa in California you so enjoyed, is my gift to you. Please ask your husband to make provision for Darold Hurley, my one friend in life. I want Darold to have everything I leave behind. Finally, I leave my soul to the devil. For God may not have enough mercy to forgive what I have done.

Conrad Phelps

Conrad folded the page. How long would it be before the police would find him? The bistro was crowded with bedraggled men talking loudly of their recent military exploits. One group spoke English. They were remnants of the volunteer British Brigade returned from Spain and the bloody Civil War. "When I get enough money, I'm going back to finish what we started," one of the men boasted. "I owe those God dammed Fascists for the blood of my friends."

Conrad pushed the bread knife aside. What had seemed his only recourse moments ago, no longer defined his fate. He still had a considerable sum of money.

Gesturing for the waiter, Conrad took a ten dollar bill from his pocket. "Will you please deliver this note to the Ritz Hotel desk for me?"

Conrad got up from the table and found a chair where the three Brits were seated. Trying to impress the men with a false bravado, Conrad spoke with all the confidence he could summon. "I'm a Yank, name's Johnson, fellas. Overheard what you were talking about. I've got a brother still down there—with the Lincoln Brigade somewhere near Barcelona. I'll pay good money if one of you would drive me down there to find him.

~

Angela awoke to the sound of several hushed voices outside her room. At first glance, everything about her in the tiny room seemed unfamiliar. Looking about, however, the picture became clear. She began collecting her thoughts and reconstructing the hours before going to bed. Everything seemed a lifetime ago. Sitting up in the narrow bed, she gazed at her reflection in a small vanity mirror nearby and smiled. She knew who she was this morning—and who she was not. Her mind had cleared, sifted out the complicated events of the past weeks. She had been in St. Paul when everything started. A pained look crossed her face at the memory of the trolley collision—the injured baby on the floor. Although some elements following the accident remained vague, she recalled traveling through the mountains to the vast ocean—the wide beach below a huge villa and a wonderful man named Darold.

The night before, Guillaume had helped her understand her days spent in Paris with Conrad. Together, they traced the Phelps' travels backward to London, New York, and California. Connecting the dates enabled Angela to realize that she had been gone for nearly six weeks.

Lying in bed, she understood that the accident had caused her blackout. An amnesic episode that took her a world away. In time she was confident every piece of the puzzle would fit together. Before getting out of bed, Angela prayed—prayers of thanksgiving for her protection and ultimate safety. And for the angels who must have been at her side through it all.

Guillaume's voice was sorted from the others beyond the door. "Thank you, God, for sending that wonderful man—that chosen guardian angel to rescue me."

Kevin, her father had promised the night before, would be calling her this morning. This morning? Angela pressed her memory, it was Tuesday here…so, it must be late Monday night in Minnesota. Kevin's voice would be all she needed to regain the life she had almost lost.

Hurriedly she dressed and combed out her blond hair. As she did so, she remembered Conrad. A cloud of sympathy rolled over her thoughts. Closing her eyes, she prayed…"God, in your infinite mercy, forgive…"

In the living room with Guillaume and Mrs. LaPointe were two strangers.

"Bon jour, mon cherie," Guillaume rose and greeted her with a wide smile. "You will be going home to America today!" His emotions were torn. In such a short time he had become incredibly attached to this spirited woman. Yet, his happiness was overwhelming.

Guillaume made introductions, "Mr. Duvalle here will be taking you to London when you are ready to travel. This is Inspector Gastau of the Sûreté, Angela."

"And from London to New York," Mrs. LaPointe added with a smile of her own. "But before anything else, my dear, you have a man waiting in America for a call from you. Anxiously waiting—I am certain of that! He's called twice while you were sleeping and I dared not to wake you."

Duvalle suggested that the group retire to the kitchen so Mrs. Moran could have some private moments for her call, "Let me get the operator and make your connections, Mademoiselle."

"Kevin…! I love you," were the only words she could say.

∼

Angela peered into the crowd on the New York dock and saw the banner held by several people clustered in their own small group. She recognized her father and Becca toward the front, and Senia. Claude and Marc Atkinson were there, too. Gary and Nora Zench were waving along with other familiar people from Hibbing. Keirnan McGinnis in his crisp blue uniform and another man she did not recognize stood as if at attention.

Emotion choked in her throat. The man she loved was holding a bouquet of roses.

"I've never seen so many happy faces, Mrs. Moran," Damian Halley said at her side.

"That's Kevin!" Angela blurted, pointing to the tall man standing several feet in front of the welcoming group. "That's my husband!" Angela waved and smiled and cried her happiness.

THE END

Epilogue

October 1942

It was already four years since Angela's return to Hibbing. Despite some lingering memory gaps which might never be fully understood, her life was back to normal in nearly every respect. The tragic love letter that Conrad Phelps had left behind still haunted her thoughts from time to time. And she never forgot the tormented man in her prayers. In a private place in her heart she forgave him, and believed her God was merciful.

Those six weeks of what she called her 'missing time' had become sufficiently resolved. Doctors at the Mayo Clinic in Rochester, in consultation with Doctor Becca, continued to monitor her 'condition' and, through the years, her physical health remained excellent.

Angela's family, friends, church and community kept her involved in the lives of others much as they had before. Jacque Grojean's former art studio (now named *Shades of White*) remained a favorite sanctuary. Son Patrick, now an eleven year old sixth grader, enjoyed his father's interests in sports and the out-of-doors; while eight year old Mary Rebecca enabled Angela to relive her own childhood. Her children and her faith anchored her life.

Angela's paintings continued to bring wide acclaim and she had been invited to numerous national art expositions. 'Winter Wisps', her latest oil painting, had appeared on the cover of *Artist's Easel* magazine. Whenever her showings took her away form Hibbing, Kevin always traveled with her. And, Angela was happy! Happier than she could ever remember being.

Kevin spent more time at home now than ever before. Through Angie's traumatic experience, Kevin had finally put his personal demons to rest and placed a greater trust in a God who he now believed listened to his prayers. He had finally learned the valuable lesson Angela had given him years before: "You find yourself by reaching out rather than by searching inside." It was, as she had promised, the most fulfilling experience in his life.

His Androy Hotel was in Gary Zench's capable hands for the most part, but Kevin remained active in local Chamber affairs and was probably Hibbing's most notable booster of economic development and patriotic causes.

The nation had climbed out of Depression and marched into World War. Mesabi's iron ore mines were churning out millions of tons to make the steel for America's war efforts. People on the Range were working and prospering again. Yet, despite the 'good times', Hibbing and the other mining communities were becoming increasingly more dependent on their single resource. Economic diversification remained an elusive goal.

∼

Kevin, Angela, and their children, had gone to California in September of 1939 to visit Darold Hurley and enjoy 'Emma's Beach' as the villa manager fondly called the wide bar of sand. Darold and the Morans had been in contact with each other almost monthly since Angie's return the year before. Angela's Mayo psychologists had been insistent that she would not be truly recovered from her ordeal until she could confront her experience directly. Returning to Sunset Shores proved a marvelous therapy. During their two weeks as Darold's guests, the family discovered sea lions and watched Clark Gable movies in the mansion's little theater.

Angela's greatest disappointment over these past four years was her inability to locate Guillaume LaBlanc. Her countless letters to the Montmartre address and his mother's home in Thoiry were never answered.

∼

Four years. In human terms, years are often marked by the vital statistics of births and weddings and deaths. Funerals commemorating the passing of friends and loved ones always left an emptiness in the life fabric of those who mourned their losses.

A sudden blizzard on Armistice Day, 1940, claimed the life of Steven Skorich who became disoriented while hunting east of Hibbing near Timo's Lake with

Tony and Rudy Zoretek. Without warning, the mild morning had turned stormy, and Steven—already in poor health—lost his bearings and froze to death.

On every Saturday mornings, Senia Arola could be seen sprinkling rose petals at two grave sites in North Hibbing's cemetery—one of those was Steven's, the other was that of Peter Moran. Two words might best define the sixty-two year old Finnish spinster—unrequited love! The once headstrong accountant had sold her firm and now spent most of her time in the reclusive isolation of her home.

Sister Anne de Poris died peacefully in her sleep on Thanksgiving Day the following year. Although no one would know it, her last vision was the happiest she had ever been given. Sister Anne saw her brother waiting for her at the open gates of heaven.

In a funeral service at the Virginia cemetery, Armando Depelo was laid to rest in December of 1941. The once handsome man died of an alcohol related liver disease which had left him emaciated. The minister, his landlord, a fellow bartender, and a woman named Florence were the only people who braved the sleety morning to offer their last respects.

And there were some who died without the recognition of a funeral ceremony. Guillaume LaBlanc was one of these. Despite his mother's pleas, the young man became involved in the anti-Nazi French resistance movement. He was killed in an obscure little village near Reims, east of Paris, and buried in an unmarked grave in March of 1942. Only four months later, his mother, Madeline LaPointe died. The widow's heartbreak over learning of her only son's death was the only explanation for the healthy woman's sudden collapse. Ironically, it was a fellow resistance comrade named Benjy Duvalle, who traveled to Thoiry to give the widow the tragic news.

After giving up his drinking habit and passing through his bout with depression, Claude Atkinson, might have borrowed a line from Mark Twain: "Reports of my death have been greatly exaggerated." To fill the long winter months, the rejuvenated old newsman took up the popular sport of curling, and at age seventy-one, began regularly playing bocce ball at the Bennett Park courts during the summer. Claude, it would seem, was a modern Methuselah. If some clairvoyant had told Claude that he would live another fifteen years, he would have believed the prediction wholeheartedly.

Darold Hurley celebrated his sixtieth birthday on February, 20, 1942. He had made his first and only trip to Minnesota in January the previous year. Hurley completed the liquidation of Phelps Enterprises, which Conrad Junior had started years before, during two contentious meetings with Calvin Hodge. Vowing never to return to frigid Minnesota, Darold established, and managed, the Sunset Foundation which would endow various charitable causes throughout the country. Conrad's book collection, valued at more than four million dollars, was anonymously donated to Macalaster College.

In March of '42 there was a birth in Duluth. Carver and Colleen Blake had their first son. Kevin and Angela were present at both the wedding of their new friends two years earlier, and the baptism of James McIntosh Blake at the St. James Church.

The Morans were in St. Paul two weeks after the Blake's baptism for a different kind of ceremony. Duane Locher was sworn in as the new Chief of the St. Paul force. (Had it not been for that event, Kevin may never have learned his old friend's first name. To him, Locher was always simply—'Captain' or Locher). And one of Chief Locher's first official acts was the promotion of Keirnan McGinnis to his own former position as Police Captain.

Tony and Becca Zoretek celebrated their sixteenth anniversary in August. Now in their early fifties, both remained active in their careers and community. Tony's contracting and real estate businesses had emerged from the Depression in solid condition and flourished with Hibbing's building boom of the early forties. Doctor Becca continued to bring new lives into the world and nurture the sick of her community.

~

Conrad Phelps left the Paris bistro on that Monday night in October of 1938 with a man named Buddy Miller. The two men traveled south toward the Pyrenees and Spanish border for nearly two days. In that space of time, however, Miller surmised two things about the visibly nervous little man. His companion was probably not Adam Johnson from Ohio, and the American traveler had more than a thousand dollars in American cash.

Near a small village south of Toulouse, Buddy Miller would do something the career mercenary soldier had done several times before. He would kill! Conrad was urinating in some roadside bushes when Miller walked quietly up behind him and put a bullet in the back of his balding head.

Conrad Phelps was left in a shallow grave without any identification on his body. The note he had left for Emma had been delivered to the Ritz Hotel by the bistro waiter. Lawyers in St. Paul eventually determined that the letter's contents were to be legally considered as the businessman's last will and testament. They began distributing the Phelps assets as directed in December of 1941—more than three years after Conrad Phelps, Junior, had last been seen alive.

∼

It had been four years since Angela's return to Hibbing. Despite some lingering memory gaps which might never be fully understood, her life was back to normal in nearly every respect. The tragic love letter that Conrad Phelps had left behind still haunted her thoughts from time to time, and she never forgot the tormented man in her prayers. In a private place in her heart she forgave him, and believed her God would be merciful in His judgement.

Those six weeks of what she called her missing time had become sufficiently resolved. Doctors at the Mayo Clinic in Rochester, in consultation with Doctor Becca in Hibbing, continued to monitor her condition, and through the years her physical health remained excellent.

Angela's family, friends, church and community kept her involved in the lives of others much as they had before her episode. Jacque Grojean's former art studio (now named *Shades of White*) remained a favorite sanctuary for the artist. Son Patrick, now an eleven year old sixth grader, enjoyed his father's interests in sports and the outdoors, while eight year old Mary Rebecca enabled Angela to relive her own childhood. Her children and her faith anchored her life.

Angela's paintings continued to bring wide acclaim, and she had been invited to numerous national art expositions. *Winter Wisps*, her latest oil painting, had appeared on the cover of *Artist's Easel* magazine. Whenever her showings took her away from Hibbing, however, Kevin always traveled with her. And Angela was happy! Happier than she could ever remember being.

Kevin spent more of his time at home now than ever before. Through Angie's traumatic experience, Kevin had finally put his personal demons to rest and placed a greater trust in a God who he now believed listened to his prayers. He had finally learned the valuable lesson Angela had given him years before: *you find yourself by reaching out rather than by searching inside.* It was, as she had promised, the most fulfilling experience in his life.

His Androy Hotel was in Gary Zench's capable hands for the most part, but Kevin remained active in local chamber affairs and was probably Hibbing's most notable booster of economic development and patriotic causes.

The nation had climbed out of Depression and marched into World War. Mesabi's iron ore mines were churning out millions of tons to make the steel for America's war efforts. People on the Range were working and prospering again. Yet, despite the good times, Hibbing and the other mining communities were becoming increasingly more dependent on their single resource. To many, the supply of rich hematite ore below the Mesabi surface seemed inexhaustible. Others knew better! Economic diversification remained an elusive goal in northeastern Minnesota.

~

Kevin, Angela, and their children, had gone to California in September of 1939 to visit Darold Hurley and enjoy "Emma's Beach" as the villa manager fondly called the wide tract of Pacific sand. Darold and the Morans had remained in contact with each other almost monthly since Angie's return the year before.

Angela's Mayo Clinic psychologists were insistent that she would not be truly recovered from her ordeal until she confronted her traumatic experience as directly as possible. Returning to Sunset Shores proved to be a marvelous therapy. During their two weeks as Darold's guests, the family discovered sea lions and watched Clark Gable movies in the mansion's little theater. And, to the thorough delight of the visiting Minnesotans, Darold arranged a small party one Saturday evening. Somewhere near eleven o'clock, there was a knock at the front door…the invited guest greeted Angela with his world-renowned smile, a warm hug, and a memorable "Welcome back to Hollywood, Scarlett!"

Angela's greatest disappointment over these past four years, however, was her inability to make any contact with Guillaume or Madeline LeBlanc. Her countless letters to the Montmartre address in Thoiry were never answered. Some angels,

Angela came to believe, are sent to us in our most critical times…and then divinely dispatched to others in need of their guiding hands.

∼

Kevin had waited for this October tenth since receiving the small parcel from California several weeks before. Darold had found Angela's rings.

While Angela was still asleep on this early Saturday morning, he quietly left the house. Under his arm was a package he had put together the night before. The autumn sun felt warm on his shoulders as he slowly walked down the long amber and red-colored hillside toward the barn. Despite the stirring of the horses, he was able to saddle his gelding and ride away without any notice.

Early that afternoon, Angela seemed consumed by an unspoken sadness. From her art studio window she watched her husband raking leaves away from the inlaid brick patio he had built the previous spring. It was nearly two and Kevin had not said a single word about their special day. Dwelling on her melancholy, she turned her gaze from Kevin to the oil painting resting on her easel. The patch of green grass beside the small pine-ridged pond, the soft blue sky, and the fringe of radiant maple trees on the canvas became blurred by her tears. Angela's anniversary gift for Kevin now seemed to have lost its heartfelt meaning.

How could he have forgotten?

Staring absently at her painting for several long moments, she dabbed her brush into a dark gray oil. Perhaps the sky in her in her labor of love should not be blue after all. As she was poised to add some new brush strokes, Angela felt a swell of emotion work its way through her body. From as far back as she could remember, she could always sense Kevin's presence in a room.

His words were chocked with an emotion of his own. "I love you, Angela Moran," drifted across the silent space between them.

Beneath a majestic Norway pine, an old plaid blanket had already been spread over the bed of soft needles. Strung from the trunk of the tree was a long red ribbon which disappeared over the ledge of gurgling creek. At the end of the ribbon was a bottle of wine and a small plastic-wrapped box.

Under the boughs of the familiar old pine, they cried and they laughed and they loved as the fading afternoon sun dropped slowly into the silhouette of distant trees.

In Appreciation

In order to make BLESSED THOSE WHO SORROW a finished book, many eyes had to pass over nearly one hundred and twenty-five thousand words. Those eyes—along with experience and wisdom and skill behind them—were purveyors of the author's third novel. This story, along with its characters and grammatical underpinnings were given its texture through those caring eyes. Providing a necessary scrutiny to an elaborate editing process were friends to whom I am deeply indebted.

    Chapter by chapter, Ed Beckers has been through every draft of every book I have written. The hours he has spent are as countless as the insights he has provided. From Ed, this book was passed to Nancy Harp. Nancy's perfectionism while editing a crude manuscript has been an invaluable contribution to this story. As with my last book, Norma Grant reviewed the final proofs in order to provide further polishing. Gail Nevalainen proofread the manuscript and her son Shawn did the tedious formatting. Once again, my friend David Wirkkula was willing to provide my story with a strikingly colorful cover. I sincerely thank all of you.

    And, I am grateful to the staff at the Hibbing Public Library for their assistance while doing the necessary research.

    Support and encouragement are essential parts of the writing process. Every simple "I enjoyed your book" provides an inspiration and motivation to continue telling stories. So, a big thanks to my readers is well deserved.

Minnesota author, Pat McGauley is a former Hibbing High School teacher. Born in Duluth, McGauley grew up in Hoyt Lakes, graduated from Winona State University (BS) and the University of Minnesota (MA).

A former mineworker and historian, McGauley has lived in Hibbing for the past forty years. In 2002, TO BLESS OR TO BLAME was published. The sequel, A BLESSING OR A CURSE followed in 2003. In addition to his novels, McGauley has written two children's stories: MAZRAL AND DERISA—an Easter story, and SANTA THE KING (2004).